One Wish

and

One Wish To Give

Part I: Rainbows

ISBN 978-1-7354472-0-9 (hardcover)
ISBN 978-1-7354472-1-6 (paperback)

*Dedicated to my parents; whose
work never seems to be finished.*

CHAPTERS

CHAPTER ONE

BEGINNING

A village is nestled inside a forest inside a desert. Inside this forest, clouds form overhead and rain. Inside the forest are animals: deer, rabbits, boars, bears. Inside the village, people drift by doing their tasks: building houses, forging metal, raising animals, planting crops and reaping them. The village is a paradise stuck in time.

Some distance away from this village, in the middle of the desert, is a man walking for salvation. Dipaka is a grown adult; of 27 years of age. He is draped in off-white clothing. There are splotches of blood across his clothes—they are his. His lips are crusted over from the low humidity. His face is bruised. He drags behind a fur overcoat. It is his only shield against the cold nights. He holds onto a pouch of water. This is his last life source. He allows himself to drink this sparingly. His stomach grumbles. He has been walking for two days now.

A young man, Quill, sits on the threshold of the forest. He is tall for his age, on the verge of becoming 16. His muscles are strong, but not bulky. They are sinewy and his figure is svelte. He wears a green tunic that's light and flows easily.

On the threshold, the sand flows into the forest like water washes up on a beach. His hand dips into the sand. The sand flows through it and falls. Done looking into the horizon, Quill walks back into the forest. Its cathedral of trees envelope him. Crepuscular rays shine through the dewy morning.

After an hour of walking, he enters his village. It is comprised of wooden houses, a fire pit, and several cut down logs on which people sit. He pushes the wooden door into his family's house.

His mother and father are sleeping. His father rises from the bed. "Son, you are always early to rise. I'll get my clothes and we'll begin." There is a forged sword leaned against the corner of the house. Muddled clothes are folded on the floor. The Father comes up to the Son and puts his hand on his shoulder, "Let us hunt."

"Today, let me hunt alone," Quill says.

"You know you can only hunt alone after your rites. Until then, you can follow me. Come, take your spear."

"I can be more than this if you would only support me."

The Son takes the spear and follows his father out of the community. He secures his spear to his back with a knot. When the spear is pulled, the knot unties and is ready to be used.

The empty clearing of the village becomes populated with trees as they head out. The fog and dew of the morning has condensed and the sun shines clearly through the forest. The scent of the flora fills the forest.

Animal tracks are visibly pressed into the dirt. A heavy animal has been here. The stench of its stool is in the air: foul and moist.

Around the forest are sounds: birds chirping, their wings flapping in flight, insects clicking. The Father and Son stand still and absorb these sounds. Somewhere among the cacophonous forest is a slight hint of labored breathing. They start making their way to the source. In motion, they move like animals. Their bare feet stomp upon the soil and rebound equally as fast. They sprint towards the bottom of a hill.

The animal eclipses the sun on the hill's apex. The Son grips his spear; its edge recently sharpened to pierce. Son and Father move slowly up and across the trees. They inch closer to the boar.

They pause to observe the beast. It is breathing and looking around. It starts walking off away from the sun. The beast starts to turn around and snorts in the direction of Son and Father. It tramples fast and quick upturning leaves in its wake. The Father takes his sword and runs towards the beast. Its tusks scrape by the Father's skin.

The Father crouches down and grabs his wounded arm. His sword slips from his grip and tumbles downhill. The beast turns to the Father, readying a second charge—its tusks pointed towards him.

The Son rolls down the hill, following the sword. He takes a rock and throws it at the beast. The beast charges at Quill. The boar lunges at his body. The Son side steps the charge. He grabs onto a tusk and in his other hand, his spear. Resisting the force of the animal, he grips the tusk and spins his body to send the spear into the animal's side. It snorts and gasps for air. The Father runs downhill. The Father grabs the sword on the ground and brings the sword across the boar's throat.

The Father stands there coughing and catching his breath.

Quill stares at his father. Quill shoulders the dead animal.

* * *

The Father and Son walk back into the community. The people around them walk to greet them. An elderly woman comes by and puts her hand on Quill's shoulder. She tip toes and whispers into the young man's ear, "You are becoming a man."

The Son turns to his father and says, "Father, I wished you would've trusted me."

"In two full moons, you'll become a man. And only after, tradition will allow you to hunt alone."

They put the carcass on a stone. The Son takes a small knife from his hip and cuts along the mid-line of the animal. They strip the animal apart. They cut apart some of the meat into thin strips and hang it off rope. Other parts will be used for that night's meal.

Done preparing the animal for food and ration, he goes back into his house and naps for a moment. Upon waking, he tells his father and mother, "I'm going to gather herbs and vegetables." It is almost twilight. The forest begins to cool down. The sun is still high up, but not for long.

* * *

The man in the desert comes to the forest in the desert. The full moon illuminates the monolithic trees. Sand flows into soil. Patches of grass show up in spots emanating from the forest. "It is a mirage," he whispers. He hobbles down a dune. His weak legs give way and he tumbles down. His body rolls to the bottom of a dune and is stopped by the soil of the forest. He lies there, unconscious.

* * *

The man wakes up. His eyes open towards smoke in the sky. Water drips into his mouth. His eyes adjust to the dark and the silhouettes of rustling trees. He takes his hands to support him sitting up. His hands press against the moist soil. He looks around. Orange embers illuminate the faces around him. The people around him bring clothing, food, and a bowl of broth.

"My son, Quill, he carried you back here. Are you okay?" the Father asks.

"I…I got lost." He looks at the son. The son looks back at him. "I'm Dipaka."

"Please have some of our food and water. You must be hungry and tired," one of the villagers says to him.

He ravenously devours each morsel of food; taking the broth and water and drinking it as if he were about to die. People bring him more clothing. "Thank you. Thank you. Thank you," he repeated over and over between each bite.

"A hungry man shames us all," another villager tells him.

One family extended hospitality, "When you are ready, we prepared a bed for you."

The young man, Quill, asks Dipaka, "Where did you come from?"

"From that direction over there," he points to the south, "that's where. There are mountains over there."

"What are mountains?"

"You don't know what mountains are?"

"No."

Dipaka takes the soil in his hand and shapes it. He creates a large pile and shapes it into a point. He points to a flat area and calls it the desert. "Here, this pile here. If you can imagine it like a big rock, that's how tall it is. It's a...tall thing—much taller than the trees here."

"How did you get lost?"

"I don't know...I was..." He touches his lips, cracked from the dry desert air, and bloodied. He removes his fur pelt coat. Underneath he wears a light white button shirt and pants. "It's warm here, it's not like outside where it's cold."

Quill's mother instructs him, "Please rest and eat. You must be tired."

* * *

Dipaka watches on as the young man chops wood with his father. The young man keeps chopping one after the other. He does not stop.

"I appreciate your hospitality, but this is not my place," Dipaka says to Quill.

"You can't survive out there," the Father says.

"I suppose you are right," Dipaka says.

The young man rests the ax by the stomp. He sits down. Dipaka goes and picks up the ax. "I owe you all for saving me. Let me do some work around here."

A villager tells him, "No. That isn't necessary."

The young man tells him, "If you want, you can come pick herbs with me."

The Father nods in approval.

* * *

They walk side by side into the forest. Quill asks Dipaka, "Do you want to go back from where you came from?"

Dipaka considers, and tells him, "From where I come from, people are afraid of crossing oceans."

"Oceans?"

"When it rains, it forms puddles," he points to a puddle on the ground, "but imagine a great body of water. Imagine that the sand out there was water. And to cross the desert back to the mountains is as difficult as crossing an ocean."

"But you came here from the mountains, crossing the desert, a journey that could have killed you. What possesses a person to cross into danger?"

"A willingness to be the first."

"Are you the first?"

"No...no... first in my family. I didn't answer your question. It is dangerous out there. I'm not sure if I want to go back. If I do, I might die on the way back."

Quill walks across a fallen tree. The downed tree is wedged into the fork of another tree. Dipaka follows him. The young man tells him, "We're almost there."

Quill continues walking up the downed tree, gaining elevation over Dipaka. "I always enjoyed this place. It's away from people. I remember setting up challenges for myself where I would test how far I can jump. Just to see if I can make it. Each jump was a marker in my life. I could tell you exactly when and how I made each one."

He turns his head towards Dipaka, "There is nothing to control you here." He climbs a tree and jumps down to a branch far below and out. High above now, Quill walks across the branches of each tree.

The growth is thick. Some trees were even cultured so as to form bridges out of intertwined branches. "See this here? I made it this way. I tied a string between two skinny branches. I made sure it kept taut through the years."

Dipaka can only follow on the ground as the young man moves through the canopy of the forest.

"You move well," Dipaka tells him.

Quill pauses in the tree and looks beyond the forest to the desert. There is a blue clearing in the distance. "I've decided. I will follow you to the mountains."

"I didn't say I will go back. Or take you," Dipaka responds from the ground. The young man descends the tree: maneuvering by jumping down and using his arms to slowly lower himself.

"We're here. Take out your pouch." They gather mushrooms and herbs from the ground. He places them into Dipaka' pouch. The young man digs several small holes with his hands. He reaches into his pouch and plants several seeds around.

Animals dash about around them. Dipaka looks around, wary.

The boy keeps handing flora to Dipaka. Dipaka asks the boy, "Why do you want to leave this place?"

He doesn't respond. "Here, take this too," the young man says. They walk back.

The young man walks forward. Quill asks him, "Why do you want to stay?"

Dipaka touches his lips. He winces. It's still cut and bruised.

* * *

They come back into the village. They spend their time preparing dinner. They eat mostly vegetables with some meat reserves and broth.

Dipaka sat around with the villagers explaining where he came from. Then, the people turn to their houses and sleep. All the fires by each pit are extinguished. He sees the young man sitting by the last fire remaining. He walks and sits next to him.

"Quill, I owe you my life." He makes the same pile that demonstrated a mountain again. "The desert is far and vast." He motions his finger across the flat ground, leading up the rising crest of the mountain. "I may have explained something wrong. I may have made the mountain seem important. That's not true…" His finger jumps over the mountain. "Here, the other side of the mountain, on the opposite side of the desert, that's where there are many things. There are so many things that I cannot find the words to describe them to you…because I owe you my life, I'll let you choose your life…

"…Quill, I'll show you how to cross the mountains."

Dipaka gets up and begins to walk to his foster family's house. "Starting tomorrow night." Dipaka disappears into the house.

Quill sits and stares at the fire, the fire becomes pareidolic—taking on forms of what may exist beyond the mountains.

* * *

"Each night, we'll see how far we can get and then we'll walk back. You have to be able to adjust to the distance. We'll also have to pick up speed. We want to cover as much distance in the cold before the day hits. Supplies will also be heavy. So we need to be ready for that too." Dipaka gives Quill his fur coat. "Use my coat for now. I'll fashion one for myself later."

On the night of a full moon, they take to the edge of the forest. Each of them holds a log on their shoulders. They start walking to the south. When they breathe, their vapor condenses in the cold night. The young man's nose starts to run. The moon rises and their way is illuminated. Dipaka instructs that when the moon reaches the peak, that is when they need to start heading back. He points to the spot where the moon will be at its apex.

"Let's keep going," Quill says.

"The moon is past its peak. If we don't return now, the people will wake up and wonder where you are," Dipaka says.

"I want to keep going. I can make it back in time," Quill spoke with exhaustion while holding the log. Sweat drips onto the desert sand.

Dipaka gets closer to the young man. "This is only our first time. We can do this again tomorrow. Your hands are bleeding... let go of the wood." Dipaka drops his log and plants it upright on the ground. "Now we know where we left off. The next time, we need to get past this point faster."

Quill plants his log into the ground too.

They turn around to the village. Quill walks sluggishly. Dipaka instructs him, "You spent too much energy coming here. Keep walking. Go on." Quill walks a bit faster.

Whenever he sees that Quill was slowing down, he tells him, "Keep walking."

Two logs stand on the sand. Wind blows sand onto the base of the logs. Their footprints will be washed over. The logs will be buried.

* * *

The next afternoon, the Son tells his father that he is going to collect vegetables. Quill and Dipaka go to forage. On their walk through the forest...

Dipaka asks, "Do you know where the large animals' dens are?"

"I do. I've walked across a cave where bears make their home."

"Do you know what it means to tame an animal?"

"No."

Dipaka explains that in order to reach the mountain, they would need to carry a few days of supplies. To do this, it would be best for animals to carry the bulk of the supplies while they walk. And to tame them, he would teach them behaviors favorable to their goal.

"Why would you do that? To control them so much?" Quill asks.

"It is necessary to get to the mountains. Otherwise you would die of starvation and thirst."

"What happens when I reach the mountains? What happens to the animal?"

Dipaka is silent, then he tells him that the animals would need to fend for themselves.

"Cross the mountain with me," Quill says.

"I can't."

* * *

Dipaka wakes up later than everyone else. He sits up on the ground. He notices rope hung on the wall. He walks out and sees the boy and his father sharpening swords. He takes note of the boar meat being hung to dry as well.

He walks up to the two of them. "Can I borrow one of the swords? I would like to hunt alone. I want to show you my gratitude by offering you an animal."

The Father considers. "Yes, of course."

The Son looks at his father, "But why can't I?"

"You know why," the Father responds.

The Father offers Dipaka a sword and its sheath. The sword is metallic, shiny, reflective. It's an odd design. The tang is the grip. The tang flows straight into the blade. It doesn't have a guard to prevent the hand from slipping into the blade. Dipaka holds onto it. He goes back into his foster family's house. He finds two coils of rope. He places them into his pouch. He puts the sword into its sheath and ties it around his hip.

* * *

They go on another run for food. After they retrieve the vegetables, Dipaka turns to Quill, "Show me where the den is."

Quill leads Dipaka through the forest. They stop behind a tree and peer towards the cave. Foliage, moss, and dirt cover the stone formation. Three cubs walk slowly towards the den. A bird flies and squawks overhead. The mother bear walks out slowly and rubs her head against the cubs' faces.

"Quill, can you put this rope in the trees?" Dipaka takes out the coil of rope and hands it to Quill. Quill puts the coil on his arm. He climbs the tree, grabbing each branch, transposing his body to reach for the one above. When he climbs, he is solving a spatial puzzle with his limbs.

"You didn't need to put the rope that high," Dipaka tells Quill when he came back to the ground. Quill silently chuckles.

"We'll observe how they behave," Dipaka says.

* * *

Dipaka sits around a fire with Quill, his family, and cousins.

"Do you have someone you love?" they questioned Dipaka.

"No. I left home looking to become rich. I didn't have time to court a partner."

"What about your family?"

"When you say love, I think of a woman, a wife. That's my first thought," Dipaka considers, "then yes, I do love my parents. Quill, do you get married here? Where two people stay together for a long time? Become bonded?

The Mother tells Dipaka, "We choose his wife."

"It's the same where I come from. Maybe one day when I return home, I'll be wed. How long have you been together?"

"I cannot count the years anymore. It has been more than enough!" the Mother laughs.

The Father hugs her close.

Dipaka asks Quill, "Quill, have you a chosen wife?"

"No, that is later in my life. A boy must become a man first. Then in time, a wife is chosen for him. And it continues like this, stretching until the end of time."

* * *

Night after night, they carry a log farther and farther. The stretches between the first logs were far. The progress was great. After the twelfth log, the distance between the logs became smaller. The beginning progress dwindled. They move faster but their speed approaches a limit. Forty logs have been placed in the desert. Full moon to full moon to new moon, they have spent a month and a half training to reach the mountain. Drawn in the sand was a timeline, an arrow into the future.

* * *

Quill climbs up the tree and retrieves the rope that he's put up there. He throws the rope down. Dipaka ties a loop around a tree and walks to the next one. A perimeter of rope cordons off around the den. He wraps Quill's father's sword in cloth, and places it on the ground. He turns to Quill, "I know you have tenets to not touch this. So please do not help me unless I give clear instructions."

Dipaka walks into the bounded area. He sees the mother bear in its den. Its eyes glint in the dark. The bear walks out with its cubs. The bear growls at him. The heat of its breath and humidity doesn't faze him. The bear stands up on its hind legs and raises its claws. Its deafening roar shakes the fur on its body. It is absolutely immense and it towers over Dipaka.

Quill stands by the trees. He glances at Dipaka and then at the sword.

Dipaka utters the words, "Pla'on dto!"

Quill whispers, "What are you doing?!"

The bear rushes him. It swipes its claw at Dipaka. He is thrown against a tree. The bear charges at him. He again says the same words, in a different intonation, "Pli'gon toh!" The bear pins him against the tree with force.

"Plo jon tuh," Dipaka utters. The bear swipes at him with his claw and he is dragged to the side. The bear crushes him. It raises its claws and swipes at Dipaka. It rips into his clothes; into his skin. Dipaka is thrown against a rock. There is an audible pop heard; coming from inside his body.

Quill unwraps the sword from the cloth. He grabs the sword and slides down towards the den. The cubs trample towards him. He swings the sword in their direction. As he does this, there is a slight fire that arcs from the tip of his father's sword. The cubs pull back. Quill brings the sword above his head and swings it down—"STOP!", Dipaka yells.

The action has already started.

The sword comes down and cuts the adult bear. Quill has tried to pull back the swing, but not enough for it to stop. The cut is superficial, but blood has been drawn. The bear draws its claws back and jabs it forward—towards Dipika's heart—a killing blow.

Dipaka looks at the claw coming towards him. He does not flinch. "Pio om toh!"

The bear stops its swipe, huffs and sits down on its hind legs. There it was, Dipaka sitting injured against a tree, and a bear bowed in obedience to him. He wipes sweat from his brow and spits out blood. He smiles, like fear has been lifted from him. He turns to Quill, and tells him,

"I have decided. I will go with you to the mountains."

* * *

They return to supper. Dipaka holds a squirrel by his side. Quill and Dipaka take a seat around a fire with Quill's parents. The Father asks, "Dipaka, what has happened to you?"

"I fell down a hill. A branch ripped into my body."

"Wait here. We'll bring you something." The parents leave.

"What were those words you said? That you were trying to say?" Quill asks Dipaka.

"I was trying to remember the words that my father taught me... He said those words were spoken before the written word. That these words were spoken long before man crafted tools from stone. I suppose those words were always meant to be transmitted down to me," he pauses, "Quill, your father's sword. There's a black mark on the hilt."

Quill examines it. There is a slight indentation of blackness on it. Dipaka wraps up the sword in the cloth again.

The parents return. The Mother tells him, "Remove your clothes." They present a bowl with green paste to him. "Spread this on your wounds," she instructed. Dipaka opens his green tunic and applies the green paste to the wounds. She continues, "Leave it on there for the night."

"Before I forget, here's a squirrel. The sword is sharp. It really is superb." Dipaka hands both squirrel and sword to Quill's father.

The Father accepts. They cook the squirrel and eat.

* * *

"With every wish realized, we move our society a little further, a little farther. We have old stories that our home was just one tree originally. A single twig in the middle of the sand. A single person came onto it. And when the sapling was pulled out, water sprang from it, then fruits, vegetables, seeds, leaves. Sand was transmuted to soil where that person walked. That person took the seeds and water and spread it around. He created this forest. And when the hungry, the starved came into this place, he entreated them to stay. He sheltered them. The story allows us to realize that a hungry man shames us all.

"There was another story of the First Man. When the forest was still young, when all the trees were still as tall as you or me, when the floor of the forest was leaves, when you could still see to the end of the forest in every direction because the forest was not dense yet...when there were only twelve people, a fire threatened the trees and food. He walked into the flames... enduring it...throwing dirt on the fires and trying to stop it with his hands. Slowly, the forest stopped burning. He saved families, strangers. It was said that when he walked back to the village, he bought something back with him, a wish."

"A wish?" Dipaka asks.

"It was said that the first person of this forest was the progenitor, the first to wish and to give a wish. There is a long line of people who are able to have their deepest wishes granted. Everyone who has completed the ritual obtains a wish."

"Your father talks to me about your rite of passage, and how it's coming soon. What's this ritual you have to go through?"

"To be recognized as a man, I will endure a flame. I will endure it until the last ember burns out. Throughout the ritual, my village will recite all the names of my ancestry back to the First Man and when I will have completed the ritual, my name will be added to it. Then I will inherit a wish from the last one to have completed the ritual."

"Do you want to do it?"

"I have to."

"But do you want to do it? You have a choice."

"I don't know...are you spiritual?"

"I was a good man. I followed all my tenets and yet...," Dipaka peers upwards, "...these gods have cast me aside. I am stuck here."

"But you're also alive, aren't you?"

"Maybe I'm not so forsaken. Considering where I am, this green place inside the dead desert, it's a type of miracle," Dipaka says.

"So you understand, that maybe tenets are there for a reason. We should follow them," Quill says.

* * *

The villagers enter into a section of the forest with large trees. Their thick roots span for paces and paces. The only way to look up is to lay down. A thick canopy of leaves shades the entire ground.

The old and elderly collect fallen fauna: dried twigs and leaves. The young men of the village tie a rope around the circumference of a tree. They take a smaller piece of rope and tie their feet together by the ankles. Pulling on the longer rope by the tree, they plant their feet by the tree. By pulling with their arms, and pushing with their feet, they're able to slowly climb the tree. A few of them are already up there. They take axes from their hip and start chopping down large branches. When they cut a v-shaped groove into the branch, they kick on it. "Watch out!" Large branches fall from the top.

Several other villagers walk to trees struck by lightning and start cutting them down. One struck down tree is toppled over. It's split at the trunk and is leaning against another tree. Thirty villagers throw rope over the tree and tie a knot. They throw the line down to the people on the ground. The people on the ground pull on the rope until a knot slips up the line and is tight against the tree. Everyone climbs down the tree. They chop the tree loose from the stomp.

Pulling tight on the ropes, a hundred people pull on the rope again and again. Creeeakkkk. Creaakkkkk. The tree begins to slowly roll off the tree it's leaned against. Their feet are firmly planted on the ground. With one pull, the tree rolls slightly towards them. "Keep pulling!" Some readjust their hands on the rope. Their fists are white-knuckled from their grip. Some turn around and place the rope on their shoulder. And they drag the log.

With a crash, the tree finally drops! With the tree on the ground, they can cut it out for firewood. For five days, villagers will come in and out of this area cutting and carrying away wood.

* * *

It is twilight. The boy walks into a clearing in the forest. There are no trees in a wide circle. If two people stood on opposite ends, they would barely see each other. Here, the ground is covered in pebbles and stones of different colors. Crepuscular rays shine through the gaps of the tree. As the sun sets down, the stones reflect purple and blue from the twilight sky. A dark gray replaces sunlight in between the gaps of the trees.

Stacked wood is laid out in concentric circles—three in total. Each ring id a body's length from the other. These circles are all chest-high and form the thickness of a wall. In the center is a sitting platform. In the gaps between the rings, there is an abundance of small twigs, already-burnt wood, dried leaves.

The entire village—all one thousand-odd stand to the opposite end of him.

Quill stands ready, in wait behind the trees. He looks forward. To him, the villagers are silhouettes. He looks farther behind the villagers and sees if Dipaka was there. There is no sign of him. He sees two people come out from the crowd. "Mother...Father..."

They each have a bag of an oily, fat-like cream. They start walking from opposite ends of the circle throwing and applying the cream into the wood. The Mother wipes tears from her face. They both walk in a spiral to the center—one of them clockwise towards the center and the other counterclockwise. The two of them climb down and up the chest-high walls when walking in the spiral. They meet at the center at the same time. Their bags are now empty of the cream. Both of them walk outside the ring. His father helps the Mother down.

His father crouches down and takes two stones from a pouch. He strikes them together. The spark ignites a tiny flame on the cream. He stands up and looks up towards the sky. The sun has completely disappeared. Night is almost here. The parents walk back to join the rest of the villagers.

The flame spreads in opposite spirals towards the center platform. The three rings are ignited. This fire is the signal.

The boy walks towards the fire. He looks side to side. The dense forest gives way to emptiness here: rocks on the floor and trees far away. He looks forward: the view of the villagers obscured by the fire. The sky is black. And the only light is the fire. It is the only visible thing. Smoke rises from the pyre. Reaching closer to it, it becomes much hotter.

He builds up a jogging pace and accelerates towards the first ring. Its heat becoming greater. The height of the flame is now apparent. It's now as high as his head. His arms cover his face as he runs now. He takes a blind leap through the flame. For a brief moment, his body is flashed in fire. "It's not so bad," he thought. He lands. Now he realizes that the first ring was the easiest. There is too little distance to do a running jump over the next ring.

The fire from the rings spills like water onto the twigs. The cream that was laid out in a spiral catches on fire. It catalyzes the burning of the twigs. He stands between the third and the second ring pondering what to do. And it's getting hotter. He takes a step forward. The ground underneath him is burning hot. He forces himself to take another step. "Keep going..." He subdues any need to scream.

A wind blows. The burning of the wet wood produces a dirty smoke. It stings his eye. The flames become larger and higher for a second. Ten steps was all he needed to walk to get to the next ring. Each step was a hesitation on his part. Step forward with one foot, then step the other foot to meet that foot. He wants relief, but knows that if he rests, the heat will just be worse. But there is just more pain in front of him. "How am I going to get through that one?" He squints to look at the second ring. Sweat beads on his forehead.

He reaches the second ring at last. Now he intends to climb over it. Where there was no fire on the ground before, all the twigs have ignited throughout the ground in the circle. More than that, it's heating up the stones underneath as well. He is standing on fire and any moment of thinking or hesitation invites more pain.

He puts his hand on the wood. It recoils quickly from the heat. He puts it there again. "Just keep it there..." Now he places more of his weight on his hands—all the while resisting the urge to pull away. His hands are burning completely now. The skin bubbles over. He hooks one of his legs up on the wood. He pushes off the other foot and rolls over the second ring.

He falls with his back to the ground. He screams. It echoes out into the forest. Dipaka hears his scream, "What are they doing to you?"

He's on his back. His legs kick wildly at the air and his arms flailing in the air. The elbows touch the ground and his body is jolted. He flips over to his knees and hands. His back expands and rounds. He coughs. The smoke is in his lungs. He looks up and sees the wall of the inner ring. More coughing. His breathing becomes more labored.

He crawls forward and then he collapses. The heat has stopped registering to his body—even though his face is now on the ground and burning. The hair on his arms, legs, head, and face all burn away. He closes his eyes. "I don't want to get up," he thought. The pain is somewhere far away. The heat: it's a distant chill. Somewhere in-between the first and second ring, that wasn't where his mind was. He hears a voice. He concentrates on this voice beyond the crackling fire, beyond the sound of water boiling out of the wood, a sweet voice in the dark. It's speaking without words.

He crawls forward again. Feelings are dull. There is a voice that grows louder in the dark. He feels himself moving upwards and sideways. He curls his body in a fetal position. He opens his eyes and finds himself in the center. In the gaps between the wavering flames, he sees the whole village—his family in front of him. He closes his eyes and reopens them. They are still there.

The orange fire now burns higher and brighter than before.

The platform matches the height of the rings. It's a square platform. He brings himself to sit on his shins. He puts his hands on his thighs and closes his eyes. There is solace in the dark. Voices are heard beyond the wind and fire. Most of the villagers recite the name of the First Man. In unison, they recite his sons and daughters. Then his sons and daughters.

The pain. Each name is etched into every painful pulse and feeling. He has never heard these names before, but now each one is becoming a permanent memory. The number of voices roll out as the ancestral tree splits from a common branch. And then it becomes louder when their common ancestry realigns again. They recite the names one by one by each generation. The volume and names continue to waver in and out.

There is a realization that occurs to him: that to know where each name comes in for one person's lineage of the family tree, each individual villager would have to know the whole tree. The effort for this feat is the true cost of family. And when will he learn each lineage? Each name?

The time between each name is longer. He sees something under his closed eyes. One of his great-great-grandfather's name is mentioned. He sees him. He sees him planting trees on the border of the forest and tending to vegetables in the dirt. His great-great-grandmother, she's tending to wounded men coming from a hunt. Now on his mother's side, her great grandfather is forging a sword, his father's sword. Her great grandmother is weaving yarn. And as though he was viewing through a curtain, he sees the other twelve of his great-great grandparents and their lives.

The orange fire is burning blue. The fires' height is lowered, but it is a hotter and deeper heat. It's a flame that is self sustaining now, a fire that re-ignites its own coals. With the lower height, If he would open his eyes, he would be able to see the villagers from afar. But he doesn't. All the wood on the ground are white-hot coals. The stones underneath are glowing orange. The blue flame reflects on his face, on his bald head.

His grandparents...He walks along a path in the forest. It's a bright day outside. It's his grandfather. He's younger...A tree up ahead splits their walking in two: he goes to the left of the tree, and his father's father goes right. He crosses it and looks to his right again: his grandmother on his mother's side. On the outside, he's mouthing their names even before the villagers recite their names. He's getting closer to an opening in the forest. All four of his grandparents, and their daughters, their sons, his cousins: they appear behind him. They push him forward!

The voices cease.

He opens his eyes. He first notices a pale blue light casting over everything. The smoke of ashes burns his eyes. His eyes tear from the sting and blink a few times. He notices the chirping of birds. They are high-pitched, cheerful, and frequent in their calls. He hears them flapping their wings, launching themselves off springy tree limbs. He looks forward again.

"Mother, Father..."

"Quill!", the whole village calls to him.

A villager steps forward. He extends his hand to him. Their eyes meet for a long moment.

This was it.

Was this ritual the sacrifice needed?

Quill extends his hand to meet the villager's. Quill stops for a moment.

His arm is burnt black. Its size is like a long, skinny branch. His fingers are like tiny burnt twigs. Somehow, they manage to move. He hovers his hand over the villager's. Quill touches his finger to the villager's. Then all his limbs go limp at once. His body has failed him.

His parents run up to catch him. They support him from falling. Quill whispers slowly, ash falling from his lips—or rather skull at this point. It is an intense labor on his part to say these three words,

"Let...me...go..."

* * *

The charred body of Quill lies on a bed of leaves. It is a body in a very superficial sense. One could even call his body a skeleton. The sunlight passes over him. There is some flesh remaining. He is a skeleton. The face looks shrunken, it is half bone and half flesh. Only the eyes hold any life left.

"Son, no one has been burned before by the fire. You didn't have to endure it." His father's words.

The green eyes look blankly into the sky.

The Mother cries and holds her son's hands.

Dipaka stands by the edge by Quill's body. He thinks of his own father's words. He was only give words that allowed him to control animals. "Father, why weren't there words to heal people? Quill, you will not pass away."

For five days and five nights, Quill has laid there in the middle of the community. Everything happens around him. Five days and five nights without food. His green eyes peered at the blue sky, the rain that falls on him, the night sky, the stars, the rustling leaves. Voices, however distant it seemed—they were actually close.

Was the blue sky like the ocean? A great body of water? Mountains? Were they like the edge of a leaf—with a peak and valley? There was a world waiting for him and he had to see it.

* * *

In those five days, Dipaka had taken the role of Quill. He had gone to the forest alone, gathered vegetation, and replanted what he has taken.

"The First Man of this forest..I wonder where the first seed emerged," Dipaka questioned the forest.

In Quill's absence, he has started gathering provisions. By the bear's den, he has started field stripping squirrels and drying out the meat in slices. He has prepared canteens out of animal skins. He is putting vegetation into canvas bags.

The bears walk towards the squirrel meat. "No," Dipaka says. They stop. He ties a canvas bag to one of the bears. "Follow me." The bear walks a few paces, awkwardly trying to adjust to the weight of the food on its back. Dipaka leads the bear on a loop. The more it follows Dipaka, the more adept it becomes in moving with the load. He looks at the cubs, and decides not to train them.

Over the past two and a half months with Quill, he has collected furs of various games. And in the last five days, he had resigned himself to tailoring Quill's fur coat. "Quill, the moon will become full soon. Your coat will be ready by then."

* * *

Members of the community sit next to Quill each day. They tell him what has been happening. If only he could see their faces. Instead, they were voices of a blue sky.

Someone had a child. Someone had a birthday. Someone's daughter had their first steps. A baby son called his father, dada. Were these stories what his ancestors saw? *Is* seeing?

A wispy cloud floats by and disappears.

* * *

It's the twilight of the fifth day since the ritual. Quill's mind wanders. In the rustling of the leaves, he hears a voice. He floats among the canopies of the forest. He felt this before. This feeling was familiar. It was just like the fire. A figure of light walks and illuminates the forest. Quill follows it around and through trees. It tells Quill, "Stay."

"Are you the First Man?"

The figure of light dims and disappears into the dark.

"The world is waiting. I have to answer its call," Quill says to the darkness.

He sees himself lying on that bed of leaves. There's a charred skeleton, a body that's half dead and half alive. Was he being prepared to be buried? Were they waiting for him to pass? Can this body be made whole?

It could be wished whole.

He saw what people's wishes could do. In a period of drought, when people died of thirst, someone made a wish to bring water. Since then, rain would come when needed and no sooner or later. That was legend.

As a child, a stray ash from a fire floated towards the forest. The ash ignited a dry leaf. And from leaf to leaf, the fire spread and grew. The next morning, the forest was on fire. With one wish, the fire was extinguished and all that was left was smoke.

There was joy too. The night after someone's rites, she walked the entire community to the edge of the forest. She told them to look skyward. And for one night, the stars in the sky shone like small suns. Each person was a dozen shadows dancing in the glow of many suns.

There were feasts. People wished for bounty. For abundance in harvest. For long days and nights of food.

There was compassion. Men were carried back from hunts with bones pierced out of their bodies, wounds that became green and yellow from disease, blood spilled. Each time there was a person, without hesitation, to wish them whole again.

It could be wished whole.

The body could be whole.

Did he really needed to say the words for his wish to come true? It was a wish seated in his heart: a deep wish that was seeded and grew by these few days. The mountains, the oceans, the shining stars in the vast desert. There is so much to see. The people, the stories that were in this place could be everywhere. There is so much to learn and understand.

Time here was stuck, but time elsewhere, somewhere else, could be boundless and changing.

"I wish...I wish...to live forever."

He sleeps.

Nature will repay its debt to him for his stewardship of the forest. On the bed of leaves where he lays, the leaves dissolve into him. Veins on the leaves become his veins. Green leaves turn red and become his blood. The yellow, sun-starved leaves rebuild his skin. With each leaf his body absorbs, his bed becomes thinner, and he sinks closer to the ground. The black and burnt skin becomes wrinkled, then becomes vibrant and elastic again as if death and age reversed. He sinks lower. His body takes in the water, the dirt, the leaves, and even the worms from the ground. These become the elements that compose his eyebrows and hair.

He lies in a crater.

* * *

Sun rises.

Quill's father walks out of his home. He sees Quill lying in a crater. It is about the same size as the three rings from the ritual. He circles around, bends down, and runs the soil through his hands. His son was whole again.

Quill wakes up. He rises and views his hands. It was complete.

The Father throws him a sword. The Father says to him, "Today, you'll lead the hunt."

Quill catches the sword. "Father." Quill is surprised he could speak effortlessly. They head into the forest before anyone else has woken up.

Quill returns to the village. He shoulders a large animal. There was a great feast that night, celebrating Quill's return. An elder woman tells him, "You are a strong man now, just like the First Man."

Dipaka turns to him, "Tonight's the night we leave. I have all the provisions ready. We cannot wait." Quill nods.

* * *

He wakes up to the sound of insects chirping. He sits back on his cot. He looks around and tries to remember this moment. The wood that sticks out from the corner, the floor, the ceiling, the smell of their home, the moonlight that pierces through the gaps in the roof—all of it.

He walks to see his parents for the last time. He quietly parts the curtain. He sees his mother. He parts it completely and..."Father, where are you?" The Father isn't there. He slowly puts back the curtain in its rightful place. This was no time for sentiments, he has to go. "Goodbye, Mother."

He walks outside. Dipaka stands ready with his bear and fur coat. He hands the fur coat to Quill. The man wears it over his green tunic. The bear is tied with supplies. There are bags with the fire starter cream, firewood, clothes, fruits and vegetables, dried meat, and pouches of water. They look forward to the emptiness ahead. They do not need a light at this point, they know their way by feel and memory.

They walk towards the threshold of the forest, farther from the village. The insects' chirping is fainter now.

The pitch darkness is starting to end. They see a blue speck in the dark. Soon, they're at the clearing: the same threshold where the man has found Dipaka. A full moon illuminates the entire desert. The sands are blue in color. The way it blows in the wind looks like water. Long white clouds are in rows all along the sky. They are only apparent because of the moon.

Quill walks ahead five feet. He sees an object planted into the sand. He falls on his knees and wipes his eyes. He takes it, wraps it in cloth, and ties it to his hip. He gets up and continues walking. It is his father's sword. For a long time after, he would wonder if he had heard the sound of leaves rustling in the forest.

* * *

Thunder rolls across the desert. From the threshold of the forest, the silent lightning strikes the sand. Seconds later, a large boom is heard. The two shadow figures take off from the forest and into the desert. Rain soaks their clothes and fur coats. Each lightning strike from the distance illuminates the desert.

And another thunder boom illuminates the desert. It flashes. Rain begins to pour across the desert. Their torch going out is in danger now. The smell of ozone permeates the air.

The rain comes from afar for them. It is raining heavily. The sand is flooded by the water. The ground that used to give way to their weight is transformed. It is absolutely hard to the touch when they step on the ground. Water overruns their feet. This rain has made the walk easier.

For a second, Dipaka imagines himself on a beach, waiting for sailing ships to take him aboard.

Over the rain and thunder, Quill yells to Dipaka, "Is this the ocean?!"

"No! We have to keep going!"

Their torches go out. "Keep walking!" Dipaka calls to Quill.

Every flash of lightning, Dipaka sees Quill's back.

They trudge along the hard sand. The water is up to their ankles. The water flows from higher sand dunes and crosses their legs. The sand flows through their toes. Other streams come from every direction, and even water falls from their elevation. The water level is rising. Streams are criss-crossing each other and crashing on their legs. There is no beginning or end, no order to how the water is moving. It is becoming harder to move.

Quill stops and tilts his head back. He takes a drink from the sky. The light comes. Dipaka sees him and does not comment.

A series of four lightning strikes comes down. The light lasts long enough to illuminate something large out in the distance. Dipaka and Quill see it. The edges, the peaks, even in the dark. Quill begins to speak, "Ar-" he is interrupted by the sound of four lightning strikes, "ARE THOSE THE MOUNTAINS?!"

"THEY ARE!" Dipaka yells over the rain.

The bear lays down. "GET UP! GET UP!" It does not comply. "Pio om toh!" It stretches its legs and falls to its side and sleeps.

Quill yells over the lightning and rain, "Dipaka! We can't go any farther without the bear!"

Dipaka stands there in the rain; lightning striking all around him; the water coming up to his knees. Quill looks at him for direction. Dipaka sits down. He takes a stick from the supplies. He fashions a makeshift umbrella from the stick and tunic. There was nothing else he could do. They sleep lying against the bear.

All night long, water swishes on their bodies. Lightning booms.

* * *

They wake up to the sound of the bear yawning. Quill opens his eyes. There was light out there. An emptiness to the desert. He stands up and feels something between his toes. It wasn't empty and it wasn't sand. He bends over and picks it up. It's a flower. A twelve-petaled flower. He looks up. The entire desert was full of flowers from horizon to horizon. He moves his head and each flower changes luminance. The desert was shimmering.

"Dipaka, wake up. It smells like the forest, but different."

Dipaka sees it. "We are blessed to see this." He bows his head.

They sit and eat before taking to their journey again. Each of them were quiet and took in the setting—even the bear.

* * *

For three days, they walk towards the mountains. For all the training they spent carrying the logs, walking in the cold desert was easy. Without the logs, their pace was astonishing. A five day's journey turned into three.

On their journey, sometimes they cross other desert traders. They exchange goods, enough to boost their supplies for further travel. During the second night, a group of three desert traders they meet spend their dinner with them.

One of them takes out a glass bottle with a golden-brown liquid. "Quill, here, take a sip. You're not a man until you do!"

"Quill, go ahead," Dipaka urges.

Quill drinks from the bottle and coughs up the alcohol. Dipaka and the other desert traders laugh. Dipaka says, "Try again, but this time drink a little bit." Quill takes a sip and then coughs. A desert trader pats him on the back, "Good man! Where are you two heading?"

"Where are you two heading?" He asks.

"Oh, the mountains. Good luck to you both, and to your bear! But for now, let's feast and tell stories!" A desert trader says.

They uncover cloth from a pit. There's meat being cooked over a bed of charcoal. A desert trader hands a piece of meat to the bear. It eats it up. They share the rest.

One of the traders point out a gazelle's silhouette by the sunset.

"Ay! You would be at the base of the mountain by tomorrow night."

"Yes, we would," Dipaka answers.

"That mountain is not so bad. You could pass over it in a day. Dipaka, fellow trader, have drink."

Dipaka takes a bite of the meat and drinks. He asks the traders, "So how did you get here?"

"We came along from the North, from Rus. Before that, we were in Gibraltar." He opens his bag and shows the trinkets he got from each country. Quill looks at the souvenirs. They were novelties. Metal was cast into intricate pieces with inlaid jewelry. Clothing and scarves were much different from what he or Dipaka had worn. This was the world, and he's being invited in. He takes the trinkets in hand.

While fiddling with it, Quill feels warm. "I came from a place that was stuck in time. Some place without adventure...without reaching...but I think I'm ready."

"Cheers to adventure!" They all drink up. "Cheers!"

The next morning, they bid goodbye to the three traders. They hug and bid each other well wishes.

* * *

They arrive at the base of the mountain.

"Thank you. You may return home," Dipaka instructs the bear. The bear walks back, where it will be reunited with its cubs.

"To reach the cities beyond, we have to cross this mountain," Dipaka says. Dipaka points his finger towards the peak. Quill tilts his head and tries to understand that there was something more massive than the trees he has jumped from. There was no end to its height. Clouds obscure the peak.

* * *

They are both slowing down. Dipaka is coughing. Quill sees that his walking is becoming labored. Quill covers his face when a cold gust cuts by him. "Dipaka," Quill's muffled voice calls to him, "are you warm?"

"Yes."

Wind begins to surround them. They walk against wind resistance from all directions. Their ankles have to torque and adjust to stay grounded. The provisions on their back rattle and pull them. As they go higher, the weather changes to a blizzard—the wind and snow cutting and biting their exposed skin.

"What is this?! Is this light?!" Quill yells over the wind.

"It's snow!"

The wind pushes Quill off track. He struggles to walk forward against the gust.

"I can't see!"

"Hold my hand!"

Quill searches in the blank white space and grabs onto Dipaka's hands. "If we lose each other, Dipaka, I want you to have this wish! Keep it! And in good season, reap your heart's desire!"

In this white place, where everything disappeared, Dipaka knew he has received something mythic and ancient, something much older than those words his father taught him. Maybe the snow is a light. His fingers slowly curl up. "Friend, I will guard your traditions!"

At that moment, a gust aims straight at Quill. It pushes him over. Quill drags Dipaka on the fall down. Quill slides down the mountain. Dipaka loses his grip on Quill. A gust tips over Dipaka too.

The sword is thrown into the wind.

Dipaka calls out over the sound of the wind. "Quill!" The cold is unforgiving. Dipaka walks around the rocky landscape being careful not to fall. "Quill! Where are you?!" His voice is swallowed by the wind. Dipaka picks up his supplies and slowly walks away, looking back occasionally. The snow and wind enwrap his vision. He could not risk his life to find his friend. "I am sorry."

* * *

Quill wakes up. The sky is clear and the stars are out. Green and purple waves flow across the sky; an undulating, wavelike sky. The firmament is moving in waves. "Dipaka, what is this? one answers.

His hands are black with frostbite. He's shivering. Ice freezes his foot. He looks around for his rations, they're nowhere to be found.

He hobbles onward. His breathing becomes forceful. He's past the peak. His body tumbles down rocks. It cuts into his skin. Blotches of blood drip onto the snow. A wind blows up the peak. Every step forward becomes heavy and without control. His knees collapse and hit a rock. He screams in pain.

He winces and closes his eyes to deal with the pain.

A voice of a friend compels him, "Keep walking. Go on." He keeps going on. He feels for the ground beneath him before taking any steps. His eyes were firmly fixed on the sky above him. The stars and moon were washed in a celestial curtain. It was like crepuscular rays shining through a cloud, but here it was rays of green and purple light shining through empty sky. He decided he didn't need to know what it was. It was enough to see it, it didn't need a name.

The snow? It's not cold anymore. The dirt? It's warm. "Am I home?" He opens his eyes. A bright sun rises over the horizon; greeting him.

Buildings are a haze in the distance. A figure in the far distance takes off a fur coat, revealing a bright green tunic. He folds the fur coat and puts it on the ground. He turns to look back and continues walking towards the city.

The man's fingers get warmer. As he opens and closes his hands into a fist, black dust falls from his fingers. His fists become white and the color begins to return to his hands. A flurry of different color dust emanates from his body: red, peach, white, black. His hands run through his legs, arms, back. There are no scars. There is no pain.

He stands in front of dirt and patches of grass. Quill recognizes the dirt, the grass, but without the trees in the way, these plains were almost unfamiliar. Gusts of wind blow through him and rise above the mountains.

This man looks out away from the city and to the east. A wind blows from the east and takes with it the sand from his fur coat. He turns to see the sand of the desert wash away. He looks back at where the wind came from.

Quill smells the air: a strong ocean mist.

CONTENTS

CHAPTER TWO

KINGDOM

The Kingdom was lost.

In the middle of a busy bazaar, two merchants talk of the King.

"I can not believe that the Prince and the King died at the same time. The palace must be in turmoil," one merchant says.

"So what happens to the order of succession? Who rules this Kingdom now?" one merchant says to the other.

Soldiers march out of the palace and into the bazaar.

The palace sits on top of a hill. It's painted red. It's surrounded by large walls in three concentric rings. On the four cardinal points of each of these circular walls are large doors. They are heavy in the sense that they are virtually immovable. On each of the doors are large bronze-casted friezes—each one with a giant animal on it: dragon, snake, horse, sheep, monkey, rooster, dog, pig, rat, ox, tiger, and rabbit.

"Where is the King?" the people ask.

"There are going to be changes," one of the soldiers says.

A person clad in armor steps forward. But his armor is different from all the others: it's regal. Intricate artwork painted in golden lines cover every armor plate. The artwork has been scratched off, worn by time and battle. He is the General.

The soldiers line and fill the streets; taking every available opening. The General stops walking and stomps his feet on the ground twice. The soldiers step forcibly apart in two lines; creating an open walkway.

"I am taking control of this Kingdom! In the next few days, you will surrender your materials when asked. We will make this Kingdom equal for all!"

In the following days, the guards seize control of the harvested crops and food in the bazaar. People attempt to protest and fight, but the soldiers overpower them. The food is taken and wheeled inside the palace walls.

***

In the bazaar, horns sound from afar. Soldiers eating in the restaurants get up, grab their swords, take to their horses, and ride to the edge of town. A dust storm approaches from the desert. Clouds of sand roll towards the Kingdom. It looks like a tidal wave. It wasn't any of these, those are men.

Each one of them comes in tattered clothes. Arrows are fired from horseback and land near the soldiers. Some arrows ricochet off the armor, others barely pierce through the soldiers' skin. Soldiers from on top of the wall fire off their own arrows. Horses crash into the sand and mangle the bandits underneath them. Still, the bandits press through and cover the distance. The dust storm approaches nearer and nearer.

As the bandits get closer, their arrows pierce through the soldiers' armor. Soldiers fall from on top of the wall. Others on the grounds fall over. Many arrows bounce off the wall.

The bandits arrive at the base of the wall. Some shoot arrows overhead. A dozen others throw grappling hooks onto the wall. They begin to scale it. They make their way onto the top. The sentries engage in combat with the bandits. As more bandits climb up, more soldiers flock from the center to defend the Kingdom. In the span of an hour, a battle of attrition was waged.

All that was left were hundreds of corpses from both sides. The bandits' horses have long fled.

* * *

At a distance far from the commotion, five bandits climbed the wall and infiltrated the Kingdom. In a week, they gather enough information about the town's layout and leave. They steal horses from a stable and ride it back towards their camp in the plains.

* * *

The General-King sits on the throne. He still wears his regal armor.

He views straight through the royal hallway, through the open doors, and on the east wall: smoke rises from the east end of the Kingdom. Black ash rises against a dark sky. The wall flashes orange from a bonfire. Bodies are burned.

He leans forward on his throne, and rubs his goatee and mustache. "Bandits. Scum."

* * *

There are rumblings along the bazaar.

"Did you hear about the glass road?"

"What?"

A buyer chimes in, "I was there by the wall. This man took a sword and pointed it at the bandits. Flame and fire came out from the end. An inferno burned each and every person. Each bandit was engulfed in a white fire."

"A white fire?"

"Yes. It wasn't orange or blue. It was as white as the sun."

The merchant looks over to another merchant, "Can you believe such a thing?"

"And where they fell? There are splotches of glass."

* * *

Dipaka walks into the bazaar with his sword held high. The black sword has lost its specular quality, its sheen. It seems more like a shadow now. A dark void that does not reflect any light at all.

A soldier walks up to him. "Bandit!"

The green tunic he wears, and a fur coat on his back sets him apart from everyone in the bazaar.

"I am no bandit! I just saved your Kingdom from those who were!"

"I'm putting you in the dungeon."

"You can try."

Dipaka takes the sword and swings it in the soldier's direction. Blue and yellow sparks fly off the armor. It's not a fatal hit, but the sword shaves the shoulder plate cleanly off. Metal is still ringing in the air. Dipaka swings for another strike. The soldier ducks under and tackles Dipaka to the ground. Dipaka holds onto the sword even while falling. While mounted on top of Dipaka, the soldier grabs onto Dipaka's wrist and slams his hand against the ground. "Let go of the sword!" Dipaka does not let go. The soldier keeps slamming his hand into the ground. Hairline fractures form in his hand. Try as hard as he might, his body has failed before his will: Dipaka lets go of the sword.

Surrounding soldiers run in and grab a hold of Dipaka. They arrest him with metal shackles and chains.

* * *

He is led towards the palace. The walls are massive. Even from a distance, you would need to crane your head up to see the top. He is led to a large gate. Sentries from on top of the wall notice the soldiers and motion for the ground soldiers to open the gate. A large counterweight on the side moves up as two men open it. The gate splits apart in the middle; opening in two halves.

A wide expanse. There are houses behind the wall. The ground is paved, and stone slabs covering the floor. Soldiers march back and forth. Other soldiers practice archery, sword fighting, horseback riding. This must be the garrison. Another wall is far away.

Dipaka is led past all these troops. It is a massive army that this Kingdom has. It was a scary feeling seeing into the true size of a Kingdom's army.

He is led to the second gate. It is a different life in this ring. Women and children walk about. There is a marked difference in clothes between the people inside the walls and outside. The people inside this place wore beautiful, embroidered silk. Their clothes were vibrant in such bright colors like turquoise or magenta.

Dipaka asks, "Are these the King's wives and sons? How rich the King must be; to have so many wives and children."

"Keep walking." The soldiers prod him along.

The women and children look on the prisoner being led through to the third gate. Dipaka looks at them. They seem scared, but not of him. Behind this gate was the Royal Palace. It is a distant object. As they walk closer, the steps can be discerned. 108 steps lead up to the Royal Palace.

* * *

Inside the palace, on his throne, the King sits.

"General! We present you a sword and prisoner!" The soldier stomps his feet. A soldier kicks Dipaka on the leg, and he is compelled to kneel.

A subordinate is summoned by the king. The soldiers walk the sword to the king. The General-King examines the sword. The blade is black, the darkest black. No sheen or reflection to it. It is a visual void. There are contours to the sword, but how can anyone tell without neither shadow or light. The King flicks his finger on the blade. There was no metallic ringing. There was no sound at all.

The General-King begins, "There are stories being told of a man who protected this Kingdom. And this man held a sword that breathed fire. He repelled the bandits from the wall. Then he walked into my Kingdom. My Kingdom!"

The General-King walks down from his throne, Dipaka's sword in hand. He kneels down by Dipaka. "I will show you gratitude for protecting the people. Let me find you food, clothing, so that you could become a soldier. Submit to my order," the General-King says.

"No," Dipaka responds.

The King walks back to his throne. He holds onto the sword. "Tell me. Who forged this sword?"

"I don't know. It's a gift. It's a sword brought from a timeless, strange land," Dipaka says.

"It is a strange object, isn't it? One that has no color, but has a form, a shape."

"Give it back."

"You will see that you have no control here."

Where was I? How did I come to this place? The Silk Road, the desert, a forest, a mountain. God-given. I was supposed to die. A miracle. I was god-gifted. God gifted...the Mandate of Heaven was mines, and mines' alone. Who was I to be controlled, to be tamed? I won't. I won't be tamed.

"What gives you power over men?" Dipaka knew what real power was. He had been witness to it.

The King waves his hands. Soldiers cover Dipaka's mouth with another shackle. They take him by the arms and carry him away. As Dipaka is led away, the General-King concentrates on the sword, "What an interesting trinket."

* * *

He is led to a garden. Bamboo grows in large heights around him. There is a clearing. It's a grove.

Slabs of stone were placed in large square tiles. Specks of sand from the bamboo groves slide across the surface of these immaculate, marble-white tiles. The sand crunches when the soldiers step on it. Each tile is about the length of a man. And in the center of each tile was a square hole about the size of a forearm. Dipaka is escorted through the middle of this grove.

He looks down into a hole. And from the light that reaches into the holes, he can make out people. There were feet that caught sunlight from those who sat. Faces bathed in harsh light that look up from below. He could see people pacing around in their cells. There was the old, the young, children, women down in this place. There were two hundred squares and souls.

The squares drop off in front of him. As if there was nothing on the horizon. He keeps walking. A large semi-circle caps the two hundred cells. Concentric, descending steps lead down to the entrance to the dungeons. It was about one floor deep into the ground. As they descend the steps, their footsteps echo out. It was a perverse open-air amphitheater.

An array of stone columns creates the entrance to the cells. He is led into the labyrinth. The air was stagnant. Stone walls were built around to support the tiles above. There were wood doors to each cell. Most of them were rotted through and through. There were a few fresh doors; replacing the rotten and broken down ones. The wooden doors seem like a recent addition.

* * *

How many weeks has it been? Months? There was the rain. The days of dry heat. Nights where I shivered. All the while light would pour from the surface.

At night, I'd hear the wind howl. And as it moves past the window, it'll whistle too. I take note of the moonlight every night. When the cell becomes completely dark, I'll know a month has passed.

It takes twenty steps to go around this cell. I can endure. My hands are raw from hitting the walls. I've seen you survive through fire and flame. Am I as resilient as you? How much longer can I go on?

You gave me a wish. What did you wish for when you died? You had a life well lived. Your family loved you. You had a house, a landscape that was your own. Isolated.

And where did I begin?

The countryside by paddies. The fields were green and sun-soaked. We always had enough to eat. My father told me to pursue the dreams I had. And my mother said when I had my fill of journeys, return and be wed.

The tenets that I learned. A pantheon of gods, each dominating specific forces of nature. That we are born into castes. Without power. What were they all for? That to say we were the world and the world was within us? This damp, disgusting place. It's in me? And these tenets, they teach that me and the world is like a flower. It is a flower that blooms into itself. And it continues this way forever in both directions. As if it was cyclical without beginning or end. And that you were me, and I was you, and we were whole with the world.

I took myself to cities far from home. In strange places, I received their clothes. I learned their customs, ate their foods. I traded spices, silver and gold. There was such a fire, a passion to life. Exchanges would be made over and over. I'll join other merchants as they cross the great desert by camelback. I'll watch them prepare meals by spreading coal on the sands and cooking meat out in the cold nights. I remembered standing before large ships with sails taller than the tallest trees I've seen. And slowly, the world will grow for me. I'll amass my own caravan of camels. Going from east to west I was poor. I remember traveling back East along the same roads with silk and gold from Italy. I was rich.

Moonlight, where are you? The damp smell of night is here. Wood. I've smelled that wooden door everyday. The first few nights in this prison had an unbearable smell. Then I stopped smelling it. There's a hole by the corner where I shit and piss. Who knows how deep that hole goes.

Then I came to the desert. I was robbed of my riches by bandits. My caravan of camels, my clothes, my bullions of gold and silver. Left with only a canteen of water, I considered myself dead. I wanted to exact my revenge on this world. Although I cursed the world and my tenets, I was delivered to a green place. There, I met you...and lost you.

Now I am here again, in a place where I am compelled to curse this world. But you taught me something, a lesson I've forgotten.

Quill, what lesson were you teaching me?

* * *

"You jail me. You let me rot here while you sit on your throne. You are not my king. I'll be the King." This was his wish. A tension in his body, a sort of weight, was released.

* * *

"Knock down the prison doors! Release the prisoners!" Horses galloped over the square holes over the cells. Sounds of metal clanging and dropping are heard. "Get out! You're freed." These words are repeated and at each repetition, the sound approaches him. His door is knocked open, just enough to show a sliver of the outside. "Get out!" someone yells into his door.

He leaves the prison. The saviors were galloping away in their horses.

* * *

Dipaka retraces his steps from the grove to the palace. It was months ago. The texture of the ground under his feet felt so good. The air was fresh.

Men in black cloaks were galloping all around. Fires were being set. The General-King fends off the men in horses. One man gets off his horse. He fights without weapons. He's able to dodge the General-King's sword. He dips under. He grabs the King's legs and throws him to the floor. The King lies on the ground. The bandit stomps on the King's wrist. The King releases his grip on the sword. The bandit throws the sword far away—landing paces away from Dipaka. The King grabs the bandits ankle and with one squeeze, the bone is crushed. The bandit's ankle was no longer a rigid structure, it was squeezed into a liquid sac. The King does the same with the bandit's head.

Dipaka takes the sword and runs at the King. He swings at him. The sword's tip lights up in fire. The King steps back. Dipaka swings again. The fire is an inferno; a column of fire that touches the night sky. The King retreats back. "You're with them?!" the King asks him. Dipaka recalls his confinement. He swings again at the King. A wall of fire rolls at the King. The King runs up the steps towards the Royal Palace while Dipaka continues to swipe at the King. The General-King runs and dive rolls into the Royal Palace.

Catching the King at the end of the dive, Dipaka strikes at his armor. It connects and an elbow plate comes off. The King grabs onto the sword's blade with his hand. "You will submit to me," the King tells Dipaka. Steam comes from the King's hand. As the blood burns and evaporates; the smell of iron fills the room. The King pulls the sword closer to him, pulling Dipaka closer. With one hand gripping the sword, he front kicks Dipaka. Dipaka is fazed for a moment, with the air knocked out of him. The King punches him in the temple, still holding onto the blade. Dipaka twists the sword. The King releases his grip, "I've defeated armies. You're only one man."

A rush of wind blows away the candles inside the throne room. It shuts the Royal Palace doors. Darkness.

An electric arc comes from the sword. The electricity seems alive, like tree branches reaching, touching, crawling on the room's walls. This was the light now.

Violent wisps illuminate randomly. Fire sparks ignite in the air around them.

There was the sound too. The crackling. The crackling belonging to the fire and to the lightning. From the sword, a bright daylight emits; cuts the room into half light and half shadow. Then the light recedes. They are both blinded in the dark.

A rapturous wind spirals out from the sword. Sand manifests from within the tornado. The sand gets blown to every inch of the room. Sand hits against the stone and wood. It sounds like rain was falling on every surface: up, down, every side, every side.

"Am I being taken inside of you?!" the King yells over the wind.

Dipaka sees something through the glow of the fire and the flashing lights of the lightning: an opening. He stabs the sword into the King's heart. Then the killing blow: decapitating the King.

* * *

Dipaka opens the Palace doors.

Beyond the ring he saw smoke. He runs down the 108 stairs. He sees the large gate and closes the distance to there. With a single slash, the sword emits a half-moon crescent shaped fire to the gate. The fire cuts through the metal gate, leaving a diagonal hole. Lightning pulses ever so briefly in the heat of the hole. He runs through the opening.

People are rappelling down the walls of the rings. They wear black clothes. Their faces are hidden in hoods and scarves wrapped by their mouths. They are corralling people. A long line of people are walking chained and away from the center ring. Bandits chase and tackle down stranglers. Soldiers engage in combat with the bandits. Without weapons, the bandits managed to disarm the swords and shields from the soldiers. The soldiers' arms and knees were dislocated. They lie on the ground unable to do anything.

The Kingdom that was promised to him was being destroyed and ransacked.

He runs to the line of chained people. Other bandits run to him. He holds the sword up to the air. There were twenty-odd bandits rushing to tackle him. He swings the sword at one of them. The bandit ducks under it. Dipaka side steps and avoids another bandit tackling him. That bandit falls to the ground. Dipaka hits one of them with the hilt of his sword. It looks like a swarm of blackness enveloping him. Instinctively, Dipaka hits the sword's point on the ground. A ripple of wind throws the bandits away from him. Twenty lightning strikes fall from the sky with incomparable sound. They hit every bandit simultaneously. Each one of them fall to their knees. They are smoldering corpses that kneel to Dipaka.

An echo comes from far away, "Do not retreat!" The yell reverberates along the ring he's in.

Some of the soldiers have begun to kill the bandits. Dipaka runs to the chained hostages. The bandits maintaining the line come at him. There was a hesitation in their movement. As they come at him, he's able to slice and dispatch each one easily. The people on the line hold up their hands. He breaks the chains. On and on until each one of them are freed—a hundred in total. They run to their houses.

For a moment, he is paralyzed. A strong scent freezes him where he is. He's in a daze. It's like the faint smell of a rose with grass touched by morning dew. He scans the people who ran from him, "Who are you?"

He runs to the last interior wall; the wall that separates the Royal City from its people. A hole has been blown out with explosives. Stone and concrete rubble lie on one side of the hole; stacked like a ramp. Archers from on high shoot at him. He dodges the arrows. The archers take aim at the other bandits that are funneling through the hole. Dipaka cuts through each of them. The ones who were not cut manage to get through.

These bandits were a plague. An endless swarm of darkness.

These bandits were quick, fast. Like a swift wind, they passed by him. They scoop up the fallen bandits. Dipaka watches as they run up the walls as if it were a floor to them—while carrying the weight of the fallen—and disappear.

He hears explosions and lights from everywhere. Walls were being destroyed. "No!" The walls and rings that he dreamed would be his were crumbling. More lights and booms. Dust and detritus fill every empty space in the air. Every ring wall came down. Dust hangs in the air. It was unmistakable that the walls had fallen. Through the dust and without the walls, he could see the faint silhouette of the palace. In the other direction, he could see through to the plains.

He sees faint dark figures—now blurred by the dust—retrieving the bodies. Swift shadows that moved. He tries to stab at these shadows. "Fight me!" he yells to them. He swipes at the air with his hands clearing his vision. He coughs. The dust has filled the entirety of the Royal City.

"What are you telling me?" He looks at the sword. He holds it up and points it towards the plains. A cyclone of wind bursts from the tip. He is pushed back by the impulsive force, and has to find his footing. The dust from the air gets sucked into the cyclone and it funnels into the plains. Tiny stones skip and scrape across the ground. As the air becomes clearer, the sunlight that was blocked was finding its way through the clearing. It wasn't night.

The smoke has cleared. Sunlight illuminates everything.

The large metal gates still hold up. They're monoliths in the open space. Twelve giant gates mark what once was. There are no more walls to separate the different classes. It was silent outside.

People cautiously come out of their homes. Blood was spilled all over. There are rings of rubble where the walls once stood. Dead soldiers are on the ground. A circle of 20 black spots lies some place in the open space. The people stare at the one who stands alone.

* * *

In the aftermath, Dipaka walks back to the grove. A crowd follows the figure with the black sword. He freed the remaining people from the prisons. The prisoners reunited with their families.

An elder priest comes from the crowd, "The King was no good. There was famine while he feasted. People were imprisoned for speaking against him. And when the King denies his people; goes against the will of the people, nature corrects. Kings and dynasties can be taken away. If Heaven deems it so, even the King may be removed. This is the Mandate of Heaven.

"I lived through a dynasty of three kings. Never before have I seen a true demonstration of the power of nature. You are truly God-given and are meant to lead us."

Dipaka walks to the Palace. The people follow him. He walks up the 108 steps. He steps into the Palace alone. The people stay outside. Sunlight casts the doors' patterns on the King's decapitated head and body. Iron and blood hang heavy in the air. It will be but a short time until the body begins to rot. Dipaka takes the crown off the ground. He realizes that he hasn't had time to get shoes.

He walks out. The crowd chants to the man with the bare feet, "King! King! King!"

* * *

Several days later, a Sorcerer meets him in the throne room. He takes Dipaka to the crypts underneath the Royal Palace. He points to a grave in the wall.

"She was a Princess that governed over the Kingdom in a time without kings. She was fair and brave in her decisions. She was never one to succumb to wars and battles. She was always the diplomat. During her rule, the world was like an everlasting spring. The people respected her; upheld her like the sun. A sorcerer, sensing that it was an auspicious time, forged something using benevolent magic.

"He created a mirror. It was small enough to fit in the palm. The rim of the mirror was a white corona, much like the crown of the sun. The light on the rim was ever changing. The mirror, itself, was a flawless surface. Its surface was like a prism, reflecting you in a rainbow.

"But it's no longer here."

Dipaka responds, "Did they come to just take a mirror?"

"It may have been one of their goals. The walls that defend us were taken down. We are left open to intruders. I cannot speak to their motives, but as your adviser in sorcery, the Princess's Mirror was one of our most prized treasures."

"Why did they take this mirror?"

"Much like your sword, it may have powers that we do not know about. Maybe the mirror holds a secret."

* * *

He takes a stroll through the Grove.

"What were you before a prison? It's peaceful here. Who would pervert a wonderful place in this way?" He brushes the sand off one of the marble squares. He walks to the end of the squares. There's a drop. He sees the semi-circle of stairs. It was so obvious what this place used to be: an amphitheater. "Quill, you said to me once that the wishes brought joy. I'll bring joy back to this Kingdom."

* * *

He enters the city to seek a blacksmith. He parts the curtain and enters into his shop. There are anvils, swords hanging from rafters, hammers, water baths. King Dipaka unwraps his black sword from cloth. He presents the sword to the Blacksmith, "Please, help me learn the secrets of this sword."

"I can tell you about its metallurgy, its composition...but secrets, what do you mean by secrets?"

"Is it imbued with magic?"

"Magic?" the Blacksmith bellows out in laughter. "I'll examine the sword, and see what I can find."

* * *

"Sorcerer, I want to lead an expedition into the mountains. But I do not know the right time."

"I cannot do that for you, but the Priest can read the stars for you," the Sorcerer says.

Dipaka walks to the Priest's quarters. He explains that he wants to search the mountains for a person. Dipaka knows that the weather is unpredictable, and will need assurances. The Priest tells Dipaka to ride with him to the Kingdom's outskirts; to where the mountains become visible. They ride to the edge of the Kingdom. Dipaka's servants and soldiers set up a large tent for him. The winds that cross the plains are constant. They shake the canvas of the tent and set torches dancing. At night, the Priest walks with Dipaka outside of the tents. Below the full moon, the mountain ranges are a pale black. The Priest examines the sky. He takes a star chart under a torch's light, and tells Dipaka, "The skies over the mountains will be clear in a year's time."

* * *

He walks in the bazaar. He talks to one of the merchants.

"It's been three days since my coronation. I've done nothing."

"Your Highness. Progress takes time. You will be a great leader, I feel it."

"In another life, I was a trader. A merchant. Much like you..."

"Your Highness must be pleased with the riches and powers he has command of."

"You are too flattering." Dipaka buys from his store.

* * *

"I want to lay out the outer bazaars in squares. I've been to cities in the West that had their towns arranged like this." He traces a grid with his hands. "Do you think we can make this work?" The soldiers hear his decree.

So he says, so the bazaar becomes reorganized according to his specifications. The people did as their King demanded, without soldiers having to force them.

ONE YEAR SINCE CORONATION

The Blacksmith announces, "We have examined the sword."

The Sorcerer presents the sword to the King, "There is nothing here. I do not feel any magic. I meditated on it. I felt its energy, until I resonated with it. I saw its history where it was forged in a forest. This must be a very ancient sword, to have been made in a forest. However, there were no methods used that were unusual."

Dipaka asks, "Are you lying to me?"

"I've seen the sword as reflective as any sword, until it was marked by drawing the blood of a bear. I've seen it cast into the wind among high places," the Sorcerer says.

Dipaka knew he was telling the truth.

"Blacksmith, what have you found?" Dipaka asks of the other.

"It behaves like any ordinary metal. I can heat and bend it. When I strike it with my hammer, it sparks. I do not know why it looks the way it does."

"Then what creates the effects that it does? I've seen light, wind, thunder, and fire come from this sword. Where is the source of the magic?" the King asks.

The Blacksmith and the Sorcerer stare at him.

"Both of you are dismissed."

A servant wraps the sword in cloth and brings it to him. Dipaka clutches it and holds it on his lap.

* * *

In the Grove, the underground prisons have been excavated. Dirt has been brought in to fill the underground as the wooden structure underneath had been taken apart. Everything related to the prison was burned. When the work was finally completed, snow settled on the bamboo stalks.

Come spring, he had invited local artisans and performers to the amphitheater. Torches light up the dark. It's a spring night that feels in-between seasons. It's not cold, it's a night that felt like it belonged to the mid-summer. Breezes smelled and felt like the mist from high mountains. The wind was dull and warm, and not like the crisp winds that cuts in the cold.

Inhabitants of all classes: the poor, the hungry, the rich, the soldiers, children come and fill the seats. And when the seats are filled, the rest stand in rows behind them. As expected, the King sits in the center.

There was acrobatics. The performers leap and bound in the air. He's seen someone like this before.

There was music. The crowd claps to the music. The loud drums compels people to move and dance.

And then the night was over.

* * *

Dipaka leaves to the Palace. There was that scent again: captivating and magnetic. He stops walking while everyone moves past him. He closes his eyes and takes it in the moment.

A woman walks to meet him. "Your Highness. You may not know it, but I spent some time here, in um, this prison. The General, he locked up the wives and children of the previous King. To the General, custom did not hold meaning neither did lineage.

"I was one of the daughters he locked up. Day after day, I had hoped that that day would be the last. Or that I would die. We did nothing wrong, but by being who we are. Then you freed us.

"I feel like you're our rightful king.

"I just want to say thank you."

"What is your name?" Dipaka asks.

"Feng Xin Zi." She leaves.

* * *

Dipaka sits on his throne. He yells to a guard soldier at the end of the throne room, "You, guard, come here!"

The guard stands before the throne. "Come closer." The guard walks up the steps to the throne. "Come closer." The soldier walks until he is face to face with the King.

"Now, you are a handsome soldier by any account," the King whispers to him.

"Um, your Highness."

"Don't be so modest. Now, someone like you would surely know how to woo a woman."

"I'm not sure what you are aiming at..."

"Well, you see I may need your help to..."

"Your Highness, you can choose any princess of any land to be wed. You can have concubines, wives. Your decree is enough."

Despite their best efforts at secrecy, their whispers echo in the room. The second guard soldier, stationed at the door, slightly turns his head at them.

"Your Highness, I believe the Sorcerer may be able to concoct a love potion for you!"

"I advise against it sir!" another soldier chimed in. "He's given me his love potion and I walked the streets smelling of decayed fish. Everyone covered their noses when I approached. I didn't even dare go to the girl I was trying to court."

"A love potion that smells of decayed fish. I have fools for soldiers!" Dipaka chuckles.

"How about a party? The King and Prince used to host parties in the hall."

With glee, Dipaka announces, "So be it, let's hold a party for the masses!"

* * *

The courtyard of the Palace is filled with light. Lanterns float in the sky. They are held to the ground by string and sandbags. When the wind blows, it seems like an ocean sways above the people.

Merchants set their wares up in the courtyard. There are people cooking food. Nearer to the Palace are the musicians. Each attendee wears a mask. The men wore masks that concealed their entire face. The women wore masks with floral headdresses above their masks.

From behind the Palace doors, a soldier points out to Dipaka that the woman in the green mask over there is Xin Zi. Dipaka wears his mask and slips into the crowd. He dances with a few women, a few men. He makes his way to the one in the green mask.

He asks her if she would like to dance. She speaks, but it's not Feng Xin Zi's voice. He dances with her. He looks around. The masks that people wore were iridescent. They were both green and blue. A shift of the head and the green masks became blue.

There were too many people. He couldn't find her.

"Fools for soldiers. I swear to the many gods!"

* * *

"I have an idea. Can you ask her to meet me by the cherry tree?"

"How about you tell her yourself? You're the King," a soldier replies.

"For a soldier to question his King, we must be becoming too familiar."

A soldier rides out from the Palace. Feng Xin Zi steps out from her house. She unrolls the parchment paper. It's an invitation for a picnic by a cherry tree. She tells the soldier she will be there tomorrow at noon. The soldier rides off.

* * *

There is a garden. Grass grows tall and is managed well. Stones are laid out in paths. The stone path leads to a grove of cherry trees. They are in full bloom, the pink leaves fall in the wind. Feng Xin Zi follows the stone path. She comes to the trees which were planted in a grid. He is alone, sitting on a rug, waiting without knowing she was here. He sits on the rug, arranging the food and drink. Leaves fall on the rug, and he takes each one and places them outside of the rug with care.

A spring wind rustles every tree branch. Dipaka turns and looks at her. He stands up and gestures her over.

"I prepared the food myself. These are some of the dishes from my country. Please sit down," he says. She notices a hesitation in his voice underneath a confident exterior. They finish their food in silence.

Dipaka mutters, "Pio om toh."

She looks up, and says, "What?"

A flock of birds fly through every tree; flies through them. Cherry tree blossoms are dragged into the updraft. They soar above the trees. Dipaka tells her, "This is for you..." The birds fly above them as if in a wave. A thousand, two thousand, uncountable birds move in a dance. Dipaka and Xin Zi tilt their heads up and watch the black birds twist, spiral as wa collective, pulling apart, coming together: a murmuration.

"Oh, it's so wonderful. A rhythm. Their wings flapping is a rhythm," she says.

Then the birds disperse suddenly as if their dance was an ephemeral cloud. A heavy volley of rain follows shortly.

"No! The royal rug. Soldiers! Come carry these away immediately! The food too. Hurry up!"

He turns to her. "I'm so sorry that—Quickly! You people are much too slow." He turns back to her, "I'm so sorry that it's raining. I just—" His face turns red. The rain becomes heavy and covers his eyes. He keeps wiping the water from his eyes. The rain splatters mud onto his cloths; his regal clothes and dignity slowly being washed down by nature. Leaves falling on his person and sticking to him.

He looks down at his shoes, slowly sinking into mud. "I've come so far." Anger turns to a sadness, but a touch wakes him from his reverie.

Feng Xin Zi brushes his arm: avoiding the rain, their heads both bowed to see each other's eyes. She asks him, "Want to hear something funny?" He doesn't answer. She asks him a question that seemed to have no answer. She asks, "Where do birds go when it rains?"

He bursts out laughing.

* * *

The skies were clear over the mountain ranges. However, Dipaka remains by the hearth in his Palace. By candlelight, their child is born. He holds him. He says these first words to their child, "Quill, our son."

FIVE YEARS SINCE CORONATION

Family was reunited.

The King and Queen had journeyed back to his homeland. With a royal caravan, they traveled to the place that was sun-soaked. How proud were the parents to see him with a crown on his head. How much love did they show to their four year old grandson. How welcoming were they to their daughter-in-law.

For a few days, the King was home. The rice fields were the same as he had remembered. It was as if time was frozen in this place. It was the monsoon season. Rain beat on the wooden roof. There, in the gray outside, the soil became saturated. Pools of water become small oceans. And in the very rooms where Dipaka played as a child, the parents played with Quill.

And when the rainy days left, and the sun shone through again, the son brought his family back to his Kingdom.

For them, the journey was world opening. For generations, their family were farmers. All they've known was the paddies and the dirt. Mountains, seas, lakes, the desert were just myths and stories. The journey to the east was a realization of creation itself.

Then their caravan came to the Kingdom.

For four years, the King has shaped the Kingdom to a cultural center. Strangers from strange lands were welcomed to trade and stay. In the four years, denizens of the Kingdom wore clothes from every foreign land. Music, food, art was a rainbow. There were no walls in the Kingdom.

Their caravan carried them to the Palace grounds. "Extraordinary," the Mother said to her son. It was theirs as much as it was their son's. For weeks and months, the parents would explore the Kingdom. This place was their new life.

* * *

Dipaka arrives at the base of the mountain. Xin Zi stands beside him. He has arrived with half of his army.

Porters hold their belongings. When they cross into the higher altitudes, they'll change into warmer clothes. Ambassadors from northern countries gifted thick fur coats to the Kingdom. The soldiers will need to make due with layers of normal clothes.

The wind carries up the mountain. There isn't a cloud in the sky. The Priest was correct in predicting the weather. After they've missed the last opening, the weather hasn't been clear for years.

Dipaka looks at Xin Zi, "I can finally bury him."

She walks up with him. There are no paved trails. There's only pebbles and rocks. They reach a height where the temperatures begin to cool. They've hiked for three hours so far. The sun shines overhead. The mountain peak cuts the sunlight into rays.

A bird flies over them. It circles by itself over them. It's almost like a lone vulture. The bird dives down at the King and his entourage. It spreads its wings above them and slowly controls its landing. On its legs was a clipped, rolled up message, "Quill is sick. Come back."

Xin Zi reads the message with him. She watches him stare up at the mountain. He sighs. "We can let the soldiers search," she tells him.

"I wanted to do this," he says.

"I know. I know. I know."

He instructs his army to scour and find any bodies at the top of the mountain. He turns around to walk back down. His soldiers will soon return to the Kingdom and will report that they've found nothing.

* * *

Fireworks sound within the palace and all at once, there were screams.

The bright light outside fades in Dipaka's view. He jolts up, but he can't move. Moonlight outside casts silhouette forms all around him. He turns his head and Xin Zi is not there. She is tied to a chair. "Dipaka!" she yells.

Three soldiers grab his arm, restrain him, and drag him to a chair. They tie him up. Dipaka counts twelve soldiers in the room—soldiers donned in the Kingdom's armor, but not *his* soldiers. A soldier stands over him. By his composure, he was the leader of the group.

The Soldier tells him, "You've killed the King. What do you know of battles and wars? And brotherhood? Tonight, I'll hold you responsible for the death of my friend."

"You can't do this! The Mandate of Heaven makes him our rightful leader," Xin Zi says.

The Soldier continues, "Beliefs and tenets are heavenly ideas. As a soldier, you grow to realize that what is earthly matters. That we, by our own hands, shape the world."

"Do you want money? I can give you money. I can give you fortune...prestige," Dipaka tells him. He notices that the Soldier's armor resembles the former King's.

"I've no need for that."

"Then what do you want? Release me," Dipaka demands.

"My name is Wu Wei." Soldiers that surround him light up lanterns. The bedroom is illuminated in an even orange light. Wu Wei takes the King's black sword and strikes the point of the blade into the ground. It stands upright before Dipaka..

"Wu Wei, please let us go if you don't want anything," Xin Zi pleads to him, "please let us be..."

"I don't want anything. There is a transgression that must not be ignored." Wu Wei takes his own sword from his back, swings it—

"No!!!!" Xin Zi yells.

Into the ground. His shiny blade was textured. The metal was pitted, the edge of the blade had valleys and peaks from where other swords have struck against it. The two swords are side by side. There was the black sword that saved the Kingdom, and the white sword that had once served it.

"Kill the false queen if he," Wu Wei points to Dipaka, "does not follow my instructions."

Dipaka and Xin Zi are quiet.

Dipaka tells him, "What transgression did I do to you? I don't know you or any of the soldiers in this room."

"I don't expect you to know our history." Wu Wei looks and studies Dipaka's face. "So I'll recount it for you. But first, take her outside." She screams and they drag her far into the courtyard.

"Long ago, this country was seven Kingdoms. This was a time before the spoken language. When the world was colder, and snow and ice covered every ocean...

"There were endless wars and battles across tribes of men. Those people fought with nothing more advanced than axes or knives. Those who had survived canonized their fighting techniques. There were seven styles in the seven Kingdoms. Through the ages, as Kingdoms merged, and alliances made, the seven fighting systems were distilled into one. This one fighting system is what we use today.

"Rulers in their time were fighters. Each ruler was respected and feared. These rulers were men that earned their place on the throne.

"Us soldiers trace our lineage back through these men, not to the kings or emperors that we swear allegiance to.

"Our General was right to rule this Kingdom.

"And who are you?

"An outsider who came here. And came to power by a Mandate of Heaven?" Wu Wei spits on the ground.

"Where were you then? Where were you when the General-King held dominion? Where were you when the soldiers of this Kingdom defended the people from invaders, time and time again?" Dipaka spoke.

Wu Wei walks around the room. Wu Wei's soldiers stare at Dipaka. Wu Wei stands by the window, looking outwards. The shadows of the swords danced in the lanterns' flicker.

"When our General took control, he tasked us with an important mission. To find and seed new land for the Kingdom. A fertile land, far from the mountains and plains. He had a vision of a great empire for our people. We walked to the ends of the earth to find fertile, undiscovered lands. At each point of the journey, our map of this world expanded. The edge of this world was farther than we even thought."

Dipaka recognized these feelings.

"We traced the edge of each ocean, coming to shores where the beach sand was black, some were red-colored even...and when we found that the boundaries were closed on the map, we walked inland."

Dipaka looked around and thought of where his son was. What were the screams?

"Our banners were white and brilliant when we left. It was four years into our journey that I came to see that our flag was weathered black. By then, we had found a land worth seeding. We left behind half our army to fortify and cultivate the land.

"The land was already full of life when we came upon it. Bison, cows, horses, rabbits made the pastures their home. There were no people."

"And you came back here to bring back the rest of my army, my people." Dipaka says.

"That's correct. But I can't lead the exodus. I can't if the people won't believe if I am the King. When I came back, I expected to be greeted by our King. Instead, I came back to see a King without ambition. A false idol. But.."

After walking around the room, he stands before Dipaka.

"But I will accept your rules, your decisions, if you can best me in a bout. This rogue army will follow your every command if you win," Wu Wei says. His finger presses down and twists on Dipaka's sword.

"I won't fight you," Dipaka tells him.

"You don't have a choice. You don't have control. Show us you deserve to lead us. Your family depends on it."

A rogue soldier unties Dipaka's hands. Dipaka grips the sword.

Please grant me the wind, the fire, and lightning... Dipaka speaks to the sword. He pulls it out of the floor. As he looks at the sword, he pauses. At this moment, he remembers the story of the Princess.

"No...no..." He holds the sword in his hand,

"This game you're playing...

"You must have killed my soldiers to get inside. You threaten my family. If I would best you in combat, and held you alive; I would despise you for these acts. We would not be able to reconcile, not even for the price of the pastoral land. I would sentence you to death...

"If you would beat me in combat, then you have a Kingdom that despises you; just as they have hated the General-King. Heaven would befall great plagues on your reign.

"This design of your's...all to just get me to fight you. Why..."

His mind was churning through the scenarios of why Wu Wei would do this. Why go to lengths to take away Dipaka's agency and choice; just to fight. Dipaka realized this:

"You came here to die, didn't you?"

Wu Wei takes the sword, walks back a few paces, and stands in a fighting stance. Wu Wei says, "Your wife is outside, your son, your parents. You must fight."

The black sword slices straight into Wu Wei's direction. He side steps it. "You're slow." Wu Wei, with one hand, strikes his sword at Dipaka. Dipaka blocks it. The force of the blow caused Dipaka to kneel.

Wu Wei: "You are no fighter. Get up."

Dipaka gets up. Wu Wei barely slices Dipaka's arm. The shallow cut was a controlled move to demonstrate precision and control. While still reeling back, Dipaka is kicked down. Wu Wei comes in closer to whisper in his ear, "Where is Heaven to stop this?"

There's a stampede outside. Wu Wei motions for his soldiers to go outside.

"Dipaka!"

He hears Xin Zi's voice over the footsteps. She yells, "I'll come back!"

Why...why won't you lend me your powers...I—

The soldiers have left, and the bed chambers hold just Dipaka and Wu Wei. Dipaka swings the black sword and Wu Wei pulls back.

Wu Wei strikes his own sword into the floor. He takes off his armor. He wears white tattered clothes. Across his body are scars, a few from animals' claws, "Come."

Dipaka tries several times to hit Wu Wei. Each time Wu Wei parries the hits with his bare hands. Outside, the two groups of soldiers fight. Over the yelling and noise of sword hitting sword, who could tell who was winning. Dipaka is exhausted at this point. He cannot hold his sword any longer. He is out of breath and sweating.

"I could push you over with a finger," Wu Wei says to Dipaka. He turns to see the fighting outside. Dipaka stands; recovering, breathing. The sounds of sword against sword seem to dwindle, until there was no more noise. Then, the sound of trampling moves closer. "I-I can't fight anymore," Dipaka mutters.

"You may not have to," Wu Wei tells him.

Dipaka readies himself to fight Wu Wei and his rogue soldiers to the death, "There is no other way out of this, but for me to fight. Even if I should die...although you despise me, don't bring your vengeance on my family."

The doors open. Dipaka's soldiers rush in. As if a pack of animals surround their prey and rip meat from bone, the same intensity was shown when the soldiers rushed in and each one stabbed Wu Wei.

Wu Wei looks directly at the King, swords lodged in-between every bone and organ, blood sputtering out of his mouth. "It was here, when he had kissed me good-bye," Wu Wei tells him. "What do you know of a friend forsaking you...demonstrating to you...that you were unwanted."

Dipaka's soldier tells him, "Your parents...We are sorry we could not have done anything."

EIGHT YEARS SINCE CORONATION

At a stone pavilion, Xin Zi and Dipaka are having tea. It is a rare, warm spring day.

Tell me by what ways do I come to this place. Three years have passed since the courtyard. You moved away from me.

Dipaka's hands touches hers, "You...should drink." Xin Zi picks her tea cup up and drinks it; her hand trembling a little.

Heaven has punished us. Pushed us apart. I wish I could tell you what I saw in that courtyard. When those soldiers carried me out, away from you, I felt I was going to die. I knew it. Instead, they hold me there, in the darkness. I looked at our bed chambers, an orange light. I feared for you and me.

I saw soldier fighting soldier as if our country was fighting itself. There were bodies and blood. So I ran away, I turned to tell you I'll return. Each hallway and passage was lined the bodies of our people. Our home became a labyrinth.

Each horror turned every place unrecognizable.
I looked for our son.

A bird lands on the edge of the stone table. It jumps on the table and tweets a few times, then takes flight again.

Dipaka picks up his teacup. The tendon of his wrist raises up as he grips the cup tightly. Xin Zi reaches across the table, and gently parts the hair from his eyes.

* * *

Dipaka walks outside. The moonlight covers the courtyard. He holds his sword close. He is practicing a sequence of moves, something he had asked to learn from his soldiers. The way he moves is rigid, abrupt—much in the same way as the General-King or Wu Wei.

Quill, what lessons have you taught me? What do I need to realize? My tenets have been tested again and again. I've tried to. I've tried to keep them. And when that sacred tenet of life was broken, did that act set me on a path to here?

He strikes at a slab of stone; the same height as him. A spark ignites. There are many black spots on the stone that have accumulated there over the years; many scars of sword strikes from previous soldiers.

What was the point of fighting, when it couldn't have prevented any of this?

He slices the sword vertically. It gets lodged into the stone slab. He struggles to release the sword from the stone. At sunrise, the soldiers find him sleeping; clutching the black sword.

* * *

The smell of incense is carried through into every room. Xin Zi lights another.

I petitioned for you not to hang that man in front of people. You were free to imprison him. The one lone, rogue soldier who was alive.

Who stood and watched. But did not participate. Who cowered and hid. And when you found him, in front of your soldiers, you insisted that he live, just to hang him as an example. An example. That was the cost of a life to you.

You took him. You leashed and dragged him like an animal. When you walked up those stairs, and tied the noose around his neck; I wanted to yell for you to stop. The crowd cheered when he was hanging... writhing in pain.

Who do you blame now, Dipaka? Who would you kill?

The smoke funnels outside, swirling in the air.

* * *

Dipaka unrolls a stack of parchment. There are ten maps in the group. One shows the continent, a fully completed map that extends to the south. Every river, every lake marked. A red line marks the place from the Kingdom to the pastoral place. There are ten X-shaped red marks along the way. Each separate map are enlargements of these red marks.

If Wu Wei's maps were correct, these places were resource rich. In his youth, he has lost so much from the bandits that robbed him. Now he has access to more resources than nations.

* * *

You yelled at him.

Their son spun a toy.

"Be quiet with that racket!" Dipaka yells, "Servants, bring Quill to the other room!"

Quill begins to cry. Feng Xin Zi motions for the servants to stop. She holds Quill's hands and walks with him out of the throne room. "Why are you so angry?" she asks.

"Leave me," he says.

I couldn't leave you. Our love was forever. It had to be. This was the bond between a queen and king. It had to be forever. It had to be forever?

* * *

I wished I hadn't yelled at you.

Dipaka walks into Quill's room.

"Quill. I'm sorry that I yelled at you." He hands him the toy that he was playing with, "Grandmama and Grandpapa went to a better place. And I'm still sad that they left. Sometimes I may be angry. But that's because...maybe..I don't know what to say

"This toy. Do you remember where you got it from?"

Quill looks at him, "Grandmama gave it to me."

"That's right. It used to be papa's. Grandpapa made this for me."

Feng Xin Zi stands by the doorway listening.

Dipaka says to his son, "I want you to have something. I didn't get this from Grandmama or Grandpapa, but from a friend. One day, when you need to, or if you're happy...you can make a wish and it'll come true. Then when you have made the wish, you can give it to someone else."

Then, Xin Zi turns away, leaving. As if to say, "What did you hide from me?"

What would you wish for, Quill?

* * *

I am lost again in a labyrinth. But it's not of place. I just feel...these memories...

...are so fragmented. So lost in time, shattered, and I'm picking them up. Looking at them. Like glass. Like mirror, I look at them but they reflect only me.

I loved you. Oh, Quill. My son, my beautiful boy. Why have you disappeared? By what godly forces?

On that night three years ago, I found you. Sound asleep. So peaceful. When I found you, the palace was ordered again. It had a sense to it again.

Feng Xin Zi sits by Quill's bed. She clutches the sheets close; his scent still on it.

My baby boy. My sweet boy.

She looks out the window, into the blue sky outside.

Bring him back please.

I am lost again in a labyrinth. But it's not of place. It's a labyrinth of time.

* * *

Dipaka leans over Feng Xin Zi and helps her light the incense.

He hands over the maps to her. "Let's build a new beginning," he says.

She looks at them. "Dipaka...I don't think I want to go to these places. But I don't want to be here."

She wanted out of the maze, and here were the maps. And maybe somewhere lost in the labyrinth of time, she'll find a new beginning somewhere.

TWENTY YEARS SINCE CORONATION

In the years after, the Kingdom expanded into an Empire. When the soldiers needed horses, they brought their King to the pastoral fields where wild horses ran. They saw how the King held dominion over them with a few words. And when the need for larger animals were needed for transporting lumber, for grazing the new lands, for kinship; those too were provided.

The ten lands that were marked on the maps were unpopulated. When the soldiers arrived with their King, the wild animals were domesticated. In each of these places, several soldiers stayed behind and became the seeds and leaders for the lands.

Villages, towns, and even a few cities developed in six years. People from the original Kingdom made their trek to the new places. For a time, the King and Queen stayed in each of those ten places. They watched as strangers came in and shaped the unique community of each place.

On that tenth year, the eighteenth year since the King's coronation, Feng Xin Zi returned to her home in the original Kingdom.

* * *

In the throne of the Far Lands, the tenth place farthest from the original Kingdom, two people are brought before the King. They are bought for judgment. The King and a few trusted soldiers are in the room.

The King begins speaking, "A long time ago, a life ago, I was not a King. I was a trader. I moved from land to land. I even crossed the desert to trade.

"Then somewhere in the desert, a group of bandits, red bands wrapped around their arms, attacked me in my sleep. And I said to myself that I won't let these people be flashes. I told myself I'll memorize each and every face.

"There were seven men. But there were, in particular, two who were the last to leave. I was already on the ground. The group was already leaving with the goods I've gathered. One of them returned and kicked me before leaving again. He had a scar across his face like this. A deep scar, down to the bone."

With his thumb, the King makes a line across his right eye to his left lip.

"And the other, the one who threw the first punch, threw my water canteen at me. 'So much for gold, huh?' He told me before he left. And this one."

He holds up his hand bends three fingers down, leaving the thumb and index finger up.

"Had two fingers on his left hand. Where is the rest of your group?"

Silence from them.

"Soldiers, what have they done?" The King asks.

"On a patrol on the outskirts of town, a man was heard screaming. It was faint. There were drips of blood on the mud. At night, we saw three people. Two of them were dragging the man. We found loose teeth on the ground...they ran. The man was bruised, beaten," a soldier responds.

"I was able to catch him," another soldier tells the King.

"So kill us. I promise you if you let me live, I'll kill everyone in this village," the one with two fingers tells him.

"You, King, do what you must. Kill us just like you've done to take the throne," the scarred man tells him.

"What if I don't?" the King asks them.

"Hah! The King with the Black Sword. That's what people call you. But look at you," the one with two fingers says.

"Send them away to the prisons," he instructed the soldiers. "I will deal with them later."

"Very decisive!" the scarred one says.

The two fingered man yells at him before leaving the throne room, "Where's your Queen? We'll show her a good time!"

* * *

A full moon rises overhead.

A bird flies into the throne room. Tied to its leg is a piece of paper rolled up. The King takes the piece of paper, and walks to the doorway. He holds it low so that the paper catches the moonlight. It says, "Harvest was well this year. Wish you could see the leaves."

He writes a message, and passes it to a soldier to send it off with a bird. "I miss our dinners spent under falling autumn leaves."

So now I am in-between the lessons of my youth and age. What do I learn now? Xin Zi, Quill, where does this life take me?
I'll find the answer.

* * *

The King walks into the Blacksmith's forge. The Blacksmith was personally invited by the King to come to the Far Lands. The forge was still in early days; waiting to be made whole again.

"I am glad that you came here. I need to ask for your advice," the King says to the Blacksmith.

"What advice could I possibly give?" the Blacksmith asks.

"You must have heard about the two bandits."

"Yes I have. But why are you coming to me for advice?"

"My father had a similar face to your's..." Dipaka says. The Blacksmith is silent. Dipaka pauses and asks, "Do I punish them? Or do I follow my tenets and allow them to live?"

"If following your tenets caused you loss. But not following them gave you kingship, these lands. Then is it not obvious?" the Blacksmith asks him. "Did the universe not demonstrate to you the effects of your actions?"

"I suppose."

The Blacksmith points to the King's sword. "Do you want me to sharpen it for you?"

The King nods and hands it over to him.

* * *

"How are the summer plays?" The King sends a bird off.

* * *

"I've examined their past. I can tell you with certainty that although they have committed acts of violence, they have never taken a life. But that's not to say that they won't," the Sorcerer tells the King.

"You can say that of anyone. Even yourself," the King responded. He pauses. "If I jail them forever, would that be punishment enough?"

"If you jail them, then you must feed them. You would have the village grow food for the strangers who would injure their own. Mind you, this is food and resource that's already scarce. They will despise you. And to what end?"

"To change them. To bring them under my control."

"Men cannot be controlled," the Sorcerer says.

"When you are done with them, please let me have their blood," the Sorcerer says.

* * *

The following correspondence takes place within the next two weeks.

A messenger bird comes to him, "The music is enchanting! Flowers are blooming around the Twelve Gates."

"It was at one of the gates when Quill first called you Mama," was the message the King replied with.

"I remember. He would be 19 years old now," was the Queen's reply to him.

* * *

"We learn that life can be taken in war. But it's peaceful now," a soldier says to the King.

"What if I send them to die?"

"No one would think any different of you," the soldier says.

"Do you believe, like Wu Wei did, that faith held no water?"

"No. I don't believe what he believed. But I also don't know the life he led."

"Wu Wei...in a way...when I look at the land around us, I understand him." Dipaka lets out a heavy sigh. He looks out to the horizon, "I never did ask why the soldiers decided to follow me."

"The General-King grew up in a time of war. So he ruled thinking there will be scarcity. We took food from the people we serve. We didn't want to. We killed people who we've watched grow up. We were servants of the King and nothing more.

"You were, in many ways, a new beginning for us. You gave the army a sense of agency. A sense of control," the soldier says.

"Thank you."

* * *

The King finds the man with the missing fingers in a small straw hut. The man sits inside a metal cage.

"What's your name?" the King asks.

The man with the missing fingers tells him, "Sol."

"Where are you from?"

"A land covered in snow," Sol says. He asks of the King, "Why are you even here?"

"Why did you leave me with my water canteen?"

"I wasn't about to kill you over treasure."

"Why should I let you live?" the King asks him.

"Lust?" Sol picks up a piece of straw from the ground.

"I do not lust for you," the King says.

"It's a different kind of lust. I took a long time to remember. But I finally remembered who you were. When I left you in the sands, I didn't see weakness or anger. I saw someone who wondered 'How can all this work be just taken away?'

"That is your only lust; to control. Control your money. Control your queen. Control your Kingdom.

"Kill me or let me live. Your only victory over me would be to control me one way or another," Sol flicks the straw at the King's face.

The King leaves the straw hut and walks to an adjacent hut.

* * *

"What's your name?" the King asks.

The man with the scar tells him, "Lo."

"Where are you from?"

"An ocean away."

"Why should I let you liv—" the King is interrupted.

"I've seen your son."

"Watch your tongue."

"The King with the Black Sword has lost his son. Oh, the armies that were in search of him. The people that were harassed and beaten for information. But they never did return the boy to his father. I suppose he's a man now, isn't he? How many years of his life did you miss?" Lo leans back in his cage; sunlight illuminating his face.

"How could you know who he is? What he looks like."

"Sol and I trekked through a dense forest. We've seen a tribe of people dressed in black rags. They sat round a fire. One of them called on the other, Quill. How many people have that name?"

The King stared through him.

Lo continues, "Sol tells me, 'Maybe he is the son of the King.' I tell him, 'We leave. In this dark forest, if they see us, who knows what they would do.' So we leave."

"Should I believe this lie?" the King asks.

Lo responds, "I offer you a story, but you take no solace in it. So you would rather believe your son is alone? Or maybe dead? Or did you accept that he could be dead? Maybe the Queen did, and you didn't."

"Faith tells me that there is a design that leads people into our lives. For one reason or another. I'm trying to parse why providence brings you two back to me. Why is there an ugliness to this circularity?" the King asks.

Lo turns to look through an opening in the straw hut. He sees a thin sliver of the blue sky, "Peace never lasts. Life is calamity after calamity. You'll learn the same lessons."

***

A full month has transpired since the two bandits were caught. Dipaka sits in a dark throne room. In the darkness, entoptic phenomena fills his vision like moonlit, white desert sands swept up in a night wind.

Dipaka holds the sword in front of him like a cane. He orients the sword vertically, and one by one, he lets his fingers go. Then he lets go of the sword completely.

The sword balances itself on the tip.

This is the first time the sword has done this. But he does not care. His mind is elsewhere. It is elsewhere understanding, meditating, unraveling a deep truth. A deep truth that can only be gleaned after asking the same question over and over:

"Quill, what lesson were you trying to teach me?"

It comes to him.

The General-King asking if he was inside of Dipaka.

The two bandits inside their cages.

The sword in front of him. A father's sword.

The look in Feng Xin Zi's eyes when he kissed her goodbye... were the same eyes that stared at her.

The sword in front of him transformed. Its blackness flaked off like sand. In the spots where that blackness had fallen off, glass has taken its place.

The money he had. And had lost. The worth, it had no worth. Life had a worth, didn't it?

He understood to a deep extent that a Kingdom would not have been worth his friend.

He looks at his own eyes in that same reflection. The sword was like two mirrors placed opposite each other. The reflections in that sword were endless. Infinite eyes look back at him—like him addressing the people of his Kingdom. The Kingdom looks at him, and he looks at the Kingdom. However...even *inside* the sword, there were reflections in a kaleidoscopic space.

The friend and the son named Quill, twice disappeared. And the grief, twice felt the same.

The name Feng Xin Zi that means flower.

There was a tenet he had never quite understood, but had taken as an axiom. There was a true understanding now.

He was the Kingdom. And the Kingdom was him.

* * *

The King walks into the throne room, with his sword.

The soldiers and all his subjects look at it. All the myths and legend that surround the King referenced him as the King with the Black Sword. It seemed as if he had transcended. The sword he now carried was both diamond and mirror; a design from higher realms.

The two bandits stand there spitting. Kicking the floor on which they stood.

The subjects boo and hiss at the bandits. "Go die!" "You deserved to be killed!"

"Can I show you mercy? Can I use these hands to reach inside your heart and transform them?" the King extends his hand forward and mimicked grabbing a heart.

"Or do I do what is just?" He brings his sword, holding it with both hands above his lap; the mirror surface reflecting glints of light on his face.

"Instead." He goes up to them. He takes his sword and nicks each of them over the heart. No blood is drawn, but an impression is left on them. The twin whirlpools of his life, the forces that stretched his conscience thin: his Kingdom and his tenets, crashed into each other.

"I will let you two walk out that door. My people, do not stop them."

The people look at the King. A murmuring in the crowd grows to an uproar. The King hits his sword on the ground twice. The crowd becomes silent. Sol and Lo look at each other and begin to walk towards the exit. A slight smirk crosses Lo's face.

"Let the thousand eyes look at you. Let the world seep into your very souls. The riches that were wasted away. The friends who lost their way. The ones you've grieved for. The ones who grieved for you, who tried to save you. The ones...you've saved."

People in the crowd look at the King. They look at the two people walking to the exit.

Lo's eyes become red. His eyes water as if dust was in them, and he presses his hands against his eyelids.

Sol rubs his arm as if he was freezing in the cold. Goosebumps pricks up from his arm.

"Family...," his throat gets choked up, "...that are in far places."

They look forward to the sun and the door that stood wide open in front of them. The grid of tiles stretch for them. They keep walking despite the irritation.

Lo gulps in air from his mouth, then exhales slowly from his nose. These are forceful breaths as if to subdue the irritation in his eyes. "You, King..." His eyes are tearing and he's wiping away the tears with his forearm.

They walk away from the King.

Sol is breathing slowly. He hugs his arms closer. The breaths he takes; there is steam that comes out as if cold air surrounds him.

"Invite every one of those people in."

Sol falls and clutches his heart. The crowd sees his pupil expand out and fill his green iris so that the whole of his eye is unnaturally black. Then life seems to disappear from him when the pupils return to their normal size.

Lo falls into a fetal position; whimpering. His breathing is heavy and labored. He keeps stammering, "I-I-I'm sorry. I'm sorry."

The crowd closes in to look at Sol's body. A denizen asks the King, "Did...did you kill him?"

"No. I don't think so," Dipaka responds.

The crowd surrounds Dipaka, Sol, and Lo. But the King seems to be part of the crowd, looking at the two bodies. For the first time in a long time, he was Dipaka; an unsure trader from a family of farmers. Dipaka looks over at Lo.

A soldier exits from the crowd and walks past Dipaka. He stands over Lo. He crouches down and parts Sol's hair. His eyes are there, but blank. The soldier takes Sol's palm in his hands and tells Dipaka, "He is gone." "I-I-I," Lo continues to stammer. The soldier tells Lo, "Stand up, walk with me." The solder helps Lo get up. "Come, I'll find a place for you."

And in the months and years to pass, Lo found a new beginning in the army, in the village. In time, the village accepted him; for they saw in him themselves: a person. One day in the future, a decade from this day, he will lay his life on the line to protect these people from marauders.

* * *

The next day was the start of the monsoon season. Rain and wind trickles across the village. The villagers opt to stay in their houses. Dipaka instructed the soldiers and guards to rest on that day. He tells them to spend time with their families. He is alone with the sound of raindrops against the mud. Dipaka looks outside and sees a small part of his empire, one that stretches back through roads and roads. He is reminded of the time that transpired to bring him here...but something interrupts him.

He hears chirping from outside the door. It's a bird that's jumping around the corner of his door. He extends a finger and the bird gently lands on it. He slowly rises up, holding the bird. He gently walks back with the bird and sits on his throne. He looks around for something to feed it. He finds a seed in a nearby jar. He lets the bird jump around the throne's armrest. He leaves a seed for the bird to eat. The bird pecks on the seed and devours it.

"Quill, I learned your lesson. Why did I tame myself? You were free, to take life and see what may come. I'll let myself...I'll let things come what may."

He takes a piece of parchment.

He asks the bird to come to him, without those ancient words, "Please send this letter to my wife." The bird hops around, waiting for him to finish his letter. He writes, "I'm coming home."

As soon the bird departs into the rain, another bird comes in. He opens the message,

"Come home, my love."

CONTENTS

CHAPTER THREE

SAECULUM

My earliest memory as a child was being led to a temple. Inside there was a line of people waiting to have their futures told. Mama later told me that the Seer let them ask her anything. People who had no direction in life, people who wanted to know when they would die, those who wanted to know what their children will be like...the Seer was someone who had all the answers.

When I was a child, I was sick. Taking a few steps or moving suddenly would leave me out of breath and coughing. Mama would tell me it was by a miracle I survived my birth. I remember being on my bed and staring into the fields through an opening in our stone house. In my memory, there were only clouds passing overhead; and zephyrs and breezes entering into the room every so often.

Mama brought me to the Seer. Mama wondered if I would ever heal. Every person who visited the Seer gave what they could for whatever information they could gain. It was not a matter of currency, but of value. Some gave their crops, some offered their services to the temple. Those that went to the Seer would inevitably turn their lives around with what they've learned.

Mama wheeled a full cart of wheat to the accountant. He counted and tallied each bundle. It was almost our whole harvest.

Past the stone pillars was the Seer in her room. Incense was lit around the room and its smoky, almost lavender smell filled the air.

My eyes adjusted to the brightness of the room. A single, small window illuminated the room. Seated on a wooden stool was the Seer. Beside her on the floor were ritualistic symbols in aged, yellow chalk. Walking up to her, the dark figure clouded in light took form as an elderly woman. There is the barest memory of her wrinkled face.

She crouched over to hold my face in her hands. And I held her face in my hands. Her eyes looked into mine. She held her hand over my heart and felt its beating.

"Seer. I've given you all that I have. Please tell me, will she live?" Mama asked her.

The Seer, eyes still locked to mines, told Mama, "Yes, she will live more than you or me. I will not take your things. I will give you this knowledge for free. More than this, there is something about your life that you must know."

The Seer's hands grasped mines tightly, "In our hearts, we hold our essence and our desires. One day your heart will be shared with someone else and your love will be a boon to the world."

Mama listened intently and remembered these very words from the Seer, "Your love will be a boon to the world. Look for a burning cloud."

In the days following, the Seer's health declined and she passed away.

Love was my burden to hold. The last words from a legend. I was supposed to be responsible for humanity...and I chose not to pursue it. And so my heart healed and years will have passed until that day when I see the burning cloud.

* * *

A two story stone house rises out of the golden wheat field that surrounds it. Inside is a bamboo staircase. I remember as a baby crawling up these stairs. Upstairs is an old bookcase by the window. The wood weathered by wind and rain. These were my father's books. Pages are here that I cannot read. Diagrams that I don't know the meanings to.

I was thirteen then.

Outside the opening, a blue sky with cirrus clouds. "Aliya!" Mama called me from the field.

I walked into the field. Wind shakes the field of wheat. With a scythe I cleaved the stalks down. I bundled each pile and laid it upon the dirt.

Mama walked close by. Her hands sometimes ache, and she cannot work as quickly as I can. "Mama, I can take care of the work. Please rest," I say. She shakes her head and smiles at me, "I am still young and I can still work."

Patches of wheat rustle. It must be a wild animal. "Here, come here!" The stalks move in waves in front of me. I run to catch the shifting of the stalks. PHEEWWW PHEWWW I whistled with my fingers. "Come here!"

"Let it go!" Mama yells.

I heeded her.

That night, I watched the August moon rising. Sitting on my bed, I observed each celestial object that appeared over the horizon. The stars faded into view. The moon was so large, it could've swallowed our field. I laid down and watched it descend. It came back to me—that same feeling I had when I was younger. A feeling of looking out into the world, but not being a part of it.

* * *

Men screaming from the kitchen, "Tell me! Tell me the truth!" Metal was clanging around and banging against the floor. Things were toppling over in the kitchen.

"Mama!"

A man was restraining her hands.

"Get out of here!" I yell. They restrained Mama and stared at me, "Did you see a little boy come by here?"

I yell again, "Get out of here!"

"A boy passed through here yesterday. We tracked his footprints to your field. Can you say truthfully that you are not conspiring to conceal him?" one of the men asks.

"What do I have to gain by hiding him? You've searched the house. You searched the field. Where else can we hide the boy?" Mama says.

And so they left. Mama's hand was purple and bruised. What did they have to gain?

"Mama, are you okay?"

"Maybe one day when you find your love, people won't be mean to each other. Maybe this boon to humanity will mean something."

I took ointment and rubbed it into her forearm. I didn't speak a word. I didn't believe in it.

* * *

A blue sky. A black veil falls from the sky. The Seer's face and my mother's melts into each other. Their voices urge me to find this boon.

A light enters and I drift away from this. I wake up to darkness.

Why is a boy sitting on my window? He couldn't have been much older than me. Short, skinny, frail at first glance. Black hair. He hops down from the window and walks towards me. It was a distinctive walk.

"Why are you here? Mama got hurt because of you!"

"Want a pomegranate?" He extends his hand. He's smiling, giggling. He hops off my window and sits on the floor. He removes a knife from his waist and starts to cut the pomegranate. The young boy plucks the seeds into his hands and places them in mines. It's almost like peeling petals off a flower.

"I'm sorry that your mom got hurt," he says.

"Who are you? Why are you even here?"

"I thought your wheat field would be a good place to sleep in. I heard you snoring, so I came in to see. You snore pretty loud," he says.

"Get out. I think if you stay, you'll just hurt us more. Please leave."

"I don't know how to get to the nearest town. Can you show me where it is? I've been staying around here because I don't know."

"What do you need to go to the town for? Just go," I tell him.

I looked over at Mama's room and didn't hear any movement. I was a bit relieved.

"I need to find my people again. Can you take me?"

"No, I'm not going to take you!"

He puts a few more seeds into his mouth, but this time, he started chewing more loudly.

"Maybe I should ask your mom then," he smirks at me.

I imagine that he won't leave until I actually showed him the nearest town. I argue with him on how it's too late to go anywhere.

"Well you have until sunrise to get back, right? You can leave and come back," he says.

So we left.

"I'm Quill."

"I'm Aliya."

I grab a cloak for myself and an extra cloak for him, some light provisions like a water canteen, a knife and a handful of nuts and berries. We leave my house. A dirt road begins some distance away from my house. It's a long road to the town from there. There are houses along the way. They're few and far apart. There are sleeping sheep in front of some of them. Others you can see horses.

"Why are you alone? Don't you have a family?" I ask him.

"I have a father and mom."

"If you have parents, then why are you here?"

"When they took me away, they told me that my parents didn't want me."

"Of course they want you. Where are you from?"

Silence.

"Your mom seems nice," he tells me.

"But she's stubborn about me falling in love."

"You don't have to do anything you don't want to do."

"Hmmm."

We walked for two hours. The gates of the town stand tall. It is an empty place. In the daytime, it's full of life. I point out to Quill where the different people are: the bank, the blacksmith, the government building...

I pause for a moment outside the Seer's temple. The town has converted it into a place of remembrance. I usually do not notice it when Mama and I head into town to sell our crops and trade. However, tonight, it takes on a new form. With the blue moonlight casting onto the temple's facade, the temple becomes solemn.

For a moment, I felt that I only shared the world with this boy next to me.

I tell him, "Well, here's the town. Now please leave us alone."

"Goodbye!" He walked off and it was like he was barely here. He was a ghost that passed through.

* * *

It is spring. Mama takes me to Father's grave. It is a few miles from our house. The grave is on a hill, beneath a skinny tree. Mama said that we bury people on hills so that the rain would roll off. Each spring she takes a walk here with me. And each spring, she doesn't speak. I've only heard a few stories of my father. How he passed when I was four. But today, Mama starts to recount the story of how they met.

"Long ago, this field was your father's and his family's. How did I end up owning this?"

She came from a place across the ocean. She was part of a sea-faring people. My ancestors could live days out in the water. Without a map, without a compass, they were able to distinguish their location. They can find islands and lands from the ebb and flow of the water. Sitting in a boat surrounded all around by water, where the stretch brings you breeze and the salt fills your nostrils...the birds singing overhead and the life underneath the ocean sound—these were the elements from which they were able to discern their location.

As a young girl, she was meant to stay on land. But as her father's only child, she was meant to be on the ocean. From a young age, my grandfather taught her to read the migration of the birds, the interference of the waves, the ocean patterns that flowed globally and locally.

One winter day on return to her village, her village was violently pillaged. Many died. In a last ditch effort to save what survived of her village, they took to the ocean. Out of the tropics, they rowed across the world. Five boats of twenty people of their tribe left their home. Although lost in an area not familiar, she took the gestalt of the sounds, the smells, the fauna and intuited in her mind: a way. She saw a way north.

A boat's trajectory marked by spirals that moved into other spirals flowing forward.

Large storms pushed them off course; delayed their migration... she sailed across ice encrusted waters. She said the ice sheets that crashed into other sounded like crackling fire. And when the bright sun set for the night stars to come overhead, the brightest star in the north rose higher and higher each night. It had meant she was heading north.

Within a week of travel, the weather became warmer. They stopped by land and stayed there for a moon phase. The time rejuvenated the weary travelers. But this was not where they had to be. Mama saw half of her tribe stay on this island. Something pulled her north. She took to the ocean.

As the north star rose further up and the sun rises ever higher from the horizon, people started becoming sick. Their skin boiled over and ripped off. People died. When they passed, she threw them overboard. Their bodies floated south from where she was. Soon even her family passed. What pulled her north had left her alone.

Isolated.

Rowing the boat by herself, she lost consciousness. And by chance, the boat drifted into land.

On days when labor was few to do, my father would walk a distance to the ocean. He had spent a lot of days looking out to the ocean. Father found her on the shore. He took her in. In time, they taught each other the ocean and the land. He learned how to sail, and she learned how to tame the earth.

It was the first time I heard about my family's past in deep detail.

We dug two troughs and placed flowers into them. We placed incense into the earth and burned that as well. We bowed three times and said a prayer for our ancestors to look after us and bless us in life.

* * *

Staring out the window, moonlight casts over the wheat fields, I pondered the meaning of the story. Father, Mother, who were you? How did you live? Why was a life of adventure neglected?

A strong gust blows through my room.

* * *

Five years have passed since Mama talked about my father. Now I'm without either one. I've managed fine by myself. During Mama's funeral, all these relatives who I haven't seen came. The procession was small. I wondered how many more would have come from Mama's side. They were strangers but they were linked so close to who I was and who she was and who he was.

Standing here in the middle of my family's field, it's so windy. The wheat follows the wind and rustles. My hair keeps flapping against my face. I weave a black ribbon in and out of my hair.

* * *

I wheel one bundle of harvest towards the market. The bazaar opens up to greet me. Busy people everywhere hustling and bustling about.

The merchants barter with me for my grain. Then I leave the busy market.

I push my wagon home. Halfway home, my legs become tired and I decide to take a nap on top of my wagon. I lay down on top and watch the sky overhead. It envelopes my vision. Seeing just the blue sky—without a hint of wind or cloud—invites me to float up.

I drift into sleep. I open my eyes and for a second it seems as if everything is gray before turning blue again.

The money in my pocket is so few.

* * *

Thunder! I wake up. I have to close the windows and cover the firewood!

No, not thunder. Horses! A whole horde of them trample across my field. My crops...

They run through the field cutting lines and curves through the stalks. That's weeks of provisions. A second round of horses is coming! They pass close to me with a wild force. There are saddles and stirrups, but no riders. Dark satchel bags of purple and black bounce up and down on each horse.

A cloud of dust. A horrible sound of a hurt animal moans from that cloud. Horses trip. They get up and continue running. I get closer to the dust. The other horses have trampled it. What do I do here? If I get close, it might hit me. I'll approach it so that I'm closer to its head. It's groaning. It kicks its legs at me. What a beast.

I cover my mouth to stop the dust. The horse bleeds, but there are no bones that are sticking out or broken. My approach is slow. I reach out my hands to its face. It huffs at me. I touch her head and she relaxes. Her temper melts away.

Over the next few hours, I feed the horse. I put salve on its wound. I unburden the horse by taking off its stirrups, its saddles, the bags that were on it. It trusts itself to get up again. I lead the horse into the shadow of the house. It lays down and sleeps. It is still afternoon.

Outside my stone house, I view the wheat fields that used to be filled and full a few hours ago. But now there are lines that criss cross through the field.

From the distance, a ragged man walks from the empty, unplanted plains towards me. I grab my scythe and walk towards him. I walk to him until we are paces away.

His clothes are tattered. And I knew him as he knew me. Before I see his eyes or face, I recognize him from the way he walked, even hobbled as he is now. How many years has it been?

"You..." I drop my scythe.

He stumbles forward. His legs are destroyed, bloodied. Blood drips from his clothes like water falling from a drenched towel. I only see his eyes. His hair is black and disheveled. His nose and mouth are wrapped around in a black scarf. I unwrap the black scarf from his face.

"I can't...I can't do it anymore. Lead me into the house," he says. I put his arms around my shoulders. He leans heavily on me. While walking side by side back to my house, his clothes soak my clothes with blood. He stumbles through the doorway, his hands supporting him. A bloody hand print is left by the jamb.

With urgency, he sits by a chair. He looks at me with an empty stare. His breath is labored. He is as much as a wild beast as the horse—no, the horse was tamed. He is something else. He averts his eyes from me. His head nods down as if almost to sleep. What am I supposed to say? Or do?

He jolts up suddenly and lunges at me. He rips a piece of cloth from my arm. He takes the ribbon and ties it tightly on his bleeding leg. Blood drops on my floor. He tells me in words with long pauses, "They'll be coming. Maybe a few days from now. They'll be coming."

I ask, "Who's coming?"

He falls off the chair and lands with a thud on the floor. He looks asleep. I lift his arms and legs so that he would lie flat on his back. I take a sponge and wipe away the blood on his face. Beneath his long hair and beard was a calm demeanor, a sort of innocence that recalls a boy who once offered me pomegranate. The bleeding seems to have stopped.

I walk outside to escape the smell of iron in the air. I look at the empty plain where he came from. It seems that my life will be chained by a prophecy once again, "They'll be coming."

* * *

Night falls and Quill sleeps on the floor as if he is a corpse. I walk around my house like a stranger, avoiding him as I step around.

The next morning, I find the horse galloping around the field. Its golden mane flows. As I step out, it walks to me. "What is your name?" I call her, "Moonrise."

I walk to where I left the equipment that I took off the horse. How did I take the saddle and reins off? How would I put it together again? I swing the saddle over the horse. Then the reins. It took me a few tries of putting straps and hooks together one way then another until I felt that it was secured.

"Moonrise, be still..."

I mount the horse. I slip and fall a few times. I cling to this horse tightly and hug around its neck with my arm. It jerks slightly as if it was uncomfortable. It would be wiser to not hug its neck. I sit up while gripping the horse with my legs. "Okay, let's go forward." My hands grip the reins tightly. She walks slowly forward. I try to counterbalance slightly by leaning back. "Moonrise, this is scary."

She walks through the lines in the field. I am high up above the stalks. As she traces through the stomped down stalks, I begin to feel more confident on top of the saddle. Is this what flying feels like? I look up at the clouds while she walks. "Oh, Moonrise, if I could fly."

$$* * *$$

I hold my finger to his nose. He still breathes. I nudge him. He does not wake up. The black cloths on him are like fish scales. Short rags that somehow make an outfit. It's been three days since they both arrived. I've taken most of his clothes off and washed the blood and dirt off. I put them back on him today. He doesn't have any scars on his leg. Then where had he bled from?

In between working on the field, going to the market, and learning to ride Moonrise, the days have become fuller and more filled. Even with the thought that someone is coming for him, it doesn't seem to matter. Lying there for three days, he seems less a corpse and more of a house ornament.

I say to this still person, "Quill, it's peaceful. Isn't it?"

"Your name is Aliya..."

"You're awake."

He rubs his eyes.

"I was trying to remember your name all this time," he says to me. I manage to smile. His mood is lighter, "It's calm here. The breeze that comes in, the crackle of the fire when you make food. The sounds of the birds in the morning. The smell of the field." He touches his clean face and looks at his clothes. He says, "Thank you."

He continues, "Aliya, the girl I met long ago, enjoy your time. This peace won't last."

"You said that they're coming. Who's coming?"

"Walk with me," he says. He leads me outside. "There is a group of men, dressed like me. They call themselves the House. They take people and things away. When they come to a place, they destroy everything."

"You're part of the House then, aren't you?" I ask. Your blood soaked face, why didn't I think to run away, to not help you?

"Yes. You need to leave here. I tried to stop them, but..." He looks away from me, "I betrayed them. I untied their horses and let them go. They woke from their sleep, and realized my betrayal. I fought them. I killed some of them. But they outnumbered me. It was by fate that a horse came back to save me.

"Exhausted, I fell into a slumber on its back. I do not know how far the horse has rode. I don't know how long it rode for. But they will track the hooves here. And when they come, you need to be gone. I may have to fight them again."

I tell him, "Then the King's army will come and fight them if they are a threat. You don't have to fight. You don't need to kill."

"This life, I owe you." He puts his hands on his heart, "I know this is your home. I know that you don't want to leave. But you need to."

What am I to do? Stay and fight? I can't fight. Leave? I can't leave.

"Our lives are not decided by us. If you stay... Aliya, I'll do my best to protect you," he tells me as if those words were comforting.

So he stands. He stands outside for days. He's like a statue. I bring him food. Sometimes he helps me make food. He tells me about the birds he sees in migration. He tells me the way the wind moves at night, the small animals that scurry about the crops. As if these ordinary things were new to him.

During those days, I decided to not work the field if everything was going to be destroyed. I spent the days upstairs, looking at my father's books. I must have memorized the characters over the years. I practiced writing them in the dirt. But I don't know their meaning. There were fifty books on these shelves...

Mama told me my father was ordinary, but he was the only one in the village that could read. Over his younger days, he had learned from the sailors near the shore. He would spend nights by candlelight reading over these books. These were books he found or was given. Although Mama told me she was never interested in reading, she told me that he had always wanted to teach me to read.

I wondered if Quill could read. One night I watch him standing outside in the night. He holds his arms close to keep the cold away. I brought down a blanket and a book. He wraps himself in the blanket. Steam rises from his breath.

"Quill, can you read?" I hold the book up to him. He takes the book in his hands. I huddle up next to him. He opens to the first page. I could feel the stories that my father read coming to me. Maybe I could understand my father, even if through his books. For a moment, the possibility of a world swelling from those pages was real.

"No," he says. I wished that he could've. I wished that he would've said yes. "When I was younger, I knew some words. I forgot all but one." He squats down and draws out a character in the dirt. I recognize the character, now he'll tell me what it means, "Fire."

These days were peaceful.

It was calm.

* * *

They say you have one life to live. They say harvest your crops in good season. They say grow your family. They say when your fortune comes, you will be ready.

I stood between my home and him. The House set the field ablaze. My field to the front of me, my house behind me. The wave of fire spread slowly through the distance. Smoke envelopes the sky and grays out the sun. The graves, too, were burning up. The tree on the hill is on fire. I have to leave.

The House was dressed in black, just as Quill said they were. They walk through the field with their torches held out. I stand paralyzed.

Quill runs into the field. The first person lunges at him with a long sword. Quill lowers himself and tackles him. Another one runs at him with a knife. They're wild animals. It was harrowing to watch them and to hope that they do not see you, and by accident, become involved. Through the smoke and stalks, I see him throw each one into the ground.

I need to rescue my father's books. It's all I have left of him.

No...my stone house...my family's stone house. It explodes. A wind rushes out from the explosion. A ring of dirt expands from it like a ripple in a pond. The ripple shakes the stalks. The permanent stone house that was mine, my family's, is gone. I wade through the dust. Maybe I could find something in the rubble. Anything. Please... please just let me have one thing.

Mama's hairpin. She once told me that this was one of the few things from her old country. This is enough...

Moonrise! She comes to me. "Moonrise, I never made you run before, but today we have to."

I ride her through the burning field. Smoke all around me. She's coughing. Moonrise does not want to go farther in. I grip the reins. She continues in. Where are you? Where are you...I find you. I yell, "Quill, you need to leave! Get on!" He continues fighting. The people from the House swarm in like locusts. But they do not attack me at all. They jump on top of Quill creating a pile. They cover him like a dark cloud...he's disappearing. He reaches his arm out at me before his face disappears into the crowd of bodies. I'm reminded of ants climbing over one another to gather their food. It was disturbing watching these people but have them not make a sound.

I approach so slowly, but more people keep running aside me to jump on the pile.

There are muffled screams coming from inside. A hand...a severed hand tumbles out of that human pile. People are falling in from the top like rice falling into a funnel. Arms are pulled inside, seemingly—slowly being ripped. I back away.

He's biting ears and faces. The skin tears from the people. Without their masks, they seem like regular people. There he is again, the man with the bloody face. He walks upon that hill made of men. He walks down, and falls. I could just go away...

Instead I ride towards him. He mounts on the saddle...and we leave my house; my life.

I headed to the roads where we walked when we were younger. Upon a fork, I take a road that was newly paved.

SHADOW IN THE CAVE

We walk into a forest. The frost comes in. I gather the wood for a fire. Larger pieces are set on the bottom, then smaller pieces on top of those, then a pile of leaves and dried detritus on top. I take a flint and set it ablaze.

"I lost it all. I lost it all. My home. My field. They burned Mama and Father's graves. They burned my father's books. I knew that I would never read them. Now I can't. You understand? I can't!"

He looks at me.

"You spilled blood on my land. You desecrated every memory I had." Why won't he say anything?!

There was no remorse in his eyes. He says, "There are much worse things."

Then I lost time. I must've closed my eyes and cried until it was dark. It was the smell of broth that brought me to my senses. He nudges me lightly, and hands me a wooden bowl. I drink from it. The fire is still crackling. A lid on a pot rattles up and down as the liquid sometimes overflow onto the fire, and singes the pot. He stands up and views the dark forest.

"I should not have said that there are much worse things. Each person has their own grief," he says.

"Who are the House to you?"

"They raised me. I'm not quite sure. I don't remember much of my young days. They took me away from my broken family. To provide me a house where I could be free and be loved. Their house was made of their people. Lost souls, old, young living together. People from war-torn lands. And we had looked after each other.

"They had tasked me to save this girl from a family. And when I looked at the family, I found that the family was happy. I understood at that moment." His lips were quivering. His voice was wavering. "I knew that when they had taken me, they took a future away from me. There's uncertainty. I'm not sure if my name was given by them, or by my family. Wherein inside me, where they stop, and I begin."

I wanted to say, I didn't know where my family stopped, and I began…

He continues, "I walked back to the camp. They have expected me to take the girl. I laid down and looked up at the sky. I thought of every person who was cared for; who found purpose in the House. And I thought of all the nameless, unborn, young, old, taken ones who would have false futures…Aliya, I loved them."

There was a choice of family and future, and did I, to selfishly say, choose the future? I understood him completely—wholly.

"Where did you find the pots?" I ask.

"I found a cache nestled inside a tree. There was a blanket. Clothes, pots, a water canteen."

"What fortunate luck," I say.

Even with his back turned to me, I heard a small "heh."

Where do I go from here?

Sleep…

* * *

We had spent the day walking. The House will keep tracking us. We have no destination. We walked to an empty field. The morning fog and dew still float in the air.

"I believe we are far enough. Aliya, you have to find another home. This is my fault. Walk far from me, and let them track me. I give you the cache."

I do not speak.

He asks me, "Do you want revenge on them?"

"Yes."

"Don't choose this life." Gentle winds stir the mist that hangs between us.

I think of Mama, having to flee her own land. I think of her, having to face soldiers with their hands grabbing onto her arm. I say to him, "If war is going to end, then there needs to be people who put their lives on the line for it. If peace is out there, then it is worth dying for."

"Then I need to show you how to remove your shadow," he says.

I dismount from Moonrise.

"What?"

He tells me a tale of a great monk. A monk had lost his way in life. So to find his enlightenment, he left his monastery. He hiked up a mountain and found a cave. Hungry, and thirsty, and without food; he had decided to sit inside the cave and meditate. He lost himself in his practice until years have passed. In that cave, he found enlightenment. And those years have impressed his shadow into the cave walls.

When he finished telling me the tale, the fog has lifted, and the sun is shining through the clouds.

Quill walks far from me. He closes his eyes. The shadow in the ground recedes into him. He walks towards me, but he casts no shadow on the ground.

"I don't understand," were my only words. I felt the world fall away from me. What...I don't understand.

He says, "It was said that the great monk had figured that if the shadow can be impressed on the cave walls, then it can be removed. The method was taught to the House to stalk prey. The shadows betray our location."

"But monks don't eat meat."

"They don't?"

"No," I say.

"If you can find the way to remove your shadow, you'll be able to avoid the House in the forest."

This was the first of three skills he needed to teach me. And when I would have learned the three skills, I would be ready to help him end the House.

* * *

He tells me to close my eyes and walk.

"Where are we going?"

"You need to find a silence in the dark, Aliya. You need to explore that space. You'll find the answer."

I've never meditated before. My family looked up to monks like heroes. But we had never taken the time to understand their precepts. Moonrise's reins lead me as I walk.

"Quill, what am I supposed to see here?"

Of course he doesn't respond. Hide my shadow? How could that do anyone any good?

"Did you have to do this walking?"

"No, I was told to sit in a cave. But we must walk so we will not be caught." He must be tying a blindfold on me. I had played children's games where my eyes were tied and I had to find the other children by sound. "I'll lift this veil in three days," he says.

I open my eyes a little to peek through. Dots of light shine through the veil. I close my eyes again. I try to find the space he's looking for. What did my father looked like? How resilient was Mama when she was younger? Instead of finding space, I just find memories.

And I just hate them.

"Quill, if I learn how to hide my shadow, doesn't that mean I run away?"

"Yes...we have to live."

* * *

He lifts the veil off my eyes. I see the forest. But I see something more...I notice the shadows of every leaf. I notice the moving shadows across the tree tops and forest floor. It is a brighter day than I've ever seen. There is something here, a solution, but I can't see it yet. It is like laying eyes on an old friend and trying to remember their name. Or recalling details of a dream.

"I feel them coming somehow. It's like a ripple in color. Like I'm standing on light and I feel their shadow is expanding into my space. It's faint...I don't know if it's real," I tell him.

I look into his eyes. So his eyes weren't black, but a deep brown. I wouldn't have been able to tell without the sun. He stares at me.

"I don't want us to be here when they come," he says.

"If we hide, we can ambush them. There can't be so many that they would be able to find us before we find them."

"Aliya, please understand. I've taught you a skill that every member of the House knows too. When two predators meet, they do not ambush each other—they fight head on. You're not a predator...you're just a farmer."

...

"And you're just an orphan, Quill."

He looks at me with those same eyes, but they lack the coldness or even innocence that I had come to know from him. With heavy steps, he walks to Moonrise, and grabs a knife from her satchel. He firmly grabs my wrist and presses the knife handle into my palm.

He says, "If you want to fight, then we stay and fight."

For a brief moment, I wanted to kill him.

* * *

Night came without a word between us. I had spent those hours trying to find the way to remove my shadow. I've gone three days without my sight, but I do not think I am any closer.

We did not eat for the day, and we will not be stoking a campfire.

I tell him, "There's five of them coming. No, they're here."

I didn't notice any leaves rustling. Instead I look up at the rising moon. Although the forest is dark, and in its own way blinding, the moon does color the tree tops blue. Moonrise is pacing back and forth. She's huffing. Quill tries to soothe her. I clutch the knife.

She takes off running. "Moonrise!" Quill catches me right as I start running after her.

Although the wind rustles the leaves above the trees, there is a lower rustling on the ground. An orange light crosses above. It whistles as it moves. It lands far from me. Then more of them get released. It's coming from so many directions. They must be arrows lit on fire.

The dry brush on the forest floor lights up. I run to stomp out the flame. It still spreads. While the arrows fly over like tiny shooting stars, I look over at Quill. His shadow is casted long and then short by the lights.

"They're looking for our shadows. I want you to hide under a fallen tree. You've walked three days in darkness, you will be able to find your way."

"I need to be here."

"Your hands are shaking. There will be a time for your revenge, but not now."

How can anyone make out a person's shadow among all the other shadows? I turn to tell him something before I go, "Quill, they say that the Awakened One could turn arrows into flowers. So please don't kill them."

There must be five of them, the directions the arrows are coming from. Where? Where could there be a fallen log? I need to find a place to hide.

Five people...There is a haunting revelation to me, that each person may be as strong as Quill... Making my way around, I hear the drawing of the bow and the *twang* sound it makes as it recoils. I can barely see the smoke in the dark, but I can smell the burning leaves in the air.

I hear Quill's footsteps moving away from me. I look over to him, but there is nothing there.

I hear someone, "Brother...this world is a passing shadow. Even though there is light in this world, our real house is somewhere else. Come back to us."

The fire makes the air rise. The leaves are lifted up by the draft, and they ignite up into flames. They're like orange fireflies that rise and disappear.

"Brother, they lied to you. This world is the real house. I've felt it," this was Quill's voice.

Another arrow strikes a tree near me. Did they see me?

"If you kill us or we kill you, the wheel will spin again and again," the other person says to him.

An arrow flies over me. My shadow, in a brief moment, is cast long against the floor. I stay still. Did they hear me? I need to find shelter from these arrows.

An arrow strikes a tree in the distance. Another arrow strikes into the same spot. Fire flakes down the trees like slow, orange raindrops. The fire illuminates the two of them talking in the faint light. In their black clothes, they look like shadows.

Even more arrows are sent near Quill. They're not coming in the same direction as they were before. They're moving. Quill says, "We can't keep taking people away."

"We? You left us."

Quill catches one of the arrows aimed at him. He throws it aside.

"We named you," that person says.

How can I allow destruction to happen? Why would I live another day? Mama, when you left home, did you, instead, wanted to stay?

Smoke and steam is filling the air; even the tree sap is sizzling. The orange glow of fire, hanging in the smoke, looks like the forest is frozen in an orange sunrise. But there is something above, that fights against the orange glow. Even though the orange fire may be everywhere, there is a blue light that glows brighter with more smoke. The moonlight is washing over the fire.

I get it. I understand. I know the method now. And there it was, my shadow looks like smoke being blown away from me.

I grip my knife.

HAND OVER FIRE

Through the smoke and orange light, the strange figures reveal themselves like blurs through a black veil. Quill had started fighting his brother while archers still fired at him.

I try to find footsteps stepping gently on the ground. I close my eyes and join in the dark again. If I cough, I would give away my location. But the smoke is suffocating. I want to get out of this forest.

The arrows still fly through the forest. It sounds like a bird's call, but the whistles are far between. So I walk around Quill, him at my center and I, tracing a circle. Maybe it was a spiral. Something nicks my shoulder. I open my eyes and my eyes are tearing. There is too much smoke to even see. I close my eyes again.

How far am I from you, Quill?

"How could I not see you through the smoke?" Who said that?!

I lash my knife at him in the dark. Words manage to leave my mouth, "Die."

"You hold no shadow. What else has Quill taught you in these few days?"

The wind was hot and brought updrafts. My clothes float in the air. The fire has ignited the forest floor.

"You must have trouble breathing," he crouches down and looks at me. His face wrapped again and again in that black cloth. Only his blue eyes are visible. He says, "To endure this fire..." The knife is burning into my hand. I strike at him again. He slaps the knife out of my hand.

"To endure this fire...," he repeated. My house was burning down. My farm was on fire.

"To endure this fire...," he says again. I choke him.

And still he says, "To endure this fire, put your hand over fire and let your touch disappear."

I don't know how. I am on my knees. And both my hands are pinned to the ground by arrows. I try to budge my hands but it feels like lightning striking me. My eyes are stung by the ash. I cry without wanting to. It hurts to breathe. The wind whirls my hair. My hair clings to my wet cheeks. It burns. It is unbearably hot. It absolutely hurts.

"Give up your touch and find yourself again. Just as the Awakened One has," he says.

They speak like they are not hurt. If there was any refuge to be found, I wouldn't want it from them. A wave of smoke crosses between me and him.

He says, "We were instructed to..." To what...

"You had slipped into sleep." Had I crossed? "We were taught to hold our hands to the fire. When we learned about the pain, our scars had healed."

My chest feels like it's on fire. I-I can't breath anymore. I manage...I manage to say, "What use was there to...to...to...that?"

"You are witnessing the proof." He sits down in a lotus position. We are face to face like a teacher to a student. "My name is Josef."

I take a deep breath and blow my hair from my face. "Ah, you can see me clearly now. Do you believe that the world was here for us?" he asks. Arrows fly across the treetops. "This world where walls fall, where calamity happens to good people, where faith isn't enough to hold you. It's uncertain."

"Then what…is…certain?"

"We don't know. But we know that the skills taught to us bring us closer to the truth. And we believe that the truth is that this is all an illusion. So hold your hand to the fire, find yourself in a place without the pain, and let yourself heal."

Why do I feel the pain leave me? Why did it feel like a pressure was relieved? I think I wanted it.

"If you join us, then we will all find the truth."

No, I need to concentrate on it. The lightning, the wet blood on the dirt. The ash in my eyes. The hard breathing. I'll take the pain. I grit my teeth—and pull my hands off the ground, the arrow shredding against my skin and bones. My mouth becomes dry and I just see white in front of me. The arrows in my hands suspend like weights that twist my bones in one direction. I press the arrowhead under my foot and…snap off the arrow head. Biting on the other end, I slide the shaft out of my hand with my teeth. I spit out the shaft at Josef's foot.

These quivering hands, listen to me and grab the knife. I stand up over him.

He stands up too. Branches creek around me. The sound gets closer. From the top, someone drops in front of me. His legs barely bend on landing. He has the same black clothes, the same quiver, the same bow except…

"The fire is taking over this forest," *she* strikes a flint and stone to light the tip of her arrow. An arrow fires off in a random direction. She turns to me, "My name is Bahiti." My fingers shake while I draw out the other arrow out of my other hand. Bahiti says, "Quill, he has taught you. I haven't seen your shadow."

While she speaks, I look at my clothes. Dirt has soiled it. Blood is on it. I look back at Bahiti and Josef. If I would keep living like this, would I end up like them in black rags? Would I stay hungry for the rest of my days? Like a ghost staring through a window?

Bahiti walks up to me. She takes my quivering hands into hers. For a woman, it was a distinctly heavy touch. It's a firm grip that she takes. Her hands seem like they have been through many battles. "Are you...my dark mirror?" I ask.

"You must be in so much pain. Endure it, you can find the way out," she says. Then she repeats over and over:

"You can heal.

"You can heal.

"You can heal.

"You can heal.

"You can heal.

"You can heal."

"I can't. I can't..."

""You can," she puts my knife in my hand. She parts the hair from my eyes and wipes the tears off my cheeks. She walks back and stands next to Josef. The moonlight shines through the smoke clouds like a summer sun peeking through trees during mornings. It shines on the mangled meat of my hands. A house...that's right...my house...

Who needed to heal anyway? I run at them with a knife in hand. The way they run from me seems like animals. Their long strides, their speed. I couldn't catch them. But still, I hear where they go. I stalk them through the smoke and fire, through burning trees. Winding and winding through the maze. Fiery sprites fly by me. They say that long before people tamed horses, people would run until their prey is exhausted...

But why does this feel like I'm playing a child's game; chasing one another until one catches the other.

I run. And I run. And I run. I see you through the smoke. I see the shadows you cast. How long have we been running for? Hours? Minutes? How long have we ran that you two slowed down to a walking pace. I hated you. I walk towards them. My pace overtakes theirs until I am behind their backs.

There is no going back.

The knife goes into one of them. Then the other turns around. I haven't even seen their eyes before I put my knife into him. They lie there face down. There are two more of them. And one more fighting Quill. I need to find them. Even though I felt them coming before, it feels like they are occupying the very same space I am. I'll trace my steps back to Quill.

Smoke passes me by. I turn my head. Two figures move and take Josef and Bahiti. They put them on their shoulders and go away. It was so fast. They had looked like a ribbon with how they moved. I begin to chase, but my legs lock up. I can't move. My body has given up on me. They had to be the other two not with me or Quill.

I feel them moving away from my space...the space that I had felt their presence in. But I still feel another person in this space.

* * *

I'll find my way to you.

I walk this burning forest; pass streams that reflect orange and blue. I find Quill and his brother in a familiar scene; lying on the ground with their blood spilled over it. Only Quill managed to speak this time, "Aliya, they left, didn't they?"

"Yes, they did."

He gets up. I tell him, "Let's leave."

We walk without knowing where the edge of the forest is. We only hope that the moon would guide us through. The fire that had roared so fiercely hours ago gives way to crackles. We were tired. We were hungry. He tells me that this is going to be one of many battles in the war we are going to fight. But we had only taken three lives. I was wrong to believe arrows could turn to flowers.

We had somehow walked passed to where I was taken. I tell him of what happened.

Quill looks at my blood on the ground, to where the arrows had pinned me. "Had your blood met the earth, and bind you to the world?"

"I don't understand."

"I don't understand either, but I feel it that it is so," he says.

I look at his face. How long had he laid there that the ash had covered his entire face in gray? I look at my feet, my shadow is there again. My hands, they are healed. I hadn't noticed that I was able to breath again. I look at his hands; wondering if he was forced to put his hands into the fire too; if he still feels a touch. Maybe if I just go ahead and just touch a finger to him...

"Aliya, there's a child here."

She lies on the ground; abandoned. He props her up on his back. The way he does it, it is so gentle. He even looks vulnerable. I brush her hair back. Her tiny nose expands and contracts. He says to me, "This child has a future because of us."

* * *

We come to the edge of the forest. The smoke rises to the sky with a pale sun behind it. It's like a pillar to heaven. The sky was gray, and it casts its shadow on us. I say to him, "This place is a grave now."

"It was so green a day ago," he says. Quill is about to turn his head. When my relatives came for Mama's funeral, they had told me not to look back.

"You shouldn't look back, Quill." He doesn't.

"We can't use this knife for cooking anymore," he says to me.

"Why would you care?"

He pauses before speaking, "It's our only cooking knife."

It was. He seemed to have hated me at that moment. What was so important about a knife?

* * *

The first night.

Her house was on the empty steppe. Just a wide expanse of sky, and no wheat to block the horizons. There are thunderstorms that roll through the sky from far away. The house is thatched in straw. The child runs to her house. Her mother and father come out to hug her.

We stayed for five days to be sure that the House would not return to her. We stood guard outside every night.

"You did it," he says. "You found the method…that to have the shadow recede, you have to take that darkness in and manifest it inside."

"No…" How could I have told him he could not have been more wrong, "I found something else."

He stares at me.

I say to him, "Shadows disappear when there is no light. So I pulled that light inside of me." I point to the moon.

He looks at the family having dinner in candlelight inside, "They look like they belong together; the three of them."

* * *

The second night.

"Was the second skill you were planning to teach me, healing?"

"They taught you, didn't they? I wanted to teach you that last. I didn't want you to learn it so early."

"Why not?"

"Hold your hand to the fire long enough and you lose feeling to your hands. Do it again and again and you don't feel touch anymore."

"Then, what is the third skill?"

He says, "Both skills you've learned until now are manifest by spirit alone. I believe, by finding something inside of yourself. The next skill would require more time. It would require building you up physically. You've seen how fast and strong they've run, how they've carried the dead across.

"You'll need to fuse what you felt before and what you feel in your body.

"The next skill is finding strength."

He continues to describe a regimen to strengthen my body. He names a list of exercises which I don't even know. I figure these won't be too hard.

For a sect believing that the world is an illusion, they sure do have a fascination with building their body up.

* * *

The third night.

"If you're cold, you can sit closer to me," he offers to me.

I sit where I am.

* * *

The fourth night.

We spent the day helping them plant seeds for spring. They offered us food. We suspended our watch for tonight and ate with them. After eating alone for years, I realize I missed the company of people.

* * *

The fifth night.

"Aliya, I don't think they will be coming here."

"If we leave, we have nowhere to go," I tell him. Then I pause. "Maybe instead of running and hiding, we find them."

"Okay," he says.

* * *

The sixth morning.

We chose to depart, but before we leave, the child goes to her family's garden. She asks me to kneel down.

She puts a yellow flower in my hair.

ONE HUNDRED FLOWERS

"Aliya. Who are you?" he asked when I opened my eyes.

I was the wind in high mountains. I was mist through valley corridors. I was clouds casting shadows over empty, sandy steppes. I was the air that whistled through the night—a name you could not say. I was the scent of pines hanging on the forest air. I was the dusk sky which you had wished would stay forever.

I was also fire. I was the water on still burning embers that reminds you of harder times. I was cautious steps walking down steep mountains. I was the hope of feasts in hungry times.

I was your first vision, your first breath, your introduction to the world. I was all those first memories—forgotten in time. I was first light—the first glint of sun that touched the earth. I was the first night after creation—when chaos had given way to quiet.

I was winding roads through time—the empty time you had felt finding your way to destinations.

I was strength, I was fire. I was a spirit that had binded the world together.

Oh, I was the sun that begins every day and the changing moon that marks the seasons!

I was a boon to the world.

I was the first flower gifted by our first saved one. I was one hundred battles, a one hundred flower crown tied by my mother's hairpin.

I was those words that didn't need thoughts to say:

"I'm your first home."

BOON

We had just fought five people of the House inside a windmill.
We've managed to win without destroying the gears inside. We've
defeated four of them before the fifth ran and took the fallen.
They've left behind some things.

I look around the inside of the windmill and see what they've
left behind. I find a stone ax, and some sharpened arrowheads. I
find a white flower growing in a pot, which I place on my crown
to mark another battle won.

"Quill, these flowers. Maybe we'll find someone who knows
their names."

Quill looks around and does not respond. He picks up a round
object from one of their pouches. Although it's night, it's radiant.
It looks like a white fire.

"What is that?" I ask him.

"It's a mirror," he hands it to me.

I hold it up. If anything could be described as not of this
world, this mirror would be it. The House has people that can
hold no shadow, can heal, possess superhuman strength and
speed, but this is a truth all its own. I see myself. I see *my self*.
The 98 flower crown; all the flowers are rendered so colorful.
Like their natural colors were dyed further in its own shades.
And each flower had its own story. Oh, but if only I had known
the names of each flower, then those stories would be complete.
I see Mama's hairpin. I can *smell* the ocean's history in it.

My mouth is dry when I ask him—was I nervous? "What do
you see in it?"

I look over his shoulder while he looks into it. I see ourselves
side by side, but I know he'll see something else.

"This can't be real, Aliya."

"What do you see?"

"My own eyes. But inside them. I don't know how to say this, what my eyes are reflecting. I'm trying to see what my eyes are looking at. They're young eyes, Aliya. Young eyes. My young eyes. I...I...I *see something.*" He emphasizes the I. "I see a golden crown."

My heart skips a beat. They had said the Awakened One had been a prince once.

"Quill, have you ever wanted to return to your family?"

"I don't think I know who they are."

I say to him, "I think you do know. It's not too late to go back."

He puts the mirror inside his clothes, "Let's eat."

* * *

He asks me, "If you were able to make one wish, what would you wish for?"

"Mama..." He places a finger on my lips.

"You've fought so long. Was it all for your mother?"

How could he not have known? "I think it was."

"Where does your journey end?" he asks.

"Don't you mean our journey?"

He sighs.

"I do not know your mother, but I do not think she would have wanted you to fight so many battles. *I* do not think you should live in the past. She would have wanted the future for you." He's sincere.

"So, what would you wish for, Aliya?" He looks away from me, into the campfire. The windmill makes those noises only giant things can make. It turns slowly, but creaks in such a deep way that it affects my heartbeat.

I consider. I think about it. The windmill turns and creaks.

I searched the depths of my feelings and couldn't find something worth wishing for.

Instead, I ask him, "What would you wish for?"

"I'm not sure of my own name, Aliya. I'm not sure what was right or wrong. But I know something was certain in my past. I have a faint memory of being given a wish."

"Have you made a wish?" I ask.

He nods.

"What did you wish for?"

"I wished for things that were necessary in our journey. They were with Moonrise, but she ran away with them." He laughs, "It's funny, isn't it?"

"What do you mean?"

"The night in that forest, you had asked where I found those pots and pans. I told you I found them inside a tree. But before that, I wished for necessary things," he laughs, "and then they were gone!" He stops laughing, "I think I had been given a truth back when that wish was fulfilled."

I ask, "What truth?"

He takes my hand.

His touch is gentle and light. I look deep into his eyes. I wanted to recoil my hands, but instead I let it linger there. He has given me something. He didn't need to say the words, but he said them anyway, "This wish, I give to you. When you are ready..."

Something surged into my heart and stayed there. Was this love or a wish?

* * *

There was a deeper skill in removing my shadow that I had found. Every time I had done it, I had begun to feel more and more in on different plane—in a different *space*. I had begun to feel the other members of the House. In that burning forest, I could only feel them near me. But now, I could feel them from far away. I had once asked Quill if he had felt this too. He said he couldn't. He had said that the unique method that I found to remove my shadow may be why.

I felt them traveling. They were headed east. We do not know where they are going. But they are heading straight to somewhere. We'll cross them on the line that they walk on. Quill suggests getting in front of them. He draws a line in the sand, with a certain speed. Then he draws a second line, this time faster. "We can get ahead of them if we spend the next half-day running."

As we close the distance to where they are, we come to a road. This road must be leading to where they were going. We slowed down and began walking. The people are asleep, but dawn is coming. A stream runs through here. There are several foot bridges that follow the stream. It's a large village, which has low wood houses. The belongings outside the houses and the tools in their yards can tell a lot about that family's job: an ax, a hoe, an anvil, cloths flying in the wind. Far away, high walls protect a palace.

"Quill, I won't let a single house burn."

"We won't." He walks around with his hands rolling around. He swings his arms in circles and paces quickly. He takes heavy breaths and slowly exhales. He rolls his head round and round. He's never been like this before a battle. He's usually calm.

I feel them approaching.

They're here. An army of them. I learned that the ones who fired arrows were just on the cusp of learning how to fight. Usually, they were recruited when they were older; and so are less experienced. The ones who fight hand to hand are the stronger ones; they're the ones who were recruited as children. But no matter which ones they are, they always try to return the dead.

A purple sky highlights the outskirts of the village.

The experienced fighters run past me. They're going to find young people to kidnap. Quill runs after them. The people with arrows are striking their flint and stone to light the arrows. They are about to fire. I jump on top of one of the buildings. I run. I run across the building's roofs. Each stride bouncing off one roof and beginning on the next. The first arrow is fired. I crouch down into a deep squat, storing energy in my legs until...

I jump high off the roof; catching the arrow in a place between sky and land. On landing, I grasp the burning tip with my hand and extinguish the fire. I break the arrow in half. Although the House members were clustered together, they are now dispersing. I'll rush to them before I lose them.

A dot of the sun lights up the sky in red.

The stream that ran through this village may be a blessing. If they go in, their arrows will be wet, so would their flint. I grab the nearest one and tackle him into the stream. But he has fired an arrow into the air on falling. Now we're both falling. I can't fly and grab the arrow.

As I'm falling, I see it arc towards a building as if time had slowed. Arm lengths away from the arrow, Quill jumps. He stretches his arm and grabs the arrow. A House member tackles him in mid-air.

I climb out of the stream. They're going to send a volley of arrows. Five of them. I run as fast as I can before they light the arrows. They're scrambling, and uncoordinated. Instead of aiming above and with the arrow on fire, they aim at me.

One of them runs into the village. Ten others are running, surrounding the village from all sides, but I have the five before me to deal with. They shoot their arrows at me.

Orange light casts the land.

Soldiers come out of the houses. They run to catch the House members that were surrounding the houses. Here it comes.

The five arrows fly at me. I only manage to catch three of them. I should have caught all five. The other two arrows fly past me and bounce off the breastplates of two soldiers.

I chase the one who goes into houses. I enter one house, and exit another. Through and through alleyways, I give chase until she turns at me. She grabs and throws me into the other house.

The wall collapses. She runs up to me and grabs me by the foot and drags me. I'm trying to break out of her grip.

Quill has taught me an exercise where I curl my body and reach my fingertips, he called it a sit up. I sit up and grab onto her hand and try to wrestle the fingers off. But no, she is still dragging me. I kick her, but I only spin around.

The sky was white for an instant.

Soldiers are returning arrows back at the others.

As I'm struggling out of this woman's grip, while being dragged on the ground; I see Quill going from rooftop to rooftop fighting other House members.

I make my hand into a claw and dig into the ground. Then I use my free leg to kick her forearm. I hear and feel something snap in place. Her grip loosens enough that I pry myself out and stand up again. She nurses her other arm in place. I can already tell she is healing.

I breathe.

Slowly.

Recomposing myself.

I run at her, grab her, and dive over a foot bridge. We both fall into the running stream. I remove a pebble pressed into my arm. The sound of calm waters running. The feel of pebble and stone under my feet and the waters flowing through them. The dull gray world not yet awake.

Like a bird or a swan running against the water to take flight, so do I. I run along the stream and kick off the stone walls to be on ground again.

They're converging. I see them jumping from rooftop to rooftop. I've seen this before. They're coming for Quill. "Quill! They're coming!" He's far from me. I see him fighting on the side of a palace. The House members are like flies swarming around a cow's wound.

The houses disappear into a blur as I run down the main street and up the palace walls. While running up the palace wall, I see the members climbing the walls. I grab and pick each one off. They are monsters who do not scream when falling. I stand back to back with Quill fighting off the House members on the high wall.

They keep climbing the wall. From this high point, I see them swarm over the whole village like locusts. In one summer as a child, I've seen locusts fly over my farm like dark clouds, eating all our crops. It looks the same. A rush of air on this high place shakes the flower crown on my head.

I look down at the wall. They're running up the wall in zig zags. All of them. I don't care anymore...

I tip myself over the edge, and drop down the wall. I load my hand back while I fall. Wind in my face, pulling my hair upwards...I punch the first person I see from above. They fall to the ground with others. Good.

I fall on their pile of bodies. With a hard thud.

This pain is different from a bruise or a sting or a welt. My back feels like something was pushing from the inside. Like my blood was flowing where it was not supposed to. I follow my hand to the pain. A bone was out of place. I try to stand and it hurts. I'll force myself to straighten up.

Like fire through my back.

They're not coming for Quill. They're coming for me. They turn back from climbing the wall and fall down the wall. It looks like a dark cascade, a shadow waterfall.

They grab my ankles. They grab my hands. There's too much pain to fight. One by one, they mount on me.

I see what they were trying to do to Quill. Block the air until he's suffocating. Until he can't breath. Until he sleeps in this darkness. I can't get out of here. They keep pushing me in, pulling me into the center. This horde was a blindfold; with dots of light through the dark. No...I won't use the wish here. I'll find my way out myself.

I can't move with their weight on me. I'm curled over in an uncomfortable stance. My arms are twisted behind me. My neck and head bent forward. My face pressed against black cloth. And they're still piling on me. I twist my arms and manage to slip out in between their grasp.

Not at this moment, but in quieter moments...I had wondered if wrapped up in this horde, all bundled together, if they were able to feel touch.

I'll pull everyone in. I won't let them push me further in. I grab every arm, every leg. And I drag them in while I dig myself out. Slowly, the light from the outside is coming through. I manage to crawl out and...

I see Quill falling from the high wall. Let me escape this horde's grasp...

Let me run fast...let these legs move as quickly as the wind...

As I catch you.

The blue sky. The day has come.

"Good timing," he tells me.

The soldiers are running and taking the swarm apart from the other side. They're dragging people off the swarm and putting them in chains.

Has it been ten minutes? The sun is fully up now.

No one died in this battle, I realized...

A ball has been thrown in the air. I immediately recognize it. Before I know it, I'm in the air, kicking it away from the palace walls. The ball explodes. The way I fall away from it, the way it explodes while moving away from me; it seemed like a comet in the sky.

* * *

"My name is Lo," someone said. He turns around to face us. A deep scar runs through his face. I hear familiar hoofing.

"Moonrise?" I ask.

"Now who is that?" Lo asks.

"My horse."

"No, these two are Sun and Monsoon."

We're on a cart. We're riding to somewhere. The cart's bouncing up and down. Was I ever so careless to my wheat bundles when I pushed my cart? Every bump is killing me. After battles, I usually rest a day and start to move again. I didn't need to be on a cart being wheeled recklessly around. I yell, "Lo, please stop moving so recklessly."

"Hahaha, you don't have a choice in the matter. Without your help, I think our village would have been destroyed. I'm bringing you two to the doctor. He'll help you two get better."

"Did any building catch on fire?" I ask him.

"No."

Ugh, my neck. I can't move my head.

I hear laughing to the left of me. "Relax. Here." It's Quill. He takes my hand and puts it on something a bit cold. At least I can move my left arm without much pain. I feel the bumps and the skin along it. I pluck a seed from it, shine it in front of me—a ruby seed, and eat it. A pomegranate. Quill is also taking from the same fruit. Our hands must be taking turns to not touch each other.

"Quill, can you move too?"

"No."

"Quill, you're not healing?"

"Every time I do, I feel farther away from this world. I want to be here."

"There's something I wanted to ask you for a long time. Why does the House take the dead?"

"We—they recite them their rites before they pass on. To give them guidance through that intermediate space. Then we burn their bodies."

"What intermediate space?"

"The place between death and life."

"Most people would say life and death."

"The rites are read to guide them to their next life, Aliya." Death and life...

"But you haven't read the rites to them in our battles," I say.

"I haven't done it because it was a lie. If the things I've learned were a lie then...the way you learn so fast, the difference in your methods, you represent some sort of truth. I can't understand it yet," he says.

"Don't make me into something I'm not," I say.

I try to relax.

I say to him, "If I die, don't read me those rites."

The wheel turns and turns...creaking...

* * *

"We are here!" The horses stop. Lo pats them. I would imagine he's walking to a house nearby. No, I know... He's meeting with someone.

"If I could only move right now. I want to see what the horses look like. Do you think they look like Moonrise?" I ask Quill.

"I looked at them when Lo put me on here. They look like her; a little bit. You miss her, don't you?"

Lo and the Doctor come up to the cart. They put Quill onto a sling and walk him into the building. Then they move me. Both of us were put on stone tables. The Doctor said they'll set my bones, seal my wounds, balance my energy.

Lo takes a chair and sits by Quill, "All along, I have heard tales of a man and a woman who traveled the land. One of them has a flower crown, and the other in black rags. They would return children, who had been forced into martial arts, to their families. They protected villages from bandits...it is an honor to meet you two."

He pauses, and looks down.

"Long ago, I was not a good man. I had traveled to cities and stole. I hurt other people. But my King had taken me, and had shown me my better self. But before he changed me, I had once provoked him with the name of his son...a son who he thought he had lost. I had seen his son in black rags in a forest once...

"Your name, what did you say it was?" Lo asks him.

Quill responds, "I don't know."

"Tell him..." I say to Quill.

"It's not my name," he tells Lo.

I tell Quill, "I think you know it is..."

"My name is Quill."

Lo bows his head, "My Prince..."

"Let them rest. You can come back later," the Doctor says to Lo. Lo leaves.

* * *

Lo came every day and night bringing food to us. He bought us new clothes for when we would be ready to change into them. He assisted the Doctor when the Doctor needed help. Lo had usually spent time telling us jokes and stories.

"Where do birds go when it rains?"

"Three new monks were asked to bring water from a well back to the monastery. They took turns. The well was on the bottom of a mountain. The first monk took a short, steep path up and ended up tumbling his bucket. So he told the other two monks not to take the steep path. The second monk took a zig-zag up the mountain, but was exhausted at the end. The third monk comes back with two buckets of water. The first two monks were so impressed, they asked what he did.

"He looks up at the sky, in deep concentration. The two monks lean in to hear his secret.

"I just asked the new guy to do it for me."

"A farmer was working in his field. His wife passes by and notices a foul odor. She asked him, 'Was that your ass?'"

"What's the difference between a robber and a merchant? The robber has the decency to let you know you're getting robbed."

Hours and days of these stories and jokes. Hours...and days...

They weren't very good jokes, but Quill seemed to laugh. And I hate to admit it, but so did I.

The days passed by quickly until we were able to walk again.

* * *

He undresses out of his old rags in front of me. For the first time, I see his naked body from behind. We were battle tested, but he had chosen to heal every time. Except this battle. I hold the scars that I chose to keep. He walks and takes the new clothes, from Lo, and puts them on. No longer wearing heavy, dark rags; he now wore a white, flowing silk shirt and pants. He looked dignified.

"I don't know what I would wish for, but I think I know what I long for," I say to him.

"What's the difference?"

"Wishing is a prayer. It's a thing that you do not suffer for. Longing is waiting, hoping that something would come. It may mean that you may work to get to it...or not. It's like a fortune, I think. A fortune you hope would pass.

"I'm thinking a lot of what you had told me. About the future. I think...I long for that one day—I'm looking forward to a peaceful life that is my own. Maybe one day, when our war is over, when our duty is fulfilled, there'll be time for leisure. For pleasure," I say.

"That is something to look forward to," Quill smiles.

I change too. My clothes are white again. There are black laces on the shirt and pants.

I muster the courage to say what I need to say next, "You were right. Our journeys are different. You need to go to your family."

"Aliya, I will fight with you until the very end."

I tell him, "You don't need to, this isn't your duty."

"I think it is."

I walk to his old clothes. The mirror is placed under a pile. Holding it in my hand, it had little weight. The white fire that danced on its circumference felt like a feather tickling my fingers. I hold it up so that both our faces are in it.

I ask him, "What do you see?"

* * *

Oceanic blue skies are punctuated by clouds. I feel young again; looking at the clouds and disappearing in it. I say to Quill, "It's spectacular." A single line of clouds arcs from horizon to horizon as if the sky was halved. The colors are brilliant and vivid. It was a rainbow, but revealed in the clouds. It's expansive and it pulls you into it. Stare at it and let yourself float up.

"Quill, can you see this? It's beautiful."

The Doctor comes out and tells us, "It's called a fire rainbow. It comes out only on beautiful days like today. It's an auspicious sign."

"Beautiful..." Quill manages to utter...

While looking at me...

If I was to deny love, but I felt it so strongly then do I give in?

I'll give in halfway. I stand to the side of him, our elbows barely touching.

* * *

Was this what a kingdom was? This palace is empty. Expansive. Lo's boots echo. In my village, I had seen a palace, but have never entered. Who would need a house this large? So many families could live here. We come to the throne, the seat of the King.

"Quill, one day, that seat will be yours," Lo says.

Quill asks, "Lo, where is the King?"

"He had gone back to the middle of his empire. It must have been 15 years ago...I didn't want to press the issue, Quill, but I'm glad that you had decided to come," Lo says.

"How can you be sure he's my father?"

"Faith is enough," Lo tells him.

Quill stands in front of the throne. He touches the wood that was so intricately cut. He sits down and looks at me. It seemed that he wanted a direction. A memory comes to me, that of soldiers coming to my house.

I say to Quill, "I realize now...I could have saved your life. When you came to my house a long time ago. Soldiers had come before. I could have told them...They would have found you. I could have saved your life."

"I ran away from home. I wanted to go to the town to get provisions. It was weeks after that the House found me. It's not your fault," he says.

"Quill, ycu have to go back." You have to leave me.

"Aliya..."

* * *

Lo had gathered supplies for a long trip. He packed them into a wagon. It was fit for a king.

"Ever since I met you, you have been unsure of your own name. I spent many nights thinking about that. A person's name gives them a story, a history. A person's family name gives them a history. It tells others of the work, the history, of the family that led you here. So because you don't have a name, you may not have a story to call your own.

"I want to give you a gift just like you've given me.

"I want to give you a name. I want to give you a name so you remember our adventures together. That our time was not in vain. And that you had transformed into...a good man.

"Before you go, I name you Lotus. And if you ever doubt yourself, remember your name."

"I'll find you again," he holds my hands and lets go as he walks away. Those fingers slip away so slowly.

I say, "Don't look back."

He looks back once, before taking off with Lo on the wagon.

Long after he leaves and the stars cast light on empty roads, I notice flowers growing on the ground. My 99th flower...a blue flower.

WHEN YOUR FORTUNE COMES, YOU WILL BE READY

I don't get to become a prince, but I'll walk this earth. I'll be an avenger. I'll be the savior.

For all the times I had visited this space to feel where they are, it has occurred to me that I can see farther since the beginning. But I also feel that I sense less shadows than before. Their numbers are diminishing.

He had asked me, where does my journey end? The future? I had resented the Seer's words for my whole life. I think I found my journey's end. It was a future without the House. I'll find a future without war or suffering.

Death then life.

I think I understood the House. They'll burn the whole world down to see the truth. Had the Seer seen the truth? She saw a future.

Losing my dad, my mom, unread books, Moonrise, Quill... Lotus...at times, I still cannot come to terms with a world without them. But somehow, I feel like I should live for them. I cannot wallow in my own misery. I *should* make these fleeting moments mean something.

* * *

Summer is hotter than usual. Or is that just where I am? The cave's walls are wet. The sun shines in. My shadow is cast against the cave's wall. And then, it was gone.

I enter into that space again. I must've been able to see the world as it was. But I saw it as both far and near now. Where are you people?

A voice. "Did it not occur to you, that every time you had come to visit this place, that there would not be someone looking back?"

What...the...fuck?

What was that?! I fall out of focus for the first time. My heart feels like it's about to beat out of my chest. What was that? It was just a voice, but it wasn't from here. What did he mean, someone was looking back. He knows where I am.

But I'm not ready to fight yet.

I lose time walking through the world. In mountain passes, I yell until corridors echo with my voice. In tall forests, I run across tree tops. I wade through rivers until its chill warms my skin. I sit under lonely trees on the steppe; watching thunderstorms roll by.

Over a lake, round as a circle, I see the full moon on its still face. The campfire still crackles. I look over the water while I carefully cut my hair short. It smelled like perfume when the hair was taken by the fire.

I sleep.

* * *

Dreams like fragments.

I see Mama tending the field, but there was someone with her. I approach but the man leaves. The wheat stalks, but here more golden, rustle in the wind. A gust throws the clothes off the clothesline. Clothes are caught on the stalks and flap. I go to pick them up.

Mama stops me. "Aliya, you're grown up now."

"Mama, I have to pick these clothes up. We're going to lose them."

"Your hair looks nice."

"Mama, help me with these clothes."

"Aliya...forget about the clothes. Look at me."

"I can't. You know I can't."

I hold these black and white clothes. I walk them back to my house. It has been years since I've seen it. The stone. The light and the shadows. My bed. The table. I sit by the kitchen table, looking outside. The bundle of clothes still on my lap, I refuse to look at the face of my mom.

I feel a hand rubbing my back. "It's okay. It's okay," Mama said. I feel her putting the crown on my head. She tells me, "Remember where you came from. But, also know where you're going."

"Mama..."

She puts her hairpin in my hand, and closes my fingers on it.

"We're proud of you."

* * *

The way forward was blurred. Without entering that space again, I could only judge from my memory. Although I was wandering through the world before, I now have to find a direction to go in. I haven't had a care of where I went before.

I walked to a lone tree on top of a hill. Its trunk looks like muscle and sinew that struck itself into earth. It also looked like loose threads hanging, waiting to be loomed into a shape, a fabric. Its skinny branches reached up to the sky and shaped itself like a mushroom. I spent hours watching the tree's shadow move on the ground. I have to judge the sun's motion.

I see myself reading my father's books under that tree. Instead, I write the only character I know. I draw four strokes on the ground: fire. At this moment, I realized I was free. I didn't need to be a farmer. I wonder about the lives I could lead. A soldier, a doctor, a sailor, a princess, a merchant, a scholar, a vagrant, a wanderer. Maybe after my war, I'll become one of them.

From on top of this hill, I find my place in the world. From the movement of the tree's shadow, I learn direction. I know North. So I know South. I know East. I know West. I recount the directions I had taken since I had been in that space. I'm trying to rebuild the map in my head. If I know how the sun moves, I can tell which direction I'm moving in no matter where I am. I recall the places I've been, and I think I know where I can find them.

By any means necessary, I have to find the House without the usual method.

* * *

That voice finds me again. The same voice from the space. The voice that I had been hiding from. A voice that sounded both old and young. He somehow entered into my dreams.

"Aliya, are you not coming to the truth?" it spoke.

"What truth?" I think I know what he is about to say, but my heart beats faster.

"You're not removing your shadow...you're removing yourself.

"In stories, we tell people what 'I' do. 'I cross my arms.' 'I sit.' 'I stand.' like our bodies are different from our minds. But we know that's not true, is it? It is the one and the same.

"Hmmm. Nothing to say? When you enter here, into this space, your mind is here. Where did your body go?" the voice asks me.

"It is here. Just as it's always been. Who are you?" I didn't even know what I just said. This place is a dream.

His voice circles me as if someone was walking around me.

"They call me the Teacher."

"I know where you are. You have the last horde of the House left."

He just ignores what I just said. He continues, "For someone not part of the House, you've done well to master our skills. But, it is a lot like a child reciting words from a book, but not understanding its meaning. Quill didn't give you the meaning, did he?"

"No, I understand where your skills lead to. He didn't have to tell me."

"Then why do you fight us? If you know, if you can feel, where you are, where you are right now."

"Because burning the world down doesn't help anyone. Because running away doesn't help anyone. Because...children need their families."

"I want to show you something. Something that made us all believe."

With the full weight of my journey behind my words, I say "I'll protect this house and everyone in it."

"Find me."

* * *

There was a courage upon waking. Where they are, I know where to find them.

* * *

On rolling green hills, where the mist hangs forever. And when you move through it, you feel the spray on your face. The mist is so thick, there is neither shadow nor each light—just gray. The mist is blown with the wind. At times, I see clearings through it where I see the grass. Sometimes I see the sun's rays. It's a dance where sometimes there is the sunlight, sometimes the grass, the spaces in between the mist, and the mist itself.

The longer I stay here, the more my clothes take the moisture of the air. The fabric hangs heavy on me. The grass is wet and slippery. I take my shoes off. Bare feet is better for traction on wet grass.

Although the mist is thick, the sun is out—illuminating everything in a soft, gray glow.

"Teacher, I've come for you!" My yell was dulled by the water in the air. The mist falls like slow rain.

A person walks through the mist, parting it with his hands. Water droplets stick to his white beard and roll down, catching other droplets. His clothes were not black, they were a shadow, a night-black silhouette without form. A gust of wind shakes the bun on his tied up hair. He is not tall or hefty, but in all ways average. But he is imposing and old. He speaks.

"No kingdom. No state. No boundaries. If there is no kingdom, no state, no boundaries, no nation, then there is no war. No war to fight. No war to lose or to win. No society.

"No society.

"This is the first step to lifting the illusion.

"No house, no people, no children, no family. No family, no attachment.

"No attachment.

"When we are led to no attachment, we become free. This is the second step to lifting the illusion.

"No society. No attachment. Then there can be no pain. No pain or grief. Then we lift our dispositions beyond the cycles of death and life.

"No world. No land. No forest. No ocean. We will be carried into the real House. This is the final step to lifting the illusion.

"Sit. Please."

He kneels down, and puts his hands on his thighs. He closes his eyes as if in meditation. I could end him right now. And the others that were around me. I didn't need to be in the space to know that they were around their leader.

I sit too. Was this how knowledge was transmitted from teacher to student through the ages? I ask,

"If you are a teacher, then do you read?"

"Yes."

"What is this word?"

"Fire."

I trace in the air another few characters. The title of one of my father's books—one burned by their conquest. Family Tree, he says.

"Why did you not teach the House how to read?"

"Words are too little to feel. To give meaning to experience."

All those words in all those pages, they had meaning to me.

"Are you their leader?"

"Yes."

"Why do they not see the space like you or me?"

"That is why I had asked you to find me. You had found that within the skill of receding your shadow, there is the deeper skill of finding a space, an area in it. There is an even deeper skill that is buried even deeper. I want to instruct you through the deeper skill so that you may understand."

He continues, "When you had spent time in the dark, you must have realized that there is also a space inside your own shadow. That your shadow is a needle through a fabric. It exists on both sides, it pulls you out, and into something else. The space.

"Please see me in the space."

I close my eyes.

"You had found this space by another method, haven't you?" he asks me inside the space.

"When I had looked at the moon, I found that the shadow can be extinguished by light. And it was by that same way that I had found the space. Like light had seeped through the spaces in between fabric."

"You must be aware that shadows, unlike light, have a special property."

"What is that?"

"May I show you?"

I consider. "Yes."

"Shadows can merge."

He steps into me.

* * *

When I went into the space, I found shadows on an unmarked territory. A landscape barren of all things. But it had a texture to it. There was a color, a shape, and a form. It was physical. I could see something in the space.

From inside the space, the Teacher pulled me into something without meaning. I wasn't in the space. I'm not sure if I was anywhere. It was deep, unending, non-physical, indescribable.

Pain. Healing. Attachment. Detachment.

Heartache.

Grief.

Change.

Unshakable faith. Duty.

All these feelings at once. It's hard to feel it, but it feels so easy to be *in it*. And it wouldn't let you leave. I want to stay here.

But I'll put something here too. A gift for them. The feelings I felt; that were easy to feel, but hard to surrender to.

The scent of one hundred flowers, blooming and withered.

Laughter.

Bad jokes.

Love in all forms.

Longing for better days.

I open my eyes back to the world.

"You felt it, haven't you? How can the world be enough? Be sufficient? Be true? When what you felt was boundless," he asks.

Every House member must have felt it. I felt it. I was wrong when I had said they couldn't feel touch.

"It's all here too. It's all here too. It's enough," I tell him.

"It's not enough."

The mist takes him. He disappears before me. I wipe the water that has built up on my eyebrows and hair. I stand up. I know what was coming. He had laid two paths in front of me before I even came here: an invitation to join or a trap to end me.

I can't shake their faith. And they can't move me from my resolve. Even when we understood each other.

* * *

A loud sound throws me against the ground. I spin on the ground on my back. It doesn't seem like they're using arrows anymore. A fist comes out of the mist. I block it. But I didn't block the kick to my back. That one is going to hurt.

Where are they coming from? I can't be in both the space and in here too. I can't know where they are and fight them at the same time. I run around to find a semblance of shadow or form around me. A bomb lands near me. I jump into the air and out of the way.

The explosion throws dirt and grass into the air. The sunlight casts the detritus' shadows against the mist—like sun rays inverted into shadow. The air around the bomb rippled out like a dome. It was a wave pushing waves out. The spray hits against my face like hard rain.

They throw their bombs at me. I can only dodge them right before I see them. The explosion spreads the mist so that for a brief moment, I can see through it. Then the mist falls back into that empty space. It was as if the world was revealing itself one pocket at a time.

Got you! I grab someone's fist. I lock my arms into theirs. "How many are there of you?" She doesn't speak. I throw her up in the air and she fades into the mist. Huh. I don't hear her falling. The bombs and the destruction scar the land under me. I feel only dirt and cut grass. The grooves in the dirt; pebbles that press against my naked sole, the craters that were rock-deep. What had they done to these beautiful hills?

The mist makes it hard to see the bombs before they come right at me. It blindsides me every time. At least seven arms reach out from the fog. I've seen this before. They're not going to catch me this time. I tackle someone through the fog and both of us roll down the hill. They disappear from sight before I could go after them. A trail of spiral-twisted mist is in their wake.

I look back. I hone in on any sounds that they might make when approaching me. Any smell. The air does smell of earth and grass. The smell does not leave and stays here like a fixture. No wind to take it away. I'll take a moment to remember this...

"I'm not going to hide my shadow, so you can all come straight and find me!"

My shadow comes back to the ground like rolling black waves. Coming back here, I cannot help but think of this shadow as a pin, a needle into the earth. Like the tree that looked like sinews.

A moment of silence passes me. The air is still.

"Fight me!!! I'm here! Your last enemy!"

Answer my call.

I take my crown off and slide the water off my hair. I forgot I had cut it. The sharp ends have dulled. I walk through the mist; making a tunnel as I go. Have they given up? The Teacher must know where I am. But I will not enter that space again. If you were here, would I see you through the mist? Your shadow? Your face?

I see a bomb coming. Another one. Then another. They're throwing everything they have at me. It's the last push. If they're surrounding me; encircling me with their explosives, there's nowhere to go, but up. I drop down and focus on my legs. When learning, Quill had told me to imagine my legs like wood held and bent over into a curve, and when I had the most tension held in the legs, to let it go quick and spring up.

The mist felt like rain when I was moving up. The water droplets flick off hard on my face. I peer down at the mist that had parted. The bombs are still exploding like fireflies lighting up on a summer night. I'm far away enough that I can't hear the sound. I see the rolling hills from up high with the mist parting. Through the clearing, the sunlight reaches the ground. Birds must be so lucky. Brown craters appeared like twinkling stars, popping up in random until a much larger circle was completed.

Approaching figures are jumping up. Seven of them. I hold my fist to my side and palm it with my other hand. On the fall down, the first one to come close will be plummeted straight down to earth. Falling down, falling down. We're going to meet in the middle. With the speed they're coming up, they're creating tunnels in the air. Through some of the spaces they've created, sun rays shone through. The wind whistles by. I see the white of their eyes. I punch one of them to the ground.

That created an opening for the others to take. Someone punches me, sending me falling to my right. The world is spinning to my right. There's nothing to grab hold of. The water droplets moving like a spray across me. The sun, a faint light in the sky, entered and left my spinning vision a few times already. Falling, the Sun blends into the rest of the sky.

A member grabs my wrist. There's only precious few seconds to get him off before the ground comes. I shove his face away from me and break one of his fingers. He leans back—dragging me with him. We entered into a spin in the other direction. He tucks his legs in. The world spins faster. He's forcing me into a somersault with him. I struggle to fix my position. I can't figure out where the ground is. I can't judge how I'm going to land.

He headbutts me. Blood drips into my eyes. The blood and the water mixing and irritating my eye. This one member is still holding onto my wrist while spinning. I see two others nearby in my fall. I grab onto one. While spinning and maintaining a firm grip on the other person, I'll curl my arms. I bring both of them together and hit each other on the head. The one who grabbed my wrist had let go.

Something is wrong. They're falling up. I should have hit the ground by now. An arm wraps around my neck, pressure in my head building. Pressing against my throat.

I no longer felt the ground. I can't see the sky or the earth. I fight fumbling against my opponent. I toss him up(?) into the air and I follow. But I couldn't feel the ground. Where I expected to fall and hit the dirt, I don't. The mist hits against my face when I move. I wipe away the water from my eyes.

But the sensation of falling stopped. The air doesn't move like if I were falling. It is still.

I can't win if I don't know where I am. Where I'm going. They come from all directions like I'm the center of a circle. I could only grab onto them for brief moments to hit them. Without a ground to stand on, I couldn't just punch or kick them; I have to hold them. But they keep hitting me because I don't know where they're coming from. One hit wouldn't end me, but if this keeps up; I may be done. If they start throwing bombs at me, I won't be able to jump. *I can't push off mist.*

No.

How lucky was I.

A bomb comes at me.

In our travels, Quill and I had come across street acrobats. They did somersaults, flips, and tumbled. I asked why he didn't teach me those moves. He said flips were not useful in fighting. If you turn your back on your enemy for even a second, you wouldn't be able to see what would come for you.

I whip my arms around, and twist out of the way just like those acrobats. It was the only way. *Of course flips can be used in fights.* The bomb rushes pass me. It explodes; making another bubble in the air. If I can see how the sunlight is in the void, then that'll give me the direction. It's just air inside...there's nothing.

A bomb whizzes through the air. I catch it and throw it back in the direction it came in. I notice something new this time. As it approached me, the air moved towards me before the bomb did. A boat moving through water, the ripple reaching the shore before the boat. There's a lesson here...

They keep coming. Different people each time. I grab them. I fight them off. Bombs. Again and again, the sound. The explosions had thrown me, against a backdrop that hadn't changed. Until I stopped. If I could only figure out where they are without the space.

The somersaults and flips are exhausting me. The House had hit me several times already. My movements are sluggish and slow. My face, my cheeks, my eyes and hair. They were blood mixed with water. How easily it had flowed and soaked half my body. My hair is suspended in this air.

Like a flash, I'm reminded of a lake's surface.

Mama...I understand you.

I look at the lines the mist makes. At the ripples that signal coming danger. At the tunnels made by the House. It is both speed and location at once. The patterns the mist makes are like an ocean but splayed all around me. The mist was a map. It has a shape, a form. Every droplet was a star. The mist itself was a constellation that was ever changing. The tunnels that they had carved while moving through the air were still there in the background, but falling. The way the mist had moved to take up empty space was a sign that the House members were there. On close examination, I notice the subtle ripples in the air; it made sense. I could understand where they were by looking at the ripples. By dead reckoning, I can tell where I am. And where I could go.

It was more than North, South, West, and East. It is also Nadir and Zenith! The water droplets swing around me like a vine. I see the lines, the empty spaces. I know where I can find them. I *see* them! I go through the air, propelling myself. I trace the lines, the edges of the ripples. I find the bodies lighting the bombs. I crash into them.

Ground again. They are no more. I watch the mist and anticipate every move. Every attack that can come. I find and end every last member.

Where is their Teacher?

I walk through these rolling hills, scarred by the craters, rocks and pebbles, bodies. "This is the end!" Blood mist from my mouth falls on the grass. I look at the mist. It is very much like a blindfold, but light against light, and the water the clearings in the fabric. The mist is so still. I pass my hand in front of me. It's not as thick as before.

"Breathe," a voice says.

I catch my breath. I find a space in this mist. Subtle ripples seem like flowing curtains. I walk through it. My breath is still.

* * *

I see the Teacher. He stands to the side of me. "You've used up too much energy. You've lost too much blood."

"I don't want to fight anymore," I told him. "But I can't allow you to keep spreading your words...your world. Look at the destruction you've created."

"The same could be said of you."

"What do I do with you?"

"What do I do with you?"

A gentle breeze blows across the hills. The mist crawls across in spirals. He points up in the sky, "You were suspended there, for a moment."

"Was I?"

"Yes...I've never seen anything like it."

"I know you'll end me. I can tell from your gaze. I suggest you heal. There's a life for you after your war."

"Healing to you...is that just avoiding the pain?...you're not going to answer? You can't spare one answer after everything you've done?"

"You have potential to be a figure of influence."

"Spare me."

"You're shivering."

"So are you."

He walks away from me. The mist is clearing. He sits down within talking distance, "Why did you fight a war that wasn't yours?"

"You're not making any sense." My clothes are red. I didn't notice, but I was shivering. It's both hot and cold. I respond, "You *know* why I fought this war."

I stand where I am. Why did he make me run so much if my chest can't keep up with my breathing right now?

The Teacher wraps his arms around himself. "It seems my time has come to pass. When the next wind blows, I will be delivered."

The spaces in between his words grow with each breath.

"Then my war is over," I tell him.

"Do you believe ideas ever die?" he asks me.

There was a reason why they call him a Teacher.

Before I answer, I look up. The sun is covered in haze. I wonder if it's made of the same things as fireflies. The sun is warm against my face. Do ideas ever die? I suppose we're taught by questions. Does he mean like undiscovered places; that ideas are not made, but found? Do ideas reside in the lessons we teach? In heritage and heirlooms? In people?

A bird flies across the sun. Its shadow casts on my face. I'm happy. I smile and look at the Teacher, "No, I don't think ideas ever die."

He smiles too and a zephyr passes both of us.

A flower. My hundredth one. Just let my hands grab it. There.

"With earth as my witness, bind me."

I can finally sit down. I take my One Hundred Flower Crown off and lay it on the earth. How many people can claim they offered their own wreath on their graveyard. "Ha ha ha haa."

"I hope that each one of you that I have saved will live in this world. Enjoy your peaceful days."

I open my eyes slightly. When I was younger, I looked through windows into the world. Now, the world peers into my eyes.

Hooves ride like thunder. I hear it, but I can only see a blur. I smell old, worn pages from books; and wheat. I glimpse a sword, glinting in many colors. I hear your voice asking me, "Who are you, Aliya?"

* * *

I said something, but I don't know what I had said. Something more important. There was something more important I had to speak in this dark. Through the parting fog, I glimpse a pale moon in mid-day.

"My only wish. I'll reunite with you when our lives are our own. I'll meet you on the road somewhere...maybe under a glowing moon."

His warm hands take mine. Oh what a light touch through this darkness. "I was supposed to be with you," he says.

"I think I had loved you."

"I was supposed to be with you. Aliya. Stay with me, please."

A golden crown. A flower crown. A round mirror.
It was three circles that told of a story.
I close my eyes and wonder
If rainbows appeared
When the mist had parted.
I close my eyes
For the last time.
I float.

And he says to me, "May you find the ways through death."

I float between love and hate.

"May you find safe passage through the dark rivers."

I float between the earth and the sky.

"May you transcend every realm, every demon, and monster."

I float between the illusion and the truth.

"May you turn the wheel and find your next life."

I'll even float between life and death.

"Aliya, I love you."

I'll float in the middle.

"May you find peace."

* * *

In the space that I'm in, I open my eyes. Scared, I do not blink that it may disappear. I find myself in the cove of my house, reading these books again. But I know every word. I must've taken something from the Teacher's realm. I read through my father's entire library without blinking. And it was wonderful, even with the frayed and missing pages and missing text.

I look outside. Quill and Mama were grooming Moonrise. Farther away were newly built houses. Maybe the families I've saved were there. Oh, there was a promise there. Of a time of peace...when we have our own house. I could imagine it as vividly as that fire rainbow.

I would love to stay here.

But I'll be brave. I'll close my eyes to open them towards the future.

I swell with tremendous pride at who I was, who I will become.

In this space, I saw time slip by...so slow...so fast. And so...a fiery light pulled me into the world.

I needed to say something before I can forget. Before I change. I needed to say...

Life was your own.

Itinerary

CHAPTER FOUR

LIMERENCE

Camille asks me, "Hey Bradley, do you want to go to the roof? I want to show you something."

I leave the party. Everyone is here in this apartment. The people I knew from our class, band, clubs. I follow her out of her apartment and into the hallway.

"I always wanted to go to the roof," she said. Camille opens the window about an inch. "Actually, you know what?" She kicks the glass and the glass shatters. She enters the fire escape and starts walking up to the roof. I part the hanging wood frame left from the destruction and follow behind her. It is night outside; yellow-halogen street lamps are on.

The roof comes into view from the fire escape. I walk to the edge of the roof and peer out. I ask, "This wheat field. Did you put this place out here?" Sunlight illuminates the wheat field. There is the night, and the day, divided in my view.

"I'm so glad to be heading off to college. No more classes that I don't want to take," she jumps up and claps her heels together. I sit on the ledge peering out.

"What do you plan on studying, Camille?" I ask.

"I always found biology fascinating. Like genetics is such a promising area. Where your entire person is made and determined by a set of instructions. And disease can be cured if we know how the game works. Okay, I'm rambling now."

"I don't think that could be the end of it. I mean your grandparents or even great grandparents' suffering had to count for something...for you. It's cliche but the whole genetics business puts such a horrible implication to life—"

"Don't tell me," she interrupted.

I continue, "I mean doesn't the whole thing imply fate?"

"Maybe, but that doesn't change what is true or that people still need to help people. It's almost like..."

"...why should philosophy stop progress, right?" I suggest.

"What if there's something else? Something not fate or free will?" I ask her.

"What would that be?"

"I don't know."

"Yeah, exactly...what are you looking to do?" she asks.

"I always wanted to write."

"Like stories? You have any good ones?"

"Not really. I have one."

"Tell me."

"Maybe one day."

"You know every time I hang out with you, it's always with everyone else. It's actually nice to know you for you," she says.

MAY 1979

Bradley Dusk is awake. Birds chirp outside his window. Wind chimes ring gently from his neighbor's porch. A warm wind, the type one would feel between spring and summer, comes into his room. He sits on the bed, looking out of his window. His curtains billow slightly. What was a dream so strongly felt?

He gets his backpack and heads out the door. He takes a bus. It is mostly empty, except with three adults and one or two tardy students in the same bus.

The bus takes him two miles from his home to Fort Hamilton High School. Built in the 1940s, it is a street away from Brooklyn's Narrows. Three stories tall, more wide than it is high, the high school is one of Brooklyn's more populated schools. Sakura trees line the perimeter of the school. With spring about to give way to the summer, they are in full bloom. The pink leaves would fall when class is in session. A football field, the pride of the athletic department, is situated in front of the school.

The bus arrives two blocks away. He exits the bus quickly and runs to the school.

"Bradley. You're just on time…again," his home room teacher sarcastically tells him.

Bradley ignores the teacher's words and sits down. Frankie, a friend, leans over and asks, "Maintaining your reputation?"

* * *

Friends come by and gather at Matt's house: Frankie, Camille, Pauline, Fiona, and Jack. Matt was personable, and always invited people to any event he dreamt up. There is not one person in the high school who hated him.

In the apartment hallway, Matt's mother and father leave the apartment and greet Bradley, "Hello."

Camille walks to open a window, "It's hot in here."

Matt takes out a board game, "So I got this German board game. I can't read the rules but my grandfather taught me how to play. You'll learn the rules while we play. It's easier that way."

"But I want to argue over the rules," Bradley says.

"You two argued over Monopoly rules last time," Camille says.

"Camille, you're the one that nudged the board *accidentally*," Pauline says to her.

"You better have some evidence if you're going to accuse me, Ms. Lawyer," Camille says.

"Okay, okay. Let's just play the game. Bradley said he has to leave in a bit," Matt tried to keep the peace.

They play the German board game with as little friendly arguing over pedantic details as possible.

Bradley seemed uninterested, "Uh guys, I have to go. My shift begins in an hour."

"Stay," Camille tells him.

"I can't. I'm sorry guys. We'll continue this next time? Or something else?"

"I wish you could stay."

"Same here. But responsibilities…" Bradley tells Camille.

The rest bid him goodbye.

PARIS, FRANCE

"Paris. Isn't this beautiful?" she says to me.

"Amazing, but everything is so empty. Where is everyone?"

"We're here alone—the two of us."

I don't know why, but we're walking to a cafe. We're walking by La Seine, following the river. We walk up these stairs. There's a café above these stairs. People are appearing now. Our friends are at this café. They're waving for us to join them.

I'm sitting inside. Sunlight pours into the place. The light touches all the walnut tables and seats. The furniture *gleans*. Windows are opened. Cigarette smoke flows all around inside and outside here.

"Tell us a funny story," Camille pulls up a chair and puts down a saucer and tea cup with grace. I don't think I've ever drank coffee before.

"Well one time, I took a train to Long Island. Out to Valley Stream to see my cousin. We drove out to a high school to explore. He calls me up to the rooftop. But the thing is I'm afraid of heights. And I'm there at the bottom. He's calling out to me.

'Bradley! Get up here' In sort of a hushed tone. I'm climbing a ladder by the side of a building. My knees were jello. I try not to look down. I get to the top and he leads me into a boiler or maintenance room. We hear some sounds, which is weird for a weekend. I hide behind a boiler. He decides to go farther in and check it out. A security guard comes out grabbing him by the arm.

"He just tells me to run. I'm standing there with my palms on my face.

"Two hours later, we're held in a police car waiting for his dad to come pick us up.

Camille, you're staring at me."

"How can I not? You're telling the story," she says. This happened before. This is a memory. I now realize her attentive stare at me.

"Bradley, that really wasn't a funny story," Frankie laughs. Camille takes a sip of coffee and places the cup back on the saucer.

A church bell rings six times.

She looks around, shifting in her seat. "I wonder where the cathedral is," she says.

"What?"

"The church, there's a bell coming from somewhere."

I ask her, "You want to go find it?"

She stands up from her chair. She pulls down her t-shirt ever so slightly to take out the wrinkles. We walk northwards, with the sounds of the River Seine behind us. The cathedral had to be somewhere.

She stops in her steps, "Um. Do you want to walk to Ireland?"

Without hesitation, I say, "Yes. You know...we won't get far. I mean we can walk. But when this dream ends, we can't resume where we left off."

Church bells ring seven times.

* * *

Bradley wakes up to a cold winter. And he is late to school. Again.

MARCH 1980

On a March day in Brooklyn, the last snow has melted. The weather is still cold. Bradley's fleece shirt muffles. His hair falls slightly out of his beanie. Camille walks behind him. She wears a black puffy jacket, bleached jeans, and a scarf.

They greet each other. The winter tree branches shake and crackle against one another as if it were October. "I always keep thinking that the trees would bloom in March, but it's in May when the leaves start growing," Bradley says.

"I do look forward to when the leaves are pink for a week or two. You're not taking the bus?"

"The snow has finally melted. Sometimes I just like to walk home."

"Looks like we're walking home together then," she says. "You looking forward to studying accounting?"

Bradley answered, "It should pay well. I hope."

Words are exchanged about graduation, on the colleges they've finally picked and decided on. He will be heading to Loyola in Chicago. When he graduates college, he hopes he'll be able to find work at Wall Street. She'll stay in the city and study biology with a focus to becoming a doctor. The conversation flows forward: the winters in Chicago, the motivations to becoming a doctor, the things that were behind them like SATs and college applications.

"Why are you always working? As soon as the last class ends, you always head off to work," Camille said.

"College is going to be expensive, and I sort of want a car too."

They arrive at her home. He stands outside.

""Are you going to prom?" she asks. She takes her key out of her pocket.

"Are you?"

"No…I don't know. Everyone I know is going, but…I don't know."

"Camille, I feel the same way."

She puts the key into the lock. She turns around, "I'll see you Monday."

"Hmm, bye," Bradley replies.

He arrives at his house; a quarter mile away.

JUNE 1980

The kids are told to march in step. This was the last graduation rehearsal. Bradley And Camille are paired up and march together.

"Tomorrow's graduation. You ready?" Bradley asks Camille.

"No, I don't think I am."

He wasn't, either.

FRANCE

Eyeglasses that were round. Sunglasses that were oversized. I put them on her. She puts a square-ish, rectangular one on me. She tosses her hair back and purses her lips, "Je suis beau, n'est-ce pas?"

I put a cigarette in my mouth and let it hang, tilt my head down, peer at her over my sunglasses. I jump inside a convertible, "Get in, we're getting out of here, babe."

Ripping through the streets of France. Taking the tight curves. The wind flapping through our hair. After getting my driver's license, the fear I had of driving suddenly disappeared. Going through the catacombs, driving alongside the Seine. I send the car into a long and screeching drift around the Arc de Triomphe. The car accelerates around the wide circle. My stomach is tensing against the acceleration. On exiting the circle, the car whips out and I bring it back to control.

She unbuckles her seat belt. She slowly stands up, one foot bracing against the dashboard, and her other foot against the headrest. "You ever see people stand on horseback?!" She yells over the wind, "It's probably like this right?!" Her black scarf unravels and is taken by the wind.

She says, "Oh well."

JUNE 1980

It's the last day of high school. The students have come back to receive their diplomas and report cards. Windows are opened. Students are not in their seats. They go up to each other and ask them to sign each other's books. "Hey Mr. O, can we go out to get our yearbooks signed?" Normally a strict, by-the-books type of teacher, he surprises them by saying yes.

They're in the hallway. There aren't any lockers in the corridors. Mosquitoes fly in and out. Dragonflies stick on the walls. The group of them walk down room to room. Camille pushes her yearbook on Bradley, "Hey Bradley, you didn't sign my yearbook." They exchange yearbooks.

He writes, "I enjoy our random bumps on the street, Bradley Dusk". He looks at what she wrote, "We've known each other for a long time. Don't lose touch! - Camille Papillon".

Frankie, takes a Super8 camera from his backpack. "Give me a second," Frankie says. He fumbles around with a film cartridge. Standing in the hallway, he uses his thigh as an impromptu table to lean the camera on. He puts the cartridge inside the camera. He turns it on and starts to record. "Okay guys, wave your yearbooks at the camera!" Bradley blows a kiss to the camera.

Frankie directs them, "Now yell 1980!"

"1980!" Everyone waves.

"Does that even record sound?" Pauline asks.

Frankie aims the camera downward. "No, it doesn't." He points it up again. He brings the lens right in front of everyone's eyes; inches from their face. Frankie wanted to be uncomfortably close and intentionally annoying. Some of his friends laughed, others rolled their eyes. "Get it out of my face," Pauline swats Frankie away.

Camille looks out the window, "It never occurred to me how special our high school was. It's by the shore. So why did we never take the time to walk there?"

"Let's go then," Bradley says.

"Let's meet by the entrance after school," Frankie says.

"How about now? We'll slip out and be back before lunch is over," Bradley counter-suggests.

"Bradley, we have to go back to class," Camille says.

"Are you guys in or not? All I need is one person to join and then the rest will follow. James?" Bradley asks.

James replies, "Really?" A few of the friends walk back to class. "We'll see you later," James tells Bradley.

Frankie walks over to his side along with Jill and Pauline. Camille stands in place. "Camille, are you coming?" Frankie asks.

"You guys are going to get caught," Camille responds.

Jill, another one from their class, turns around from the window. Everyone turns and looks. With authority, she says, "I know a way out."

Camille fidgets her fingers. Frankie, Matt, Jill are moving to the staircase.

"Come on," Bradley pleads. Bradley starts walking towards the staircase. "Camille, this is your idea."

The other classmates are out of sight and are back in their classroom. Are they going to tell on them? Surely, the teacher would find out they're ditching class. It was inevitable.

Camille tells them, "Let's go."

* * *

Jill leads them to the bottom of a flight of stairs, right before it turns into another flight of stairs. She points out the window, "We're going to take that exit. We need to hug the wall so that the teachers won't see. Now the back entrance is big and closer to the shore, but we won't be taking that. We're going to head by the pool entrance, there's a small exit. We'll take that and walk to the next block. Then we'll head to the shore from there."

"Wow Jill, guess you're putting knowledge of those spy novels to use," Frankie comments.

They get to the bottom of the staircase. Jill cranes her head through the door and looks both ways. She signals the others to move ahead. They get to the exit. Dumpsters are to the left of them. They cover their noses while making their way along the wall. Frankie records 10 seconds of this with his Super8. He aims the camera above to their classroom.

Some of the students are by the window and take notice of the people below them. James shakes his head disapprovingly.

Right before they turn a corner, they hear a door open. Jill looks around the corner. "Jill, hurry up. Someone's coming," Frankie said. She confirms there is no one around the next corner. She walks forward. Now on the side of the building, they could not be seen from windows. "We'll take that exit by the indoor pool," she points to the gate, opposite the entrance to the indoor pool.

"Matt, don't you love swimming?" Jill asks.

"I hated that class," Matt replies.

"I wished I learned to swim," Camille says.

"I didn't like the teacher. But then again I did learn to swim in the end," Jill says.

They come to the gate. Jill is unbinding the chain from the gate. Someone comes out from the indoor pool, "Hey, aren't you guys supposed to be in class?" The swimming teacher takes a pack of cigarettes out from his pocket and begins to remove one. He lights a cigarette up and starts smoking.

They stand in silence. The swimming teacher looks at her. The pressure is on Jill. He flicks the cigarette's ash away. "Well, uh," Jill begins to speak.

"Well, I'm looking away now," he turns away from them. "I know it's the last day of classes and all. Don't get into any trouble."

Jill continues removing the chain from the gate and walks through. "Thanks," Jill says. The swimming teacher waves his hand to acknowledge her.

She takes the group up to the next block and turns again towards the shore. Cars go by the Belt Parkway underneath. They walk over an overpass bridge and take the stairs down. The Shore Parkway is paved with asphalt. There is a railing which separates the road from the Narrows.

"That was fun escaping. What now?" Bradley asks.

Camille tells him, "Let's just walk."

The group of them walk with backpacks down the Shore. It is a hot June day. Humid air blows from the water. The Verrazzano bridge rises high in the distance. They walk to the bridge; about a mile or two from the school. Then they head back to the high school, where they slip back by lunchtime. There was talk of a future: bright, hopeful, a promise that was to be fulfilled.

For a few of them in their class, this will be the last day they will see each other. Some friendships would last the summer, but lose contact entirely by college. For others, they'll keep in touch through college for two or three years. For an act of mischief, a memory was made.

A PARK BENCH

I sit on a bench. Flurry falls all around me. The sky is gray-cast. I don't even know where I am. The world in front of me is grayed out. I only see the immediate space in front of me. Are we still in France?"Where is the promise of adventure?" she asks. Skin touching skin as if our masses were relaxed into one another. I peer down. She takes my arm and holds it close. She relaxes and lays down with her head on my lap. I don't know what to do.

She tells me, "The bed curves down and I feel the pressure of someone lying down. It gives me great comfort but when I opened my eyes, there is no one there. And I feel so much more lonely."

"Does presence give you comfort?" I ask her.

"If someone you knew for a long time fell away from your life—even if they weren't dead—wouldn't that create a hole?"

"I hadn't done the things I wanted in high school, Camille." She asks me again, "Where was the promise of adventure?" I close my fingers on Camille's hands.

* * *

The fingers close onto themselves. His eyes open up to the streetlights outside.

JANUARY 1982

"Celtic knots tangled
"In between the crevice blacks
"Were never ending"

"Was that a haiku?" she asks.
"Yes, East meets West," I answer.
"Bradley...Bradley?"
A voice comes out of nowhere. Camille looks puzzled.

* * *

Bradley wakes up with drool on his mouth—which he promptly wipes off. The professor asks him, "Your snoring was waking the class. Something boring about Bayes's Theorem?"

"No, Professor. I just had a late night..."

"Please solve the equation."

He proceeds with the steps on how to solve it. He does it correctly. Radical two. Greater than. Less than. Equal to. Over.

He exits the building. It's another school situated by the shore—Loyola University. It is February and cold. Bradley walks to the shore. Lake Michigan was an abyss. It wasn't like his high school. There, the New York and New Jersey skylines was a ring that circled his view. Here, it was a horizon that has no end. Intellectually, he knew that on the opposite shore of Lake Michigan was land. He stood there and looked out for so long that the gray sky and water had blended; and he had disappeared.

Winter vacation has just ended. New York has winters, but it could not compare with Chicago winters. And it would be months until spring comes.

Bradley sees his roommate Jim sleeping, while getting his own textbooks for the next class. Bradley nudges him, "Jim. Class is in 10 minutes." Jim walks to the bathroom sink and brushes his teeth.

"You got to start waking up yourself," Bradley tells him, "you can't always be coming in late for class."

Jim puts on gray sweatpants, a t-shirt he picks off from his "laundry pile", a jacket from his chair and a scarf that he wraps around his mouth. "I forgot my textbook," Jim takes a pile of crushed dollar bills and coins from the table. He slips into his flip flops. After three semesters with Jim, Bradley had learned to stop telling Jim that it's "damn cold" outside. Bradley admonishes

Jim, "One of these days, you're going to die of hypothermia, and it won't be because of me."

After exiting the dorms, Jim runs across campus to the lecture halls. Over the clipping and clopping of Jim's flip flops, Bradley wondered how this maniac is top of the class.

Class after class and then lunch. Then more classes. Then to the library. He heads back to the dorms. People are playing a board game in the common area. They're sitting on a floor with multi-colored cards spread out. They invite him over, "Bradley! Come play!" He takes a seat.

APRIL 1982

Bradley brings back groceries from the supermarket.

Jim puts batteries into a flashlight. He opens and closes the switch, shining the light on Bradley's eyes. Jim asks Bradley, "Blizzard's here. Now what."

Bradley flips through radio stations on his blocky portable radio. "Massive snowfall rips across Chicago. All public schools and universities are closed. Residents are advised to stay in." Bradley takes the radio from his desk and sits on his bed. He flips the antenna up, telescopes it up, rotates the dial back and forth finding different stations through the static.

Jim parts the window curtain fully open. The howling wind whistles through the sub-par insulation of their windows. "Pull that back," Bradley tells him. Jim suggests that they wrangle up the people on their floor for a snowball fight.

The next afternoon, thirty-odd people descended on the quad. The wind picked up again. The fell snow is blown up into the air. It's a white out. Bradley looks at the footprints on the ground. He covers his eyes. A snowball hits him on the shoulder. He bends down and packs a tight snowball. He dodges another snowball. Through the white out, Bradley stalks through the trees, looking for people. The snowball whizzes through the whiteout. He hears a thud, and an "Ow, my ass."

Jim finds Bradley through the white out and tells him with a smile, "This is college." A sentence interrupted by a snowball to Bradley's mouth.

Bradley brews some hot chocolate. He drinks it. And collapses onto his bed.

CALAIS, FRANCE

I sit here. A light projects onto the screen. Smoke reveals the light. Camille taps me on the shoulder and leans over to my ear, "I don't know any French. We could just watch this movie without sound and I don't think we'll miss a thing."

I yell. I yell loudly, "WHY ARE YOU WHISPERING. IT'S ONLY US HERE. Besides, we took seven years of French."

She shushes louder than I even yelled. "Taking French is not practicing French," she says. She leans in and whispers, "What movie is this?"

I whisper back, "Jim and Jules. It's all fun games until real life comes."

"That doesn't sound like my type of movie."

"So what's your type of movie?"

"Here's Johnny!" she looks at me while speaking, but I'm the type that prefers to keep my eyes on the movie.

"What?"

"The Shining. You know, the Shining?"

"Oh. I don't watch horror movies..."

"I love them. Let's go see one sometime. A scary movie."

A large part of me wants to tell her I don't want to, "Okay. Let's go see one sometime."

Why did I say that?

Fin comes up on screen.

"That was pretty dark," she says.

Coming outside after being in the pitch darkness is a small pleasure. It's the feeling of lost time being regained. The sun is out. It felt like night inside the theater. She says, "Doesn't it smell like the ocean? It sounds different here." There is a large park in front of us. I see a sign called Calais, France.

There are a lot of roundabouts on these streets. We go inside a Fine Arts museum. And then to the Second World War museum. By way of our combined knowledge of French, we were able to make sense of most of the placards—even over bickering on verb conjugations. This town has such a history of war and occupation. It was decimated in World War II, but looking around us, no one would know. The town is a testament to human resilience.

At the coast, we see a beach to the left of us, and a port on the right. "Feels a bit like Coney Island, doesn't it?" I ask her.

"It definitely feels like a seaside town. You want to head to the port? I mean, unless you want to head to the beach."

I look at the beach, "Let's go on the boats."

Tall, small ships bob in the water. There is no sign of seagulls or any type of life. We put money into a machine and it spits out a ticket. She pockets the ticket. Our feet clank on the boarding plank. It's a large ferry ship: white, with two rows of windows that shimmer in the sun.

She walks to the back of the ship deck. I walk up to the uppermost level. Before I know it, we are moving. Horns blare out one after the other. Pass the steel beams and floors, I can hear the hum of the engine churning. I walk down to the deck. The ocean sprays mist against us.

I have trouble maintaining balance while the boat rocks up and down on the waves. I grab onto a bar. Camille says, "We have to get you a pair of sea legs."

She hugs her spring jacket close to her. I should offer her my sweater. "Crud," I said.

"What?"

"I forgot my sweater at the theater."

"We'll get something in the next town."

"This should be a short trip anyhow. I hope," I said. I really do hope. I grip the handrail tighter.

I walk up to the top. "Camille, I want you to see something top-side." She looks out, and says,

"I see the cliffs..."

AUGUST 1982

Today is the last day of Bradley's internship.

A man dressed in a well-fitted business suit puts an orange helmet on. He slides his backpack over and empties his pockets' contents into it. He wrangles his tie and loosens it. He walks his motorcycle out from an underground parking garage in Wall Street. His breathing is muffled under the helmet. He straddles the bike, slides his visor down, turns the ignition on, and takes off.

The bottom of his jacket flaps violently, trailing him. On acceleration, his cuffs pull back slightly on his arm. With his elbows pointed out, and his upper body leaned forward, the tightening of his shirt on his arms and upper back becomes a small joy.

He takes the same route he takes everyday: he rides by Trinity Church, circles the old stone City Hall for the view, u-turns on the street when the red light comes on. It was a 50/50 chance if the cars would honk at him. Usually he had biker boots on, but since his internship was over, he didn't mind ruining his dress shoes u-turning.

He follows a yellow taxi onto the Brooklyn Bridge. Over the wind, he added his own sounds. Every overhead crossbeam he passed under was another "thump" in his head, like a drumbeat. "Thump thump". Between the wind, his inner voice, and the road ahead, riding was a song. Today, there is a particular shimmer of the Hudson River that sparkled and is reflected on the beams of the bridge.

White wakes and lines were left by boats.

On exiting the other side of Brooklyn Bridge, he takes a corkscrew curve into the Brooklyn-Queens Expressway. He takes the inside lane and leans the bike sideways into the acceleration. In the straightaway, he accelerates again. His hands become numb for a second in the impulse.

Leaves and trees. Street lines, and cars. Both blurred by an afternoon sun and speed.

He passes by an old friend's house. Between his house, and her house was someone familiarly dressed in an orange t-shirt and bleached jeans. The motorcycle wheels squeak across opposing lanes. Car horns beep at the illegal maneuver.

She looks at the person before her. A businessman in an orange helmet with a leather backpack. She knew who he was before he even said,

"Hey."

He takes his helmet off.

Traffic moves again.

"Hey.

"Hey. So you're back in the city," Camille says.

"Yea. You came back from work?" he asks.

"No, I was taking summer classes. I just came back from the University library."

"You doing anything? You want to grab some coffee?"

She looks at the motorcycle and responds, "Sure."

"Let me put my bike away."

"Actually, can you take me to the diner on your bike?"

They walk to his house, he comes out with an extra helmet. He sits down on the motorcycle. She puts on her helmet and gets on. She puts her arms around him, and leans on him. He takes her hands and brings them above to his sternum. He quietly says, "I'm a bit ticklish." She squeezes a bit harder when he takes off on the bike.

$$* * *$$

"You're looking refined. How long have you been back?" she asks.

"The whole summer actually. I don't know how we keep missing each other."

"What is this for? You're a bit crinkled here," she grabs onto his lapels and smooths them out.

"This internship at Wall Street."

"Oh okay, Mr. Fancy."

"How are things on your end? You're studying biology right?"

The waiter places two cups down, and two pieces of cake, "Would there be anything else?" They both wave no.

"That's right. Studying biology." She points to the coffee cup, "This gets me through long days at the lab. I need a vacation, Bradley."

"Where would you go?"

"I would love to go to Europe. You know, just shopping at Parisian shops. Eating French croissants and chocolates. Seeing the cliffs of Dover."

"It must be so beautiful over there. This time of year. It must be so alive with activity. I imagine it's like Central Park, but all over Paris."

"Yeah," she says. In her periphery, she sees cars passing by the diner.

"Camille, life gives us signs right?" Bradley looks at Camille, tilting his coffee cup back and forth with his fingers.

She looks at her cup, "That's one of my few beliefs I have that I won't give way to logic. I have to believe that some things are outside of logic. No, that's not a good way of putting it. We should allow ourselves to wonder."

"That's wonder with an -o, and not wander with an -a, right?"

"Yes. Wooonder," she emphasized the first syllable. "I mean, that's not to say, we shouldn't also let ourselves wander."

"I sort of feel the same way—about life. Some signs, uh, coincidences just seem so improbable. So improbable that they should have some meaning," Bradley says.

"What kind of signs are you talking about?"

He pauses. "I don't know," he answers.

She looks out the window, "Wow. Feels like I'm back in 7th grade again."

"What?"

"Remember our history teacher? She would let the class go on these wonderful tangents. Spend the whole class just discussing things apart from history."

"This does feel nostalgic, doesn't it?"

"How long have I known you for?" she asks.

"Too long..." Bradley answers.

"I wrote in your yearbook to keep in touch."

"Did you? Here." He writes his number on a napkin and hands it to her.

"Shouldn't the girl be the one writing the number down?"

"It's a new age."

They spend the rest of their time talking about what they do at their work and school. Mundane details such as where they eat lunch, what they eat for lunch, their co-workers' habits. He brings her home.

"I really loved catching up with you," she says.

"Same here. You'll call me?"

She replies, "I will. Oh I forgot to mention, I go by Cammy now. You can call me that. Cammy. I wanted a new me for college."

They hug and say their good-byes. He walks forward, holding onto his motorcycle, with a pull that tells him to look back. He wondered if she had looked at him leaving from her second floor window. He walks his bike all the way home wondering. Just wondering.

The meeting unraveled thoughts in his head. He should have mentioned he was only back for this weekend. He should have made plans with her before leaving again. He still has her phone number, and she still has his.

Did she? Did she look back?

DOMESTIC LIFE

An older Camille is helping a child put on their coat. The child looks about five years old. She has auburn hair just like Camille. He is older too. He's wearing a black peacoat. She wears a beige trench coat with a business suit underneath. The child turns around while I (?) put a backpack on her.

"Are we excited for our first day of school?"

"Yes, daddy!" She holds his hand while he leads her outside.

I watch from a distance: my apparition and Camille's.

The apartment is accented by rustic furniture. Shelves that look like reclaimed wood are stacked on the walls. Walls are painted in pastel colors and decorated in local art. Plants surround the apartment on countertops and tables. On the tables are utility bills with crayon pictures drawn on the backs of their envelopes. I hear another set of footsteps go upstairs.

Camille's apparition sneaks into a nursery room and picks up a baby boy. She whispers, "Don't cry, don't cry." I look at the far side of the room; the Camille I know stands there. I head downstairs and watch as I put my daughter into the car.

Camille puts the boy into a baby seat.

Both of us pause in our steps. The amber autumn leaves rustle loudly. Leaves fall slowly from the branches.

He looks on at themselves. He exits the house and sees all this.

She looks on at themselves. Camille walks and stands behind a tree.

There is a recognition, as if this was some moment that has been lived. No, it was much stronger than recognition—it was an *expectation*.

The family rides out into the street. I take a seat by the porch. Camille leans against the tree, looking at him. We stay where we are, glancing at each other, at the street, at the house, back to each other. Hoping that maybe studying this would bring some sense to us. Neither of us approach each other.

I look a long way down the road.

Low, high pitched noises reverberate all across the street. What was this noise? Wind chimes. It's coming from their door. It hung by their porch. There was another sound too. There was a whisper in the wind: "Bradley."

I look at Camille; standing in the shade of a autumn tree. Her brown eyes stare at me. I call back in a whisper, "Camille."

* * *

Bradley wakes up in cold sweat. He takes a damp towel and wipes off the sweat. His heart has been beating through his chest, but his hands were numb, and his breath is quickening. He walks to the window and pulls the curtain apart. Over the motel balcony, he sees his motorcycle bathed in orange-halogen lights. He pours tap water into a hotel cup and takes small sips.

Bradley had scheduled his internship company's trucking service to take his bike. He would follow the precious bike's transit from state to state on Amtrak. Due to insurance reasons, he could not ride with the truck drivers. During some truck stops, he would take his motorcycle and ride along the highway. Then he'll ride to the next truck stop, drop off his bike, and take the Amtrak to the next state.

"You know, your company must really love you a lot to let you transport a bike for free," the truck driver tells him. The bike is the only cargo on the freight truck.

Bradley tightens down the straps on D-rings on the truck floor. He grits his teeth and pulls a bit harder. Sweat drips from his forehead in the summer heat. "Yes, I suppose so. Let me buy you something to drink. Bottle of water?"

"No, son. You don't need to do no such thing," the truck driver laughs. "I remember when I had a speed hog when I was younger. I was a devil on the road. I know how it is. I'll take good care of her."

"How about I buy you a 6-pack."

"I'll accept that."

The truck driver leaves, pulling his horn and waving to Bradley on his departure.

* * *

"Train boarding. Last call for passengers. Train boarding. Last call for passengers."

Bradley walks through the aisles. He takes an empty seat by a window. A man with a newspaper tucked under his arm stumbles onto the next seat. He's a bit heavy set, has a bit of a beer belly. He smooths out his pants. He pulls his suspenders forward and airs out his shirt as if there was no company near him. He wipes his glasses with his pocket square. He lets out a large yawn and unfolds his newspaper loudly.

Bradley looked on, slack-jawed at this person's behavior. He has another sixteen hours on the train with this guy.

"Young people inherit the world we old people made. You'd best to remember that," this guy says to Bradley.

Sixteen hours.

There was not another empty seat around him. People were coming in and filling up the seats.

"What brings you on this train? My name is Eddie," Eddie asks while looking at the paper.

Eddie asked the question right when Bradley was putting on his earphones. "Kids these days can't hold a conversation," Eddie flaps the newspaper. The folds and wrinkles are still there.

Bradley looks at the seat in front of him, with one earbud on his ear, "I'm Bradley."

"Now what do you do, Bradley?"

Bradley takes out his earbud, and switches off his cassette player. "Student."

"No, son. What do you do?"

"I'm not sure I understand your question. I'm studying to be an accountant."

The train lurches forward. The wheels on the giant machine turns and turns. Eddie folds up his newspaper and tucks it by his armrest. Bradley knew he was ensnared by this old man.

"I had a cousin who was an accountant. He got heavy into gambling in his later years. Old Tommy loved going to Atlantic City, playing the slot machines until the day breaks. Poor bastard died of liver failure. He couldn't resist a good beer."

"I'm sor—"

"Oh, you're sorry. Hahah," Eddie's laugh bellows throughout the train. Bradley wanted to sink into his chair. "You didn't know him, but no worries."

Bradley decided to take the offensive, "Eddie, what do *you* do? Why are you on this train?" He straightens up in his seat and wraps up his earbuds around his cassette player.

"I was a teacher. I'm retired now. Around this time of year, I would start teaching school. But it's been five years since I taught. I miss the looks of misery on those poor students on the first day of class. But as for why I'm on this train..."

Bradley knew. He knew it in his bones that a long, *long* explanation was coming.

"My wife and I started taking road trips after our kids left the house. This was-oh, I would say maybe 20 years ago? We'll take our beater car and travel across the states. How many states have you been to?"

"Three if you don't count the places in between."

"I've been to all 50 and some of Canada. Not bad for someone from Long Island, huh?"

"No, I guess not. But you didn't answer my question about why you're on this train. Where are you going?"

"My wife's at her younger sister's second baby shower. Now you see, I don't have a great relationship with her sister. So Melissa, my wife, said don't even bother coming. She said, 'It'd just be drama.' With no kids at home, nothing to do, I figured I'll buy a ticket to Chicago. Figured I'll get there in time to see one of the Cub's home games. My dad was a big fan, you see."

"I was bringing a bike across states."

"So where is it?"

Bradley explains his agreement with his company.

"Why did you take a train? Why didn't you take the airplane?" Eddie asks him.

"Needed time to think about things," Bradley tells him.

"With young men, it's always one thing on their minds. Is it a young girl?"

"Maybe."

"I see a smile there. Tell me about her."

Bradley talks about how they were in the same classes in middle school, in high school. Always with other people. But he had met her recently on the street and she gave him her phone number. Bradley described her as driven, smart, funny.

"Want to hear my opinion?" Eddie asks him. Bradley says yes. Eddie replies, "It doesn't sound like you know her at all. Maybe you should give her a call when you get back."

What did all those dreams mean then?

"Yea, maybe I will."

"Melissa was the girl next door. She grew up next to me. I was a shy kid, you see. A very shy kid. I was 18 then. On a winter day, she had rolled her ankle while shoveling snow. I saw her hobble outside the window. Know what I did?"

"Went to help her?"

"No. I stayed inside and watched her stumble up the porch to her house. Through my window blinds, I saw Veronica and David open the door to help her in. Uh, Veronica and David are my mother and father-in-law." He sighs. "That was a low point in my life. Still a low point. The snow kept building up over the night. I couldn't sleep that night. The next morning, I walked over to her house with a shovel. I cleared up the entire porch and driveway.

"David walked out and asked me, 'Eddie, what did you do this for? Your house is over there.' I tell you, I tell you...my face was red. I-I-" He belly laughs again. "I had nothing to say."

Eddie continues, "I heard someone yelling from inside, 'Invite him in for breakfast, Dad!'. Over the breakfast table, she gave me this look of, 'I know you saw me and didn't help, but I'm grateful that you did help.' They were putting food onto my plate. I just ate it without saying a word. David offered me 10 dollars for the shoveling I did. I said I couldn't. This went back and forth for a while until Melissa said, 'Eddie, can you help me to my room?'"

Eddie had picked up her crutches and headed to her room. He saw her books, her gymnastic trophies, a sketchbook of unfinished drawings. He recounted how in the weeks coming, he drove her around while her ankle healed. They went to the movies. When she had gotten better, they went dancing. He recounted the long years thereafter: their marriage, their kids, the career changes in-between. It was sunset when Eddie finished telling Bradley his story.

LONDON, ENGLAND

A red double-decker bus arrives at a bus stop. I'm sitting on the outside seat of a two-seat bench. She walks in and sees me. "Late again?" she asks. Inside are blue seats. A silver pull-cord runs along the windows. It's a bus from New York.

"I remember being late to class, and you came onto an empty bus. you sat in front of me and said a few words. I wanted to reach out and talk with you," she says.

She takes a seat in front of me. Eyes forward.

"I wished I had scooted over," I say...

"I wished that I would have asked you to. I was trying to find reasons to talk to you," she said with eyes still forward.

"Words are too little."

The bus goes through the streets of a familiar neighborhood with stores we frequented. On the periphery: London architecture. We sit a row apart. I look at the back of her neck, her hair. She looks towards the front. Neither of us makes a motion towards the other. The bus passes by the delicatessen where kids hung out, the park where we learned to ride bikes—each at separate ages, the library where I used to skateboard for a few months and then had lost interest in, the pharmacy where Camille's mother had worked. A bell chimes as a silver cord is pulled. The bus pulls into a stop.

She stands up and walks to the entrance. I follow her. I hold onto the pole.

"Guess this is where I get off," she says. Only later did I realize her eyes were glancing at my fingers. My thumb taps on the pole. She says, "I'm waiting."

"What's that?"

"Nothing," she says.

"Bye. I'll see you later."

* * *

The train had stopped in the middle of the night and shook Bradley awake.

Bradley exits the train. The train station is outside with views of fields around. He sits on a bench. The summer air was humid near Erie, PA. He looks above him, the stars twinkling, shimmering. In the fields far from the train station, the sounds of cicadas rattle.

I can't sleep. I can't take care of my parents. I'm looking outside to these yellow streetlights. I need to go for a walk. I need to collect my thoughts. Why do I feel so sad? It's not because of my family. Cammy? Are you there?

Where did this feeling come from? My future? That I deserved this? Even the shops are closed now. How late is it? The night sky is purple. Heartbeat breaking through my chest. What's my future? What hope was there to an internship I didn't feel passion for? Why had I spent these years away?

How many more years would I spend away in my indecision?

How am I supposed to create a well lived life? A fuller life? Hold it together.

Keep it together.

It's guilt. No, it's me feeling undeserving. How can guilt feel the same? I sit on this bench. I deserve this. I deserve this because I've wronged so many people. There's blood on my hands and...

I just...don't deserve the happy things that come to me.

I put my hands on my eyes. Maybe if I block out the world, it'll disappear.

He opens his eyes. The lights on the train bloom into view. Eddie tells him, "I brought you back here. Let's go back to sleep, okay?"

Bradley does.

OXFORD, ENGLAND

She walks along the shelves running her fingers along the books. Dust accumulates on her fingertips. A gray sky outside casts ribbons of blue light along the floors. Footsteps echo in warm tones along the high arched ceilings.

A stack of books are on a reading table. Green reading lamps with brass pull chains are arrayed along the reading tables. I glance at the spines in front of me. They're adventure novels, and they're mines.

I follow the sound of footsteps to a wall. She climbs up the ladder and picks a book from the top, "Got it. Sir Isaac Newton's Principia."

"I got it. Drop it here."

She climbs down. She takes the book from my hands and flips along the pages, "This book is one of the greatest scientific achievements ever."

"You understand this?" I asked. The pages inside are Latin. They are filled with diagrams and equations, which seem like proofs and theorems to the Calculus I've used in class.

"I understand the math. I wouldn't say that I understand the words. It's just that this is a piece of history. Without the type of math that Newton derived, we wouldn't have many of the machines we have today. Or understand the equations that govern the motions of the planets," she says. She takes a seat and flips through the pages of the book. "Seems familiar doesn't it? Books with words you don't understand?"

"I wish I could share your enthusiasm," I tell her.

"Oh. You don't have to."

"But we would have more to talk about."

She looks up from her book, "Friendships aren't conditional on shared interests. I don't think."

I get up and walk along the stacks. I turn and turn. Although I feel like I'm walking forwards, I start to see her again in the distance. As if this labyrinth folded onto itself. I look forward and I see her sitting by the table, and I look back and see her reading the book.

"You want to become a doctor to help people, right?" I lean by a bookshelf.

She looks up from the Principia, "That''s a pretty direct question."

"I've changed my mind over the years. I've wanted to become a doctor, but...I'm going to pursue biology. I think science uncovers mystery. It leads us deeper into the center of the labyrinth. Understanding the biological process will help to develop treatments.

"A few weeks before she passed, my grandma told me, 'You're a smart girl, Camille. You'll be someone yet. You could save us all.'

"Well, that's how I feel anyway."

That's too much pressure for one person. I ask, "What was she like?"

"Kind, devout. Sweet. Oh, but she could nail you to the wall with her biting remarks." She looks back down at her book, "I miss her."

I look outside. How far does the sky go, in this dream? I look back at Camille and ask, "You know where you're going, don't you?"

"You don't know who you are?" she asks.

"I don't."

* * *

"Bradley, can you buy me a soda from the dining car?"

"I will," Bradley says to Eddie.

Bradley returns with a can of soda. He opens a water bottle and takes a sip. He asks Eddie, "I want to ask you something. What made you want to become a teacher?"

"To be honest, Bradley, I fell into it. I was working at my dad's restaurant for a bit after school. Veronica said there was an opening at the school for a shop teacher. So I took it. Who knew I would be a good teacher?"

"That's not much of a story."

"Do you know what you want to do?"

"I finished interning in a Wall Street firm. They paid me pretty well. I was able to make enough to buy a nice motorcycle."

"You enjoyed the work?"

"Well, it was just shadowing people, going to meetings and taking minutes. Sometimes I make coffee runs. It is what it is."

"Hey," Eddie pauses before speaking again. Eddie leans over and puts a hand on Bradley's shoulder and looks into his eyes, "It doesn't matter what you do. It doesn't matter how much money you make. Do what makes you happy."

Eddie leans back in his seat, "Tell me what you love to do."

"Speed. I love speed. Cars, bikes. Um. Pranks. I enjoy pranking people."

"So car and pranks. Your generation is really leading the charge."

"Of course we are," Bradley says. "When I was in middle school, I enjoyed writing poems and short stories. I think I still have those notebooks somewhere. Uh, in high school, I entered into a spooky story Halloween contest and won first prize in that."

"You should take that up again. Melissa is always trying to get me to paint with her. I couldn't get into it. But she had always said, 'Life is brighter with art'"

"I don't know. I feel like guys and poetry..."

"You know how I said I used to be pretty shy? There's one lesson in all of this. Being happy, finding your own way...once you stop caring where you stand in comparison to other people, then that's it."

Bradley repeated for himself, "Then that's it..."

* * *

Night turns to day.

The rest of the train has fallen asleep. Eddie has put down his newspaper. He pats Bradley on his hand. Bradley removes his earphones.

He whispers over, "Bradley. Last night, you were on some kind of trance on the bench. I tried to reach you. You wouldn't respond. I had to help you come back in. I didn't want to ask when everyone was awake, but is everything okay?"

"I don't know. That's the first time it's happened."

"I don't know if you have too much pressure or whatever. I'm not good with words. Look...you're a good kid. Just...take it easy, okay?"

"Okay." Bradley's voice cracked a bit.

CHICAGO

A history textbook is opened up. On another piece of paper, I'm writing down notes. Important people, events, documents, laws, ideas, Supreme Court cases—PEDLIGS for short.

"Jim, isn't it amazing?"

"What is?" Jim is laying on the floor reading a book with his legs propped onto the bed.

"How I'm supposed to take these outlines and write an essay off of it. But somehow I do. Something comes out of this nonsense of notes."

"Why are you philosophizing?" Jim says to me.

"What?"

"Stop thinking about thinking. Just get it done. Jeez," he says.

"When are you supposed to hand in your paper?"
I tell him, "Two weeks. I'm trying to get a leg up on this."
The phone rings.

ON A TRAIN RIDE

"Where is this train heading?" I ask her.

"You choose," she says.

"You have a map?"

She says, "I lost it."

I look outside. Green leaves and landscapes pass by so fast that it has become impossible to see which way is forward. We were sitting in the same row. She had the window seat, and I sat by the aisle.

"I had my fun in Paris. Where do you want to go?" she asks.

"How about Stratford-Upon-Avon and Stonehenge?"

"Shakespeare's birthplace?"

"I was never a fan of Shakespeare in school, but maybe that would be different now that I'm older. Maybe I'll appreciate the work he's done. You think there'll be plays over there?"

"Probably. Would be a waste if there weren't any," she replies.

An older woman is knitting on the train: black and white yarn all mixed up. I can't tell if she's unraveling the threads or interweaving them. The dream doesn't let me scrutinize it. It doesn't let me see the details. The flow of time is going both ways.

She says to us, "You two have to choose."

"What do you mean we have to choose?" Camille asks.

"You want to go to Ireland right?"

"That's right," Camille says.

"You'll be double backing if you go to Stonehenge," the older woman says. "How can you know how long this dream would last? It may end anytime, so choose what's precious." She continues knitting.

"On the one hand, I may not like Stratford. On the other hand, Stonehenge is something I've always wanted to see," I say.

"I'll leave the decision to you," Camille says. She looks out the window, "I'm getting a bit cross-eyed trying to see if we're going forwards or backwards." She turns around and she shows me her cross-eyed eyes. I groan.

I decided. "I've always wanted to go to Stonehenge too...but let's head to Stratford."

* * *

The train pulls into Chicago. It's rather late in the afternoon.

"Do you know what to do yet?" Eddie asks.

"No," Bradley answers.

"I think you do."

Eddie hands him a quarter and points to a payphone. Eddie watches him put the quarter in. Bradley takes out a crumpled piece of paper. He dials the ten numbers.

The phone rings. Each ring reverberates into a sound that goes on. Each ring enclosed into the other. Like sound was wrapped around sound. Heartbeat breaking through his chest. The rings end, Bradley mutters, "Hello?"

A silence.

Eddie whispers to him, "You'll be alright, kid." Eddie pats his back and leaves with his newspaper under his arms.

On the other line, Camille's voice: "Bradley?"

MARCH 1983

"Hey Cammy. I just got back from seeing Videodrome. You owe me a few friends. I think I lost a couple after making Jim and others come with me to see it."

"Oh, you *loved it.*"

"Yeah, the part with the gun and the stomach was a real show stopper...you know, with all these horror movies you watch, what are you actually afraid of?"

"Large animals. Like animals that weigh more than me. Or at least as much as me. You can't fight them. Bears, whales,..."

"I get your fear, but that doesn't make it any less ridiculous."

"Hey, I know you were busy last winter, but are you going to come back for the summer?" Camille asks Bradley.

"No, I think I'm going to take that internship in Chicago. They said they might have a job lined up for me after graduation."

"..."

"Cammy, you there?"

"Yeah."

"I know I said I'll come back..."

She interrupts him, "I think I'm going to apply to the program at New Paltz. There's a professor there who's doing research that I'm interested in."

"I thought you wanted to apply to MIT."

"Uh, I didn't make it in."

"I'm sorry."

"Uh, don't be. I...I got to go."

"Bye then."

"Good night."

STRATFORD-UPON-AVON

Camille introduces her friends, "So this is Cindy. And this is Kate."

We greet each other.

I introduce Jim, "This is Jim. He's a real piece of work." Cindy remarks that he doesn't look that way. I had to disagree.

Cindy takes the same curriculum as Camille, but a year ahead. They went on jogs when the weather was agreeable. Kate is another person at her college who had the same interests in horror movies and was majoring in philosophy.

We exchange greetings.

I wanted to get a brochure and follow it. Jim preferred to go without a plan. Camille agreed with me, Kate with Jim. We looked at Cindy. She decided to go without a plan. At one of the white timber-framed buildings, I saw Camille swipe a traveler's guide. I fetch one while no one was looking too. After walking up and down Stratford, we stopped at Bancroft Gardens.

It's a small park. The Swan Theater of the Royal Shakespeare Company is in front of us, the small River Avon to my left. Camille points out, "It feels a bit like the River Seine, doesn't it? Maybe not the size, but the setting of things. Like the placement."

I say, "Feels like Battery Park. Well, except that it's a stream. You're right. The setting of things seems the same. It feels like a metaphor; in a sense." We decided that after lunch, we'll see if there's any plays going on at the Swan Theater. They set up a picnic blanket on the grounds. Somehow, we had food in front of us.

I wander away to the stream and sit down; my legs hanging over the edge. Camille comes over, "Hey, what are you doing?"

"Thinking."

"What do you have there?"

"Trying to think of the last lines of this poem."

"Oh? Let me hear it."

"I think some poems feel larger when they're read silently, instead of being recited." I pass her the piece of paper. I watch as she moved her lips across the words.

"It's sort of morbid. What's the meaning?"

"I don't know. No meaning. No meaning, but the one you want it to be."

"You sort of really settled into your writer persona. It's sort of disturbing how you went from a bad boy on a bike to a writer."

"Bad boy on a bike? That's how you see me?"

"In a way."

"Oh, I don't think I'm a good writer."

"Nonsense."

Jim, Cindy, and Kate are laughing and giggling. They seem to get along well. Jim comes over. This can't be good. Jim tells Camille, "Hey, Bradley finds you cute." I can feel my face going red. He has the nerve to run back. What am I going to say? He always does this at bars, but this time it's true.

"I...I..." I managed to say.

She chuckles.

She stands up. They turn to her. "Ahem," she clears her throat and recites my poem.

HEART SONG
By Bradley Dusk

One, in fire, in flame, is not there at all.
Anxious phantom suffering with your tears.
The heart was ash; there is no air to fall.

Decayed one, drowned in an ocean's lull,
Feeling wave by wave; there is no time here.
One in fire, in flame, is not there at all.

Frosted body under canopies tall,
Remained a spirit, lesson found and seared:
The heart is ash; there is no air to fall.

Wind twist about you on that cliff edge: soared.
Look up from great heights: this blue view austere.
One in fire, in flame, is not there at all.

Love held you tightly, hear its waiting call.
Answer to learn that it had held no flare,
The heart is ash; there is no air to fall.

Bent, broke, withered, wasted, and ego small,
Find your feared courage, and destroy those war gears.
You. One in fire, in flame, are not here at all.
The heart is ash; there is no air to fall.

I was wrong, poems can feel larger when they're read.

SEPTEMBER 1983

"Hey, how's my journal going?" Camille asked.

"Well, you shipped it to me back in July for my birthday, so I'm using it. And it's mine now. When is your birthday?"

"I'm turning 21 tomorrow. I'm sure I told you."

Bradley replied, "I would have remembered."

BIRMINGHAM, ENGLAND

"Nice to see you again," I say to her.

"Nice to see you too."

"Drink?"

"Don't mind if I do," she runs to the nearest bar. "Let's drink to me turning 21. Although I think I already did. I might be asleep right now."

We go back and forth teasing each other on how much we could drink. I walk behind the bar and take a tumbler. I grab a tall bottle, and another bottle with a metal tip on it. I pour both liquors into the tumbler and shake it. With my other hand, I scoop some ice into a tall glass and pour the tumbler's contents into it. "So what do you call that?" she asked.

"It's, uh, it's uh Brad's uh cocktail."

"That's the stupidest name for a cocktail." She sips it, "This is horrid."

I challenge her. "Let's see you do better."

She steps onto the bar counter and jumps down to the bartender area. "Breaking windows, stepping on bar counters, you really don't have any dream manners, do you?" I ask.

"Dream manners?"

"Yeah. Dream manners. You know, manners in your dreams. I don't know about other people, but I act like me in my dreams."

"No, probably not. I started teaching myself lucid dreaming so I could play around in dreams," she walks while she talks. She seems like she knows what she's looking for. She grates lemon and lime. I ask politely, "Now, don't get any pith in my drink."

She talks to herself while assembling the cocktail, "Let's put a bit of cherry, and some cherry juice. Oh, slice some ginger in here. Whiskey...whiskey, where's some whiskey. Here we go." She's at the end of the counter at this point. She pours the whiskey into a stout glass and slaps it down the counter like an old time cowboy flick.

I take a sip. My mouth is so dry. I take another and another sip and my mouth is still dry. "It's pretty dry."

"You're dry."

"I'm pretty sure you were making it up as you were going along."

She says, "Nope." She's a bad liar.

We stop after a couple more "cocktails". We walk outside. I'm glad there's nobody walking around. I'm doing cartwheels through the streets. Cammy keeps trying to kick into a handstand, but keeps coming back down. I cheer, "Commit to it. Come on." My words are slurring together, but whatever. "Yes!!!!" she screams. She holds it on top for a good thirty seconds, or it was...uh... ten seconds.

"Hold onto my hair. Oh god." She runs to a trash can and starts vomiting into it. I can't stop laughing. I offer her some napkins, "Oh, I can't breathe! Oh! Hahah! Oh no." Yellow stains on my sneaker. And some of the pizza I ate earlier.

She laughs; acid still in my throat. "Want to get some new clothes?" she asks. I walk to a fountain and scoop some water into my mouth. I try to dry out the floor with my napkins. "So how about those dream manners, Bradley?"

"Ugh, don't," I say. She laughs.

I say, "Let's—let's get those clothes."

* * *

We're in a shoe store after replacing our outfits. I ask her, "Doesn't it feel so weird that we're the only two around?" She's in the backroom scrounging for her size. She's on the floor with shoes strewn about her; empty boxes all over the place.

She sits next to me on the shoe bench, "In class, I learned that there were two kinds of touches..."

She slides closer to me. Her nose lightly grazes my cheek and follows the curve to my ear. Her warm breath. She whispers in hushed tones—every syllable is clear, every small sound piercing, "The light touch: sensitive, unnoticeable."

"...and the deep touch: apparent, hard." Her hand grabs onto my thigh. I turn my head to look at her. I look deeply into her eyes. Her eyes move ever so slightly.

The store fades to black. An orange glow flickers on her face like a movie projector's flicker. She turns to look at the light. The glow accentuates her skin: smooth, imperfect, slightly freckled. A sliver of hair rests over her ears. I gently slide it back.

"It's a campfire," she tells me. Her hands aren't on my thigh anymore. Insects are loud around us. Clicking, whistling. Frogs are croaking.

"It feels like, what's the opposite of abundance?" she asks.

"Scarcity?" I suggest.

She says, "It feels like that. It feels like two people alone in the world. It feels like all that is needed is here.

"Bradley, I can't see any of your clothes. I can only see your face from the fire. Everything else is dark."

She breathes the cold air. She throws a few wood logs into the fire. The smell of campfire is so familiar, but I've never gone camping before. She says, "My dad used to take me camping. My mom never wanted to come along. So it was just me and my dad. I always loved making a fire. Collecting kindling, tinder, leaves, cutting wood. Mom would've freaked if Dad told her I was using an ax. We would scare ourselves silly telling each other ghost stories."

"Is that why you like horror movies?"

"Yeah."

"One time at night, we walked to a beach in the state park. All the sand was lit by this blue glow. We skipped rocks for a while. I started throwing rocks into the lake. It hit some night swimmer and we just cut and ran."

"How'd you know you hit him?"

"He yelled, 'Ow! My arm!' in this high shrieked voice. 'Ow! My arm!'" She laughs heartily. She breathes into her hands and rubs it together. The fire crackles, and a loud explosion pops from the wood. I become startled. "That's just build up of gas from the wood," she explains.

She asks, "You've never camped before?"

"No."

"We should go sometime."

"Oh sure."

"Hey."

"Yeah?"

"Look up," she says. The trees sway in the breeze. The way the branches bent and made crackling sounds like the fire, the way the leaves made the same sound as the fire in rustling; it seemed like a symmetry in life and death. She says to me again, "Look up." My eyes adjust to the dark. Faint blue dots come into view. The stars are so plentiful.

"We should go camping sometime," I tell her.

"This is reminding me of something," she says. "Something old, something unremembered." I turn and look at her. She has tears in her face, but she's smiling.

She says to me, "These aren't our names."

NOVEMBER 1983

Sometimes there are phone conversations. And if either Bradley and Camille had to recall who said what, they would not know where ones' words start and end. All memories seem to be entrusted into one another's. For example, during a lull in a conversation, a long pause, one asks the other,

"What do you think true love is?"

Who could've known lightning could strike hearts through phone lines.

"I think it's two people in their twilight years going to see movies they've read about from the NY Times."

"I think it's finding small restaurants on side streets."

"Dining al fresco!"

"Trying new foods."

"Wind chimes in small towns."

"Castanets."

"Like the Ronettes?"

"Like the Ronettes."

"It's adventure."

"It's comfortable long silences."

"In the car."

"At home."

"Someone willing to do anything."

"To go anywhere."

"Despite how tired they are."

"Or what commitments they may have tomorrow."

"Just to spend time with one another."

DECEMBER 1983

Bradley approaches the entrance to his house. He takes out the keys. How strange it was to come back. It's like this after every break from college. Even more so now, to stand outside during noon. It was jamais vu: a feeling that the familiar has become new; strange.

It has been over a year and a half since he had been back home. The front door which was once chipped and grayed had been painted white. The gate was oiled and no longer squeaks when swung. There was the aroma of baked goods in the kitchen. Through the long hallway of this two story home, his mom walks around the kitchen while his dad reads the newspaper. He opens the door slightly.

His father, a burly man, comes and hugs him, "Your mother's making apple pie." As if no time had passed, Bradley took off his jacket and sweater, and starts washing the dishes and cleaning the counters. There was a lot of extra food after eating.

He fills a ceramic plate with the apple pie and puts aluminum foil over it. He walks to a place near him. He enters the atrium, and looks up at the doorbells. Fl. 2 Papillon. No answer. He rings again. He pauses and listens as if footsteps were moving. Someone's coming to the door. "Oh, who are you?" she asks. The footsteps belong to an older woman. She adjusts her glasses.

"I'm sorry. I wanted to ring the second floor."

"Oh, they're on vacation. They drove up to Maine to visit family. Is that for Camille?"

"Actually yes."

"So you must be Bradley. These ceilings are thin, you know. The way she talks to you...oh, I think you'll make a good couple. Don't be afraid to make the first move."

"I don't know about that."

"I've got experience, honey."

"Um. Well, my family made a lot of extra pie. Please be welcome to have it."

"I couldn't."

"Think of it as an exchange for advice," Bradley says.

"Come by tomorrow, and pick up the cookware. It smells absolutely delicious."

"I'll see you then...uh, what's your name?"

"It's Veronica, dear."

"Huh. Seems like a familiar name. Goodbye."

STONEHENGE

It was a dark night, and I awoke to cold and wind.

I see Camille sitting opposite to me. On top of the stone columns of Stonehenge. She had been here for a long time; looking out. Did you will yourself to dream this?

"I think I understand religion and philosophy as I grow older," she says.

"What do you mean?"

"People are lost. Everyone becomes lost. Dante became lost in the forest. Purpose and meaning are obscured. I understand the consolation that faith can provide. Science can be cold sometimes..."

We sit on top of columns facing each other. I ask, "Is everything okay?"

"I'm just...I don't know...tired. I haven't been sleeping well lately. And I feel like no matter how much I study, I'm not understanding what I learn at an intuitive level. I'm passing the tests, but I don't know."

I say, "Let yourself be here. Here, come down." I jump down. She does too. I don't know what words I can say, "Look at the wide space in front of you. You're here. Now. You don't have to worry."

Cold wind blows across us. "They say Stonehenge is a calendar. A way of marking the passing of time," she says. She puts on her mitts. The cold wind had turned her nose and cheeks red. "What if they're doorways? To other times? Other places?" She looks through between two stones. "Sometimes I just want to run away, Bradley. If these two stones are a door, maybe I'll be transported if I step through it..."

She takes a step, walks through it—

And comes out the other side, unchanged. Relieved, I ask her, "Where did you wanted to go?"

"Far."

Her eyes were looking fully ahead. There was a slight crinkle above her brow. It seemed as if she was fighting against her own expectations and being present. If only I could help her in some way. To lessen her load.

"I'm here. Just. Just if you want to talk about stuff," I offer.

"I don't know, Bradley. Can you remind me that this is a dream?"

"Hey. Can you feel this?" I move my hand over the face of the stone columns. I feel the cold and the pits in them. She walks by and presses her cheeks against it. She says, "It feels real. It doesn't feel like a dream, does it?" The cold wind found its way into my chest. I adjust the scarf around my neck.

She tries to push against the stone column. The grass is pushed back by her heels. "It's like punching against people in a dream, but they're not hurt and you don't feel a reaction," she said.

"Can I try something? I want to see something," she asks me.

"Sure?"

She punches me. Hard. She yells, "FUCK! I think I broke my wrist."

"Did that make you feel better?" I ask while rubbing my shoulders.

* * *

Camille woke up mending her hand.

JANUARY 1984

"Did you get my Christmas present? I left it with Veronica," Bradley asks Camille over the phone.

"The apple pie I didn't get to eat? No I didn't get your present," she responds.

"Oh, is that right?"

"No, I have it right here. I wanted to call you while I open it. Hold on."

Over the phone, Bradley hears crinkling paper, the faint slip of the ribbon as she unties it. She is silent. She finally asks,

"Where did you find it?"

"I was walking through an old bookstore in the city. It was in the basement level of the shop. The bookshelves were hand built by the owner. It was like this old, dried wood. I was browsing, looking for anything that looked interesting. It's the first printing from 1884. It's two hundred years old."

"The Language of Flowers. Kate Greenaway. She has a beautiful name. It's appropriate to the book," she says. She opens the pages. There are two columns of text: one listing the flowers, and the second listing the meaning of the flower.

"There's probably over a hundred flowers in there," Bradley said.

"This would make a great coffee table book. Thank you. I wis—I should have gotten something for you. If you were here right now, I would hug you."

"You don't have to. I'm still writing in that journal you gave me, but I'll gladly accept the hug," he says. Each of them in their own places peered in their empty rooms, hearing the ticking of the clock, twirling their fingers into the coiled telephone wires; trying to find the next words to say.

Camille breaks the silence, "Before I go to sleep, can you read me something?"

Bradley speaks, "This is an old one:

"Celtic knots tangled
"In between the crevice blacks
"Were never ending"

After they hung up, Camille sat with the book in hand. She looks at the fainted colors, the pages that were stained at the edges. It was the oldest book she has ever held. She puts the book down on top of her other textbooks.

The next day, Saturday, she walked a few blocks over to Bradley's house. TVs were glowing in the curtains of houses. In the summer, TV dialogue would mix in with the sound of children in the streets and fire hydrants at times. But the streets were barren now. It was quiet. Her pace slowed when crossing Bradley's house.

She listened intently without looking; as if a passerby. There was the faint sound of a TV playing. It must have been his parents. Or maybe it was the neighbor's TV. Along the short block, two story houses line the street; each of them starting where the other ended; and each of their walls shared. She imagined that the rooms were larger than the apartment she lived in.

The door began to open and she briskly took to walking again. She had barely passed the property line when she heard, "Camille?"

She turns around. Bradley's father was outside. He was a burly figure with a white beard. She asks, "How do you know my name?"

"Lucky guess. Bradley told us about you. When we call his college, he's usually on the phone with you."

"Well, I'm sorry about that. I'm just passing by. Haha."

"Were you looking for Bradley?"

"No, just um…passing by," Camille says.

"Don't be a stranger. Come over sometime."

* * *

She comes back home to find that the mailboxes had been filled while she was gone. On her family's coffee table, she sorted out the different envelopes to her and to her parents. She saves the large envelope, that was folded into the mailbox, to be sorted last. She knew it was for her. The day passed until her parents came home from work in the evening.

"Mom, Dad. It came," she opens the large envelope in front of them. "I got in!"

"All your hard work has paid off," her mom says.

"Camille, we're going out to eat tonight. Your pick," her dad says.

Camille continues looking over the papers, "They're giving me a full scholarship, room and board…"

She would call Bradley in three days.

CROSSROADS

"You told me on the phone that you didn't want to do this anymore. Didn't know what *this* was. I-I just accepted it…

"Sometimes I walk up to this fountain near my work. I'll go there after every paycheck and throw a coin in with the other coins there. I remember that you wrote in my yearbook with your phone number. I was too afraid to call you. And I was too afraid to even say that I wished I would see you. I just hoped we'll cross paths again and I think it had come true," you say.

"Unrequited love…I would meet you halfway if you would too. But you didn't. So I can't. How many times have I seen you in my dreams? Too many. Today will be the last time. I can't fall for…this. I have to deny myself love," I say.

You say, "It doesn't have to be a dream. Don't deny yourself."

I look out and see the city that we walked far from, and the roads that stretch far from me.

"Camille…Cammy, I don't want to give up on you," he says to me.

"This hurts too much," I say to him, "good bye."

"Good bye."

MAY 1984

The sun was already high in the sky when Camille woke up. She turns off the alarm off her clock before it rings.

She marches down the aisles of Radio City Hall in her blue graduation gown.

Outside, in the midst of camera flashes, a familiar thought comes to her: where was the promise of adventure?

OCTOBER 1984

Autumn leaves are colored fire in New Paltz and Chicago. Leaves were transforming into orange and red hues. Camille walks through downtown. Leaves fall in slow motion. On such a day, they take a stroll around town and end the day getting coffee.

"Beautiful, isn't it?" Olivia says to her.

"Autumn is so different here. The air is fresher. It's like from a dream. I've been so busy holing myself at the university, but… to take the time to look around…it's something else," Camille looks at Mohonk Preserve which rises from behind the small town shops.

"After prodding you for three months to come out of the lab, I'm glad that you did," Olivia says.

"Well, you're a terrible lab partner so..."

"You know...I'm the one holding the coffee so it would be a shame if I tripped and fell."

Inside a record store, Olivia asks what kind of music Camille likes. Camille answers, "I guess the Carpenters. Be my Baby by the Ronettes. Not really a big music fan. I feel like my taste is just songs from my parents."

"I totally get that. I have this theory that we find some old songs romantic because our parents would play them in front of us. Like it's leaving an imprint on us. I think you'll like this genre," Olivia said.

Camille looks at the placard behind the row of vinyls, "Adult Contemporary."

They walk back to Olivia's car. Camille rolls down the window. On the highway, Camille sticks her head out. The wind finds its way through every crevice of her short hair. She breathes in the air that once passed over the mountains.

She returns to her dorm room and opens the window. She thumbs through the pages of her textbook; sitting on a bed so soft that she is absorbed into it. Autumn winds enter the room and caressed her. She looks at the large mirror above her desk. Her reflection stares back at her. Gone are the bags under eyes from sleepless nights and stressful evenings. She is now glowing.

She smiles back at her reflection.

OVEMBER 1984

CHICAGO

I exit a showing of Paris, Texas. As usual with these arthouse movies, I go alone.

Their relationship was so strained. There was so much adventure in their younger days. Who could have said if their lives could have been better if they had ended up together?

Jim asks me, "If you hate accounting so much, why don't you just quit?"

I reply back, "I've quit other things before. I need to see this through. It's just another year."

Jim, you're sitting on your desk and sending out resumes. You're top of the class. You stand there on a podium thanking your parents, the faculty. You even thank me for being a great friend through the years. I put my thumbs up in the air. And like that, our college adventures have come to an end.

Just as you said, you never wanted to go to graduate school. You are flown to Virginia and receive a job as an analyst at the Department of Defense. "You don't have to do this," you've said to me. You never had to say it. I've seen you look at me. "You're meant for something else," Jim had told me once.

Nails. Shingles were interlinked. Frame, tenons, and mortise were built interlinked. "This is going to be your house," my dad tells me. What? I keep hammering the nails in. One slight hit to keep the nail in place, then another to drive it into the plywood. I've gotten pretty good at construction work. Sawdust kicks up while I cut lumber on the miter saw.

"You can work with me during your gap year. But come in on time."

"There is a job lined up at this company for when you graduate," my internship company had said to me. It hadn't even taken me a second to say, "Sorry, but I can't."

Sometimes my dad drives the van to work. Sometimes I do. I had started taking the subway again. Not having the motorcycle feels like a big weight taken off of me.

"So what are you going to do?" my dad asked.

"So what are you going to do?" Jim asked.

"So what are you going to do?" my boss asked.

The wall is flickering.

OCTOBER 1986

Camille demonstrates to undergraduate students on how to use a pipet. She walks around the lab giving notes on proper technique. Adjacent to the professor's office, she grades papers, answering students questions when the professor was busy.

Olivia comes knocking at the door, "Want to head to Minnewaska tomorrow?"

"I'm surprised we never visited. Isn't it pretty close?" Camille asks.

They took weekend trips to nearby hiking spots. These hiking spots were at least an hour away, and never quite close by. Over the past year, her hatred of inclines has been tempered. She was even peeved when the hike at Minnewaska turned out to be mostly flat and short. They walked around the gray cliffs that jutted out of the lake. Camille took a few pictures of the waterfall on the lower grounds. She comments to Olivia, "It looks like it's out of a dream."

Camille sits on a wooden fence on the cliffside, "Olivia, I think when I'm done with my masters, I might transfer back to the campus in NY."

"Heh. I wanted you to stay here with me. Finishing my PhD without you will be pretty boring."

"You'll manage. Hey..."

"What?" Olivia sees a look on Camille's face.

"I'll give you something to remember me by," Camille says.

Camille vaults over a fence. She steps warily near the edge.

"Wind twist about you on that cliff edge: soared," Camille whispers to herself. She looks up at a blue sky. Olivia follows along. They both yell out into the chasm.

READ ME SOMETHING

Echoes. But echoes of a whisper.

There are words being spoken.

"I saw her in a territory, *a space*, made of light and shadows. I had given a mirror to a king, and he had given me a sword of mirror. He told me, 'Follow your heart.' I took a horse and rode." It was a strange voice. Something familiar, but it felt new.

I walk along the stream barefoot. I see the small goosebumps on my arm. I walk on gentle steps along the stream. The cold water flows through my toes. I take care not to slip on the rocks.

The stream stopped flowing. It had turned to still waters before me. I walk through this still water. There was no ripple or crest or valley or eddy in the stream. It seemed like glass. I keep walking; following a sound. Weren't these dreams about finding a sound?

A full moon is large against the sky. I come to a view that I've seen before: a large waterfall emptying into a small body of water. Awosting Falls. Only this time, the large waterfall seems like glass shards from a chandelier; hanging in time. As I walk, the moonlight glints in the frozen waterfall.

I walk along the shoreline. The words become clearer. I make out the words from the whisper.

"I rode far until I reached a place not quite the ocean, and not quite the land. A place where mist had made both land and sky disappear. There was a figure suspended in the air. She looked like a trapeze artist. The way she twirled, glided in the air. She falls.

"I rode between bodies that laid on the grass. On the rolling hills. Each a shadow."

There, I find Bradley sitting on a tree stump; he's holding his journal. He's looking at the lake that reflects the stars and the moon. It seems we were suspended in the sky. He continues telling the story,

"She laid a wreath in front of her. I wanted to bring her back to life. I wanted her to come back to life by her own wishes. I knew she was stubborn. She had lost so much blood. She closed her eyes and told me she was my first home.

"She had stopped breathing.

"Her heart had stopped beating."

I sit beside him; looking at him while he looks into the water. It felt like chemistry, the symmetry of this situation. He saw me reading in the library. I'm watching him read his writing.

I ask him, "What happened then?" His brown eyes catch the light of the full moon. With his eyes still downward at his journal, he continues speaking,

"I placed you on my horse. In a nearby village, I traded gold for someone's wagon. I placed you on the wagon with your arms crossed over your flower crown. I put a shroud over your face. When the sudden spring showers came, I stood over you with an umbrella, I didn't let a single raindrop touch you.

"Camille, they say, in a hero's journey, the hero always returns home.

"I bought you all the way to your home.

"There I read your rites. I hoped you found peace. You were buried beside your parents, on that hill.

"I returned to my father. I told him that the Palace wasn't my house. I placed those instruments of war, my clothes, the mirror sword, the Princess mirror into a chest. I told my mother and father that this Kingdom wasn't mine. I had my own life. They had their own life without me for so long. They would carry on fine.

"It was spring again when I returned to your house. Flowers had grown on the rubble of your stone house. Weeds had taken root between the wheat stalks. I rebuilt your stone house. I lived there till the end of my days.

"You told me these weren't our names," he says.

He looks at me, "Your true name. The sound it had. I move my lips trying to find the shape. The form of my tongue to express the sounds."

"How is the world perceived when we have two minds? Two lives?" I ask.

He closes his journal and puts it on his lap. We look at our reflections in the lake. The dream keeps going. I hear it. The water has begun to fall again.

MAY 1986

Blood spills onto Bradley's jeans. A man shrieks in a high pitch. A large figure has jabbed his arm through his torso. A second man spits out blood and collapses. The large figure reveals itself under a single light hanging from the cabin's ceiling; and the figure is grotesque.

"Print! Hahaha that was awesome," Frankie says.

Bradley licks his thumb and tries to get out the blood stain on his jeans. It's not going to come out. Frankie tells Bradley, "Well, my lens didn't come out unscathed either."

Frankie looks at his clipboard. The sketches are mottled by the blood spray. He flips back a few pages from the script. He scratches his head. "I think I got everything we needed for today.

Let's just get a few insert shots," Frankie says. Frankie sets up the lights and mounts the camera onto his shoulder.

Kacey says to Bradley, "I should have worn one of those ponchos they give you at Niagara Falls, you know?" Kacey is part of Frankie's crew. She sports a very punk rock look; wearing a flannel shirt, ripped jeans, and dyed blue hair, "What gave you the idea of the Soap Man anyhow?"

"So when you're stuffed inside a scuba suit, and it depressurizes at a great depth, what happens is an anaerobic process…" Bradley begins.

"Haha, I haven't heard that word since exercise science class," Kacey replies.

Bradley continues, "Your body becomes soap."

"That's dark. So that's how you got the idea for an astronaut becoming a monster."

"The work you've done on the suit is pretty disgusting. It's better than I imagined. How did you get it that way?" Bradley asks her.

"I took a fat suit and put some silicone on it. I was aiming for a sort of wood slash soap look. There's like little veins and blood vessels I put into the suit, but I doubt that's ever going to show on camera. You chose a good day to come on set. Sorry for the over pressurized blood spray," Kacey says.

"Forget about it," Bradley says.

"You should come on set more often, Mr. Screenwriter."

Frankie stages the corpses to film them.

"Kacey, can I peel off my makeup?" Elly asks.

"I'll help you with that," Kacey unzips the fat suit from Elly, the person under the Soap Man costume. Elly climbs out of it, puts it on a hanger. She walks outside and hangs it off a tree. Elly explains to Bradley, "It's going to take a while to air out."

"Are you going to be unbiased when editing the footage together?" Bradley asks Elly.

"I'll manage. I hope," Elly says. Kacey starts peeling away the face prostheses from Elly.

Peter, one of the men who was mangled, puts on a set of headphones and runs the sound back to himself, "Sounds good."

Ang, the second man, starts taking down each set light until the dim light of the cabin's hanging light bulb was left. Everyone banded together to wipe down the fake blood from the walls and floor.

* * *

They clean up the cabin and drive back to Frankie's parent's summer house. It was a lakeside house in rural Pennsylvania; a short drive from New York City.

Bradley walks outside. He looks at the moon over the lake. "We're going to film a few more things in the city. You sure you don't want to join us?" Frankie asks him.

"Maybe."

"You looked like you had some fun today."

"I guess I did. You still keep in touch with anyone else from high school?"

"No not really. How about you?"

Bradley doesn't say anything.

* * *

They left the door to the back porch open. Through the screen doors, the wind swept through the room. Exhausted as they were, they forgo drinking and set up sleeping bags across the floor. The lights were closed. The moonlight breaks the bookcase into blue and black colors. Outlines of board games...where the old creases had...

FRANKIE'S BASEMENT

"Been shrouded in the static vision of the dark." What did I say?

Frankie puts in a VHS tape. There's static while the images run forward in lines. He adjusts the tracking on the remote. An image forms as those lines flow backwards to make something coherent.

It was the video he had recorded in high school, on their last day.

I didn't want to be reminded...of how young we were. In the video, I glance at her and she misses it. Then I see her eyes dart—for a second—towards me. What sounds were there if it could have been recorded. What did the hallways sound like?

She waves to me across time.

* * *

Bradley opens his eyes to the dark again. He had barely slept a minute.

"Anyone else awake?" Kacey asks.

"I'm still getting used to the floor," Ang responds.

In the quiet moments before falling asleep, they spoke in low tones even though they were the only ones in the house; and none of them were asleep. These were quiet conversations that were spoken in half-broken thoughts.

Frankie rustles around in his sleeping bag, "I'm still awake. And what's wrong with my floor?"

"Your floor is shit," Ang responds.

"Haha. Shut up," Frankie says.

"I'm awake too," Bradley sits up.

"You guys believe in fate or free will?" Elly asks. "Director, what do you think?"

Frankie takes a deep inhale, "I think...free will..." and takes an audible sigh, "I mean, shouldn't my choices matter?"

"I agree with that," Peter replies.

"But how about fate? There's just some things in life that seem so coincidental. I think that fate gives hope. That despite our indecisions in life, there is a plan for us all," Bradley said.

"I think free will also gives us hope. That we're not bound," Frankie replies.

"But if I push a ball, it rolls. That's cause and effect. So if we think all the way back to the Big Bang, that sort of caused everything after. Including the very chemistry firing in our brains," Bradley had thought about this after hearing Camille talk about organic chemistry. He fell into her existential crisis over chemical equations. Camille floated the heady concept that thoughts had to come from somewhere. And the brain probably went through the chemical reactions before the thought existed.

"Einstein said God doesn't play dice, but he was wrong about that. Quantum mechanics is random. Doesn't that imply free will?" Frankie says.

"Well, as far as we know," Bradley says.

Kacey said she had been reading books and pondering about it. And that to some people, it's neither. Life is interdependent. "It feels like all these layers," she raises her hands in the air and interweaves her fingers. The moonlight hits her hands at just the right angle. "There are forces outside of us that control us from the very moment of our birth. Like our social class, our privilege, our family."

"But it sounds like we also make choices despite those forces. Like finding our own family," Frankie says.

Frankie's words lingered in the air until everyone had fallen asleep.

* * *

Frankie dropped everyone off in New York. The last stop was Bradley's house.

Bradley sits in the car seat for a moment before leaving. He tells Frankie, "They say that in college, you'll find your people, but for me, I never really felt like I belonged. But this weekend. I just...I was happy to be there. Thanks for having me."

"Look, you wrote the thing. You deserve to be on set."

"You know, since I have access to my dad's stuff...if you or Kacey need any help with building things."

"Give me your phone number. I think we're going to film some more next weekend."

1987

DUBLIN, IRELAND

I walk from Stonehenge.

I find a map. From here, I'll see if there's a port at Holyhead to head to Dublin. That looks like the shortest line to Ireland.

I make my way to Holyhead. I do see a port. No one seems to be around. I'll just commandeer this rowboat. I get inside. The boat rocks and jolts suddenly. I grab hold of the boat.

Olivia kicks it off the dock. "I don't go on this adventure with you," she smiles in her lab coat.

I grab the paddles and begin rowing. The boat spins around and around. The waves are coming in at an angle to my boat. The boat feels like how a car feels when swerving hard into a turn. The spray splashes over into the boat. I row directly against the current and the boat straightens out.

In the middle of the ocean, the seagulls glide down and touch the surface's water. I fear that if I fall off, I may die of hypothermia. Sometimes I think that life was rowing boats from one shore to another. The paddles dig into my hands, the more I row, the more the wood splintered. When I get off this boat, I'm going to set it all on fire. The boat was only there for my travel.

Somehow, I find myself transported onto a road. I wanted to burn those paddles, but sometimes I can't even completely control my lucid dreaming.

CAVAN, IRELAND

"I hate this van," Frankie was holding onto a bucket of tools. Ang, Peter, Elly, and Kacey were *all* holding buckets of tools. Elly and Ang had to bend over their backs to avoid hitting their heads on the ladders hung over them. It was pretty funny looking. They were lined up in the center of the van. The film and sound equipment were in boxes and bags that filled out whatever space was left.

The van bumps up and I hit my head on the roof. The twilight hour has come. Frankie told me he wanted to film something during this time, but never had the right idea for a scene. The sky was purple and yellow and red. The sky set against the Irish grass was a sight. White clouds in long stripes absorb the light of the setting sun.

Elly and Ang gets out of the car. They live close to each other. Then Peter and Kacey together. And I dropped off Frankie last. I help him haul the gear into his apartment. I've noticed his three story walk up is in the middle of a field, by the shore. I don't usually dream of buildings being in other places. From his third floor window, I look at my dad's van. Still safe.

I go to pee. Nothing comes out. Fine I guess.

I head back down and my van is rolling down the hill. Shit. I forgot to put the parking brake on. No no no. Stop rolling. It's rolling down the curved road. Okay. It'll just stop against the grass. NO! STOP rolling down the road.

I run to catch up. Going downhill, I pick up some speed and jump onto the hood. The van's bumping on the rocks. I have to grab onto the door pillar. I can't swing the door open. I'm on the opposite side and the door will just slam shut. The window is opened a bit. But not enough for me to get my hand inside. I climb to the side of the driver's door. It's unlocked. The van bumps onto a heavy hump. The door slams shut on me and the door locks itself.

I look to my right, the van is 100 feet out from going off the edge of a cliff, and into the water. I see the water over the edge. I pull on the driver side door. It's not budging. 20 feet. The sun glints over the water. I grab onto the roof and quickly shimmy to the back. I didn't lock it! I throw open the two back doors. I hop over the buckets, put the key into the ignition, shift the gear to reverse, and floor it.

I saved the van.

I haven't had that much fun since I had my bike.

I drive back onto the road. The grass was torn up by the van. The tools are on the grass. I go pick them up and put them back in their buckets. I inspect each one to make sure they're not damaged. I continue a leisurely drive.

On the drive, I notice a castle in the middle of a lake. Gorgeous.

Frankie's house on the Irish hill comes into view again. He looks at me from on top and waves. I keep driving until I hit a fork in the road. There's no cars around me. I park the car. The sun is still at the same place on the horizon. My dad usually keeps several maps at the back of the driver side seat.

They're just road maps of New York. These aren't going to help me.

I'll just take the right road.

LONGFORD, IRELAND

Grafton Street is so desolate without people there. I've heard that when it's filled; it's lively with buskers, merchants, musicians. The warm and white-colored brick buildings, the tiled streets made for walking feels like a house twisted inside out so that the outside felt like home. I could stay here, but there's somewhere I have to be.

I enter into a shop on Grafton Street. I browse the shelves for a tourist map.

Transported again.

The sun is in between the sky and the horizon. The sky is purple. The houses are few and far between. And each house had large fields. It reminds me of the rural areas in New Paltz. I would imagine that Bradley would talk about it as if it were a simile. A simile where the locations were self-similar.

SLIGO, IRELAND

Driving for two hours now. I'm getting sleepy.

Wait, I'm already asleep.

It's like driving through Pennsylvania, except I'm on the left hand side. What's that noise? The fuel gauge is at E. I pull the van off to the side. Well, there's nothing I can do now. Except maybe to wait for help. I hope when the sun sets, it won't be too cold. I shave a carpenter's pencil until it's dull, and I write on a piece of a paper in bold letters, "NO GAS. HELP."

A white van is parked on the side of the road. I shouldn't approach it. I walk on the right side of the road so that I won't have to cross it. There's a white towel hanging off one of the windows, and a sign posted on the driver side window, "NO GAS. HELP." I wonder if the driver left to go get gas.

I've cleared out most of the cargo area of my tools so I can lay down and try to get some sleep. I find myself staring at the roof. There's rustling outside. I grab a screwdriver. One can never be so careful. I come out from the back. I turn the corner of my van and see a woman with short hair standing there. She turns around.

I hear a door open from the back of the van. I turn around.

"Camille..."

"Bradley..."

"It's been three years, hasn't it?"

Weren't you there at Minnewaska? Didn't you tell me that story? I ask you, "Hasn't it been a year? You read from the journal I got you."

"Let me think," recalling a memory of a dream is a poetic notion.

"Did you just say your thoughts out loud?"

"Did you hear that?" Can you hear this? I think back on the dreams I had. You smashing the window in your apartment. Us walking step in step in our high school graduation. When you told me about camping with your dad. When you implored me to share my writing with you, "I don't remember reading to you..."

You may not see it. But I'll recall the memory for you. I close my eyes and imagine. Instead of destroying, I'll bring back something. I bring to my mind the frozen stream, the chandelier-like waterfall. Your words in your voice.

"I see it now. The ancient lands. The smell of flowers," I say to her.

I imagine. I conjure these memories, "I see shadows bathed in light. I see crowns...horses. So many things that weren't in *that* dream."

"There was only sadness in those memories."

"Yes, there was..." *I say to him. It reminds me of uncertain times.*

"We found our places in life, haven't we?"

"Yeah. I think so. I'm...happy. I know who I am. I know where I'm going."

"Did we have to become someone so that people can love us?" I ask her.

"No."

All those years lost to fear.

"Camille, I think you changed my life. I had started searching for something. Although I'm still lost now, you've made me start looking for something meaningful—in the same way that the sciences are to you."

I didn't know. I didn't know my actions had so much meaning.

"You helped me find peace. You were there on the phone when I needed someone to call," she sighs, "it would have been easier if we had all those years together, too."

She said what I'm feeling right now, at this moment. I say, "I shouldn't have stayed in Chicago. But we make our choices, and keep going forward."

"Hey, let's walk to the fence over there. We can get a better view of the sunset," *I say to him. We walk to a wooden fence, and sit side by side.* The wind rolls over the grass like a wave.

Birds go across the sky in a V formation. Their wings' flapping was just slightly audible. In the quiet moment between us, I notice the blue flowers growing on the field. The German Iris. It has two levels of petals. One reaches to the sky and seemed closed; and the lower level drapes low and is opened. "Those flowers over there. In the book you gave me, they represent flame."

"The thing about fire is that it hurts, doesn't it? That it requires a bit of courage, a bit of adventure to control it," I feel the fear and scoot closer to Camille. "The adventure you wanted all along, did you get it?"

"I don't think I ever wanted an adventure. I just wanted to find my own place in the world. When people say they've found themselves, you think they meant a job? An occupation?"

"No."

"I don't think so either. But I can't begin to understand," *I pause.*

"I've been trying to understand what that means, finding yourself, knowing who you are," she says to me.

I take a breath. I pause. I contemplate. Because I've been dealing with the same struggle. "When people say that, I feel like they talk about the future. But it's mixed up in fate and free will. Lives are threads. We are knit together. Life is a tapestry."

Here was a person that sewed herself into my life; like a needle threading in and out of fabric. In turns finding myself with her, and in spaces without her, briefly thinking of her. And when I stepped back to see the whole, life was a ragged, loose, tapestry held together by her stitches.

I say to her, "And if life was interdependent; if *lives* were knit together. Then maybe finding yourself was really finding something you loved; someone you loved..."

He takes my hand in his. His hands are so rough and calloused. What sort of life had you lived in these years?

I take her hand. Even through her palm, I could feel her pulse: so steady but it's quickening. I notice her chest expanding and contracting. Who are you? So beautiful, your brown eyes in so many shades?

I want to kiss you. "I want to kiss you."

I tell her to close her eyes.

I close my eyes. Waiting...

I bend over and cut a German Iris off its stalk and slide it between her fingers. I kiss her on the cheek.

I open my eyes. The sun breaks through, and every shadow is lit up. The field, and the blue flowers are golden. It looks like a wheat field.

What we thought was twilight was sunrise.

LONGING FOR A DANCE

I have memories of you sitting on the floor; by our credenza. Flipping through old vinyl; your hair basked in white draped-filtered sunlight. You put on a record. How you tap your feet to the warm sounds when no one else had noticed.

I had asked you if you were going to prom. You said you didn't have the money. Why didn't I go? Even when my parents said they'll pay for it? Why are you sitting there reading, your black hair highlighted by a noon sun? The stubble of your unshaved beard waiting to be touched.

I look through these records. I find one.

She sits there while the song plays. I mouth the words without singing. Sitting here. Looking outside. Birds are flying around a water tower. She walks closer and bends over. Her long hair falls in front of me like textile; sunlight shines through the empty slits between your strands.

What should I play? I run my fingers through these softened vinyl sleeves.

"The Lamb Ran Away With The Crown" by Judee Sill plays.

"I love this album," *he said.*

"Oh, it's Sunday. The neighbors aren't home. Let's dance," *I extend my hand out to him.*

This dream feels so real. That even years into our marriage, the passion will still be there.

"You hear outside?" *I whispered.*

"Hmm...yeah."

The world was full of people. There are children in the streets screaming their heads off; playing, riding bikes. There are sounds: an ice cream truck with its song, friends hanging out on fire escapes talking over cheap beer, water rushing out of fire hydrants making shallow ponds on concrete, truncated conversations when people passed by.

We sway while the music plays. We feel the rug under our bare feet; the breeze through every opened window. Oh, if we had socks on, it would have been electric. Our feet moving like same charged particles: pendulums of a Newton's cradle in the same motion, in repulsion, never touching. When the song's bridge plays, spin me around...

"Lopin' Along Thru The Cosmos" plays from the same album.

The moment pulls you in. Last, last forever. Is your hand gently gliding over the contours of my face? This charged frisson when you hold me close? The goosebumps on my arms? Are you pulling my hips closer? Are you creating this moment, Camille? Hold me close, this is enough. Just let me be lost in this moment, forever. Lost, lost forever...

"I think I found you in between lyrics of a song, an exhale of a breath," she says to me.

The floor creaks on the same spot. We take turns stepping on it while spinning.

SUMMER 1987

"Dad, I'm going to stick around the city for a bit," Bradley tells his father.

"Don't forget your backpack."

He changes out of his steel toe boots and into his sneakers. Bradley takes the journal from the car seat and puts it into his backpack.

He walks along Midtown, looking at the window displays. Walking through the streets, people crowd around him; so many different people. He comes to Central Park and sits on a park bench on the outer perimeter. Joggers pass him by. He notices all the people in cars. He used to ride between the cars in his motorcycle, didn't he? He imagines his t-shirt flapping in the wind, the rumble of the motorcycle engine beneath him.

It's 5pm. There's still at least three hours of sunlight left. He'll find something to do in the city. He stretches out and yawns. Two days off this weekend. There were so many buildings he had done work on, so many apartment remodels, so much that he could look in any direction from his bench and he could point to at least one place he's been at. He'll just relax here and take the subway back later.

"Can I sit here?" That was a question never asked before on a bus somewhere. Bradley looks straight ahead, as if the voice paralyzed him. He grabs his backpack and puts it on the floor; withholding his glance from looking at her. She sits down. He feels the weight transfer across the wood planks. He felt her presence.

He turns to look at her, "Hey."

"You look bigger...," she says.

He says, "You wear glasses now." He looks deep in her eyes and recognizes their color for the first time. Her eyeshadow is recognizable and he falls into her gaze. Jet black mascara accentuates those brown eyes.

In an instant, he had conversation topics lined up in his head: what are you up to? did you get your masters? how was New Paltz? are you seeing anyone? are you happy? Instead, he says,

"You've been in my dreams."

The surprise that she had given him on this summer's day was returned to her. Those words were so unexpected. They turned to each other, looked at each other in silence. Neither had the next word to say. They examined the years on each others' faces. She responds,

"Do you want to come over for coffee?"

She had taken up an apartment in the city. They walk across Sheep Meadow in Central Park without a word, but it was a comfortable silence. She lived in a high rise building on West

64th st, a short subway ride from the university. Camille opens the first door.

Bradley stands there while she unlocks her mailbox. The small atrium threatens to squeeze the already small space in between them. His backpack with his boots pushed him towards her. She drops her keys. They both reach for it and bump their heads together.

"Ow!" Camille rubs her temple.

"Smooth moves, Bradley," Bradley laughs. "This is why I wear hard hats."

It's a homely place, comfortable. Books and assignments are on the coffee table, a half-full glass of water on the kitchen counter, dishes in the sink. It's lived in. There is a bouquet of flowers on the round dining table: skinny, tall, blue, green; flowers of all kinds. His gift of The Language of Flowers is beside the vase. The vase divides the sunlight into rainbow bands onto the book. She drinks the remainder of the water, "How'd you want your coffee?" The sunlight back lights her hair.

"Some sugar is fine," he sits down on the couch. "What's the pink flower called? It's massive."

"That's the Lotus flower. In the book you gave me, Kate Greenaway says that it means estranged love. But I like to think of it as something else."

"What's that?"

"It's a flower that grows out of the mud, and it blooms above it. Isn't that beautiful?"

There's a vinyl record player, and a milk crate of records in front of him. Camille says, "Some students gifted me vinyl records before I left. I haven't listened to all of them yet. You been writing in that journal I gave you?"

"I take it everywhere I go. I'll read you some new things, if you like."

She boils the water. She takes two mugs and puts a teaspoon of instant coffee and sugar in each. It's quiet between them as if each were searching for words to bridge the gap of years.

Bradley yawns, "Sorry, a bit tired from work."

"You do construction work now?"

"Yea."

She realized she didn't want to talk about their jobs. It doesn't matter. She looks out the window, avoiding his gaze, "I dreamed about you too."

The couch was so inviting. It just swallows you. Weightlessness. His tired muscles relaxed into it. He became light. His arms lay limp by his sides. He falls asleep, a very deep sleep instantly. The kettle whistles. She turns it off. She turns to look at him. Peaceful would be a good word to describe it.

She walks towards him.

She sits beside him. He opens his eyes for the briefest time, and closes them again. In half trance, he says, "I want to kiss you."

She reaches for a kiss. As their lips get closer, the distance widens. With closed eyes, he anticipates the kiss, but how the distance grows. Did he know she had kissed him?

In his sleep, he asks in between shallow exhales, "What were you afraid of?"

"Love," she responds.

She finds space on his body and lies on the groove on his chest. She takes his arm and puts it around her. "Your hand is so warm," she whispers. She looks out at the window blinds. A breeze shakes it. Wind chimes sing somewhere deep inside. The weight of his arm presses against her. Church bells ring six times. Hypnotized; she falls asleep too.

BEN BULBEN

Words followed me from the world, I hear it clearly as the church bells from Paris, "What were you afraid of?"

I say to the wind, "I was afraid of the future." Camille would hear it.

It is twilight. I'm here on a paved road. Small cottages are on either side. Something large is in the distance, a mountain. But it's covered in green. The top of the mountain looks eroded, scarred. Am I supposed to climb up there?

A purple sky was above the mountain. It was twilight in two places: both New York and Ireland. The sun is setting. The mountain seemed cut in half by the light.

There are bells. Wind chimes from unseen places.

"Bradley. In my guide book, it says there are twin paths up this mountain."

Voices from unseen places.

"Hey, Camille."

"Hi."

I start walking, "What's the mountain called? Are you walking to the top too?"

"It's called Ben Bulben. I'm at the base. I'll meet you up there?"

"Okay."

"You dragging the phone line to your room again?"

"No, you know I have my own apartment now."

"That's right. The bouquet you made looked beautiful. Beautiful's a common word, but I don't know how else to say it."

"It's enough. But what other words could you call it?"

"A bit messy? But that's just your apartment."

"Haha, you're terrible. Oof!" I hear a scuffle on the other line. She says, "Just slipped on some rocks. I'm okay."

I reach the top.

"Oh my. Do you see this? I'm looking at the other side of the mountain. It's like standing on top of a lake where the water is just pulled out and dried out. I can see the curve of it."

"That reminds me of something I thought of."

"What's that?" I ask her.

"After traveling with you, through these places, I sort of—had this feeling. It feels like a simile," she says. I pause in my walking to listen to her. She continues, "All these places are alike somehow. They're all roads connecting place to place. The architecture may be a bit different, but even in every place, each has...aspects of other places. When Olivia drove through roads to get to a hiking trail, it felt a lot like traveling on our trips."

"It sounds like you thought it meant something."

"Maybe..."

"I see you," *I said. He waves.* "Well, the figure of you."

She waves back. We're on the top of the mountain. I peer out. The world was out in front of us; laid out in square tracts of land and roads. A sword is stuck in the earth. Sand and dirt had encrusted the sword. "I thought I had put you in a chest. I don't need you anymore."

"You know what you're wearing?" she laughs. She's in front of me. She wears a white shirt with black laces, and white pants.

"Well, no. Why don't you tell me?"

She says, "You're in black rags." Of course I can't see myself in my dreams. She'll be my mirror.

"I guess I am." I look at myself. It wasn't rags. It was layered clothing like fish scales. I laugh too. "It's warm though."

"Why don't you take your sword and come here?" she walks to get the overlook view.

"Well, Aliya..."

"I haven't heard anyone called me that in a long time."

"Well, Aliya. I don't need the sword anymore," I walk to the overlook. The sun had descended. The moon shone over the roads, the lakes. Her white clothes are dyed in blue moonlight.

"Quill, my Lotus, Bradley...the names and the places didn't matter," *I say to him.*

"You are my home," I say to her.

"This doesn't feel like a dream."

"No...it doesn't."

I looked at your eyes while the grass swayed in the wind. I stared at you for what seemed like forever. *The grass felt good against my tces.*

I say, "I want this moment to stretch forever. That it will never be a memory."

I saw you stand up. You were tall against the moonlight.

"How do we get back?" *I ask him.*

"I don't want to go back."

She tears a blade of grass from the ground and ties the back of her hair with it. I take a flower and gently slide it into her hair, "You're radiant."

I kissed you. I kissed you...and...in the darkness...

* * *

She wakes up and feels the flower in her hair.

A whisper follows her upon waking, "I deemed you a dream, Aliya."

* * *

Somewhere in that New York night, along the clotheslines that span from window to window, house to house, black fabric—lingerie, towels, tulle, dresses all—loosen from their clothespins and fly along the wind. And the wind has blown this way and that way through the maze of buildings. Fabric would get caught on flagpoles; on gargoyles with wind still blowing. But as if wind were to arrive at a solution, it would blow the other direction and release the snagged clothes again.

As improbable as two people having the same minds, as improbable as four people having the same minds, even lost scarves and sweaters from Europe found their way here.

In its flight, the sewing on the clothes unravels. Laces, bands, hems, textile break apart into its base components—that of the thread.

BROOKLYN 1987

"Where are you?" she asks.

Her nude body is on the sofa: skin beading with sweat. She walks to the bathroom mirror, her hair is braided with a blade of grass and a flower. She puts on her clothes, her shoes. Outside on the street, she looks for any signs of Bradley. Once upon a time, she could have manifested a map inside of her, an internal compass that pointed to people she wanted to find. That skill had been lost long ago.

Rewrite.

Rewrite these endings.

She runs back inside her apartment. She walks up floor after floor after floor. On her rooftop, shards of a mirror are broken from its frame. The broken mirror sits by the ledge. A piece of glass still dangles like a cocoon off the skewed wooden frame; staples and nails exposed. The mirror shard spins and spins. She picks up the pieces and piles them near the frame. She'll gather them for disposal later.

The streetlights look like fireflies frozen in air. People walk in groups. They walk alone. They walk in pairs. They hang out in clusters. But she just needs to find one person.

She looks on top of the building next to her's. Music is playing over loud boomboxes on the roof. Cirrus clouds catch sun fire and glow yellow against the twilight sky. To get a wider field of view, she climbs up her building's water tower. The crosswinds shake the ladder. The rusted nuts and bolts that hold the ladder together creak and shake under her ascent. At the top, she circles the walkway. At this greater height, the world looks distorted. Horizons are bent into arcs. Buildings seem to peel apart on concrete skin. In a few moments, the sun will shine along the avenue, casting long, long shadows.

But you...you're going to be there.

Camille runs back down the building. She runs across streets. Cars seem frozen in her path. People seem to not move with the speed she ran. Even street lights are frozen. Meanwhile the moon is appearing, and the sun dips below cirrus clouds. What she felt was real. Time was frozen—for her. Crosswalks turn to walk signals. Streetlights turn to red. Engines cease to work for a moment while she runs past cars. People are frozen at their spots unable to move. They can only watch. They can only move their eyes to see what they're about to see—a wish becoming fulfilled.

As with a conductor's final movement, all the sounds in New York City—music, traffic, talking and whispers, the sound of air conditioners, wind—are snapped up in a single moment. But in the silence, they watch this singular woman walk past them.

Camille says, "We became each others' mirrors in our dreams. We had indecisions in our lives, but it all dissolved, didn't it?" He actualizes into the space in front of her. It looked like a flicker of light from a projector when he appeared. Had she materialized the same way?

The people regain their agency. They walk and crowd around her.

There, his broad shoulders are noticeable. His clothes are gone. City lights and orange street lights cast on his nude figure. The people were quiet.

And from the sky, black threads find their way to him. They wrap around him, threading into flowing fabric. Clothed in black layers, he removes his hood. He removes a scarf that covers his mouth. This outfit was an ancient design.

He speaks in a trance, his consciousness in a delicate balance between a dream and a reality.

"I wanted to propose to you in your old house. It would be you sitting on a wood plank swing holding the old, twain rope. And when the first wind of the night rustles the autumn leaves, and the amber leaves fall, I'll fall to my knees and ask you that question that binds together the past and future."

A tree and a swing flickers into the world. It's faded, in a half light. She walks to the swing. *How could it still be here? The twain rope mended soft by time and weather. The wooden board smells of earth and petrichor.*

She sits down...

"And I'll say yes, yes, over and over."

A strong wind blows through the street, shaking the leaves of the dreamt tree.

He walks to Camille. The direction the city lights reflected off her glasses created a rainbow on the inside of her lens. He pulls that rainbow out of the lens like how a person would gently remove a piece of thread off clothing. He curves the band into a ring and from his breath, blows into the rainbow ring. Specks of diamond flow like snow from his breath and crystallize onto the ring. The bands of color were in stacked rings which moved with the wind.

Here was a moment in time, in the liminal space between past and future, where anything was possible. They were in the threshold.

He bends at the knees.

A single leaf dislodges from its stem.

It falls

For

What

Seemed

Forever.

When the leaf touched the floor, the dreamt tree faded into the street lights. The clothes that were black rags had disappeared and in its place the clothes he had worn earlier.
"Will you marry me?"
"We were afraid, weren't we?" She begins to tear up, "I welcome our future and love together..." She slips her finger into the ring.

1988

Their daughter sleeps in a crib next to their bed. She wakes up crying. Bradley puts down a book in the living room. He comes over to pick her up, "I'm here now."
Camille rises out of her rocking chair; waking up from her nap, "Me too."
Bradley rocks their daughter gently back and forth. He brushes aside the book and sits down on their sofa.
Camille leans over; the baby grabs onto her finger.
Camille tells her, "May all your wishes come true, Sara."

CONTENTS

CHAPTER FIVE

MILLENNIAL

Cold wind rushes outside Brooklyn, New York. It's New Year's Eve 1999. Gray video game controllers are on the ground. Game cartridges are strewn everywhere out of their boxes. Three teens sit in front of a large 36" cathode ray tube TV. They're wearing 2000 New Year glasses; the zeros standing in for the lenses. The TV station is tuned into WB11.

The kids are Sara Dusk, Sam Dusk, and their friend Lindsey Lovitt-Chen.

You think they fixed all the Y2K stuff?" Sara asks. She's a bit taller than the two boys and about a year older. A ratchet noisemaker is beside her sleeping bag.

"I hope they don't. I want to see what happens. It'll be fun if everything shuts down," Lindsey says. He wears a black tee shirt with a skull on it, and pajama pants.

"That's mean. I'm sure they fixed all the computers. I hope they did," Sam says. He's wearing a t-shirt that's a bit oversized for him; a t-shirt which he had said he's going to grow into.

Sara and Lindsey are the same age. They're about to enter their first year of junior high school. Sam is a year younger than both of them.

A commercial ends with a frog doing a jig. The hosts huddle in the cold over their microphones. Sara and Lindsey took turns mocking the poor hosts. "Brrr. I'm so cold," Sara says.

Away from the children, Camille and Bradley pop open a champagne bottle in the kitchen, and pour the contents into wine glasses. Camille asks him if he was scared of the Y2K bug. He chuckled and said not at all.

They all gather and sit around the television.

"We're beginning the final countdown," the hosts stopped their chatter. Even from the TV, the collective voices in Times Square are heard. The kids yell out in unison, "10, 9, 8..." The lights on the Times Square ball shine out in all directions. "7, 6, 5..." Camille and Bradley continue counting. The ball descends further. "4, 3, 2..." The sound of the crowd gets louder and the whistling gets louder. Together, everyone yelled, "1!"

It's 2000.

Confetti is cannoned into the air and falls like snow. Fireworks fly into the air outside the Brooklyn neighborhood. Bradley kisses Camille, and they drink the champagne. Sara takes her noisemaker and spins it around. "So I guess the Honeymooners will be on in an hour," Sam says. And like that, normalcy returned.

Then the lights go out in the living room. Total darkness.

Voices search in the dark. "What's happening?"

"Nothing's on."

"I think I have a flashlight somewhere."

Sam takes the flashlight and shines it across the entrance of the living room.

"BOO!" their dad jumps out laughing. The lights come back up. "You guys worry too much! The world won't end."

"Dad, aren't you too old for pranks?" Sara asks.

Their dad says, "Here, look. I got some fireworks from Pennsylvania. So how about you all get dressed and we can ring in the New Year like real people?"

They grab their jackets and scarves and hats and walk out into the street. The cold Brooklyn air bites their lips and freezes their hands. There they join others in celebrating the new millennium. Camille walks out with a camera. Bradley takes an old glass bottle and a bag full of fireworks. Camille instructs the kids on safety when setting off fireworks in a very matter of fact way; and says that anyone who does not follow the rules goes back inside. "Sara, tie your hair back," she tells Sara.

Their mom made sure everyone didn't have any loose hanging clothes.

"Let's let our house guest go first. Lindsey, don't tell your mom," Bradley says.

"I won't," Lindsey sets fire and the firework shoots up. The Dusk kids go next.

Fireworks explode in the night sky; signaling that the new millennium has arrived.

* * *

On a spring day before the kids are home, before the parents are home, sunlight warms the room. Dust falls on the mantle of their living room. It falls on a photo of their wedding day: Frankie, Jim, Kacey, Ang, Peter, Elly, Olivia, Cindy, Kate, Bradley, and a pregnant Camille. It falls on a picture of Olivia and Camille at Minnewaska Lake. It falls on a picture of their family by a campfire, their large tent in the background. It falls on a baby picture of Sam and Sara running down a hallway; both laughing with chubby cheeks.

Sam comes home and puts his book bag on the sofa. He takes his books out and starts his homework. He looks at the sunlight that falls onto his mom's PhD.

* * *

During late springs and summers, the family had gone to Frankie's vacation home in Pennsylvania. On this particular trip, Sara rode a bike alone to a park. She stops behind some trees. She watches from a distance as cheerleaders practice cartwheels, backflips, and catches. They were barefoot. They went airborne—flying. Falling, falling gracefully. A smile crosses her face as if something called to her. Sara rides pass an overpass into a secluded forest. She walks alongside a stream. She takes off her shoes and starts cartwheeling. She tries to kick herself up into a handstand but her body falls and crumples every time. Her clothes are muddied. She finds time to clean it before her parents come back to the vacation house.

Back in Brooklyn, she asks "Dad, can I get gymnastic lessons? They're $100 a month." She produces the brochures in front of him.

He flips through the pamphlets to look at the pricing. Camille picks up the brochures too. She tells her, "Sara...we can't afford it. I'm sorry, but it's too much."

"Okay..." Sara says. And she walks into her dark room. She plants her face into her pillow and screams into it.

* * *

With Sam or Sara on their annual summer vacation, Lindsey spends the time by himself skateboarding in empty handball courts in the early morning. In the afternoon, he would spend five dollars on pizza and a can of soda. Then more skateboarding, and it would be at the comic book shop or at the library computer until it was dinner time.

* * *

Vinyl records are stored in the basement. Sara shows her dad how to rip music off of CD's. Her dad scratches his head and tells Sara, "This is too much. Can you just put this album into the computer? I'll pay attention to the next one."

After learning of Camille's pregnancy with Sara, Bradley took up a second job in addition to his construction work. After an exhausting day as a general contractor, he would head off to work another four hour shift at the convenience store. Eventually, he swallowed his pride and went back to Wall Street. He worked the same sixty-hour weeks, but was paid much more. After Sam was born, he had enough savings between his finance job and residuals from his screenplays with Frankie, that Camille finally told him to spend more time with his family. By then, Camille was bringing in income as an assistant professor at the university.

"Well, all the songs from this CD are on the computer now," Sara tells her dad.

Bradley tells Sara, "Awesome."

* * *

Their mom is sitting on the kitchen table with black horned rim glasses. She's grading papers. She has two piles of papers set up. Sam walks in. She asks Sam, "Hey Sammy. Do mommy a favor? Can you take this pile of exams and put smiley faces on them?"

He takes a red pen and starts drawing smiley faces, "Can I write good job too?"

"Sure."

He looks over the material being graded, "Mom, there's still some wrong answers here."

"I know, but they did pretty well, even without the curve."

"Apply yourself!", "You can do better than this!" She starts writing on the second pile of exams. Sam continues drawing happy faces on the non-failing papers.

JUNE 2001

School ended for them in mid-June.

It's Saturday afternoon. The three kids are by the park. Sam and Sara rest their bikes on the grass. Lindsey has a skateboard and is riding down a concrete slope.

"Hey Lindsey!" Sara calls down to him, "Let me ride your skateboard." Lindsey walks up with the skateboard and hands it to her.

"You've never rode it before. You know how to do it?" Lindsey asks.

"I've seen you fall enough times. I bet I can do better."

Lindsey laughs at her and says, "Okay, let's see."

Sara stares down the decline. She puts her left foot in front and steps in with the other foot. She tries to maintain her balance. She pushes off with her right foot and she is going downhill. She picks up speed. She shifts her weight back. "Oh crap!" She shifted her weight *too far back*. The skateboard flies off in front of her. She lands on her butt and her hands brace the landing.

Lindsey laughs.

She rubs her right wrist with her left hand, "Uh, guys."

Sam walks over, "Sara, we have to get you to a hospital."

"No!" she yells back.

Lindsey runs his hand through his hair, "Um...oh crap."

A bone is sticking out from her wrist. It is white with hints of red blood on it. Sara's disbelief overrides her pain.

"I think Sam is right. Sara, we gotta get you to a hospital. Ugh! That is disgusting to look at," Lindsey shields the sight of the broken wrist with his arm. He runs off, "I'm going to look for someone with a cellphone!"

"Sam, what am I going to tell Mom and Dad?" Sara asks.

"I don't know."

"I wish this would heal right now. Oh crap, it hurts."

And so it does heal. The bone slides back into its place. The sinews and broken capillaries realign themselves. Blood flushes in and the pale hands turn flesh tone. Nerve endings function correctly. After the pain subsides, her hand tingles. Sam looks at Sara. She looks back at him, then to her hand.

Lindsey comes back with an adult, "He said he's a doctor. He can help before the ambulance gets here." Sara shows Lindsey her arm. Lindsey looks at the adult, "Uh…"

"Emergencies aren't a joke. You can't lie about these things," the doctor scoffs and leaves.

"Sara, what the hell?" Lindsey says.

The three of them look at her left wrist. It is immaculate, clean, just as before.

"I don't know," she responds.

"Sam, is your sister a mutant?" Lindsey asks.

"Uh…all she did say was that she wished it would heal," Sam says.

"Yeah, but you know sometimes…" Lindsey continued.

"She's not a mutant, Lindsey!"

"We should take you to a hospital to get you checked out. This is kind of serious," Lindsey suggests.

"Okay, so let's bring her to a hospital. Then what? Look, nothing happened," Sam points to her sister's wrist.

"Well, we don't know that!"

Lindsey and Sam argue back and forth on whether to get her checked out.

Sara yells over them, "Tell me when you guys figure it out. I'm freaking out here that my wrist HEALED ALL BY ITSELF. I felt every single thing being reconnected inside my hand. Ew."

Lindsey sits by Sara, "Okay Sam, let's say you're right." Lindsey starts poking her, "Can I get a wish? Can I get a wish? Can I get a wish?"

"Here! Take it! Take all of it!" She slaps his shoulder a few times.

"I wish for a new skateboard!" Lindsey jokingly says. Nothing happens. "So I guess you're a mutant after all," he says. He walks down to the bottom of the hill to retrieve his skateboard. Sam and Sara look on. Lindsey picks up his skateboard and holds it high over his head. He comes running up the hill.

"Look at this. The bearings are—I've only seen these in magazines! Check out the artwork on the bottom," Lindsey announces. On the bottom of the board is a skull on fire and beneath the skull; a grenade in mid-explosion.

Sam goes, "Sara, I want one too! You're a genie!" He pokes her. "I wish my bike is black." The three of them stare intently at his bike.

Sam stares at Sara, "You disappoint me." His bike is the same as it ever was.

Lindsey punches Sam. Sam replies, "Lindsey, why'd you do that?"

Lindsey tells him, "Try now."

The bike's chipped red paint dissolves slowly into a flat black finish. The rusts on his wheels' rims begin to shine chrome again. All the small chips and dings on his pedals become smooth. The chain is black and lubricated.

They all went home; scared, but not of what they had done, but scared of possibilities.

* * *

"So...Lindsey Lovitt-Chen..." It's the rare occasion that Kacey addressed her son this way, and it has always been a bad occasion. "Do you mind telling us where you got your new skateboard?"

"That's not a new skateboard," Lindsey stuffs broccoli into his mouth. He knew his mom had an uncanny memory, which made her great at both maintaining film continuity and dissecting his lies.

Kacey squints at him, "Oh, okay, I trust you."

* * *

Lindsey and Sara are playing a match in a fighting game. Sam is in the corner doing pushups on his knees, "Did we use up whatever we had?"

"Just call it a wish. So what we did was slap or punch each other, and then we passed it on. You think we used up our chances?" Sara asks.

Lindsey sends Sara's character off the stage. He says, "It feels pretty cheap if the same person can get more than one wish."

Sam switches to doing sit ups, "Who had the wish last?"

None of them remembered. Lindsey asks Sam, "Well, what would you wish for, if you had it?"

"I don't know. More games?" Sam says.

"Your parents aren't going to notice if you have new games?" Lindsey asks.

They said they would hide the games, or keep them in rotation so it's the same number of games out. "But that's kind of boring, if we could do anything, but end up just getting video games," Lindsey says. The point was moot if they couldn't remember who had made the wish last. Caught up in their own wishes, yesterday was just individual moments: they only paid attention to what was happening to them.

They settle into a game of combinations. Sam, Sara, and Lindsey divided themselves into pairs. Each one in the pair would tap one another and make a wish. And if nothing happened, they would reverse the direction. They'll go through the combination of pairs until they find out who has the wish.

"Wait wait, but what are you going to wish for?" Lindsey asks before this game of combinations started.

Sara listened to Lindsey talk and his words came in one ear and went out the other. "New games!" Sara yells.

Lindsey and Sara switch off, each wishing for new games. Lindsey says, "Maybe the wishes only work if you transform something into something else. The skateboard and bike were already there."

Sara and Sam switch off. Sara taps Sam. Nothing. Sam taps Sara.

"I'll wish for a new...hat!" A white and red cap appears on her head. She was grateful that this wish didn't have any body horror that was associated with it. Sara reasoned that because she could make a wish, that it had meant that one person could make a wish at least twice, and maybe even more. "Okay, whoever can beat me this round can get the wish next," Sara says.

Lindsey wins the game. The siblings ask him what he wants. "Well, I can't bring back home what I wished for. I'll think about it overnight I guess."

"Well, we only have the summer," Sara says. "Why don't you wish for something now, and then give it to Sam."

"So he can give it to you?" Lindsey asks.

"Yes."

"I always wanted a trampoline...but I can't really hide it. I'll wish for a pogo stick. I'll hide it under my bed."

All three of them end up wishing for pogo sticks. They walk to the park. Sam gets onto the pogo stick, but keeps falling over. Sara and Lindsey get the grasp of it quickly. Sara holds up Sam's back while Lindsey holds onto the pogo stick for him. Sam tries to steady himself while Sara and Lindsey prop him up. Sam falls over a few times before getting the hang of it.

At the end of the day, the wish goes back to Lindsey. "Let's see how far we can take it," Lindsey says to them.

* * *

Bradley and Camille had gone for a walk after dinner; which meant Sam and Sara were allowed to be online. Sara goes onto the living room computer. Lots of music files are scattered on the desktop and with horrible naming conventions, like "01-Cassette.mp3."

"We really have to teach Dad how to name the music he burns," Sara says.

Sam turns off the television and goes to his room to read, "There isn't anything good on."

The 56K modem goes through its rhythms and mechanical sounds.

SARA: did you wish for anything yet?
LINDSEY: no..
LINDSEY: still thinking
SARA: hurry up
LINDSEY: no...
LINDSEY: almost didnt hide the pogo stick in time
SARA: hurry up lol
LINDSEY: omg ill talk to you later.
LINDSEY: im going to watch tv

Lindsey has signed off.

"Oh, come on," she mutters under her breath. She eats a bowl of ice cream while browsing through joke sites; mostly transcribed bits from famous comedians. Sam reads from a stack of pop science magazines that his mom brings home from work. Loose toy bricks and completed models are on his headboard.

At Lindsey's house, his parents drag milk crates inside the house. His dad asks, "Lindsey, can you help us bring some of these inside the house?" The minivan's back two rows are folded up. They haul in old boxes of vinyl records, cardboard boxes labeled film developing equipment, Grandpa's old clothes, a guitar, a keyboard, a synthesizer.

Lindsey asked them where this "junk" came from. "The '80s," his dad says. His parents had cleared out an old storage shed. They ask Lindsey to make some flyers for a yard sale.

* * *

"What are you doing?" Sara asks Lindsey. Lindsey opens doors, goes inside them, stays there for a moment, then exits again.

"Stop going through my house," Sara tells him.

He continues going into rooms and closing them. He walks into the basement and closes the door.

"Is what you're looking for in there?"

No response from Lindsey.

"Hey Lindsey, this isn't funny."

Sam comes home from the library. "What are you doing?" Sam asks Sara. Sara tells him that Lindsey has locked himself in the basement. Lindsey comes back out.

"So my parents brought home a lot of stuff from a storage shed last night. Which made me think, why don't I have a storage shed? Go inside."

"This...is your storage shed?" Sara asks. "You're putting your things inside my house?"

"Not really...Come on. Don't bring any flashlights."

The three of them go down the stairs. It's pitch black. And with a sudden rush of light and sound, they're transported to a place that Lindsey named, "The Bubble. Well, I was thinking of calling it the sac, but that would have been dumb."

They're inside an empty; warmly, evenly lit sphere. The top and bottoms are slightly flattened; and there are hand prints along the circumference. Lindsey had been pushing against the boundaries of the sphere the entire night. He managed to make it larger: it's about as large as a pantry now. The three of them stand crowded with the pogo stick and his skateboard slipping off the surface of the sphere.

"Now we can just put whatever we wish for inside here. No one's going to know or hassle us," Lindsey tells them.

"Pretty cool. So is this like a parallel universe you made? You know, like how some kids in books go through a closet or a thing in their wall?" Sam asks.

"No…it's just a storage shed." Lindsey enunciates, "The- Bub-Ble." He had wished for a secret storage place to go inside. It was instinctual that he had to find a dark place to go into. He carried his skateboard and pogo stick on his arms. Then, he was transported. And it was also instinctual that to get out of the Bubble, he would stare at the 'wall' for a few seconds.

"Can we come into here whenever we want? Without you?" Sara asks.

"I don't know…" Lindsey says. "Want to help me make this place bigger?" They agree. They push with their hands and feet to shape the surface. The way the surface moved seemed like the consistency of clay or fabric, but with the tactile feel of a glass surface. In between pushing out the boundary of the Bubble, they wished in a large television set which—oddly enough—had reception, a foam pit, and a giant slide which materialized sideways since that was the only way it could fit. To remedy that, they crudely shaped stairs onto one side so that they're able to walk up and push against the ceiling.

It occurred to Sam that just shaping stairs won't make the ceiling higher. Shaping stairs would only push the Bubble forward and up, but they can't expand the ceiling over their heads. Put in another way, holding your hand up while walking up stairs won't make the ceiling higher. Sam suggested that they either have to make switchbacks like on hiking trails or make a spiral that would go around the sphere. In that way, they could go up and also push the ceiling higher up.

The process would have been easier if the surface could be pulled back, but their manipulation was irreversible. They found that once expanded, the surface was not able to be grabbed back.

For lunch and snacks, they bought into existence a walk-in fridge, a full kitchen, and a soda fountain.

Over the course of a day, they managed to expand the Bubble to about the size of a school gym by walking around the sphere in a spiral. They carved out a spiral ramp on the perimeter. The ceiling was still too short to erect the giant slide upright. It laid on its side next to the foam pit and took up valuable space.

"Lindsey, I'm tired. How do we get out of here again?" Sam asks. Sara mentions she wanted to get going too.

"Just stare at an empty wall for like 10 seconds and you'll pop back into your basement."

"You're not coming?" Sara asks.

"No, I'm going to stay here until I get the ceiling higher," Lindsey says.

Sara's suspicious, "You're not going to pop back into my basement, right?"

"No…"

Sara holds out her hand. Lindsey seems puzzled and slaps it. Sara says, "What are you doing? It's my turn."

"Oh," Lindsey slaps her hand again.

Lindsey stays behind. When he decided to leave, he emerged in the Dusk's basement. He may not know how the Bubble works.

* * *

Sam and Sara materialized back into their dark basement. Beneath the door, they see that the kitchen light was on. They hear their dad chopping vegetables and pounding meat. It's chicken cutlet night. They walk to the front of the basement. Sam looks through the window and sees that no one was walking by the front streets. They exit and enter back into their house.

"Where have you two been all night?" Their dad was cooking two simultaneous dishes on the four stoves, "After dinner, can you two show me how to continue burning my CD's on the comp-ut-er?"

Sara rolls her eyes.

Camille walks through the door. She puts her backpack down on the couch. "It's a hot day today, isn't it? Sam, can you open the air conditioner?" She smells the meal that Bradley was cooking. Even after a hard day at the restaurant, he still finds the time to cook for his family.

Sam had set the plates while Sara helped her dad put the food on the plates.

"You two have been studying for your high school exams right?" their mom asks them.

Sara looks at Sam. She responds, "Yeah, we've been in the library reading books."

After dinner, Bradley and Camille washed the dishes while the kids ran off to the living room.

Bradley sits in front of the computer while Sam and Sara keep pointing to the screen telling him where to click. He takes out a piece of paper and writes down the sequence to burn his CD's onto the computer. "Okay, it's me time now!" Bradley closes the programs. He opens up a word document, titled "First Draft - 6.8.2001." He types at a rapid pace, stopping at times to contemplate, and continues typing.

Camille, Sam, and Sara sit on the couch watching game shows. "Oh, Mom. Lindsey said they're going to have a yard sale this weekend and want us to come," Sam says.

At 10pm, Bradley and Camille had gone to bed. Sara stayed up watching late night shows with her brother. Their dad had gotten up for the bathroom and asked, "You're still up?" That was a regular occurrence every winter, and every summer vacation day. At about 1am, Sam went to bed. Sara waited a bit to make sure her brother had fallen asleep. She goes to get her blue school t-shirt with a yellow eagle emblem and sweatpants; which were about her only athletic clothes.

On this particular hot night, she sneaks outside her backyard. The neighbors are watching soccer in an adjoining backyard. Air conditioners are on and humming. Sara tip toes to a dark corner of the backyard where she could be sure no one would see her. A warm wind sweeps across her. She ties her hair back, looks up to the sky, and she says, "I wish I can fly."

* * *

Sam stands inside Lindsey's room. He hears a thud inside the closet. He opens the doors, and finds Lindsey lying down. Lindsey half-opens his eyes, and then closes them again. Sam walks into the closet and closes the closet doors behind him.

Sam is back in the Bubble again. Lindsey is sleeping inside the foam pit; his mouth full of drool. Sam nudges Lindsey, "Lindsey, I'm at your house. Your mom said you went out early and I couldn't find you at the handball courts either. Hey! Wake up!"

Lindsey rolls over. The foam pit undulates while he crawls out. "Never knew that the bottom of a foam pit was a trampoline," Lindsey says. Lindsey sluggishly walks to the kitchen. He pulls out a skillet, eggs from the walk-in fridge, and a ketchup bottle. He starts frying an egg. "I've been up last night crawling on my legs, making a spiral around this bubble. Say, you want some eggs too?"

Sam looks up. The ceiling wasn't much higher. The giant slide was still sideways on the floor. "No, your mom asked me to give you this," Sam takes out a stack of flyers and hands them to Lindsey. "I have the tape in my backpack."

Lindsey squirts the ketchup onto a plate and scuffs down the eggs. He tosses the plate like a Frisbee into the sink; which *obviously* breaks. "Didn't really expect that to happen," he says.

They reappear in Lindsey's closet. "Oh, I forgot my skateboard," Lindsey goes back into the closet, back into the Bubble, and comes back out with his skateboard.

After Lindsey taped a flyer onto a telephone or power line pole, he skated to the next one. Sam follows him by jogging from pole to pole. Although he's able to rest while Lindsey puts up the flyers, Sam is still out of breath when he begins running again.

When they ran out of flyers, and made their way back to Sam's house, they find Sara eating cereal in the kitchen.

"Finally awake?" Sam asks her. Sara looks at the clock, which shows 3pm.

She says, "I was watching TV late. You guys want to bike along 3rd avenue?"

***

She stops biking when they reach an overpass. She sits on the ledge.

"Sara, what are you doing?" Sam asks.

"How fast do you think these wishes can be granted?" Sara asks. She leans back over the overpass and falls over. The boys try to catch her. "I want to fly!" echoes across the road.

She does fly. Her figure goes fast and far. From where they stood, Sara's movement sounded like a whistle while she pierced through the air. The pitch of her flight shifted lower after the air settled. The boys watched this dot circle around them from miles away. She flies back. They watch while she comes in above them. She falls. Rather—she drops out of the air. Her body flails; looking for control. Sara slows down *while* she falls to the ground. Her foot touches down, and she collapses into a body roll. Her t-shirt gets scuffed up and she gets a bruise on her elbow.

Whoa," Lindsey says.

She says, "Not the best landing. Haha. I actually did this last night. Did I scare you guys?"

Later at night, after dinner, Sam tells her, "What you did today...
that wasn't funny. I was scared for you."

* * *

Lindsey carries out a small table. He puts a box of vinyl on top. His
dad sets up the keyboard, the synthesizer, and guitar for display.
Kacey hangs vintage clothes on a rolling rack. Reluctantly, she
puts out the film development equipment. These bulky items
were precious to her. There were the other common yard sale
items: unused gym equipment, kitchen appliances, cookware.

Two musicians walk by and ask to jam. Peter runs an extension
cord to plug in the instruments and gear. A person walked by
and requested them to play, "Take on Me." They play it. Soon,
more people walk by and request more 80's songs. If it weren't
for the two passing musicians, they may not have drawn the
crowd that they did. Between songs, Kacey tells Peter, "Maybe
we didn't have to put out those flyers after all." Lindsey overheard
that and was not pleased.

The Dusk family came closer to 5pm. Camille looks at the
film development equipment, "Kacey, I remember the mess I've
made when you were teaching me how to use this. Yikes." Kacey
offers to give it to her for free. Camille said there was no room in
the house. Camille tells Kacey, "This is Brooklyn. There's bound
to be a photographer willing to buy it off you."

Peter hugs Bradley. Bradley says, "I haven't seen these in use
for a while. When was the last time you played a show with these?"

"Oh wow, it's been years. Not since Lindsey," Peter says.

Lindsey asks his parents, "Hey, can I go now?" Kacey looks
around and sees that most of what they had put out were sold,
"Sure."

Lindsey leads Sam and Sara into his closet, into the Bubble
again. The Bubble was shaped into a sphere with a spiral ramp
that wound around the circumference. Before it was low and

wide like a cavern or cave. Lindsey had made it expansive. The acoustics inside were different: sound has echo, reverberation. The acoustics and warm light created an atmosphere of reverence.

The three of them pulled and pushed the giant slide into place. It was fifteen feet tall and three feet wide. The structure was tall and skinny. It seems like it could snap or twist if the slightest load touched it. Lindsey climbed between the pitches of the spiral ramp to get on top. He stares down the decline. There was a non-zero, non-negligible chance that he could seriously injure himself. But that was the point of the wishes, he thought.

He slides down. Faster and faster. Faster and faster. Until the speed he built up shoots him past the foam pit and hurls him against the Bubble's wall. A small tunnel was extruded in the shape of his sideways body. He crawls back out. Sam and Sara just laugh. "It's like a cartoon, your body. It looks like," Sara puts her hands up, "Like you didn't know what to do." Lindsey's digits were splayed out in the tunnel's imprint.

"Sam, are you going to go?" Lindsey asks.

Sam looks up at the slide's top, and decides against it. Sara, obviously, goes. Her exit follows the same trajectory that Lindsey was heading down. It was going to shoot her into Lindsey's imprinted tunnel. She overshoots the foam pit, just like Lindsey. But before she hits the wall, she engages her flight and attempts to fly off and avoid the wall. The impulse of trying to change direction quickly throws her across the floor like a skipping stone. Her face becomes imprinted in the ground like it had been dragged through clay.

Lindsey and Sara continue taking turns down the slide. Lindsey tells them, "We should probably go back." They emerge back into Lindsey's room.

The smell of charcoal comes from outside. It crackles too. Burgers and hot dogs were cooking. "Where are the kids?" Bradley asks.

"Not a bad haul. We got $400 all said and done. We still got some things to donate," Kacey says.

Uncle Frankie was outside too, "Kacey, Peter. We've done some great things together. We're really going to miss you when you leave for California."

For Sam, Sara, and Lindsey; they didn't have the same worries.

* * *

A day later, the Dusk siblings sit at the dining table. Their parents had gone out for a post dinner walk. It's Sara's turn to wash the dishes.

"Maybe we should come up with some sort of test. Like to see if the wish went through or not?" Sam suggests.

"Why would we do that?" Sara asks.

"I'm sure some things won't happen. Like I can't just wish for a black hole in the kitchen."

"How about we wish for something small? Something that would be easy to be granted."

"How about food? Like candy or chips?" Sam says.

"I think I have the wish now, so let me try. "

"Wait, but what if we wished for candy and nothing happens?"

"I guess we'll try wishing for something else? That's the point of the test."

Like many conversations during chores, this one, unfortunately, will be forgotten.

* * *

"Chase me," Sara flies into an alleyway. She floats rapidly up. Her wake creates a vacuum in which debris catches up. The boys are floating up rather than flying. Above the house, she spots power lines.

As the boys float up to roof level, they see her fly straight through the gap between the power lines. Lindsey speeds up and passes through the gap. Sam flies behind. Right as he approaches the opening, he loses control and his body bounces back against the line. Sam ricochets back. He falls towards the ground without control.

"There's nothing I can do," Sam says to himself. Without one thought, but multiple simultaneous thoughts, this was what he felt—if total despair could be given words. He was milliseconds from hitting the pavement. His arms stop flailing as he gave himself over to dying.

Sara is several miles away. She spots the Manhattan Bridge in the far distance. A form with trusses of triangles layered several planes deep. There are two narrow passageways for trains on either end and a large middle road for cars.

She accelerates not above the structure but through it. Her sudden acceleration causes a vortex to open up behind her. Ice forms in the vacuum and snow follows her. Her path draws a contrail in the air. She threads through the first train passageway. A train passes on the opposite platform. The heavy machinery grinds and rumbles while it moves.

As if she was a gymnast in total control of her body and intuiting how to manipulate the dynamics of her situation, she opens her body up. Her open body faces entirely parallel to the length of the train as if she were to hug the windows. Her sudden expansion from a closed shape to an opened shape causes air to knock her back. She uses this air cushion burst as a springboard to tuck into a flip. Her body is tucked into a fetal position, her body curled tight. She goes through a gap through the other side—blindly.

Lindsey flies above the bridge. He spots Sara flying towards the coast of Brooklyn Bridge Park. His speed picks up. He flies in and around the contrail that Sara had created. Lindsey closes the gap and almost has his fingertips on Sara's shoes. Sara whips her body in a different direction. The air current blows Lindsey away; farther behind her.

Sara yells to him, "I'm going to head back."

Lindsey follows her when she flies just on top of the water. He notices the salt spray on her clothes. He yells, "You're going to have trouble getting the salt out of your clothes." They fly all the way back to Sara's house.

Lindsey catches his breath, "How did you do it? You were flying too quick. I couldn't catch up. How could you manage to just go through these tiny holes like nothing. You were even flying fast but you still, like, touched the wall with your fingers."

"I… don't know how to explain it. I don't think. I mean I do think, but I don't think or think about thinking. I just go with it. Hey, uh, You seen Sam?" Sara wrings out some water off her school sweatpants; which has become her de facto flying clothes.

"He was with us when we took off."

"You think he's in the Bubble? Can he be there without you?"

"I don't think so."

They search Sara's house. He wasn't there. He wasn't at Lindsey's house either. Not in the Bubble. Not in the library. Sam had the wish last, but he didn't pass it on. Couldn't find him that way.

Where was Sam Dusk?

* * *

Sara bikes home from surveying the neighborhood, asking former classmates if they have seen Sam. She comes home soaked with sweat. Her dad was home cooking again.

"Hey."

"Hi, Dad. Where's Mom?"

"Your mom's out with her friends tonight. Is Sam over at Lindsey's?"

She pauses. "Yeah."

This was odd since Sam usually calls if he's not coming back for dinner. She turns on the computer.

SARA: did you find him?
LINDSEY: no...
LINDSEY: crap...
SARA: i told my dad he's at your place...so if anyone calls pick up the phone
LINDSEY: okay
SARA: im going to look after dinner too
SARA: where was the last place you saw him?
LINDSEY: i think it was the alley where we took off
SARA: ill check there later tonight

"How was work, Dad?"

"It was a busy lunch hour. A group of people came in all at once. I don't think you want to hear this."

"Oh come on."

"No. You don't need to hear how Kevin almost chopped his finger off."

"Can I drive the car later?"

"Hard no!"

"When are you sending your script to Frankie?"

"You're asking a lot of questions tonight. What are you hiding?"

"What are *you* hiding?" She squints her eyes and examines her dad's face. She usually does this as a joke, and they would both end up chuckling; but her dad definitely sensed something was wrong.

"Is everything okay?"

"If I asked you to help me, can you not tell Mom?"

"Okay," he says.

Dirty dishes are left on the dining room table.

* * *

Lindsey walks outside. His dad is drinking a beer outside. They look at the furniture they had dragged out into the street. A pickup truck arrives after some waiting. A man exchanges dollars with Lindsey's dad, and hauls a sofa and dressers away.

Sara looks out from the passenger side. Lindsey sees her and waves. Sara's dad looks ahead on the road and hadn't taken notice of Lindsey's house. "Sara, so you just wanted to see me drive around?"

"Yeah," she says. It was not much of a plan. If there was one. Sara and Lindsey had covered every place that Sam may have went to. If they couldn't find Sam, Sara thought maybe exploring the neighborhood through random streets may turn something up.

"Well it is nice out tonight," Bradley says.

* * *

A pebble at Lindsey's window. Lindsey sneaks out of the front door. Walking far enough from Lindsey's house, they started arguing on whether to go to the police or not. Sam was missing, that much was true. It was apparent to them that his disappearance was magical, not physical. Sara didn't think the police could help. Lindsey didn't know what else to do.

A police car stops on its patrol. A policeman comes out, and shines a light on Sara and Lindsey, "Hey, you too. Shouldn't you be at home? We'll drive you back." The two of them run into an alleyway and fly up to the roof. The policeman gives chase to the alleyway, but finds no one. Lindsey watches while the policeman goes back to the car.

"What am I supposed to do?" Sara asks Lindsey.

"I don't know."

"We're an hour away from sunrise. We have to find Sam."

Over the curve of the earth, purple sunrise touched the roofs on the east; while orange street lights still criss-crossed in squares over the parts still in night. They arrive at the alley where they saw Sam last. They're in a different part of Brooklyn. One where there are many, many fire escapes on the sides of buildings.

"When I get my brother back, I'm going to be more responsible."

"Sara, we'll get him back."

"Did you see him fly up?"

"Yeah."

The concrete in the alley was clean. There was no sign of any fall. Garbage cans were immaculate. As immaculate as they could be for garbage cans. It didn't seem like Sam crashed into them. No damage on the fire escape. No sign that he was ever hurt. There's nothing on the rooftop either. Lindsey yells down to Sara, "We have to go back, it's sunrise."

She kicks a garbage can.

Sara walks home alone. She turns the corner on her block. Sam is jogging to the house. His t-shirt is drenched with sweat. Sara runs to him. She hugs him tight. "Sam!"

"I just want to sleep."

"I'm never leaving you again!"

"Oh jeez. I'll tell you what happened after I wake up. I really need to sleep."

They walk into the house. Sam walks to his bed sluggishly and collapses face down on the pillow. Sara lies face up on her bed; unable to sleep. The drop ceiling had dimples to count. Through counting, her mind wandered through scenarios where Sam hadn't have come back. Then to memories of them playing card games on lazy Saturday afternoons, to rewatching the same videotapes over and over again when they were much younger, to when they would race bikes down hills on summer vacations. Then she was back to counting dimples on the ceiling until she falls asleep for half an hour.

* * *

"Shapes!" Sam yells.

"Hold on Sam. What?" Lindsey asks.

"What happened to you?" Sara asks.

Sam stirs a cup of hot tea, "I took off flying. I was behind Lindsey. Then when I just got over the roof, I freaked out. And I fell. I thought I was dead." He sips the cocoa. "My mind went totally blank. Then all I saw was darkness."

"That's how I feel when flying. The mind is just empty," Sara says.

"Me too..." Lindsey says.

"I realized I wasn't dead when I could touch stuff in the dark."

"What..." Sara seems confounded.

"I don't know. It felt like whatever the Bubble was made out of. Weird stuff. I couldn't see anything. But I felt things. And I could think."

Sara laughs, "Well, that's what you're good for. Thinking."

"So what did you do? How did you get out and back?" Lindsey asks.

"The thing was that I couldn't walk. It felt like flying. In a weird way. So I floated around until I found some shapes. I think one was a cube. Another was a cone. I think I flew through some strings too. I grabbed onto the shapes to propel myself. Some of them came loose like I was holding onto a rock. So now there's shapes floating around me."

"Shapes you couldn't see," Sara replies.

Sam sips more hot tea. "Yeah. That's when I realized maybe I could just stare at nothing for ten seconds and get out just like from the Bubble. But then again all I was doing was staring at nothing. I wasn't able to leave like that.

"I ended up just grabbing the shapes and playing with them like building blocks. I was going to be there for a while. They fit together in specific ways. I could bend them. It was odd. I knew what each shape could kind of do. Some of them were like batteries where it held energy. Like a rubber band. I took a cylinder, and some loose string. I tied it around and around. Then I tried to throw it like a yo-yo."

"What," Lindsey is in disbelief.

"I wanted to see if there was gravity. Or if there was a ground."

"Was there?" Sara asks.

"When I threw the yo-yo in front of me, it kept spinning and spinning until it lit up. It was like a lantern or candlelight. The shapes there were shimmering. Like everything was a prism. The cylinder snapped back to me. It hit me in the forehead. When I came to, I ended up in South New Jersey. I saw the New York skyline and started running back."

"You didn't fly?" Sara asks.

"Uh, I didn't think about it. Figured I'll just run back."

"Can you take us there?" Lindsey asks.

"I don't know how to take you guys back there. Honestly," Sam says.

There was a certain disappointment in the air. Wishes had afforded them possibilities, but being able to wish for anything loses its novelty. Sam found a new playground that they could never get to.

"Oh, there was something I was thinking about," Lindsey produces a giant book from his backpack. "It's a book on weather. But I just marked this page for us to look at." He flips to the page. It's an illustration of world-wide wind patterns.

"So I was thinking we can spend less effort on flying by following the wind," Lindsey says. "It'll make things easier when we have to fly longer distances. I made photocopies for each of us."

They spent the rest of the day spending time getting better at flying. This time, Lindsey and Sara didn't let Sam fall behind.

Their one goal was more speed: more distance in less time. All three of them wanted one thing: to break the sound barrier.

* * *

Lindsey puts his suitcase into his family's car.

"Lindsey, we're going to miss you eating our food and taking up space in our house," Camille says.

"I think what Aunt Camille is trying to say is that we're going to miss having you around. You're a part of our family," Bradley says.

"We've babysat you when you were little. You're so grown up now," Camille tells him.

"Oh, Mom, stop. We all packed a gift for you. Don't open it until you get to California," Sara says.

Bradley and Camille go over to Kacey and Peter. Bradley tells them, "Goodbye isn't goodbye forever." They give Kacey and Peter a gift as well: a framed picture of the barbecue.

Sam whispers to Lindsey, "Lindsey, that thing we talked about. Sara and me are trying to figure it out."

Everyone exchanged final goodbyes.

The car turns over. With three suitcases and a skateboard in the back of the car, they'll start a new life in California.

Brooklyn becomes a paradox. It is becoming smaller. But it is becoming larger. The streets become imbued with meaning. With memories. When people leave, we rationalize. We'll see them again. We'll be in contact. We'll never be too far from here. Goodbye didn't mean goodbye forever. It was especially true for Lindsey, but still, he still felt...

Goodbye didn't mean goodbye forever.

JULY 2001

Fireworks are in the sky. The family sits around the TV watching fireworks on the Hudson River. They didn't need to turn on the TV to listen to the fireworks right outside their house. It's a quiet day for them. In the past years, they held small get-togethers, but everyone's schedule was busy. Instead, Bradley had prepared sundaes for the family.

It would be another few days until Lindsey would reach California. Sara asks over the phone if he's near New Mexico or Utah yet. Lindsey had just passed Oklahoma. Road trips with his father were not for him. Every night, he had to hear his father snore. Last night, he really wanted to just sleep in the Bubble. He didn't care if he overslept. Sam asked Sara to ask Lindsey if he was at Utah yet. Sara told Sam no.

"What's in Utah?" Camille asks.

"National parks?" Sam and Sara replies in unison.

"You two want to go there?"

"To the national parks? Sure," Sara replies.

"Dad, how about you?" Camille asks.

He looks up from typing on the keyboard, "Uh yea sure."

* * *

In their backyard, Sara shines a flashlight on a map. There are fifteen lines drawn emanating from Brooklyn. Next to the lines are times marked in hours and seconds; and scribbled math calculating distances and time. The longest line is from Brooklyn to Harrisburg, Pennsylvania. About 180 miles, and 1hr 5 minutes. There are much shorter lines: Brooklyn to Harriman State Park. About 60 miles, and 30 minutes.

Sam peers over at her map. "Your handwriting was always better than mine," he says. Sam puts on his hoodie and gloves.

"This was Lindsey's idea...anyway." She folds back the map and puts it inside her jacket pocket.

"Sara, can you wish for a GPS?" Sam gives the wish over to Sara, and a GPS appears in front of them.

"I figured we can find our way back home if we get lost," Sam says.

"I have my own way," Sara replies.

"I know you do."

The destinations would always be cities. It was easier to fly to cities where the night lights would be brighter. There would be more noticeable skylines and larger monuments to use as waypoints. No matter where Sara was, she could always find home by the light of the New York skyline.

Sam preferred certainty. Sara understood after what he's been through; after he disappeared. She hands the GPS over to Sam. Sam goes through the menus in the GPS, "Where are we going?"

"Pittsburgh." She puts on her wristwatch. Then puts a sweatband over it. The last time she flew, her wristwatch loosened and dropped over a lake.

"370 miles from here. About 6 hrs, 22 minutes by car," Sam smirks.

"You ready?" she asks.

"Yea."

She starts the timer. They take to the skies.

Sam tries to yell back to Sara that they're flying at about the top speed of a car. The wind overtakes his voice. It's all muffles. The landscape moved so slowly underneath them. It felt like molasses. The patterns of lights on the highways, on cities, reminded him of where he had disappeared to; like webs and vines. Above, the sky moved even slower. It appeared to not move at all.

Sara keeps an eye on Sam from behind. But that didn't mean she didn't have fun. She alternated poses to break up the monotony of flying. She twists her body like a gymnast's full twist. She extends her fist forward, and the other arm back. Or both arms extended forward. Chin in. Chin up. Sam catches her lampooning a swimmer's butterfly stroke in slow motion. She promptly returns to a more tighter, *cooler* form.

But her favorite part of flying were gusts of wind. In the moment before a gust hits, there is a warning wisp of wind. She could prepare and anticipate. When a gust did hit her, she used it as a springboard to push off of and tuck into a flip. She has a sailor's intuition on how to tack into the wind.

They find an empty field to land onto. Another line is drawn on the map. Brooklyn to Pittsburgh: 370 miles, 1hr 30 minutes. 246 miles per hour. Sara says, "It's a little slow."

"It's a marathon, not a sprint," Sam says.

"Feels like a sprint to me. Ready to head back home?" Sara replies. She yawns.

* * *

"My parents are out on the town so I got some time to talk. They gave me my own room. There's one road that leads up to the Four Corners Monument. There are four red awnings. So you should be able to see it from on top," Lindsey tells Sam.

"I'm looking at a map from the library, there's also a river nearby?" Sam asks.

"I think we passed by one. In my parents' car. I couldn't see from inside the site." From inside his hotel room, Lindsey looks outside to the bright lights of the Las Vegas strip. People walk around in a tiny world in front of him. Stand in's for Paris, New York, and Rome are spread out on the boulevard. If he flew over the strip, it may have well induced the same sense as flying over the actual places. "There's not much else I can tell you from being on the ground."

Lindsey continues, "Were you and Sara able to get to Mach speed?"

They were well short of hitting it.

Lindsey commented on his own training, "Oh. I hadn't been able to practice. My dad's been driving us around. I haven't had any time for myself. When I left, you said you were trying to get back to the place you were in."

"I decided to call it the Field."

"Good, the Bubble is taken. So did you and Sara figured out how to get back?"

"We tried wishing to get in, but it didn't let us." The wish didn't let them enter. The wish didn't let them enter. Lindsey ran that through his mind a few times before Sam started talking again. Sam and Sara had walked to the alley at night. Sara set up an air mattress on the ground. Sam recreated the conditions: he flew up, he consciously took a fall, and Sara raced to get the air mattress under him. He hasn't disappeared. He hadn't entered into the Field.

"'It was the fear.' Sara said to me. It wasn't the fear. And I don't think it had anything to do with the alley," Sam says.

"You're going to keep trying right?"

"Yeah."

"Hey, can you give me the wish?"

"Over the phone? I don't think it works verbally."

"Try."

"Hocus pocus, I grant you a wish."

"Nope. It doesn't feel like I got anything."

"Let me telepathically send the wish to you. Anything?"

"Nope. You said in the Field, the shapes you felt—you said they felt like the Bubble to you?"

"Yeah."

"I'm going to investigate. I'll talk to you later."

"Bye."

The blinds are closed. He goes into the bathroom, and shoves several towels into the gap under the door. It's been a week since he went inside the Bubble.

Everything was still in its messy state. He sits on the counter of the kitchen overlooking the foam pit and slide.

He mutters to himself, "In every wish, we say something, and then it's fulfilled. But it gets fulfilled by what we think the wish is going to be. So...so it's not like peace on earth means you killed everyone to get peace on earth. When Sara said she wanted to fly, there wasn't a trick that made her into a fly. What does this mean for you Lindsey? Come on think. You know this. So even though the wish becomes fulfilled, then what does that mean? What does that mean? Can the wishes become more than what I originally wanted them to be? Can they evolve?"

Lindsey looks at the cartoon-like imprint of his body against the Bubble's wall; from when he slid straight into the wall. He walks forward; clawing his hands in front like a dog pawing at sand. "Lindsey...The wishes can evolve. Sam and Sara were able to get faster in their flying."

The tunnel he burrows becomes deeper. Still, the warm glow light of the Bubble surrounds him. It was more apt to describe it as a corridor. Animals burrow tunnels, but their tunnels aren't light-emitting. Lindsey thought of office workers. Humans are the only animals that burrow lit up corridors. He looks behind him. The slide and the foam pit are a dot in the distance.

"And if wishes can become more after it has been granted... if wishes mattered more on how you felt when you made them, then when I called this place the Bubble, can I *pop* it?"

* * *

Sara says, "Sam, what you said yesterday. Thinking this was a sprint or marathon."

"What about it?"

"We're not going to fly faster if we're not going to push ourselves. Let's make it a time trial. Like instead of how long it takes us to get somewhere, let's make a limit."

"I don't know. What if—"

"Come on Sam. Let's push ourselves."

"But we have the return trip too."

Sara runs to her room and returns with the map, now with more lines coming from Brooklyn. The lines converging onto Brooklyn are much, much denser. She taps at the Four Corners Monument, "Sam, let's *try*."

Sam takes a ruler to a line that they already flew. 1 hour on the map is 2" at scale at their current speed. He starts counting off the time as he slides his finger along the ruler; extending the ruler beyond the line: one hour, two, three, four, five, six...eight hours to Four Corners Monument.

Sam emphasizes the math, "We double that by going back. We won't be back for sixteen hours."

"Sam...Sammy. Sam. Sam. Listen! I'll set my timer for four hours. We'll get there and back by then," Sara says. Sam groans. Sara gets dressed and heads out the door, "I'm leaving Sam."

She takes off. Sam makes a mad rush to get together the GPS, the map, and some water bottles and follows his sister into the sky.

Boredom. Just plain boredom. It's been three hours of non-stop flying, and they're just over Kentucky. The initial rush of enthusiasm has been replaced by drudgery. Land looks like land looks like land. Sometimes they cross a shimmering river. Squares and fields. Mindless.

"Sam, you know what that is?" She points down, "Look side to side."

It's a long river. The sun's glint runs along the blue river. The river reaches horizon to horizon; never ending. It's a compass that runs North to South; that demarcates the two halves of the United States. The Mississippi River beckons them: go west!

* * *

Foam blocks, taken from the foam pit, line the Corridor. The Corridor had become so much longer that the sound takes on a different tone from the Bubble. Lindsey took a 25 foot tape measure, extended it out all the way, and dragged it along the ground. He placed a foam block every 25 feet. After many intervals, he started losing count. He placed a second foam block on every tenth one. Then when the Corridor had become longer, he placed a third on every 100th foam block. The foam blocks are like the different demarcations on a ruler. After a while, he lost count of the distance. The Corridor was at least a mile now.

Through the hallway, he flies back to the Bubble's core. Eddies of air build up around him; causing an almost imperceptible loss of speed. He picks up a knife from the floor; an attempt at popping the Bubble. He stops a couple of steps short of the Corridor's entrance. He had known that from inside the Bubble, he could not pull the surface back. But could he push it from the other side? Could he create a shorter hallway connecting the Corridor to the Bubble? Something akin to creating the third side of a triangle?

Lindsey walks with his face pressed against the surface. It was definitely weird, but he wanted to see the Bubble appear as he emerged through the other side.

* * *

"Crap!" While pressing his face against the surface, he had inadvertently stared at it. He's back in his empty room. His luggage of clothes is split open on the floor.

"Lindsey!" His mom calls out from the other room, "You got a phone call from Sara!"

* * *

Farther than they've ever gone, they still have farther to go. The Mississippi River has given them a new hope. Their speed has increased to where their updated time of arrival is three hours instead of four hours.

The four red awnings appear in view. The highway is a very thin line on the ground; the yellow divider lines are even thinner. There are people coming out from their cars and moving in groups of four, five, three, two's. About thirty people exit from a long, yellow rectangle. Lindsey lands on the highway; far from people's sights. He takes his skateboard and goes along that smooth asphalt. The vibration of the wheels underneath him, the landscape in its brown and yellow hues goes past him in a blur.

Sam and Sara walk around. It is one thing to view landscapes from overhead. It is another thing still to be *inside it*. Lindsey rolls in.

"How long did it take you guys to get here?" Lindsey asks them.

"Five hours? Six?" Sam answers.

"You won't make it back to NY until Midnight..." Lindsey replies back.

"Well, that's what I told her," Sam says.

"We'll make it back. Don't worry. Well, this is why we're here," Sara says. She holds her hand out. Lindsey reaches out to grab her, but she pulls it away the last second. Lindsey's hand passes through thin air.

He holds out his right hand, clasps his fingers back and forth, "Gimme, gimme."

They walk along the highway while Lindsey attempts skateboarding tricks. For Sam and Sara, who had only known cities and small towns even when they flew, to see long stretches of empty land like this was a whole different experience. For Lindsey, he was acclimatizing to California and its roads.

"So how's your new home so far?" Sam wanted to know.

"Not much is really happening. My parents don't start work until September. We've been going to like different places like the beach, restaurants, taco places. I help with house work sometimes like painting. It's fun I guess. I kind of wish I was back in Brooklyn."

They're halfway down the road. A car leaving the monument passes by them. Sara watches it go by and when it was just out of sight, she wondered if she could catch up to it in less than a few seconds by flying.

"Hey, Lindsey, can you bring us into the Bubble?" Sam asks.

"You can't shake that feeling of being in the Field?"

"No."

There was barren land around them. Not even a place or a room without light. Three teens in the middle of Middle America close their eyes, then put their hands over their eyes.

"What did you do?! What is that!?" Sara notices the tunnel. The last Sara saw of the Bubble was the cartoon-like imprint of Lindsey's body into the surface. Now it has depth and dimension.

"I call it a Corridor. I can make up names for stuff too," Lindsey says. He glares at Sam. Sam rolls his eyes. While Sara walks through the tunnel, noticing foam cubes on the ground on either side, Lindsey tells her what he did. Sara takes off flying to get to the end of the tunnel; spiraling as she does so that the air current does not have a chance to create eddies.

"This is long-lo-lo-lo—on-on-on-ong!" Her yell echoes back to Lindsey and Sam. She flies back.

"Oh yeah, I was working on something when you called me today," Lindsey shows the second Corridor he was constructing. It was an experiment he was trying; to see if he could push the surface out from the other side if he couldn't pull the surface. If he could pop the Bubble.

Sam keeps his reservations for himself. There is a slight fear that everything could go south if Lindsey walks through it and does manage to pop the Bubble. Sam was trying to work it out. If the Bubble was only able to be pushed, then pushing the surface in from the other side is more like pulling, but it's also pushing the surface but from the other side. It was a paradox, and it was not something that he could predict the results of.

Sara walks back into the core Bubble area to see what's going to happen when or if Lindsey emerges on the other side.

Lindsey smiles and yells, "Here I go!" The impression of Lindsey's face was still on the second tunnel he was burrowing. He walks forward creating a line from the Corridor to the Bubble; the third side of a triangle. "Still don't see you yet!" Lindsey hears Sara from inside. He keeps walking while waving his hands in front of him. Lindsey has created a clear screen. In front of him looked like a paper towel filled with grease. It was a thin membrane; a thin window where he can see in front of him.

Sam and Sara lean in and examine the thin membrane. "This is really weird," Sam says.

"Well. I'm coming through," Lindsey announces.

Anticlimactic. A disappointment. "Nothing happened," Sam noted. The surface did not push forward—or pulled towards them. It seemed more like emerging out of the surface of a pool or parting the vapor of a fog, where the medium surrounds the person.

"You made a donut," Sara observes. Lindsey cocked his head to the side, stares at her for a good section before blurting out, "What?"

Sara says again, "A donut has one hole in it. So you made a donut."

Sam scratches the back of his head. His sister usually says some far out things but this one just didn't make sense. Lindsey points his finger toward the direction of the Corridors. From above, it looks more like a lollipop than a donut according to him. Sara maintains that it's a donut because it has a hole through the center. Sam says a donut has the dough on the inside, and traces a circle with his index finger. Lindsey argues back that no, the Bubble wasn't a donut, and the dough—or, in his words "the good stuff" is not the Bubble. The Bubble was empty space.

The argument continues on between them, in overlapping voices. "What's the 'good stuff' inside the Bubble?" "A lollipop does NOT have a hole it's not a lollipop!" "What hole! What hole are you talking about there's no hole!" "I have to agree with Sara now, that's definitely a hole." "If it was a hole wouldn't it have popped; look at the size of the sphere and this giant slide inside here and look at that tiny cylinder of whatever space it takes up how is that a donut; a donut has an outside and inside there's no outside here." The arguing goes on for a bit. It's even escalated to animated arm and hand moves demonstrating different shapes. The crux of the argument was whatever inside or outside was, and in a way to differentiate if the inside of the Bubble was the dough of the donut or nothing.

Lindsey hovers over to the tunnel. He clips out the entire top part of the "hole" or "cylinder" (the naming would depend on how you view the circular space made by creating the third side of the Corridor) or any other name. The triangular boundary that had defined the hole was sawed off by Lindsey's travel through it. Now it's a spike that raises out of the ground but doesn't touch the ceiling, almost like an upside down stalactite. He yells, rather triumphantly as if he won any argument at all, "There! It's not a donut anymore."

Sara cuts through the bottom of the stalactite; turning it into a disc floating in mid air. She lands and announces, "Hah! It's a donut now."

Sam asks, "You guys ever notice how we can push the walls and ceiling, but not the floor?" They all nod. "Is that a floor too?" he asks. Sam points at the floating disc in front of them.

"Don't start," Lindsey says. He walks over pushing the floating disc in on itself from all sides until it was a small sphere dangling at about the height of his forehead. "Done with these arguments," Lindsey says. And with that said, he claps the small sphere.

In school, we've learned not to divide by zero. We were taught that push and pull were opposites. That North, South, East, West, Up, and Down were the only directions. That directions didn't include Inside and Outside.

It was true that if you clapped, there would still be the microscopic gaps in between the grooves of the skin and the space in between the hands. It would not have been enough to collapse the sphere. The sound, the pressure wave that pushes in on all directions, was enough force the sphere into a singularity. And then into nothing.

A violent expansion. The floor seemed to have stretched in all directions. The three of them try to fly back towards the center. It didn't seem like they could propel at all. It was not that they could not fly, but that everything was stuck in place. Their visions: they saw the Bubble dividing into multiple domes connecting to the main one. Like a straw blowing bubbles in milk, but they're on the inside. On the round surfaces of the emergent bubbles, it reflected their Bubble and every other bubble reflecting theirs. Multiplying again and again until the white glow of the Bubble is taken over by shadow; until the sum reflection of their bodies had darkened the glow of the Bubble; until the multiplying bubbles had snuffed out the light into infinity.

The same fear that Sam had felt, multiplied by three people...

It was completely tactile. And they floated. And who could have said if they were together or apart. There was no sound in the Field.

* * *

"Oh no. What happened. I shouldn't have clapped that sphere. Can't even see anything here," Lindsey thinks to himself. "I was still right though." Lindsey propels himself through the dark void. Objects impact onto him. Strings like net latches on him.

He stops moving. "Twelve sides—maybe. What is this thing? Twelve sides of five pentagrams. I have to put you together with something else. Didn't Sam say something about making a yo-yo?" Lindsey feels his arms stretching out in front of him, searching for a cylinder shape while holding onto his dodecahedron. He grabs onto a solid and rolls it between his finger tips and his palms to discern the shape from one hand. It's a disc. He tosses it away.

"Oh wait I have pants. Why didn't Sam tell us we have clothes here?" Lindsey stuffs the dodecahedron into his jean pocket.

He twirls a string around his finger, and puts that into his pocket too. Unlike the Bubble, this was a darkness that led to nowhere. "No one should end up in here."

A powerful wind gust pushes him. He feels shapes slam into him from behind, bounce into, ricochet off his skin.

"What was that?" A solid bounces off his forehead. It felt like the edge of a coin. It must've been a cylinder. He reaches blindly around him, taking great care to not accidentally push a solid out of the way before grabbing it.

A skinny cylinder. He wraps a string around it.

* * *

"Damn it Lindsey…is this…the Field you were talking about, Sam? Sam? Guess he's not around. Lindsey, you there?! Well, he's not here either." Spoken words that had no sound. Sara didn't even know that her words were only in her head.

A sphere lands into her hand. It's about halfway between a marble and a tennis ball; about the size of a golf ball where her fingers could wrap around it. She squeezes it delicately. It felt like an egg shell cracking. It multiples—not divides in two—into two of the same shape and size.

"How did Sam get out of here? You hit your head, didn't you. If I go fast enough…maybe I can knock myself back awake." She waves her hands around her for two reasons: to recognize the size of these shapes, and to understand the distribution of the shapes. It wasn't clear from Sam's recall if the shapes were densely packed or if they were sparse.

She continues squeezing the children of the sphere. Between the shell-cracking feeling and the multiplication of the spheres in her hand, it was a sensation not unlike popping bubble wrap. There was no doubt she was going to get out of here, so she took her time fidgeting with the spheres. It wasn't exponential in that way that every multiplication was in two's: 2, 4, 8, 16, etc. It was addition since she was just adding one sphere every time she "broke" one.

Then she stops. "Okay, back to the plan. Knock yourself out."

Flying in the Field was a different experience. It wasn't quite the air, but the way the wind felt. It was mist that touched her skin and evaporated through flight. It could have been shapes that dissolved on or off of her. Without a frame of reference, she might as well be in a wind tunnel. She could have sworn that the shapes began to take on light; a type of shimmering. The mindset was always that to fly faster, she had to let go of any thinking. The Field was trying to teach her a different way.

* * *

"I'm back here again." Sam gets to work. Minutes or even hours had passed while he tried to find a cylinder and string. Sam finds a shape. Six faces, all of them square. As he holds onto it, his fingers felt like they were stretched and torn off, but without pain. He touches his right hand with his left and confirms that indeed, his index finger was missing above the first two knuckles where it grabbed around the edge of the cube. He was calm because there was no consequence when you have the wishes. After all, Sara was able to heal her open fracture.

There's a condition called phantom limb where an amputee would still feel the missing limb. Sam felt both the phantom limb as a finger on his hand, and the sensation that his *missing finger* felt. And his missing finger was feeling the inside of the cube. And his missing finger felt like it was being turned around and around. Without a frame of reference, or sense of gravity, feeling direction was truly disorientating. The authentic and the phantom sensations converged again when the finger reattached onto his hand.

Sam holds the cube on his left hand and makes a fist with his right. His fingers were all there. The cube had sucked in his skin. Inside the touch blending cube, he felt every vertex and edge grinding against one another. He tried to parse out the cube's structure through what he felt. The cube was in this cyclic transformation, and it was definitely folding everything inside and unfolding back out.

This cube gave him an idea. Lindsey's Bubble had given him an idea. Something in his head told him he could *transform* the Field.

* * *

An in-depth concentration. She estimates the speed by the objects that hit her. To try to pay attention to each one. Like rarefied air in the sky that she flew in. To understand her place in the Field.

A light shines for a moment; like a sparkler. So intensely bright from a single point that long lines of shadows extrude out from each shape. The background was a gradient of dark to white. The shadows were arrows pointing her to the light. She turns her head to find the source right as it extinguishes. Even when the light had faded out of view, and only the afterimage of a red spot remained, she knew where it was.

A burst. An incredible haste to go there. Before the light leaves.

Faster than she had ever gone. The shapes that bounced off her felt like sharp fragments instead of dull punches. She chased the red afterimage. Going so fast that wind bursted into a ring around her; rippling out. A discontinuity so unnatural that it literally broke the sound barrier: the Field has sound now. A low-tone, almost imperceptible static becomes audible to the three of them.

Sara yawns to pop her ears.

Closer as she gets, she hears someone mumbling and muttering to himself. "If I shove this cube in here. Or maybe it goes here. That feels more right," he says. It was Sam, but this wasn't the source of the light.

"Sam!"

"Sara?"

"Did you see Lindsey?"

"No, I was trying to build something here."

Sara couldn't see what he was building. Who would build in the dark. He should be more concerned about getting out of here. "Did you see that flash of light?" Sara asks.

"No."

"Did you notice we can hear now?"

"No," he says. Sara hears his busy hands manipulating the shapes.

"Do you want to go find Lindsey?"

No response.

Sara calls out, "Lindsey!" Her voice goes out into the Field. The farther out it goes, the lower the sound becomes. The Field flashes into the spherical, starburst pattern of shadows again. Sam takes in the variety of shapes in the brief moment: spheres, cylinder, cones, a glimpse of the cube he has on hand—which was less a cube and more of two cubes folding in and out again in both directions, strings in loops and strings in lines. Sara scans the Field quickly for where the shadows are pointing to.

She grabs Sam. The wind ripples out again.

The shapes tumble into one another. Some of them coalesced. Where once the Field was still; there is now two apparent waves of motion. Sara's two sonic booms had set the shapes in motion. The waves moved in opposite directions so some of the shapes had collided and interacted; creating new objects. Cubes bounced off of cylinders and took on angular momentum.

The light has not gone out yet. The closer Sara goes to the light, the more it seems like the warm glow of the Bubble instead of the Field's vacuum. Light so bright that it fills the whole vision.

Division instead of multiplication. Lindsey looks at the light he created. The multiplied bubbles, the edges of these near-infinite bubble reflections are made visible. Lindsey thought of soap bubbles popping together. The light had begun to snuff out the shadow. The near-infinite reflections started converging. The reflections became more clear and *countable*. Lindsey's creation flickered its last light. Only this time, the warm light of the Bubble replaced the Field's darkness.

The floor that was stretched and elongated returns to its normal dimensions. The teens are standing, not floating, in the Bubble again.

"Damn! Almost had it," Sam still has his hands in front of him as if he were still constructing something.

"Well, I'm never doing that again," Lindsey looks at where he had collapsed the small sphere.

Sara catches her breath. "How long were we in there?" She pulls down on her wristband and looks at her wristwatch: six hours have passed. It's midnight. "We have to go Sam. It's midnight. Lindsay, we have to leave. I'll see you soon."

Lindsey watches them flicker out of the Bubble.

* * *

Sam and Sara are back on the highway. They take a long look at the stars overhead. They've never had so many back home. Never even had seen so many when they had camped. Sara tells Sam what happened to her in the Field, "I broke the sound barrier back there."

"I felt it," Sam says.

Contrary to what she had originally thought, it wasn't about being mindless to the flying. "We go faster if we pay attention," she tells him.

Sam nods. He takes out the GPS and judges the direction east. Sara takes off into the night sky. Sam looks back before taking off again. Sara must have been going at least twice as fast as before. She is a point among the stars. The sonic boom is becoming familiar when it does come.

Go home faster? Pay attention to what's around him? He couldn't get his mind off of what he was working on. He takes off in a sonic boom.

* * *

They had left the Bubble unexamined. When the Bubble multiplied and converged again, it transformed. Three corridors extend out from where Lindsey stood. Each corridor was about a mile long, with the same foam blocks lining the floor. He walked a minute into each corridor before returning into the Bubble. The Bubble was not the same, and it wasn't something he had *intentionally* done to it. Being lost in the Field was enough of an uncertainty that the same fear could infect your life.

A few moments have passed before Lindsey works up the courage to go all the way through one of the corridors. Coming through the corridor, he appropriated Sara's technique of spiraling through to save some effort. On the other side: a giant slide, a foam pit, a kitchen, a spiral ramp that goes around the circumference. He was not hallucinating. He definitely went through the corridor. On his right were two other corridors. He goes through the first one to his right. The same Bubble again; with the same corridors.

"If I keep going through these different corridors, I'm going to end up lost. I'll just go back to where I came from."

He made a wrong turn back. Although the bubbles seemed similar, the corridors were in different orientations. He may not have noticed, but although the layout of the foam pit, kitchen, slide, etc were the same; where he had entered in relation to them and where the corridors were in relation to the layout were different. It would have been easy to go the wrong way.

"I'll investigate this sometime later." Lindsey stares at the light to exit.

And Lindsey made the easy mistake of going the wrong way.

Red and blue lights flash around his vision. It was Sam and Sara's basement. The same washer and dryer. He closes his eyes and re-enters the Bubble. He walks in a U to go through another corridor. He exits. It's not the highway. It's his room from New York. More specifically, from his closet.

A little girl's voice speaks up, "Is someone there?"

"Crap," Lindsey mutters to himself.

Process of elimination. Just go to what you haven't gone to yet. Another bubble, another exit. This time, his room in California. A small victory, but that's not where he needed to go. A black marker from his bedroom table. This will be useful. He goes back into the Bubble. He stands in the middle of the three corridors, and judges his sight line on the floor. With large arm wide strokes, he writes "California Room" on the ground.

He goes through one corridor, then another. Sam and Sara's basement again. He writes on the entrance, "Dusk House."

This was where he needed to go. He's back on the highway. High above ground, he follows cylindrical holes in the clouds.

Two separate trails follow out the clouds. The holes turned into white contrails against the moonlight. One contrail started earlier than the other. There is a break in the longer contrail. A ring of condensation had fallen over time. A sonic boom must've occurred here. He hovers there. He was not going to be able to catch up and tell them he has a shorter way back.

He stood inside a bubble; and there was another bubble replica in front of him. The floor had started sliding towards the other bubble. The two domes were coming together. The giant two slides were merging into one. However, he noticed that the bubble he was in did not have "Highway" on the floor. It wasn't the same bubble. Lindsey felt it around him. It wasn't a double vision becoming focused, it was a focusing of material.

Nevertheless, he had to go home. Going through the corridors, and getting lost in them was a) a waste of time since each corridor was a mile long and even though he flew, it still took a minute or two, and b) an annoyance. He made a mental note to create signs when he would come back.

* * *

"No. We don't know where they are."

"They're usually home by 7."

"Yes. We called all their friends. They're not there."

"They're usually at the park in the afternoon. Yes. Yes. They weren't there either."

"I don't know."

"Cammy," Bradley hands her a cup of coffee.

"Blue shoes. Yeah. Sam has blue shoes. Sara wears red."

At 2am, the lights are on in Sam and Sara's rooms. They stare at clothes to see what isn't there. They leave for work early. Usually, they would see their kids still in their night clothes. Old t-shirts and pants. They hadn't noticed the large rubber storage box with its lid ajar, with missing hoodies in the middle of summer.

Backpacks were gone. Photos? Who has photos of their kids backpacks? Can't you do anything?

Camille gets her keys.

"Where are you going?"

"I'm going to find them."

"We've been around already."

The coffee is wearing off at 4am. The police are still standing outside. The red and blue lights are still swirling around. There's only so much two parents can do. They've already mobilized their network to look for their kids: friends, friends of friends, family, extended family, police.

"I never knew that when I met you, we would have a life together. I couldn't have imagined children. I remember them being born. Their tiny heartbeats in my palm..."

"I had dreams months before she was born. They told me she'll be a boon to this world. And she would be a gift. A precious one. Bradley, I need to find them, but I'm so tired. I'm so tired. I don't know what else to do."

"Cammy, we'll find them. We'll find them. They're our kids. They'll be fine. They're our kids."

They reminisce about them until the spacing between words became long and the words no longer came. The father and mother held each other until they fell asleep on the couch.

* * *

Diving through the clouds, the warm air rising from the ground. Red and blue lights flashing like a pulsar. Worry, not for them, but for their parents. Less a free fall than a concentrated effort in landing fast and quick. Their backyard becomes a landing pad. Their landing throws dust through the open, screened windows. Sounds like thunder break through into the house.

Running through the rooms. To just see if their parents were okay. A crash from the front door.

Camille and Bradley open their eyes in a half sleep to their two children in fall clothes, and the two policemen in front of them. Camille's heart is beating out of her chest. Bradley felt like he had aged twenty years in a moment when he felt that he was out of season, his kids standing tall before him, the police by their side, in an unfamiliar room.

"Mom. Dad..." Sara spoke.

"Is everything okay?" Sam finished her sentence.

A situation that was felt on the opposite end. It was reunion. A faint memory in old times. But this time, it was a reunion *for them*. Bradley and Camille clutches their kids close. No questions for now, they were just glad that they returned.

The two policemen had questions for the two kids. The parents asked the police to leave. Their children were back. What else mattered? The policemen searched around the house for the source of the gunshot. None was found.

* * *

Lindsey pops in from the Bubble into the Dusk's basement. Bradley thought he saw a ghost from the corner of his eye. Bradley rubs his eyes again. Lindsey is gone. Bradley asked the empty air, "What was that?"

Two weeks since he has left Brooklyn, he returns on a sunny afternoon.

A child, a girl about seven years old, in his old room asks Lindsey, "Where did you come from? I thought you were a monster." She holds a doll and continues brushing its hair.

"Uh...you never saw me," Lindsey opens the window and jumps out. Walking through the old streets, he tried to imagine where Sam and Sara were. He had not seen Sara or Sam online, and when he called, their parents said they were grounded. His parents had been working that night that he came home late, and had lost track of time to call Lindsey. No repercussions for him. Not a lot of parents would leave their only child to fend for himself, but he could be trusted. Besides, they knew he'll be at the beach skateboarding. They didn't know that he had started flying over to South America during the day. They didn't know that he had been logging his flight times and velocity. They didn't know that when they had called him, he had a *magical* cell phone that has the same phone number as his home phone.

They didn't know that he had been sleeping in late, having nightmares with cold sweats. He could only talk about it with Sam and Sara. To make some sense.

* * *

"Yeah. Our parents were glad that we weren't missing but..." Sam pulls a book from the cart: 616.895 B. He scans the Dewey Decimal Code and looks closely at the row of books above him. He inserts the book between two books. "We had breakfast at a diner. Then my mom asked Sara where we were."

"What did she say?" Lindsey asks.

Sam continues putting the books back on the shelves.

"Uh. We didn't get home until 6 am. She was probably coming up with an excuse from the moment we landed. So that was... two hours. I'm sure she was still thinking about it while eating eggs and bacon."

"Okay, but what did she say?"

"She said we were playing hide and seek and lost time."

"That's not a great excuse. I mean, really? Where is Sara?"

"Well. After she said that, my dad looked disappointed at us. My mom did too. They knew we were lying, but it didn't seem like they were worried," Sam takes a book from the top of the cart and puts it into the middle shelf of his cart. It didn't belong in the 900's. "So my mom told us that we're not to spend the day at home. That she wants us to volunteer at the library and go to our grandma's house. And we'll take turns. And we can't go anywhere else because she's going check in on us. Fun's over for the summer."

"What if you make them forget?" Lindsey asks him.

"That doesn't seem right."

"Just a suggestion."

"You wouldn't make your parents forget, would you? What if someone did that to you?" Sam is thrown off center. "I mean this is my mom and dad. It's just not right."

Lindsey changes the subject, "Sorry dude. We need another way of talking. I got a cellphone. Maybe you could get one too?"

Sam calms down after putting another two books back in their place, "How about telepathy? You know, mind communication."

"I don't really want you inside my head."

"It'll be fun."

"I'm going to wake up screaming because you're going to decide to scream in my mind one of these nights."

"I don't scream. When have you ever heard me yell?"

"I guess not. So what are you going to do after you're done with this cart?"

"Read some of my summer reading. There's an adult computer class coming in later. Librarians make me help them."

"This just sounds like work."

"I get a break where I can go get pizza."

"Can you still sneak out at night?"

"That's the thing that sucks. Sara figured out how to break Mach 1. We can get to places faster, but what's the point if we can't go anywhere."

"Well, that's kind of why I came."

"You flew here right? Must have taken a while."

"I didn't fly here," Lindsey smirks.

Sam extends his arm and criss crosses them in a scissor motion across Lindsey. He wasn't astral projecting like Sam thought he was. So what was he talking about? A librarian walks over and says in a low voice, "Sam, you can take your break now."

* * *

"I watched Grandma knit for four hours. Four hours, Sam!" Sara tears into a garlic knot. "I don't think I can do this much longer. I want to be outside. It's summer! Mom said, 'You're going to learn about service.' and then Dad said," Her face turns stern and she stands up looking over at Lindsey, " 'You heard the boss. You get your pick of the library or Grandma's.' "

"I spent the entire morning looking at book numbers. I read books but I might need to get glasses after today," Sam sprinkles pepper on top of his pizza. Sam and Sara look at Lindsey, anticipating his complaint.

"Uh. Parents didn't even know I was gone. I woke up an hour ago, ate yogurt, and then came here," Lindsey says.

"Wait, one hour ago?" Sara piqued up, "What do you mean *one hour ago?*"

"You guys want to travel tonight?" Lindsey asks them; clearly withholding information.

Sara pushes the issue, "Not again. Last time it took us like four hours to get back. But what do you mean one hour ago?"

"Tehehehe. Here you go. Sorry about holding you back. If it wasn't for me trying to prove you wrong, you guys wouldn't be grounded," Lindsey touches his fingertip to Sara's. "Sorry for ruining your summer."

"Don't worry about it. So what do you mean one hour ago?" Sara presses.

Lindsey tells them, "You'll see tonight."

They spent the rest of the half hour together talking about games they're looking forward to on different consoles. On cartoons. If Lindsey had fallen on his ass lately skateboarding. If Sam and Sara were having fun, which they obviously were not.

Then lunch was over. Lindsey flies over to NJ; just far enough that the Verrazzano Bridge was the size of a postage stamp. Far enough that the bubble would not merge back into the other bubbles.

* * *

Sam goes to sleep early at 9pm. Not because of volunteering at the library for five hours, but because he needed to dream. During dinner, he asked his mom if there was anything that could change an entire environment.

"Like a desert into a forest? Not that I know of. Tiny organisms might be able to change things. Uhm. There's something else..." Mom said.

"Do you mean terraforming?" Dad chimed in.

"That's the word. Terraforming." His mom talks about it. An old idea that a whole planet can be transformed. Astronauts could land on other planets, and then set up a machine to transform its atmosphere, its ecology, its geology to make it habitable.

"Oh," Sam said.

Sara looked at her brother. What was he thinking about? He was definitely considering something. Only thing that came to her mind was the word *arrogant*. Good thing she was holding onto the wish for now.

* * *

In the dark Field, he assembles the string and cylinder. He lights it up. He collects other cylinders and strings. It's a work station in zero gravity. Points of light surround him like Christmas lights without the strings. It was enough light that he was able to see the surroundings. He gathers the other shapes. Quick! What were the shapes again?!

A sphere. The transforming cube. Strings. He finds these shapes. Like writing an essay or solving a math equation whose solution is just slightly out of reach…he forces the sphere into the cube. Under the light, it's clear how the cube was grinding the sphere in its interior. Two spheres come out. Because those two spheres still had touched the cube, they become four spheres. An exponential increase. Sam peers through the illuminated cocoon he was in. The shapes were still moving in opposite waves. He does *hear* its motion. It has the same tone as still clouds. It sounds the way the sky does: an emptiness, a vacuum with cloud moisture that gives it a quality that can only be described as soft. Would the Field sound like waves if it had more shapes that collided?

The strings he had collected tangles itself into the spheres. It was a topological/geometric perpetual motion machine. Under the glow of his light bubble, he was witnessing all these shapes become alive. The strings branched onto the spheres like roots, or vines, or a weed. The cube keeps breaking apart the spheres and creating identical ones. The strings continue growing.

Sam didn't notice at first but the Field seemed less a void. He looks outside his lit workstation, and he couldn't be sure, but he could barely make out the edges of shapes.

* * *

Lindsey leads them through the Bubble network. "Uh, don't try to get out anywhere. I don't know if you can come back in. I also don't want to go out and fetch you. Also don't try to force me to grab you. I don't need any other places popping up here. Not any that I didn't add. Every place that gets added creates a whole new set of tunnels in every other place. Tunnels which I have to start marking. Seven places are fine. If I start adding more. When is it ever going to end?" Lindsey continues talking at a hundred miles an hour. They walk through a tunnel, and see "South America" on the floor.

Lindsey explained to them how the network functioned. It's different experiencing an exit. Usually, when they exited, it had always been at the same place they had entered. To emerge out of a place they do not recognize was the same as waking up in a strange place.

Streetlights are bright on Avenida Revolucion. Groups of people in clusters of ten, eight, five move along talking; laughing. Heels click-clack along the tile streets. Colorful paper flags are strung high from street to street. They sway in the wind. The three teens sit outside. Tacos flow over the brim of their paper plates. Glass soda bottles catch the shimmer of car headlights.

"What use is money if you can wish for anything?" Lindsay asks Sara. Sara had used her wish for an ATM card. Inside the financial systems that accounted for every dollar and cent, an account had been opened in her name. Databases and numbers and computer code were updated. Dollars materialized in vaults to back the funds that were in Sara's name. Consistency was maintained in materializing her wish; even while the money was fake. A moment later, the ATM card appeared in her hand and the PIN number in her memory.

"Wishing for tacos isn't the same as ordering it. Is it?" Sara asks him.

Lindsey looks at the palm trees swaying. "But it's still the same thing isn't it? Eating tacos?"

"Buying it feels different from wishing for it. Like you're trading for things. Giving thanks for things. I think," she says.

Another group of friends line up outside the restaurant's pick up window. Lindsey tells her, "I don't know. I think if you have wishes, you don't need money."

Sam only ate one taco. He notices a woman who was staring at them from the time they sat down. She walks over. Lindsey and Sara turn to her. The woman says, "Hey, uh, where are your parents? You three shouldn't be alone."

Lindsey begins to speak, but Sara intervenes, "They're at the hotel over there. We told them we headed down here for food."

"Oh, okay." The woman walks back to where she came from, says a few words to her boyfriend or husband, then walks off in another direction. The boyfriend keeps his eyes on them.

"So, South America," Sam starts.

"What?" Lindsey responds.

"South America," Sam repeated himself.

Sara turns around in her chair and places the plate of tacos on her lap. She studies the geography of the place: the inclined roads which Lindsey hadn't noticed but would be great for skateboarding, the low buildings which allows a sight line to the arch monument, the bend that continues the street in a different direction. The art of stores' signage. The mingling of different cultures.

She didn't notice that Sam was teasing Lindsey for getting South America wrong. Mexico was not South America. Sam lectures on, "South America is like Peru or something." Lindsey conceded pretty quickly.

The woman returns with two policemen. She points them to the teens. The three of them walk slowly over to a trashcan and dump their plates. The policemen's pace quickens. The three of them pick up their pace too. They run into an alley and disappear from their sights.

They land in a secluded area south of Tijuana. Sam takes out the GPS from Sara's backpack. The screen is grayed out, with "No map available for the region" on the screen. Lindsey used Sara's method of locating interesting places by their light pollution. He didn't need a map or a GPS. The only place he could get lost in was the Bubble, and even then it was easy to find his way back.

The green glow of Sara's watch illuminates her face. They could probably travel an hour or so before returning home and catch some sleep. Running from the police and walking around in circles in Tijuana had disoriented them. They huddle around Sara while she points her flashlight at the compass. In the beginning, she had always oriented the red arrow to match up with the north on the compass. Then she had to remind herself where the other directions were. Now she just pulls the compass out, and knows every other cardinal direction. If she had been able to navigate by the sky, she wouldn't need the compass. If she had looked up, she would have seen Polaris. If she had flown North instead of South, she would have noticed the North Star that she was inadvertently chasing. And if she could have lived forever, the stars would shift and the constellations would no longer be the same, the earth's magnetic poles would move. If she could have lived forever, she would have to find new methods to find true north.

Polaris to her back, she flies south.

It wasn't enough to go due South. They could fly over the Pacific. Instead, they trace the coastlines.

Sara's wristwatch beeps. One hour is up. They go back into the Bubble. Lindsey goes through each room. He marks each location. Lindsey watches them disappear from the Bubble and go back to their house.

* * *

Summer had become a continuous string of late-to-start days, sleepless nights and vivid dreams. Traveling without end. Building something in his mind. Taking a nap on high mountains in a parka. They were moving to California, so why would they bring a parka? Sunglasses with mirrored lenses reflect the sky in golden tints. He had put on an inordinate amount of sunscreen. But that was more because of the California sun on his skin than for the thin atmosphere on the mountaintop. A book from the local library sticks out from Lindsey's backpack, which he had borrowed. He had wanted to take a large geography book from the reference section, but he settled for a book on South America. The book will be returned with snow-soiled pages.

His mouth is agape while he dreams. The bright sun reflects in a starburst on his sunglasses.

Inside his fever dream, Lindsey imagines the squiggly lines from his eyes being projected out. Being removed from him. But simultaneously they were already there floating. Heat. Light was heat. The entoptic phenomena were braids and knots. Edison bulbs with their coils. These eye floaters reminded Lindsey of organisms moving underneath a microscope. He looks at them with a deep intent. If he could concentrate enough, they would move to each other. These lines and strings are magnetized to each other. They touch and pulse. A sort of bioluminescence. That would be the word to use if these shapes were alive. He remembers. He has already gone through these steps.

He breathes into the void. Because to get these shapes even closer together, they should be compressed. Yes, like an object stuck inside a balloon. Or like a person in deep water. He cups his hands around the shapes and breathes into the tiny space. Rays of light spill out through the gaps in his fingers. His hands glow red. The light was so bright that bones become visible in between his pulsing veins.

The light is extinguished again. Again.

Somewhere in the dark, he searches for his other dying star.

Flying through the Andes Mountain, the cold passes him. There simply was not enough time for his body heat to be lost. He followed Sara's directions. To view his flight path with intention. Ice crystals fall behind his sonic boom. He didn't think much of what he is doing. He struck out new locations, creating new waypoints in the Bubble while Sam and Sara were grounded. Years from now, he would look back and realize that he was not only a pioneer. He was more.

In his college years, he would have an epiphany dangling from a cliff. He'll have a tank top drenched with sweat, a hammer, a drill, rope and clips hanging from his hip. After setting one clip into the rock face, he'll rappel down to install another. When he was younger, he couldn't describe the geometry of the Bubble network. With all the places he made into waypoints, he couldn't visualize how all the corridors could not interfere or overlap. The clips traced one route up the cliff. He'll install the clips all the way down the rock face. At the bottom, his belayer will give him a fist bump. Lindsey'll put his tools back into his chalk-dusted gym bag. All afternoon, members of the rock climbing club will go up and down the clips he had put into the rock. He will remember his youth, but in a way that gives him a different perspective. Rock climbing will remind him that they were humans crawling along an ancient thing.

He reaches a mountain peak that was warm. It started drizzling. Lindsey reaches inside his parka and unfolds his binoculars. He puts his parka over him to cover himself from the rain. Mist rolls off the parka. He didn't want to go any farther than he did. He'll save the actual journey there with his friends. Before disappearing back into the Bubble and creating another waypoint, he takes a second look at Machu Picchu.

* * *

A loud snap. It might have been wood. Sara hears the echo propagate through the sky. She slows for an instant, scanning through the dark night.

You're falling. You're frozen in mid-air. No, not frozen. Falling so slowly. Rushing over these cliffs. A tiny moment. Instants. An instant to save your life. I have to go faster than I've ever had before.

From afar, Sam and Lindsey see her vanish. She must have disappeared into the Field like in Sam's first flight. She didn't.

She didn't vanish.

The world is wrapping around me. The world looks like it's covered in blue. I notice you closely. Your friends are reaching to save you.

They're leaning too far forward. You're not even grabbing the ledge. Your friends are going to fall too if I don't come in an instant...

There was a blue bloom that is dissipating from where Sara "disappeared". The bloom was an explosion of blue light. It fades from view like gas dispersing until the blue bloom was the same dark velvet as the night sky. And who could say if it was actual material that had dispersed or an after-image of luminance.

Your backpack strap peels away from you. I see you trying to grab the ledge. Your eyes are on the ledge. Your hands are outstretched but you're not going to reach. The wood plank that you were using to cross the gap. It's right below you. Your feet still touching both halves. I'm almost there. Splinters are frozen in mid-air. It looks almost like glitter.

"No!" Isla yells. Instinctively, she throws herself forward to grab Eric. Fiona holds onto Isla's arm. In a crucial moment, a bright light flashes from their periphery. Their biological instinct betrays them. For a split second, they looked away to the blue bloom and they missed their window of time to grab Eric's wrist. Even in Isla's and Fiona's point of view, time had begun to slow down.

The world is fully blue. I reach him. It looks like they were crossing a wood plank across a gap. The weight didn't support him. I caught him!

The momentum carries her straight into the wall of the mountain. A pile of dust explodes out from the impact of Sara and Eric against the wall. They both ricochet from the wall. Eric bounces like a rag doll off the wall. He loses his grip on Sara. Sara manages to catch Eric's hand. The dust swirls in a spiral downwards almost like a tornado. Sara is grabbing onto Eric while he drags her down. She's falling so fast to the bottom. Eric was caught in a type of spin. Sara is pulling Eric up, or trying to. Eric weighs about 160 lbs. For a teen, for anyone, to hold up a person of 160lbs on one arm, their shoulder would be strained. Sara's shoulder dislocated.

What was that pop?

Sara screams when she notices.

Isla watches from on top of the gap. The girl was like a sycamore seed spinning down.

I can't hold on any longer. I'm losing my concentration to fly. "We're going to fall. I'm sorry."

They start plummeting. Quick. Sara has lost all control. The far fall to the ground is nearer. Sara screams. Sam knew that it was her scream. He speeds up. The world closes onto the gap. Lindsey follows close behind. Isla and Fiona hears two loud explosions from the same direction as the blue bloom. This time, they do not look. In the dark night, Sara and Eric had fallen below their sight.

Lindsey and Sam couldn't cover the distance in time.

Sara and Eric had fallen to the ground.

Lindsey and Sam see two figures standing on the edge.

Two missiles with contrails seem to be launching towards them. Fiona is paralyzed; looking down at the abyss. Isla turns her head towards the projectiles. Eric has fallen and has probably died. And two missiles are coming to obliterate the mountain. Isla is stuck in some terrible dream. The missiles arrive.

The person, who she'll learn as Sam, asks her "Did you see a girl about this high?"

Fiona points down. Isla crouches down and peers down into the chasm. These two kids told them not to worry. Why should Isla and Fiona worry about them? After all, the two kids managed to fly here. The two boys jump off into the chasm.

"Your wrist, a bone is sticking out of it," Eric tells Sara.

Sara shrugs, but also winces when she says, "Happened before. It's no big deal. Are you hurt?" Eric holds onto his ankle. It's twisted, but that wasn't a problem. The problem would be to get back up there. He yells to his friends up above, but his voice does not carry. A few feet away, the cliff drops off again. Sara looks over to the outside of the mountain. She sees two sonic booms with contrails leading to the top of the gap. Eric studies Sara for a second. He asks, "Where did you come from?"

She didn't hear the question. She stands up. Her right hand clutches her left shoulder. Eric watches her feet rise off the ground. She drops out of the air. The weight of her arm pulls down on her dislocated shoulder. The pain doubled by her open wrist fracture. Rising upwards has the same effect as going on an elevator—it had made her arm feel like it was being dragged down. "Won't be doing that. My friends will come," she says.

A faint, diffused orange light searches across the ground. Sara peers up and looks at the orange dot. If it was a helicopter searchlight, she would need to put her hands over her eyes to cover the blinding light. But the light was far from blinding, or even effective. She knew it was a red plastic flashlight taken from her kitchen drawer. She waves her hand, the weak light barely shining on her. The teens are lower now. Lindsey shines the light directly in Eric's eye. When Lindsey pulls the light away, Eric sees a red afterimage. Sam walks over to Sara. Both the red afterimage and the dark masks Sam's healing of Sara. Sam looks over to Eric and touches his ankle, then Sam puts his hand on Lindsey's shoulder.

Lindsey looks away from Eric and mumbles something underneath his breath. "Hey uh...I'm Lindsey. Are you okay? Okay, it looks like you are. So just climb this ladder over back to the top okay? We'll be right behind you to make sure you don't fall again." The faint flashlight moves to shine on the ladder. Lindsey hits the flashlight on the side when it flickers. Lindsey tells Eric, "Let's go then."

The three teens glide behind Eric. Occasionally, Lindsey shines on the next step of the ladder. Eric presses down onto the ladder with his foot to test his ankle stability. It's strong. It's better than it has been for years.

"What just happened?" Isla asks. Fiona leans against the mountain face. They were walking along a narrow path that had a drop on one side. Both of them look out at the two rings from the sonic booms. Eric's hands crawl out of the chasm. He sits there. Dumbfounded. The three teens fly over to the opposite end of the chasm.

From Fiona, Isla, and Eric's point of view, one of the teens touches another one. Lindsey taps Sara's hands. A rumble in the mountain. The older triplet feels the ground shift and sway just slightly back and forth. They hold onto each other. Rocks, earth, soil, and trees slid down like raging waters. Pebbles skip down and bounce off like hard raindrops—making similar sounds as they tumble. Large tree roots slide across the surface as if caught in a flood. Boulders clash into each other; clapping like thunder. But the flow of the dirt, the debris wasn't loud. It was terrifying because it has the same low, heart-shaking rumbling of a thunderstorm about to break. The chasm, the ladder, the plank all gets filled up. The debris was packed tightly, too. There was no chance of a second rock slide or accidental fall by another person.

The younger triplet was even more stunned than the older triplet. This is the first wish where the kids have seen the enormous possibility of what they can reckon. Not one of them had a word to say to the other.

Sara walks on the new path that now connects them to the other side, "Hi, I'm Sara."

Eric begins to walk forward to introduce himself. Isla steps forward. She looks deep into Sara's eyes. This little girl was only a bit shorter than she was. She stares at Sara: her ponytail, her backpack, her ordinary clothes. Isla wipes her brow, and props up her glasses. She brings her lantern closer to Sara's face. Sara averts her eyes for an instant. Cautiously but also confident enough to not telegraph her caution, Isla extends her hand, "Thank you. I'm Isla." Isla flips Sara's hands over examining it closely.

While Isla was with Sara, Lindsey and Sam introduced themselves to Eric and Fiona. Eric, Fiona, and Isla were recent graduates. They planned a hike to Machu Picchu before heading off to different schools. They wanted to go their own path far from the crowds. Which meant unmarked trails, and without a porter to carry their gear. But that was fine for them. They had a day until they reach Agua Calientes, a stop-gap town, before ascending to Machu Picchu. They chose this route. The shortest route was up through this mountain, and then down. There was urgency to their travel since they were a bit behind schedule and had to hurry to make it back for their flight. In this urgency, they made a few compromises and choices like crossing this particular plank.

After introductions, there was a prolonged silence. What are they supposed to say to the ones who rescued them? To these kids who looked so ordinary, but clearly not. How was one supposed to reckon with something so *magical?*

"Uh. I guess I was a bit arrogant back there. Sorry for all this trouble I caused you all," Eric pointed to the filled in area.

Fiona: "How are you? How did you? You three can *fly?*" She rubs her eyes.

"You have to excuse Fiona. She's heading to flight school. But how can you?" Isla asked.

There wasn't a way to respond without giving away the secret of the wishes. They could trust one another, but these were strangers. "Hey, do you guys need a lift to what was that town? Agua...we can get you there quickly," Lindsey says. Lindsey was eager to bring them into the Bubble, to get them to where they need to go, but not to share the wish.

It was okay that the younger three didn't want to share their secret.

Fiona: "That's all right. It only counts if we get there ourselves."

Eric: "We like to earn our way there."

Isla: "You three have done enough. We're thankful, really. But uh," She turns to Fiona and Eric. "We don't have much, but maybe you can eat dinner with us. We should be bumping into a small town soon to restock. It's no problem. We'll set up a fire in a safer spot."

The teens accept the offer. Isla looks down at her map, up at the sky, and back at the map again. They find their way into the trail again—or lack of. The older triplet picks up tiny twigs, branches, loose wood. Fiona sets up three hammocks in between trees. Isla places rocks in a circle. Eric ignites the wood. Sam and Sara have gone camping with their parents before, but never had to carry their belongings on their backs before. The three is a well oiled machine working in sync to ready noodles, cutlery, bowls without speaking.

Lindsey was about to make a move to wish for more food, but Sara stops him.

Wrapped by the warmth of the fire, they sit inside a small bubble of orange light. Eating food that was scarce. Eric offered some information about themselves. They graduated from Florida State University. Fiona received a Bachelor's in mechanical engineering and is heading to the Air Force. Isla studied anthropology for her undergrad, and heading off abroad to study in Italy for a few years. And Eric, he himself was looking to get his Master's in biology up in the northeast.

Lindsey slurps on the noodles—pretty loudly too.

"Our mom's a biology professor. Where are you going?" Sam asks.

Eric replies back, "Um. Where was it? I'm still a bit disoriented. I'm heading to New Paltz College."

Sam says, "Oh...our mom works at Cornell."

Fiona to Sara and Lindsey, "Those two rings back there. I... uh...heard loud sounds. Were those sonic booms?"

Lindsey tells her, "Yeah, sonic booms. Sara taught me. Well, taught us."

Fiona asks, "How does it feel?" Fiona turns to Sara with wide eyes, "Breaking the sound barrier?"

Sara thinks about it for a second. She responds, "Like a roller-coaster that keeps going down."

"If you can't tell, I can't wait to fly an airplane," Fiona is entranced.

Lindsey asks Fiona, "What's so cool about airplanes?"

Fiona to Lindsey, "You like cars?"

Lindsey: "Uh...I like skateboards."

Sam to Eric: "What are you going to concentrate on?"

Fiona: "You know that rumbling that happens when you go really quick? Like you're almost about to lose control?"

Eric: "Well. For me, it was either curing tinnitus or studying plant life grown in microgravity."

Sam: "Why microgravity?"

Lindsey: "Yea. It's pretty fun."

Fiona: "But imagine that feeling flying to Mars. On a rocket. Just leaving Earth!"

Sara: "What does an anthropologist do?"

Isla: "They study...humans. Not just biology, but humans and society. Almost like history but more...it's studying where we came from, and where we could go."

Sara: "Oh, so like psychohistory from Asimov's books."

Isla: "Oh, you read the Foundation series?"

Sara: "I borrowed it from my brother."

And like that the conversation splinters into separate ones—at times one of them interjects or answers a question from another conversation. Isla peers over at Sam who's in deep conversation with Eric on how Eric's going to study microgravity without heading to the ISS. Fiona explains aeronautic principles and cosmic velocities to Lindsey. Sara and Isla are engrossed in conversation on anthropology and what it means for the future.

Isla: "How did you all become friends?"

Sara: "Well Sam is my brother and we've known Lindsey since we were babies."

Lindsey: "How did you all meet?"

Eric pauses and laughs, "Star Trek fan club." Even though they hadn't said anything, the younger triplet did not think of the older triplet as people who watched Star Trek. Sam watched Star Trek. Sara usually watched a few episodes of the Next Generation before Saturday afternoon movies. The older three have aspirations of space travel. Out there, there is a possibility of unimaginable adventure. Backpacking was practice. There was something in the thrill of improvising as you go, and in succeeding. It was finding comfort in scarcity or rather finding pride—that you could hold your own against the universe. It was to find humanity's place in the stars and to share it with the world.

Fiona was hungry to reach the stars. Isla and Eric had no hurry. They believed that there will still be mass space travel within their lifetimes. Eric had a notion of how to grow high yield plants on space stations. He wanted to become a "space farmer." Isla wanted to go to space, but was less in a rush than either of them. She would be fine with visiting the moon. Her primary interest in the moment was people on earth.

Isla: "But if aliens come, I'll be ready to figure them out."

Eric chuckles, "You already speak their language." He turns to the teens, "I'm not going to be an adult and ask what you guys wanna do. What do you guys like?" Eric drinks from his water canteen.

Sara: "Does TV count? I watch too much TV. I like late night comedy."

Fiona: "Did you guys watch the Friends finale?"

Lindsey did. Isla chimes in that her guilty pleasure was video games. Even after Eric or Fiona would leave her room, she would still play till early morning on Friday night to Saturday. They relate funny stories of how they bested each of their friends in games. Fiona yawns. Sam follows. There was so little energy to talk about the things they loved most. Conversation is slowing down. The moon had passed over them.

Isla checks her wristwatch and walks away to a clearing in the trees. Sara watches her walk away from camp.

The four of them broke into separate conversations again: Fiona and Lindsey on adrenaline sports; and Sam and Eric on things they read from Scientific American. Isla was still gone. Sara slowly walks away while the four of them are still enwrapped in their conversations. She walks into the dark forest, lost.

"Sara, is that you? I'm over here."

Sara follows Isla's voice. She comes into a clearing on the side of the mountain. Moonlight washed over the trees on the mountains. The blue light gave form and dimension to the landscape. Each mountain going back into the distance becomes more darker— like someone cut out paper mountains of different blue shades. A strong gust makes the faraway trees shake like an ocean wave.

Isla asks Sara, "Did you ever think moonlight could be so bright?"

Sara didn't have any words.

"What you three are able to do...there were two sonic booms. But before that, there was a flash of blue light. I was distracted by it before Eric slipped." Both of them stare at the blue mountain range. Isla asks Sara, "Was that you?"

Sara didn't say anything. Isla checks her wristwatch. It's close to 3am. Or about 2am Peru time. They've been talking over the campfire for 2 hours. Looking behind, Isla can still see the orange embers in the fire.

Sara: "Maybe. I don't know."

She pauses, looks at Sara, and back out into the mountain range. "In every culture..." Isla pauses, trying to consider her words. "Sara. There are many cultures in the world...who share the same idea of..." She stops again. Sara sees Isla's brows furrow, her lips move without saying anything. "There used to be an ancient culture near Australia. They were sea-faring. They traveled from island to island trading. Uh, jewels, gems, precious metals, food. They would gift away large gems and jewelry to strengthen their ties with other island-nations. But they don't exist anymore. We only know about them from other culture's records, songs, poems."

"Sounds like Atlantis," Sara says.

"It does, doesn't it? You know what colonialism is?"

Sara recalls World History from last year's classes, or what she remembers of it. "Yeah."

Isla continues, "Out of all the islands in the archipelago, their island was the only one which had these precious metals. Trading ships from Europe came to the northern islands first. They've noticed that these islands had these giant golden flower sculptures with jewels inlaid into them. All fashioned in the same style, even though each island's art was different from each other. Guides from one island-nation led them to the rich island. These trading companies saw the ores that were available. Then they returned to Europe."

Isla asks Sara, "Can you guess where this story goes?"

Sara has already finished the story in her mind when Isla said they returned to Europe. They came back to the archipelago, took over the lands, the people, their resources. Wiped out their culture, their ring of trade and gifting.

Sara answers, "They took everything."

Isla asks, "Do you know what I'm saying?"

Sara understood. She didn't say yes or no to Isla. But Sara's mind turns elsewhere. The ring of trade. Origins. Something upstream.

Isla advises Sara, "Be careful." They stand looking at the mountain range for a moment.

Sara asks Isla, "Um. When I fly. Usually when I try to find new places with a map, I have to tell the cities apart by their light pollution. And then I have to use a compass to figure my way back home. How did you know the direction you were going on the map without a compass?"

Isla smiles. "The same way you do it. But my lights are up there. See the red one over there? Yeah. That's Mars. That way is West. So now you know the other directions. Oh yeah. The North Star. Since we're not too South, you can only see it during twilight. In the South, you usually use the Southern Crux." Isla draws the different constellations into the dirt. "Well now you know how not to get lost."

Sara replies, "Well, not at night anyhow."

Meanwhile, Eric uses a trowel to smother the fire. Fiona asks how the younger three are going to get back to where they came from. They have a way. Eric and Fiona didn't push for an answer.

Fiona tells Sam and Lindsey, "You all can change the world if you want to."

"Don't put that on them," Eric replies.

Fiona: "They can."

Fiona and Eric definitely figured out that these teens' skill set was not limited in any way. Fiona continues, "Well, you *will*. You don't have to change the world *now*."

Sam and Lindsey stand in silence. The wind shakes the trees around them. "Maybe," Sam says.

Lindsey asks them, "But if you want to change the world, why are you going to outer space? Like aren't there people here on earth too?"

"That's very perceptive. People have been arguing the same thing since the space race. But humanity as a whole. Not just you and me. Everyone. Humanity can do both. We can go to space and help people," Eric says with a smile.

Fiona adds onto what Eric said, "When science pushes a little forward, we all gain its benefits."

Lindsey asks another question, "But what about nuclear bombs?"

Before Fiona could offer a response, Sara and Isla walked back to join the rest. They noticed the other four had already smothered the fire. They've been talking under moonlight for who knows how long. The night was late. For the younger ones, it would be their first experience of having to learn to not overstay their welcome. To know when to stop, and to leave. Eric, Fiona, and Isla wanted to keep talking. Sam saw it in their faces. So did Sara and Lindsey. They were fatigued. It seems more that their tiredness was from their expedited hike than the near-tragedy of Eric's fall.

Sam says, "We should be going. I think we all need to get some sleep."

It didn't seem like either group wanted to leave the other.

Fiona offers, "You three should come to our end of summer bonfire."

"Wouldn't you be drinking?" Lindsey asks.

"We've outgrown drinking. Here." Fiona goes into her pack, writes her address into her journal, and tears the sheet out. The sheet was almost blinding under Fiona's headlamp. The blinding light takes all of them out of the night for a second. She hands it to Lindsey. It's an address on the shorefront. They would begin the bonfire at 7:00pm on August 31st. They'll meet again.

Eric tells them, "Thanks for showing us how to be young again."

Everyone took something from tonight. Or rather, gifted experiences to one another.

"When you come, look for the light, Sara," Isla says.

Sam says, "I guess we'll save the world." He chuckles. "Bye."

Lindsey bids them farewell, "See you guys soon!"

Sara says, "Bye!"

Sam, Sara, and Lindsey take off into the sky. They were weightless going up. Seemed like bullets creating a trail of dust and vapor behind them. When they had finally gone over the horizon, past any visible mountains, Eric, Isla, and Fiona fell to sleep.

Over night, it turns to August. Extra food in their hiking backpacks has formed with the rising sun.

AUGUST 2001

A short respite from watching their Grandmother's TV and putting back library books. The family's busy putting groceries into their rented cabin. Oddly enough, birds fly through the treetops. Outside, a group of briskly walking senior men and women pass through an adjacent hiking trail. Sam imagines their packs must weigh a ton, with how big they are. He returns to help Grandma unload the car.

After lunchtime, Sara and Grandma go on the nearby hiking trail. Grandma wears a large sun hat that has a floral silk scarf tied to its band. One can't notice the slow creep of age when we are at our homes. But Sara remembers last summer vacation, Grandma used to walk much faster. Sara could see that her shoulder was starting to show signs of beginning to hunch over. "Here, Grandma." Sara helps her up from her squat. Grandma puts mushrooms into a red plastic bag. Grandma's a firecracker, a recreational tennis player that used to run circles around Sara when she was a child. She shouldn't have to struggle to stand.

* * *

"Mom, if there was one thing you could do to save the world, what would it be?" Sam asks.

"Well, I'm trying."

"How?" Sam peels back corn husks.

"By raising you two monsters."

"No, but really, Mom."

Mom continues peeling potatoes. The skin falls off onto the newspaper. "I tried once. Still trying." She tells Sam how they had a theoretical framework for gene therapy. Her team wanted to target and resolve genetic defects after they've expressed themselves. "Um. We have our genes fixed from birth. There are ideas to change the DNA of the fetus. From within the womb. Or in-vitro. But that doesn't help people who are already living with afflictions." Their team took their work to mice trials. They were able to succeed and reverse heart disease in adult mice. "Then we modified the procedure for pigs. It just didn't take. None of them. We decided to stop animal testing and go back to the drawing board."

"Were you confident that it could work?" Sam asks.

"As confident as we could be. But we may have been too arrogant."

"But you couldn't see the difference could you? How could you know that it wouldn't work?"

"Why are you asking?"

"I'm thinking of what to become when I grow up," Sam says.

His mom tells him, "I want you to be arrogant."

Sam is taken back.

"Young people have the luxury of arrogance. That's what will let you change the world. But it's not on you to solve the world's problems right now. You'll learn the things to let you change the world. Then arrogance will transform. I know you and Sara will do well. But for now..." She points to the basket of husked corn; waiting to be peeled.

* * *

After dinner, Sara and Bradley walk down to the beach to view the sunset. On her person is an astronomy book with a fold out star chart.

"Nice to see you reading a book. Seems like the library is paying off."

"Dad," Sara groans.

"Look at it this way, you only have to do another month before school."

"Ugh..."

Bradley is enjoying this.

A young boy, about Sara's age, enters the beach holding a long, hefty canvas bag. The bag is as long as he is tall. He's at that age where movements are still uncoordinated. It's so large he has to hold it under his armpits with both forearms. He fights against the unwieldy weight of the long bag—walking backwards to counterbalance the bag, and then suddenly pacing forwards a few steps to keep it from falling. Who knows how he managed to carry the thing so far from his campsite. Or why there wasn't any shoulder strap. The bag is almost comically large against his small frame. Sara couldn't be sure she wasn't watching a slapstick comedy.

The boy puts the bag on the ground and begins unzipping the different compartments. The way he was pulling zippers one after the other gave Sara a strange synesthetic feeling: like the sound of a zipper pulling was the image of a line. Lines popped up all in her mind. When he finished unzipping the bag, the boy took out a tripod and unfolded its legs. He adjusts each collar on the legs to the correct heights. He pulls out a large white cylinder, rendered amber by the sunset, and mounts it on top of the tripod. The boy screws on an eyepiece and other fixtures onto his telescope.

"He looks like he's going to assassinate the stars," Sara chuckles.

"You should go talk to him. You could see the stars from your book."

"I don't know. He seems kind of weird."

"Okay. We can just sit here. I hope the library and Grandma's aren't too hard for you."

"I don't mind it anymore. I used to hate it, but I think I'll keep going," Sara tells her dad.

"Grandma told me she really appreciates you and Sam going over. Even if it's just to watch TV."

"I think I'll just go over to the water." It was getting too sentimental for Sara's liking.

Bradley watches his daughter walk up to the boy and smiles. She takes out her book and points to a page in the book. The boy readjusts his telescope, checks the view on the eyepiece, readjusts the focus, and lets her look at it. She puts the book down as she looks through to the sky. Night seemed to have come quicker than usual.

* * *

Kacey takes out a DVD, and puts it back into its cardboard disc case. Peter puts down his popcorn, and turns to Lindsey. Lindsey knew the interrogation was about to begin. Unlike other people's parents, Kacey and Peter did not hesitate to let their son watch R-rated movies and allowed him to drink wine. Unlike other teens, Lindsey didn't see the novelty in films with nudity, or even drinking. After sitting through countless "prestige" films, he prefers something with explosions or comedies. That's not to say he didn't appreciate films. He does. In trying to introduce culture to Lindsey, the parents had instead pushed him towards video games and skateboarding.

Peter asks his son, "What do you think of Mr. Watanabe?"

Lindsey responds, "I think he wanted to make things better because he was dying."

Kacey says, "I kind of see it like he was wanting to change, and the illness gave him a push."

"I like how Kurosawa showed that gambling, drinking, the night life never fulfilled him. Or how he thought Toyo might save him. But it was actually trying to find purpose that made him happy," Peter says.

Lindsey felt sort of uncomfortable and a bit hopeless. He didn't know why. He says, "Nobody changed at the end. After he made the playground his life's work."

"Hmm...someone did change, Lindsey," Kacey tells him.

Lindsey chooses the last chapter on the DVD, and replays it. The movie ends lingering on the playground and holds on a shot of a person overlooking it. He couldn't describe why, but he began quietly sobbing.

A CRISIS

Speed was becoming less of an issue; much like the wishes. High above waters that look frozen. Long white lines are drawn by ships and disappear with the waves. His body traces the same lines through the sky. Even at high speeds, the horizon is still unending. Unknown to him, he was throwing national agencies into a panic. Their phased arrays, and experimental satellite programs were being put through its paces. War generals needed to make the call whether this fast moving UFO was an act of war. In similar situations, their predecessors had decided to not retaliate. And each time at the precipice of apocalypse, they were correct to not pursue mutually assured destruction. These were false alerts caused by operational errors, misreadings of what sensors meant, power outages both natural and caused by faulty circuits. Their trillion dollar machines, their intelligence agencies, their boots on the ground, their next generation tech are failing to account for Lindsey. These arrogant war machines could not identify a boy.

On long stretches of flying, he took up time singing songs to himself. His mental playlist was usually Rage Against the Machine, Blink 182, and songs off of the Tony Hawk Pro Skater video games. Today, he sings Yakko's World, a fun song listing off the nations of the world, while governments are scrambling. Must've been his 20th time going over Yakko's World today. He'll mark it here: his third waypoint along the Atlantic. He closes his eyes, falling fast to the ocean. Lindsey emerges in...

* * *

A car rumbles on the highway. Loose bushings shake and vibrate miscellaneous components. Without anyone to look at him, Sam was gone in an instant.

The shapes around him were still moving in waves from Sara's sonic boom.

The cube he had fed spheres into was continuing to churn out spheres. It seemed like a fountain that threw out balls into zero gravity. And those spheres were floating there; right above a floor. The strings that had been branching along had grown thin tendrils above this floor. And when the tendrils had touched the spheres above, they pulled the spheres back forming the floor. The floor, or geometrically speaking a plane, in the Field seemed like a tiny picturesque island—the type of cartoon island with a single palm tree and land area of a small house. Shapes were falling into the island as if they were meteors. They were changing the island's growth rate, its colors, morphing spheres into other shapes.

"It needs something. It's missing a *thing*." He flies around the perimeter of the island. Soft points of light illuminate the island. When he flies across the floor, pushing the island in, light falls on and off of his body. He forms it into a sort of clump. It becomes obvious why he chose to fold the floor into a sphere: the more the cube spits out spheres, the spheres would spill over the curve, and the strings would pull it back in. It is more controllable than an ever expanding floor. Floor, plane, island, planet. Change is happening quickly. *Accelerating*. The shapes continue to slam into Sam's Planet even after he leaves.

While the minivan goes along the road, the camping gear rattles in the trunk. She looks up from her book. She was reading about the Big Bang, but she was concerned with origins more contemporary. Her little brother is in the back seat, her father was driving, her mother is looking at a map, her grandmother is in the seat next to her's. Her mind wanders. It wouldn't be Grandma. Mom and Dad didn't seem all that shocked when she and Sam returned home, even after having disappeared for the night. *Could it be them?* She promises herself to talk to them. But what was she going to do *if they knew?* What would—could it mean? *I'll know when I ask.*

* * *

Summer was ending. But not before they turn night to day. They've traveled directly south. A simple geographic change. With the waypoints that Lindsay had set out across the Atlantic, Europe was a short way away. In the open ocean, they could play tag with each other without consequence. It was a game where they chased each other east starting in sonic booms and halting. They were the only source of sound for hundreds of miles.

They fly up to the clouds. Where it rains and drizzles, but the rain evaporates before it falls to the ocean. It's as if it was a waterfall without a source. From this height, if you tilt your head so slightly, you can see a rainbow form. The rain falls. A gust of wind blows a misty spray towards the three. Drops of water stay on their canvas backpacks.

Sara wanted to recapture what she had felt. Sam disappeared before. Lindsey and Sam both told her that she disappeared. But what she experienced was a continuum, without discontinuity. A line without breaks. She wanted to find herself back on that line, where time slows.

While they flew eastward, the earth was moving with them. Dawn is coming twice as fast.

Ahead of them were dark clouds. Just as flying above made the ocean waves look still, floating here from a distance made the *tower* of clouds look frozen. As with large things in nature, like elephants or whales or planets, even fast motion seems slow. There's no mistaking what those dark clouds were. From their far vantage point, they could feel the wind being sucked into that cloud tower.

Just several weeks ago, these wind gusts would have toppled and rolled them.

Ever the daredevil, Lindsey goes straight into the hurricane. Once inside, there's no direction anymore. There is nothing to see in the wind and dark clouds, but everything was tactile. Color was taken away from the world, and the world was left in charcoal tones. The raindrops cut through his face and skin. The sound wasn't the empty tone of the sky. It was a deep rumbling. And the wind was pulsating in steady tempos, or it was for him. The shearing force of the rain was hell on his eyes. He closes his eyes and covers his shut eyes with his left hand. It didn't matter if his eyes were open or not. His other arm is outstretched to feel the direction of the wind. Water droplets are like pebbles being flicked into his hand. Thunder roared around him. The winds shook him; tossed him. Until it doesn't.

There is an instant where he feels nothing on his outstretched hand, but he still hears the wind and feels the rain on his cheeks. He opens his eyes. He realizes he's on a thin line; an edge. Nature does have many edges like sand meeting the ocean, mountain ranges that separate steppes from deserts, the atmosphere between Earth and outer space; the times in transition: the blue and golden hours, springs and autumns. In the future, Sara will mention a word to him that describes all these conditions: liminality. This edge was not only a liminal space in-between the severe winds and rain, and the calm eye of the storm; it was also a threshold in-between gray and color.

Lindsey hovers into the eye of the storm.

Sara pierces into the eye. Clouds followed in her wake.

Sam flies into the eye at an arc; matching the spin of the hurricane.

They turn to each other with their hair wet as if they were sweating. Their clothes were damp. Water droplets still rolling from their hair.

In the future, they'll have their own memories about this moment. Sam'll have dreams where the hurricane's spiral structure dissolves into a double helix. Sara will find the same frisson in holy places of the world and be reminded of this moment. Someone important would ask Lindsey what the eye of the hurricane was like…Lindsey would call it being inside a mandala.

The earth envelopes the hurricane which envelopes the eye of the storm.

All of them emerged from the turbulent gray into quiet, calm. Few edges in nature are as abrupt a change as going from the eyewall into the eye of the storm. It was calm. It was serene. The clouds are wrapped around them, and move in slow motion. It was an infinite summer zephyr inside this hollow tower. The breezes swirl in a circle over and over inside this tower. It is a wind engine. Their faces and hair are cooled by the wind. An ultra violet sky is above them; a gradient of purple that meant morning is rising over the Atlantic ocean. The navy clouds held white potential. The earth wrapped the whole sky into a cylinder. They stayed there silent and hovering until the sun touched the rim of the eyewall. Like a flashlight casting shadow from above a water well, the sun casts a long shadow from the eyewall against its opposite side. The eyewall is split into light and dark.

Lindsey thinks back to what Fiona had said to Sam and him. He flies into the hurricane again. *If the hurricane turns counter clockwise, then I'll turn it the other way.* Lindsey also had Superman on his mind when he took off. With his speed, he is carving, sculpting tunnels into the hurricane structure. He spirals down to the ocean. He circles the 10 mile radius at a faster-than-sound speed. He grits his teeth and tightens his face muscles. The acceleration should have ripped his body into shreds. Sam and Sara catch onto what he's doing. They dive down. They produce three separate high frequency sounds.

Bullets don't stop trains.

So they'd whisper some words, and the hurricane will be gone.

A hurricane hunter, a research plane, was making its way through the dark clouds and into the eye. Sudden contractions and expansion of the air were happening along the eyewall. The hurricane continues moving eastward. Small clockwise cyclones form along the bottom, but the hurricane dissipates them easily. Air explodes inside the hurricane. These explosions happened all around the rotating mass. Although the explosions had violently exploded and pushed football fields of air apart, the hurricane still propagates. Hundreds of these explosions occurred.

The hand of nature moves over the hurricane. Like a never ending shock wave, or a sonic boom, a massive curtain of air tears through the rotation. Slices into it. Another curtain of air comes from the north. This curtain was less a blast of air, then an unending stream; of a strength equal to the hurricane's. It collides directly head on with the hurricane's center. Again, and again the stream hits against the storm. When the curtain's air hits against the hurricane's tail where the storm speed was not so hard, the result was tiny cyclones that come and go—not unlike the vortexes surrounding a paddle's shaft through a river. These rushes of air have the same effect as a hand staying turbulent water. And in parts of the world, there'll be wind blowing in directions it has never blown before.

The thunderstorms are blown away. They are blown apart. Lightning had tried to chase its way between the parting clouds. It could not.

The three are thrown through the gusts. Needled through the parting lightning and thunderstorms. The red sunlight shining through the gaps, casting shadow rays in large blades. The blue sky peeking through the black clouds and violet lightning torn apart like frayed fabric. It was such a rainbow of visual chaos.

They could not fly in these winds. The winds rolled them. Tumbled them into the now-wispy clouds. Blown them far *on* course. When the wind became gentle again and they regained control, they found that these winds had carried them to their destination: Europe.

* * *

Today, Lindsey decides to sit by the beach. The hurricane was too much adventure for yesterday. He packed an umbrella and a towel, and skated his way to the beach. The ocean reflects on his mirrored sunglasses. He sweats through his black tee shirt and jeans. He stares at the ocean, and imagines islands. The view of sideways rain and bent trees from caves. Islands ravaged by hurricane winds. Tsunamis. Catastrophe. Earthquakes.

Rolling waves. The crest and valleys of water. A blue horizon unending. Dark through his glasses. What do you see?

A star to bring light to this dark place. A star that keeps breaking in my hands. A star that I keep breathing into. But the light keeps going away.

Feelings are hard to put into words. It's hard to quantify sacrifice. It's hard to capture abstract ideas in words. We only know what was right at that moment.

Lindsey looks at the dim light he holds in his palms. "There's a price, isn't there?" He pauses before he says these next words, "I'll give you a year of my life."

So a year was squeezed into seconds. Inside his palms was such a fusion. Space was being crushed into a small point. All the shapes inside of his palms squeezing together. Time too was compressed. The reaction no longer had a moment to dissipate or to rest. To him, there was so much to be done—that can be done in this field. Now that there is light.

* * *

Sara is "busy" watching syndicated cartoons, when Sam receives a message.

> LINDSEY: [url link]
> LINDSEY: you should get sara to look at this too
> LINDSEY: you there?
> SAM: Yeah.
> SAM: We're reading it now.
> SAM: Is this website even real?
> LINDSEY: looks like it

"Hey, what are you guys looking at?" Bradley asks from the kitchen. To lie to parents, never say nothing. Instead, let them see what you're "looking at." Bradley watches a strange video game montage with a robotic voice repeating, "All your base." Even though this isn't Sam and Sara's first or even tenth time watching it, and even though it's a ruse, they still laugh like maniacs at the thing. Bradley walks back to the kitchen and tells Camille, "I think I'm finally out of touch."

Sam brings up the images again. Three figures are blurs in the images. The video continues downloading while they talk. "The pictures the plane took were pretty good. We should get a camera," Sam tells Sara. Sara points out the eye of the hurricane. "It was really amazing, wasn't it?"

LINDSEY: did you guys see the video yet?
SAM: Still downloading.
LINDSEY: people say it looks fake
LINDSEY: but then im not sure if it would be a bad thing if people knew. you done downloading yet?
SAM: No...

Lindsey links them to some other articles. One of the news media videographers on the research plane had a blog. The plane was blown away by the hurricane-wiping wind and tailspinned down to the water. The broadcast was cut short since the radio communication severed. The plane managed to float on top of the ocean, where they awaited rescue. On return to land, the on-board media was transcoded and viewed back. The producers called it big-foot malarkey and the footage never went to air.

After an hour of downloading, Sam calls Sara to the computer. He hits play on the media player. The video is from the POV of the airplane's right wing. Lindsey was floating at the other end. Sara comes in about 30 degrees from Lindsey. They're both way out from the plane at the other end of the eye wall. The camera zooms in on them, but the lens's zoom range was not enough to get them in clear view. The camera zooms out so that it has a wider field of view again. Sam's face flies past the camera's view. It's a blur, but it definitely was a human and almost definitely Sam.

"Well, there it is..." Sam says.
"Yea, there it is..." Sara says.

Would it be so bad if people knew? Sara walks to the kitchen with conviction to talk to her parents about origins, "Hey. Mom, Dad."

They look up from reading. "What's going on Sara?" her mom asks.

Sara says, "Oh, nothing."

"Okay then," her mom replies.

* * *

"Sam, do you think it's the same thing? Being lost and trying to find out where you came from?"

"I don't get what you're saying."

"Hmm. Good night, Sam."

Sara went to sleep earlier that night, earlier than Sam. Later when Lindsey popped into their house, Sara was already gone. Sam and Lindsey agreed to sleep rather than go on adventures that night. When Sam woke up, Sara had already gone to the library for volunteer work.

* * *

"I've been jogging a lot lately, but you're killing me here," Sam pants heavily trying to get his words out. The summer sun is not helping either. It's a humid day and his clothes are drenched in sweat. He feels like garbage and looks like it too.

"Feeling schooled, young man?" Grandma stands tall over him. She spins her tennis racket on one finger and bounces a tennis ball up and down on a racket. *Arrogance, huh? Grandma just wiped out any I had, Mom.* Sam wants to burp, but it'll be risky. He slides his hand slowly to the water bottle, careful not to put pressure on his diaphragm. Tiny sips. Tiny sips. To not throw up.

""Want to go another round? No? Okay then. Just wait here," she laughs and challenges another player on the courts. Sam'll have time to recoup and not throw up his grandma's baking. Grandma was moving with startling agility. Hitting dramatic poses, angles. Planting her feet, driving off of it. Shifting her weight from heel to hand. Time had turned back. Sam wonders about all the other people who they can't get to. How long would it take to give the wish person to person? So he wishes for diseases to be healed.

He wonders if his great wish worked, and wishes for something else trivial. Nothing happens.

* * *

In her history class, Sara learned that some ancient civilizations are still undiscovered; even in present day. Only the few who venture out into the forests and jungles are able to find old ruins. There are civilizations in high places and oceans. She could reach those places easily. However, flying over a forest does not allow you to see inside. Therein lies the challenge. One has to be inside the woods to find their way through. And if one would be so lucky, they may find ruins there.

The sky booms with thunder when she arrives. A blue bloom of light explodes in the sky. To those who saw it, a shooting star had flown into the forest. The tree tops were lit in a halo. But when the shooting star touched ground, the light did not extinguish.

"Holy crap." Sara flicks her headlamp angle up at the sky, down at the ground again. Up, then down. Up and down. When she wished for a super headlamp, she didn't it expect to shine like the sun itself. The view in front of her was pure white. When she pressed the on button, it wasn't circuitry and batteries providing light. It was pure, raw electrons bouncing to higher energy states inside a headlamp housing. It was also freaking hot on her forehead.

The light beam is blinding. The super headlamp is so bright that it made the darks darker and the brights so much brighter.

The forest might as well have been white and black. It shone straight ahead, but the light stops at trees and goes no farther. The super headlamp wasn't an x-ray. At least she can see the ground she walks on. She walks ahead through the dark forest. It's dizzying to walk without a horizon. Trees overlapping trees overlapping trees. If black lines keep overlapping in her view, it should just look like total darkness again. Instead, she can see depth and dimension in front of her. She walks between the slits.

Slow steps through random directions to try to keep herself oriented. She winds her way through the woods. It's almost unending. What was she hoping to find? It can't just be random walking to find some semblance of ruins. Didn't nations send out explorers for expeditions? To map out the terrain? The logical thing would be to go up. To notice things. Look around for signs. Nothing worse than plain, level ground. Listen. Wind, a breeze. Smell. The leaves and soil. Ahead of her, the shadows on the trees have a different quality: they were on a hill. So she'll go up to the top, then to the next top, and the top after that. Exhausting. Like walking up way too many stairs. It wasn't like flying was an option. What was she going to do? Fly and hit her head in the dark? Nope. No more bodily injuries for her.

She catches her breath. She shines her spotlight down to the ground below and imagines a farmer leading a goat through the forest. And then the farmer slaughters the goat. A sacrifice to remove the sins of the village. Lots of civilizations did the same too, didn't they? The Aztecs had heart sacrifices for their god. How horrible it must be to have your heart taken out. Must everything have a cost? Including these wishes of her's?

Her spotlight catches a night bird in flight. Its wings flash the light back at her. The flashlight shines from spot to spot. When she swings her field of view, she tries to memorize the lay of the land. Trying to build the map in her mind. But there's a quicker way, isn't there? Why yes. Yes there was. She takes off her super headlamp. And tosses it up. It illuminates as it goes through the air. Sara scrambles up on all fours for the hill was steep. She spins the headlamp on her finger; illuminating 360 degrees around her. Her map gets filled much more quickly.

These lights that have illuminated her summer: the cities that guide her way, the stars, the blue cloudless skies—they were all waypoints. Each of them giving her a bearing to head to. To amazing places. But they weren't directions. They weren't any sort of *map*. What if there could be a more powerful map? In Peru, time slowed down for her. She and her brother figured out that she was experiencing time differently. No map she knows has time as an element. No guide on the *spectrum* of time. No map she knows has outside and inside. No cartographer sent to the worlds of the Bubble and the Field. No direction for right or wrong for these wishes. No map for home or destination. She needed a tool to allow her to navigate without landmarks or waypoints. To diminish indecision. To no longer depend on the lights of far off places and become a lighthouse upon herself.

A double vision of lights before her. Of spotlights. A larger light and the lesser light. A planet in revolution around a burning star. A light to give form to the tactile reality that had scared them all. A light to join the sound in the Field. And what had been dark is now light. And what had seemed like a dark veil is lifted.

Falling stars of many shapes collide onto the white planet emitting rainbow detritus. The star pulls in shapes into its gravity—gravity which is newly made.

Fly to your tiny planet, little brother. Solid. This is a firm ground. Sam, does it weigh anything? Shapes fall on my face like raindrops.

Fly to your star, Lindsey. I go through it. It's like a cloud. This light is so warm. You made this, didn't you? It's pretty cool.

Can I make something too?

The shapes dispersed in the field were geometric: cubes, spheres, discs, polyhedra. There were also natural-like forms floating in the Field: branches, stems, petals, rain, rocks, even gaseous clouds. With the light from the planet and star, all these shapes are rendered translucent; having the same quality as deep ocean life. The two waves of motion in the Field are visible, but are changing into different wind patterns. The two "celestial" bodies are pulling the shapes into a ring around them. The Field is looking like a stream or babbling brook; where the shapes are flowing around the two bodies.

Flying to the stream, so fast, so fast that there is no sound following her. So fast that a blue light bloom exploded behind her. Sit by the stream between the star and the planet, gravity winds rendered visible by the shapes: looking for the correct ones to forge together. Outreach her hand and touch, and feel these building blocks.

To put ideas into form. A cube, a string, a branch. Push this branch inside the cube, and to tie an endless knot; a Moebius strip to bind all these elements together. It looks like a terrarium in the way that all enclosed plants look like. Inside, all the branches are multiplying in place, and growing into each other. Root spreading inside an enclosed cube, inside, through, under, and over one another. Pushing into the edges of boundaries that keep on folding; making new boundaries inside of itself. Her warmth gives color and opaqueness to the bare branches like these objects were waiting to be revitalized. There is brown color and bark to these small roots.

The string is a gold band around this small terrarium. Without its binding, the roots would come out of the cube. A way for infinity to be held in a finite space. That's what a map is. It is encompassing infinite perimeters to a finite space. Much like the coastlines or boundaries on a map, or like the infinities of numbers between 0 and 1, these growing roots are bounded-infinities. Who could map out a coastline whose length increases the more you walk along the shore, whose length increases the more you try to measure out each turn and twist.

In her hand, the terrarium bloomed tiny leaves from brown to red to yellow to green. From her view, these were like tiny dots. Time passes inside, old branches withering and returning to dust, to grow again inside the boundary. It's cyclical.

People have died to learn the directions North, South, West, East, zenith, nadir, outside, and inside...

You're mine. Aren't you? I want to take you back.

Water dowsing rods, compasses, sextants, crystal balls, global positioning systems were all wayfinding tools. *Sara's Map* is not any of these things. It does not follow in the tradition of guiding towards tread paths. Its heritage is different. Its crafting methods are ancient. She has fashioned an apparatus that exists in a long line of crafted jewels like a transmutable sword and a Princess's mirror.

* * *

The kids flew over the Irish plains. From above, they looked like slow motion birds away from their flocks. They flew through Paris and remarked on how all the buildings were flat and close to the ground. They flew to China where they traced the serpentine path of the Great Wall from start to sea. They went to Japan. Then crossing the Pacific back to the United States. To touch down on Madagascar, walk between its wild plants, and to be back in bed the same night. To fly so fast to outrun the sun.

Fly at the speed of summer, you daring ones.

There are so many waypoints inside the Bubble. Every time Lindsey makes a new waypoint, he spends half the day relabeling the ground of every place. But with how fast they could go now, waypoints are not needed anymore. Any place in the world is a few hours away at most now. Even when grounded, they could spend their nights in days in faraway places.

Sam is catching up to Lindsey. They knew his tricks when he is about to be tagged. Both Sam and Sara close their eyes. Then reopen them to the Bubble. The abrupt rush of three supersonic beings into the Bubble sends everything into chaos. All the foam blocks explode into the air and bounce off the walls. Kitchenware from the open kitchen cling and clank on the ground when dragged by their wakes. Even the walls expanded a bit from their air pressure. Chase him through the tunnels and lighted corridors. Moving through his maze. They can't find him there.

But there's a faint pulse, wasn't there? A tree was growing its paths too. They all felt it. Which meant Lindsey was not safe in his maze. Follow the pulse. This smell of a blooming flower. He closes his eyes the moment, a second before Sam manages to touch him. Lindsey sends them all back out in the real world. They're in the middle of the Pacific Ocean. It's odd how they never think about what direction they come out of the Bubble. Guess they'll find out.

Lindsey can sense that Sam was inches from him. He speeds up. Bad decision. A terrible decision. Especially if you're moving at supersonic speeds. Downward towards the ocean. Sara has already corrected course and flew off. Lindsey realizes that he's flying head-on towards the water. Lindsey slows down with such deceleration that it feels like the whole force of a hurricane was pushing against his organs. Sam touches Lindsey with his fingers before flying straight past Lindsey. Sara was too far to save Sam from himself. And Lindsey has already changed his trajectory. Sam is going to have to save Sam.

Sam is going to have to save himself quickly. Do you know what happens to a high speed moving object when it hits water? It gets worse than wet. He's not going to disappear into the Field again. So slow down. So slow down. The turbulence, the cutting force onto his body. It was a storm inside his organs. He rolls his body sideways into the ocean so that at least he'll keep his head on after collision. He spins over and over; skipping across the ocean like a stone. A blue sky mixing into a blue ocean, the horizon disappearing in his blender vision. He stops. He leans back and takes a big breath to float. He looks up to the sky.

A boat slowly rows to Sam. Sara flies to meet them.

"Give me a second. I'm healing my hand," Sam said. Sam heals his hand underwater, away from their view. It was too mangled and gory for anyone to see. He was lucky to get away with that much.

"Doesn't feel good, does it?" Sara asks.

"No."

Sara carries Sam onto Lindsey's row boat. It's painted black with lightning strikes. Because of course it is. Lindsey asks if Sam was okay while Lindsey rows the boat into a circle. Turning around and around from nautical inexperience.

"Can you stop rowing for a second? I think I'm going to throw up," Sam says to Lindsey. Not from the rowing, but from being skipped and spun like a pebble.

Lindsey puts his hand on Sam's shoulder. "You're it."

"We agreed no tag backsies!"

A few miles away, a large patch of garbage was swirling around. If the teens had noticed it, they would've gotten rid of it. Sara notices a faded bag of chips floating by the boat. Lindsey stops rowing the boat. He takes out a thermos full of coffee and pours some into a cup. He's developed a sort of quasi-addiction to decaf coffee. After all, what else do you do when you have a fully equipped kitchen and a messed up sleep schedule? He exhales gleefully after a swig.

"We sure grew up this summer, haven't we?" Lindsey asks them in a sarcastically upbeat way.

Sam was wringing his t-shirt out over the water, "It's ending soon, isn't it?"

"We could have done more if we weren't grounded," Sara leans over the side of the boat and draws swirls in the water.

Lindsey lays down on the boat and props his leg on the boat's rim. He yawns. The boat rocks a bit. The waves carry them a bit eastward. His thermos rolls on the floor back and forth. "You know I realized it's still light out."

"Must be because we're between California and Japan," Sam says.

Sara lazily checks her watch and it's 3am NY time. There's still daylight. The longer summer days are a blessing. The ocean air is warm, and the wind is only slightly cool.

"I have to start school soon," Lindsey says.

"Same here." Sam has made his t-shirt and pants are dry as they can be.

"Then high school in a year after next," Sara says. Sara is still drawing into the water. She finds her own end of the boat to lay down in and watch the sky. "You're going to be bored without us, aren't you?"

"Nah," Lindsey says. "We're still going to see each other. How else am I going to get the wish?"

Sam yawns and lays down, supporting his head with his elbow. Sara immediately imagines a ring of trade between the three of them occurring over and over again. Except it wasn't trade in any sense of the word.

"That's true," Sara says. Cirrus clouds wipe away slowly with the wind.

"The bonfire is in a few days, isn't it?" Lindsey asks.

Sam: "Oh yea."

Sara: "Hmm. Three days I think."

Sam had already fallen asleep on the boat. Sara sets an alarm for 6am on her watch. Sara takes two shallow breaths before sleeping too. Lindsey puts his forearm over his eyes to cover the light.

The boat rocks again and again. Large shipping boats are near to them. If their shipping routes were closer, then they could see pass the horizon and spot the black painted boat with lightning. With their heads pressed close to the boat's hull, the ocean sounds low and alive. It's a spectrum of low rumbles, and the gentle babble of streams. Winds blow over them; Sam's wet clothes air dry. The oars and the boat creak while its wood shrink and expand so slightly. Waves splash against the boat. Water droplets land on their faces and clothes. They are carried by the ocean; at least until 6am NY time.

This time it would be Sam and Sara sleeping over at Lindsey's abode. And it would be one of the last sleepovers of their summer.

Sam traveled to the Field. Sara traveled to the Field. Lindsey traveled to the Field.

It has been some time since the three of them had come here. Especially for Sam and Lindsey who have last been inside when it was dark. So your planet was full. You had thought it was a small sphere. You didn't think it could grow so big. Oh, how near you fly to it and see its circumference become a line; a horizon.

The light you make. The year of your life you had so sacrificed. You didn't expect the light to extinguish the dark inside the Field. You didn't expect to make a star.

Lost in this field somewhere was Sara's Map. Only lost for a second. Trees have room to grow in the center of planets. They have light and space. These three gardeners fly to Sam's Planet. Wind lines made visible by the shapes. Traces curving and winding their way through the streams and gravity fields that exist now. With its white surface smooth, the planet's map would not have the coastline paradox. So find your way through its featureless, perimeterless face. But be careful for its surface is imbued with the permutations of many geometries. Trade one complication for another.

From different directions, they come to the pole that Lindsey's Star shines on. Shapes flow through their bodies. If wind had a shape, it may have been these shapes: the piercing winds of winter like needles across the lips, spring breezes that are more present than they may have felt, the dull winds of early summer that were humid and seem to roll off like spheres, the autumn winds that settled like snowflakes through porous clothes...

Each of them felt where the Map was. But that's because they were using it. Each had the sense of whose creations—whose *machines*—these were. No one knew who came up with their names: Lindsey's Star, Sam's Planet, Sara's Map in the first place. But they share these terms all the same without having to speak with each other.

These machines they've created here: they can't be shared. Not like the wishes. And they grow; become bigger—just like the wishes they had made.

They looked at their lives through a cube. Unfolding. Through the summers to come. Of branching paths of lives they could lead. Their different occupations they could take in life. No They looked at their lives through a cube. Unfolding. Through the summers to come. Of branching paths of lives they could lead. Their different occupations they could take in life. Not viewing the Map. Or experiencing the Map. Or being in it. The Map was fracturing their time like a prism does to light. They hadn't care for the lives they could lead. A map doesn't have directions in it or destinations. Like a prism, Sara's Map reveals all the shades. Time was a topography inside the cube of which they could move freely. t viewing the Map. Or experiencing the Map. Or being in it. The Map was fracturing their time like a prism does to light. They hadn't care for the lives they could lead. A map doesn't have directions in it or destinations. Like a prism, Sara's Map reveals all the shades. Time was a topography inside the cube of which they could move freely.

Nor could a person explore every second and inch of the Map. To experience every possibility. To understand every choice that is and that can come. Time was fast and slow in the same way ocean waves rumble low and high. Simultaneous and chronologically dialectic in their experiences.

Watching the trees turn to dust. To cycle back to this moment, nearer to the end of summer than to the beginning.

Wake up. Wake up to the wrist watch's beeping.

They're back floating on the ocean. The boat catches a rolling wave and it undulates the boat up then down. Lindsey brings the boat back into the Bubble. He drags it alongside the foam pit. Water from its hull drips onto the Bubble's floor. Sara and Sam follow the signs on the floor to Dusk House. Lindsey walks with them through the corridors.

Sara turns to Lindsey, "I want to get my map out of the Field."

Lindsey: "Let's do it."

* * *

Cup noodles, bread, ham, candy, soda. Sara and Sam packed clothes into their backpacks. At least two days worth. They've put eggs into a camping freezer. Summer was ending and they did not have days to spare anymore. They could ask for forgiveness later. Sara would explain it all to their parents. With Lindsey, he was busy with preparations from his end too. He cleaned up the Bubble, put things in order. He appeared at their house to grab their sleeping bags. Also, to haul a whole 24pk of water bottles. Mr. and Mrs. Dusk wouldn't know it would be missing from the pantry.

"Sara, you're going to write a note?" Sam asks.

"No, we'll tell them when we come back."

Sam takes a notepad and writes, "Sara, Lindsey, and I are safe. We'll be back in a bit. Tell Grandma and the library we couldn't make it today. - Sam"

Lindsey stares out through their windows to Brooklyn. It doesn't feel like home anymore. California didn't feel like home either.

"You all ready?" Lindsey asks Sam and Sara. They nod.

The project will be underway.

They organize their belongings in the Bubble. Each of them set up their own space inside. They unroll their sleeping bags. Sam prefers sleeping under the giant slide. It feels secure almost like a bed's canopy or having your feet face a door opening. Lindsey had gotten used to sleeping by the spiral ramp perimeter. At least now he has a sleeping bag. Sara throws the foam blocks out of the foam pit. She puts her sleeping bag on the trampoline underneath. The way they had set up the Bubble was almost like a proto-dormitory—a view of things to come.

Their book bags, food supplies are on the kitchen counter. That's their home base. That's where they plan their heist. Sam sets up a chalkboard at the counter's end. Sara changes it to a whiteboard since she hates the sound of chalk against chalkboard even if it's not screeching. Sam draws three concentric circles on the board. The outer circle is labeled Earth, then the middle circle is labeled the Bubble, then the third is labeled the Field. Inside the Field, he draws the planet and the star, and the Map on top of the planet.

He studies his chart. To get it out, it'll have to be bought back through the Bubble.

"That's wrong. Your map is off," Lindsey says. He gets up from his seat. He erases the Bubble and the Field circles from inside the Earth. He draws the Bubble and the Field as separate circles, and draws lines connecting them. It looks like a network. His drawing was an apt description based off of his experience in the Bubble.

"Let me take a crack at this." So she does. She erases the board. Her concept of the spaces was overlapping Venn diagrams.

They each explained their own logic. Sam believed that since you started on Earth, each level was inside the other. That it was especially true when they had burst the Bubble and entered into the Field, and not come back out into Earth. Lindsey's experience had told him that these were destinations and separate places. Sara had her own mental model that they were all the same or in a way had shared a common space.

The shape of things can determine how they get something out. Without knowing what a labyrinth looks like, you may wander into the center by accident and not find your way out. Lindsey compared it to moving a couch through a stairwell. Once you know the space of things, then it's easier to get things out. Sam and Sara called him out for referencing a Friends episode. There's a certain level of irony in that they had to create a map to get a map out.

Understanding the shape between the Bubble, the Field, and Earth was a hard thing to crack. The edges in nature did not exist between each place. They were abrupt. Stare into light, stare into the dark, emerge in one place or another. And what if these edges in these spaces were time? Slow down time when he fell, and emerge in the Field. Take a moment to stare into the light, and come back to Earth.

"We need to take time figuring out what to do," Sam says.

"Yeah. We can go in and get lost in it. Then we don't know how much time has passed once we come out," Sara responds.

"You'd get grounded again. That would suck. No fun during the school year either." Lindsey mulls over the situation, "Do you guys wonder if it matters if we get into the Field from Earth or the Bubble?"

Sara: "We've only went into the Field once from the Bubble."

Sam: "Every other time was from Earth."

Sara: "Maybe we can create a machine that brings the Map out."

Lindsey walks to the board, and erases Sara's model. He draws Sam's concentric circles, his network, and Sara's Venn diagram. He puts on a pot of water. They all study the three models until the water boils. Lindsey puts coffee into a mug.

Sam: "Pour me one too."

Sara: "Same here."

Lindsey: "I'll brew you guys some decaf. The pot I just made is pretty strong."

Sara: "Maybe we should just go into the Field."

Lindsey: "We agreed we'll work it out first."

Sam seems flustered and frustrated.

Sam: "I just don't get it."

The three teens are at their limit of understanding. In school, math problems in tests were applied rote learning. Swap out one number for another and run the formula. Formulae which took mathematicians their lives to work out and derive. Figuring out their heist has to become conceptual instead of applying what they knew. If the edges weren't there for them to identify, they have to define them.

Lindsey: "This is ridiculous. Let's just wish for the answer."

Sara: "You have it."

Lindsey: "Oh boy. I'm hoping this doesn't collapse anything." He mutters under his breath: "I wish that the Field's location comes to me."

Sam: "Nothing?"

Sara: "Anything?"

Lindsey: "Nope."

Sam: "I think there can't be any shortcuts. Eric, Fiona, and Isla were right. We have to do the work. And maybe the work has to be like...going inside the Field and figuring it out there? Even if we're afraid. Or don't know what we're doing."

Sara didn't know if his brother went completely bonkers or if he was growing up. She checks her watch. Only an hour has passed. Time does slow down without television, or games, or volunteering, or getting beat in tennis by your grandma.

Sara tells them, "I have to go think."

She walks away. Lindsey walks around the perimeter; going up the spiral ramp. Sam stands in front of the whiteboard hoping to get an epiphany or a sign. The way into the Field was easy to them now, even if they cannot completely control their access. Having been sleep deprived for the better part of summer, they were entering into the Field through half-awake dreams. Sam knew as well as anyone that if they wanted to get in, they just had to sleep.

Lindsey sits with his legs hanging over the ramp. He's at least two stories up if it was a house. He sips on his coffee and exhales. He misses lazy days like today with Sam and Sara. He thinks back to when he would lounge around their house. He won't necessarily be doing anything. Sometimes he'd be at Sam or Sara's room. Sometimes he'd be in the living room with one of them while the other was in their room. There's a spot on their couch that has his imprint on it. Mostly, it's his body upside down so that his back is on the seat, and his butt is up on the back. He takes another gulp of coffee watching both of them spend time in his domain. He yells over to Sam, "Got anything yet?"

Sara walks in a corridor that exits to Atlantic Ocean (1). Lindsey told her how he had to give numbers to each ocean's exits since it took him several trips to cross them. She mutters to herself, "What would you do, Isla? It looked like you had things figured out." She slides her five fingers along the side, marking five lines while she walks. The next bubble is in front of her and it's almost identical to the one she came from; but without the changes they've made. "Jeez Lindsey. How do you keep track of all these places?" She flies back to Sam and Lindsey.

After their short time apart figuring things out, they come back with new ideas. Lindsey summoned another whiteboard to the Bubble. This board had two sides for them to write on. They bounce ideas back and forth on how to best get the Map out. They wondered if the Field was alive and had thoughts. If it could think, then they could try coaxing the Map out of it somehow. If Star Trek was to be believed, anything you touch would come back with you by teleportation. But they couldn't control when they come in or out of the Field. They would have to stand by and keep holding the Map.

"If we can get in and out, then there has to be a way to get the Map out too," Sara says.

Time. They were running out of time in the summer. Sara's Map itself was fracturing time, exploring it.

The teens gave a name to their project to lend it significance. Project Millennium. Project Map. Project Deepdive. They've agreed to calling it The Work. Work is something old people do in their cubicles with hot steam humidifiers on the floor. If these office workers were adventurous, they'd have a houseplant on their desk or a funny calendar with a joke of the day. Which, to be honest, Lindsey gets a kick out of themed day-to-day calendars. That's how they thought of workers. But The Work is fun.

Lindsey asks, "So what did you guys see when you were in there?"

Lindsey saw that he was going to snowboard in the future, so that's what he thought he was going to do. But he also saw himself going around a loop-de-loop on a skateboard. He also remembered being spun around and around in a gyroscope contraption. Sam stood on the floor of the New York Stock Exchange, ringing the bell in front of a thousand people on the floor. His parents and sister were beside him. Sara rowed a boat in a river flanked by mountains. Looking behind, she was lugging a lot of camera equipment on her boat. Another person in a cap held an omnidirectional microphone up to the air. If they could spend more time with the Map, they could definitely see more and more.

Sara: "If we can get it out, I think we can see what the future can be."

Sam: "I don't think that what we saw is really what will really happen. Like um...it didn't feel—"

Lindsey: "Like it was one life."

They all nod, and say "hmm..." at the same time.

Sara: "I've been thinking a lot about our wishes for a while now. I don't know. Just like thinking about Grandma and how she wasn't able to walk well. I know you healed her, Sam. But I don't know, what about everyone else?"

Lindsey: "I was at the beach a few days ago. And all I could see was hurricanes. And earthquakes. There were so many houses damaged. We never took the time to think about the damage we could undo."

Sam: "I've wished for diseases to be cured, but I don't think it was fulfilled."

They didn't know that some wishes, like seeds, have roots that take time to hold; like trees, have branches in shadow growing to the light.

Lindsey: "It's scary. We undid the hurricane, but we didn't know about the airplane."

Sara: "I don't think we can control nature, but with these wishes...I think we have to do what we can."

The Map has transformed into a form of insurance for them. They could see possibilities and shape the future with their wishes. Sara's Map suddenly became more important not just for their own futures, but everyone's. Their realization put a grave responsibility on all of them to retrieve the Map. They look at each other. They blink slowly. Time seemed to stop. It had come for them. Before their eyelids had time to close, they saw a brighter light than the Bubble, a brighter light than the day. Then their eyes close completely.

The Field used to be still. It used to be silent. Shapes only existed in the space and nothing more. Now in the Field was sound, light, wind, gravity. Above all, the Field is in motion. And if something was in motion, it required change. In the Bubble, they had expanded space according to their whims. In the Field, they've given time onto its existence. Finally, in front of the Field, with the chaotic activity before them; they understand the placement of the Bubble and the Field. They are not separate. They are not contained in each other. They are not linked or overlapped with one another. They are time and space. They are twins: both singular and separate.

The sleep that they deprived themselves of have caught up to them. No more volunteering while half asleep. No more adventures making anymore waypoints. Now they can dream freely. And when they awake, they will no longer be kids.

Time changes all things. Even for two days when they hadn't entered the Field. The stream of shapes that were moving through the gravity field has grown. Other shapes had caught up into the stream. Or rather, it was like a river of shapes that flowed in between the star and the planet. The shapes, which were set into motion by Sara's sonic boom, kept colliding into the planet. They left dents on its surface. The river had decimated the planet. It runs through the planet's surface, eroding its shapes and bringing them back into the river. Sam's Planet looks like an apple with its core exposed. In a way, the shapes created a larger shape.

As one body has its material ripped from it, the stream brings the material to the star. They arrive just in time to witness a moment that is meant for them.

The star is bright and white. They see the rainbow of wavelengths from the star. The three of them were not here when each shape had been added to the star's surface; increasing its size dramatically. Small spheres grow exponentially.

Now the star's gravity is stronger, and is sucking in material much more quickly, but it does not perceptibly grow in size. The star must spread the new material over its large surface; like water washing over a beach ball. Its circumference dwarfs the planet. The star is growing larger. And larger. The three are present for its inflection point when it seizes to get larger, but instead it becomes *denser*.

Sam asks, "Is it shrinking?"

A variety of noises emanate from the star. Clunking noises spread out from it. Noises that sound like branches rubbing against one another. Sounds like mosquitoes; a buzzing that's an epiphenomenon of the star's shrinking. Fly closer. Fly into the stream that catches you. That moves you faster than you've ever gone. View out from the stream and see that the Field was a blur. To see vision skewed not by motion, but by color like everything was cut through a prism. Each shape in the Field stretched into lines. They are delivered to the star. But they are only there for a split second. A tiny fraction of time before they are slingshotted around the star and away.

During the transit, they see that the shapes flowed over the star. Some shapes burrowed deep into the star. Some shapes tumbled and skipped across the star before they settled into its gravity. Their view lasted a moment, but they had enough time to feel how strong the star's pull is. After they are slingshotted around so that they end up in opposition to where they were, they spot three broad, blue streaks painted like wide shooting stars.

The star sounds like heavy machinery grinding together. Like car detritus and steel beams were tearing apart into a high, screeching whine while also folding together, crushing and emanating in sounds that clunk and clack. Percussion fills the space. It was an accelerated percussion: magnets snapping into each other or wood lumber falling onto wood lumber. The sound was inelastic and abrupt. The star was rippling across its surface.

Lindsey: "It looks the way a stomach ache sounds."

Sara: "It's shrinking."

It's like watching the minute hand on a clock. The second hand turns turning the coupled gears turning the minute hand. The seconds are quick. It takes patience and a keen eye to see that the minute hand was also moving. The star has shock waves over its surface again. Material is swallowed into its center. The star is collapsing into itself. The decay is accelerating. The circle of the star is shrinking. Its apparent circumference seems like it's moving away, but the unwavering brightness belies the illusion. They float in space, seemingly stuck, while they watch the destruction of Sam's Planet, and Lindsey's star. Summer was coming to an end.

They came here for a map. They have to fly to Sam's Planet and retrieve the Map before it passes into the stream. The whole planet will be carried into the stream, and the whole stream into the disappearing star.

Summer was ending in more ways than one.

Sam's Planet is at least a few hundred thousand miles away if not more. The view is not dissimilar to the view of the Earth from the Moon's surface. There is a sort of weird math at work: the speed at which they fly towards the star, and the rate at which the star's circumference shrinks, they synchronize in a way that made the star's size stay the same. They come to Sara's Map and touch it. They close their eyes and hope to be transported out of the Field's chaos. They open their eyes again to the Field.

Their hands still on the Map, the star collapses onto itself. In an instant, the light goes out. Like the dark had come from behind them and towards the former star. The star reduces itself to a singularity; an impossibly small point of light. With its mass concentrated to a point, the machine-like sounds come to an end. The Field is black. Dark. A shadow.

Their hands still touch the Map. The Map is safe.

A point of light expands out in thin, laser-beam rays. The point expands out as a disc. It spins. It cuts through the stream that had been feeding it. The disc severs the feed of shapes. A hole expands out from the center, becoming an iris. A column of light grows from the spinning disc. Shapes shoot out at terrifying speeds leaving traces of blue lines. The shapes coming out are not geometric or natural, they looked crystalline and jewel-like. The star had crushed and formed the shapes into lattices. The disc spins and spins while these lattice bullets shoot out. Blue lines seemingly flash into the Field and stay there; the lattices are cutting across instantaneously. Sara looks to her side. Sam is gone. Only a scream is dragged away. Lindsey disappears from her. Wires of blue light zigzag back and forth heading away from where he was.

Snatched up by a lattice's motion. These pressure-formed shapes of shapes had their own gravity. Revolving, spinning across the empty field uncontrolled; the three are spirited far from each other. Another lattice shoots out from the iris. It makes a line across Sam and Sara as points. They are jostled and accelerated to other places. In two trips, they cannot see the white iris anymore. Time is cycling again.

Lindsey has been dragged twice...four times already. These lattices fly past them. He only hopes that they do not go through him. He cannot see his star. He only needs to feel the part of him that he imparted into it. He just needs to find *his time* again, and he'll be able to freely navigate in this space. How far they were, they were astronomical units away from where they were. He flies with a purpose back to the center. Lattices fly past him, dragging him with their gravity. He's farther away.

I can do this. Just a bit faster.

Sara is in a standstill. The instant, the very instant she felt an outside pull, she accelerates in the opposite direction. The area around her pulses blue. The lattice continues on its merry path. She is pulled by the lattice, but she is not slingshotted away or dragged by its gravity. Sara tries her best to control her way away. If she had not tried, she would go farther away from the white iris. Through her efforts, she keeps pace with the lattice. From the frame of reference of the lattice, Sara was keeping the same distance. Outside of her immediate space, her situation is similar to a tugboat pulling another ship; gravity the invisible towline. She puts all her effort into pulling away and cannot break free. She pulses brighter still.

In his head, Sam visualized a cone with its tip at the iris. The cone was the possible trajectories that the lattices could shoot out from. If he could fly in an orbit until he's out of the cone's eye, he would seize to be slingshotted. Then, he can try to make his way back to the planet. Sam experiences a different sort of acceleration. The type where it feels like the arms are going to rip off instead of your head. He flies radially. The blue lines left behind by the lattices form a sort of vector field; a mathematical construct showing velocity—speed and direction. He feels like he's viewing trees from a car. The blue traces do seem to be in a cone. He continues flying.

Sara sees a faint blue ribbon flying in an arc. Sam sees both a pulsating blue dot, and a blue line slowly flying towards one direction. Lattices scatter like a sandstorm; a gust across every direction. The pulsating blue dot is gone, the blue line stops. They are moved farther away from each other. And they keep accelerating farther out. Farther out than they've ever been, they feel the presence of other people. A gift was hiding here. Another gust, they fly farther away. Not everywhere was black and dark. There are places where colors needed new types of eyes to perceive its vividness. There are places where mathematicians haven't the terms to call the geometry of the shapes they've seen. Oh, to be beyond where you've ever been. Farthest is not a descriptor, but a place you're about to reach.

So lay down the rainbows of summer across your Field. Feel the map everlasting in your youth. And find your way back.

Branches grow unbounded inside a cube. They feel it. They see the gestalt of space and time, the motion of all things. Of all things interdependent in their motion. Of change through every moment. The needle thin path they must thread through is felt by them. They felt the Map inside their heads. Fly through the holes in-between the lattices. *Rush* through until the wind is unheard. They do not need to calculate velocities anymore, they intuit the correct move. Fly at your terrifying speeds that not even gravity can begin to hold you back. Galaxy-sized blue trails begin to converge. Three shooting stars that blink bright blue head to a point. They maintain their speed, but they do not collide, they fall in. Three different hands take the Map, dive through all the shapes inside Sam's Planet, tunnel and shape a corridor through its core, the white iris shining brightly for them, the lattices do not deter them, the white iris's aperture opening for *them*, fall into, fall through, fall inside...

Inside out.

Nature abhors discontinuities. Singularities. Sonic booms. Light blooms. The thin, liminal existence between waking life and sleep. Creating bubbles in space, and bubbles in time—both of which have begun to ripple out and create unseen crests and troughs. Like water seeping into cracks, or impurities in panes of glass, when these discontinuities are not healed—they shatter. They cause avalanches. They cause storms.

They took off. In seconds each of them broke into a sonic boom. Each air particle cutting into their skin. Soon their views become warped as they approach light speed. Their vision of the world seemed like a flower unfolding. Each light ray blossoming and folding into itself like a blooming and dying flower.

As they reached nearer to the city, their bright light burns and casts shadows from the skyscrapers. Like a meteor flashing light upon the city. A large blue bloom forms around the light points after they passed. Then wind and sound rushes in.

The spike in air pressure blasts a shock wave from the sky. From mid-air, the shock wave expands in a growing bubble; shattering windows around the metropolitan area. Glass of different compositions break in their own ways. Some of them crack and maintain in one piece; looking like spiderwebs. Other buildings' glass shatters outwards in a mess of pieces. It sounds like a thousand wind chimes when glass falls on the ground.

The three streaks of light cross outside the city limits. Along the Interstate and Long Island Expressway, windshields, headlights, mirrors break. The sudden drop in pressure causes some car tires to explode. If it were not for air conditioning and rolled up windows, many more would be injured. Cars crash into another.

Then the wind rushes in and turns cars over.

Sam flies through a coastal city. There's a shipping yard and boats. Shipping containers are stacked tall and high. There are different colored cranes. He passes in between their trusses. Tons of electronics, food stuffs, furniture are on the ground, spilling out of toppled-over, sheared-opened containers.

Through their map, Sam and Sara were able to enter into the Bubble at will. They meet each other in passing through the different waypoints. With the Map, they know every turn to take inside the Bubble without reading the ground. By going through the Bubble to teleport out, they save precious *picoseconds*. They were also able to make new waypoints without needing to label them. The Bubble network was expanding in ways that they could not use unless they had the Map.

Midway in flight, Lindsey crossed them in the Bubble. They asked him where he was going. Lindsey said he was going to his house. There was no time. But they hesitated a moment before deciding they had to confront their parents.

Time had passed in the Field. Time passed in the real world too.

They flew to the bubble that had Dusk House written on the floor. They close their eyes and come out of the basement.

* * *

Lindsey flew directly to California from the Bubble. It hadn't felt like a home to him before. Many things don't seem precious until it could be taken away from you. A blue contrail forms behind him while he flies over the California coast. They were chasing around the world catching falling stars.

A shape that looks like a fireball changes and morphs colors under the effect of gravity and wind. From the farthest places in the Field, they've dragged strange matter back through the white iris. There is a danger, an immediate threat in how these shapes could interact not in a vacuum, but with the world they know. They've introduced sound, light, time, gravity to the Field. What events could transpire? Now that these shapes can be exposed to so much more. They use the Map to hunt down these treasures before they touch the ground. The fireball wobbles like a water droplet suspended in zero-g, but it's traveling almost as fast as Lindsey. Through the haze of the clouds, the view becomes gray, highway lines are sharp, the world becomes demarcated into city and suburb. In the wind patterns, he intuits a gust that steers the shape towards him. The gust of wind won't come for a few seconds, and it won't occur at his current trajectory. It's going to happen at ground level and at the roof of his house; of all places.

They knew these shapes could change everything.

Minutes. It was minutes that they took to hop around the world. In those minutes, blue trails and blooms are impressed in the sky. For these three, the question of how much time has passed in the Field will be answered. In their first excursion in the Field, what seemed like a few hours was several hours back home. But on this last trip, so much has happened in there. It didn't seem like much time has passed, which usually means more time has passed than was experienced.

"You were gone for three days," Camille tells Sara.

"What's going on with you two?" Bradley holds onto Sam's note. Sara glares at Sam.

Lindsey grabs the fireball; crashing through his roof and breaking his hand.

Sara looks up. Shapes were crossing from one end of the sky to the other. They were falling while Mom and Dad were staring at their children. It is a devastating moment when your parents look at you in a way that conveys: I'm disappointed.

Kacey and Peter stand over their son. Through the roof opening which was dripping plywood and sheet wall dust, Lindsey watches diamonds sprinkle from the sky. Through the Map, he felt that Sam and Sara were in a similar situation. Lindsey massages his hand. There was pressure where there wasn't supposed to be. He's had this same injury before. Just a normal hand sprain. He stands up. He can't. His knee was sprained and it was too weak and painful to stand. His mom and dad help him to the couch. Kacey and Peter were stunned by their son blasting through the roof and couldn't form a response to this non sequitur in their lives.

"Where were you? For three days?" his mom asks him. Sweat beads from his forehead. He wonders who has the wish. He needs to heal himself so he can fly out.

"We got a call from Sara's parents. They were missing too," his dad says.

Sam: "There is something happening. We can't stay here."

What happened to their boy?

Bradley: "What are you talking about? Why did you two run away? Like last time..."

Camille: "We trusted that in time, you two would tell us why you left last time. But for three days, we didn't know where to look for you. You owe us an explanation."

A sting in their hearts. They've betrayed their parents for their own adventures.

Sara: "Sam's right. We got to go. Don't you see all those things?"

Peter: "What did you do to the roof? What's happening?"

Kacey: "Are you okay?"

There was worry in her voice.

Crap, Lindsay thought. He remembered he last made a wish, but didn't give it to them. Oh boy, he's going to have to deal with his injuries until he can get to them. Meanwhile he has to get through this interrogation while the world was ending.

Sara points behind them. They turn around.

Lindsey points to the ceiling. Peter holds Kacey's hand. They're waking up from a psychedelic trip in the back of their camper van. Peter rubs his eyes in the afterglow and sees stars of the form he's seeing now. Kacey's mind is recovering from the inertia of total ego destruction. She touched the camper van's roof to ground herself. Presently, she looks at Peter. Then she looks at Lindsey. She looks at the hole in the roof again and feels right back in the present.

The Map felt warmer in the real world. Sara has her hands in her pockets. Partially out of nervousness, but she wasn't going to let this cube out of her hands. Her parents had their heads turned towards the sky show. She could get out of here in a blink and be where the show is happening.

"I'm transported," Bradley says to Camille.

"Where are you?" Camille was in a trance.

The strange shapes begin to remind them of mist and shadow. Sara felt her mom's worry shut down. The feeling didn't subside. It just felt like it was replaced. Sara taps her mom's hand, "Mom, are you okay?"

Their dad starred out. Sam looks at him from the front. His dad's eyes are glazed over. "Dad? Dad?" Sam nudges him. Their parents didn't respond. Somewhere inside, Bradley and Camille were trapped in their youth waiting for adventures to come. They're sitting together outside in a cold Pennsylvania valley. Bradley pours hot chocolate into a thermos cup and hands it over to Camille. Meteors explode over the valley's tree line.

Sara: "We should get them to a safe place. Then we can do what we need to do."

Sam: "Lindsey's also injured. We could take the Bubble."

Sam spoke about it in the way someone would mull over whether to take the train or taxi. Sara turns their parents away from seeing the shapes. Their parents glimpse at their house.

Bradley: "That's right. We're here."

Camille: "Sara...Sam...what's happening?" Their mom didn't seem disappointed anymore. She tries to understand them. In this world which begins to keep changing quicker and quicker, they place their trust in their children. They are led to the basement where they are told to close their eyes.

Sam & Sara: "Open them."

They are given the privilege not many parents receive, which is that they are invited into their children's private lives. In a very literal sense, they are invited into their world.

Sara tells them, "Lindsey actually made this place." They look at the slide, the gymnastic foam pit, a kitchen, the spiral cavern of this place.

"We need to pick up the pace," Sam tells them.

They walk through a long corridor into another copy of the place before. Then another corridor with another copy. Destinations and place names were written on the entrance of each copy. They've noted that each copy had several corridors connected to them. After walking through some of the copies, the place labels were not on some of them. Even if every location was named, the children would have to memorize the stops. They've taught them how to navigate the subway so there should be crossover skill. But it's one corridor one after the other without labels. Until they reach the one labeled, "My ~~California Room~~ House."

Sara: "Mom, before we go through. Can I ask you something?"

Camille: "What is it?"

Sara: "You gave us these wishes right, Mom?"

Bradley looks at Camille. Sam never thought about the wishes' origin. Sara didn't know how to explain what happened this summer to her parents, and this question was the only way she knew how to even begin to discuss it.

Camille looks up at the Bubble's surface, contemplating, trying to remember.

A sharp exhale of air leaves Lindsey's mouth. Camille watches Sam's hand hover over Lindsey's knee and hands. The opening on the roof splits Bradley's body into light and dark halves. The sky looks like rain to him. Peter offers them water.

Peter: "Bradley, what's happening here?"

Bradley: "I don't understand any of this. Kacey, do you know?"

Kacey: "You four just appeared from my son's bedroom. I don't get it. I just don't get it. The world is ending, isn't it?"

Out of sight, Camille's engagement ring swirls in rainbow bands. The diamond, formed by *his* breath, weighs heavy on her finger today. She looks up through the broken roof.

The three teens are renewed and refreshed. Lindsey rolls his wrists, and limbers up his knees with some toe touches. "Mom, I have to go," he says. The Dusk teens go through the same warm up motions.

Kacey: "Where?"

Lindsey couldn't say an exact place in words. It was like he had the language of it in muscles. It was something he feels in the movements he's going to take to get there. How can anyone express their intuition in words? And how could they even tell their parents that they were causing the shape-fall in the sky.

Sam: "All those shapes falling from the sky...we broke something somewhere."

Sara: "We have to fix it. We are going to fix it."

Lindsey: "We'll be back soon."

Camille: "What are those shapes, Sam?"

Sam: "We don't know. We just know what they do. And we... can't control them."

Kacey: "What do they do?"

Lindsey: "Like building blocks. Strange things...that interact, but we don't know how they work."

Sara: "I'm going."

She goes through the roof. A blue light holds still in the living room; like an afterimage from a poorly exposed picture. It dissolves into the sunlight. The parents just experienced teleportation. They just witnessed flying. Meanwhile, the two sets of parents walk outside. Meanwhile, the shapes touch upon the materials of the world: water, earth, concrete, asphalt, mountains, sand, soil and sediment, time. They touch upon the imperceptible:

radio waves, networks, light and sound, minds. Transforming. Shapes catch on radio waves, TV signals. A reverberation, a ripple across the world.

"How do these seeds unfold?" Camille thought to herself.

A shape like a glass shard shoots through a woman's head on the street. Sara was too late to catch it, but she catches the woman before she falls over. There is no wound on her head. The woman opens her eyes. She seems lucid. Sara has to move onto the next shape that will fall. Through the Bubble, through the tunnels, she emerges in the ocean to catch a petal and bring it back to the Field. Out she goes from the Field back into Earth.

"I wish for the shapes to stop falling," Sam says out loud. They keep falling in front of him. Camille looks at her son. The interactions between reality and the shapes start expressing themselves on a macro scale. On Lindsey's front porch, an advancing *wave* of asphalt comes towards them. Concrete rises and falls, like geometric, sharply cut granite caught in the undulation. A geological surf rolls across houses breaking the foundations of every house. A strand of electricity crawls across the sky from where Sara is to the sky above Lindsey's house.

Tundras appear where rain forests are. Lakes are inverted into deserts.

Bradley: "Sam, you have to go. You have to go now."

Camille nods in agreement.

Kacey: "Lindsey, do whatever you have to do."

Peter: "Fly."

They leave.

* * *

They can find these rogue shapes forever. Catching them, returning them to the Field. Watching as any threshold between Field and Earth dissolves. An hour has passed. The shapes that are entering the world, and those that they return to the Field are not caught up in a loop. That is a small blessing for them.

Swaths of people gather around sites that look incongruous to their surroundings. A permanent solution needs to be found. The three are flying around the world. To them, the world is shrinking quickly. When they touch down, they remove the seeds that create the aberrations. Lindsey allows himself to drown into quicksand. Surrounded by the dark and the pressure of the sand, he feels around for a stone. He brings it back to the Field. Above the dark, the people of the plaza watch while the sand dissolves into the brick road again.

Some shapes are material. Some shapes are earthly and have a body. When they crash, they shoot like bullets through rain forest trees. Height is relative when you can fly, but coming down through the forest canopy, it's striking how tall trees can get. After picking up the shape from a puddle, she looks up at a tree that was split in half, splintered and glowing like lightning had struck it. The tree is parted almost to the ground. The split is about her hand's width. It looks like it could fall in any direction with a slight push. She wishes for the tree to be healed.

The shape in her hand phases through her skin and bones.

Another shape escapes Sam's reach. Over him, clouds are laid out in white lines. More shapes pass over him; optically shifting the clouds. The sky is refracted and refracted again, like viewing an image through many panes of glass where each layer is askew from the layer underneath. The sky over him might as well have been multiplying. He follows the shapes to where they go.

In the Bubble, Lindsey watches the corridors and each bubble room breathe. The room is flexing in and out. He touches the surface. It's never done this before. The last time the Bubble behaved weirdly was when it sucked them into the Field. The surface of the room ripples. He felt uneasy about what it could mean, but he has no time to investigate. He feels for the next shape that is going to move through the Earth. With great speed, he exits the Bubble and flies through blue skies.

Going through deserts, leaving behind a setting sun. Sam and Lindsey fly to the forest where trees are split. There, the three of them watch the shapes that they chase stop. The fall of shapes stop. Chaos gives way to order. It organizes. Under words. Light rays draw out in lines between shapes. Like fine threads, the lines appear in broken dashes of sunlight. The shapes become points where lines connect to each other into a tessellation. These tessellations surround them and flicker; appearing and fading again. New fiber grows across and bridges the split. Only a scar is left when the wish is fulfilled.

A wind flows through the trees without obstacle. Dew cascades from leaf to leaf until the water drops land on their heads.

All these thresholds are not really there at all. So they have to put thresholds where there are none. They have to put doors in every place. Separate the Field and the Earth. To lock out spaces and freeze them in time. All these steps are laid out in front of them. To separate these places is the only way to stop the chaos. They know what it means for them. They have to do it anyways.

Enter into the Bubble. They felt it. The same energy that was held inside of them was in the Bubble. They could only recognize it now because of what happened on Earth. They weren't able to connect it before. The shapes were passing through here too. They couldn't see them, but they were moving through, shooting through these corridors. The Bubble was a membrane. It was a highway, the network by which the shapes passed through to the real world.

Shut off every exit. Catching shapes in mid-air for them to materialize. Mixed inside the Bubble with everything was their thoughts. And they thought of the material and the energy. They bring these shapes together. They fuse them together in front of every exit. They close off Paris. Peru. Mexico. Patagonia,

Madagascar, Australia. At every exit, the warm, amber wall of the Bubble repeats what happened to that split tree. Thin lines seemingly emerge from nothing. It's only with a tilt of the head that they come into view. Every time they blink or shift their eyes at the corridor, a new thread is there, suddenly and almost invisible. Goodbye to China. Japan. All these corridors that led them to places where they had late night adventures are locked off. And up with the walls at Atlantic Ocean. Lindsey fondly remembers setting up those exits.

They meet between the last two exits to be locked off. One to New York, back to Dusk House, and one back to California.

"Well. It's your house," Lindsey says.

"Do you think we'll still be able to fly after?" Sam asks.

"I don't know," Lindsey responds.

"We should keep California open. Our parents are still back there. We might need a way back to them," Sara says.

Lindsey: "I mean I don't know if we could go back after we're done. Back to Earth, I mean."

Lindsey watches Sam and Sara seal up the New York exits. First their house, then his. Maybe he'll still be able to fly to NY when this is all over. Locked behind those amber walls were copies of where they were standing. Cut off from shortcuts to faraway places. There is one more thing they have to do. They have to close off the Field.

The white iris still spins. It still takes shapes from the Field and releases it into the Earth. If they close off the iris, they may not be able to reopen it. If they stitch it together, they may not be able to go back. But just as the summer began with a sacrifice, it needs to end with one. They roam. They fly into the dark of the Field. They find their materials. They understand not what these shapes do separately; but only what happens when they synthesize.

Sara: "It's all burning down there."

Sam: "We have to get to work."

Of all these machines they've made in the Field: machines to make light, to create land mass, to guide them; this last machine is purposeful. They know what it will mean. It means separation of the wishes from the Earth. It means not seeing their parents ever again. Even so, they begin their alchemy.

It seems that these things they make didn't seem to matter what shapes are being put together. It takes the thought to create their machines. Thoughts like a sun, a planet, a map. Once they synthesize the curtain, they're stuck in the Field. That was their thought now. Those walls they put up in the Bubble were made of threads. They were stitched in place. What's a stitched wall but a curtain? They'll do the same to the white iris. A patch to cover the shape-fall. They were able to get out of the Field before the iris appeared. They'll do the same now.

They cradle these massless shapes, building blocks on their tiny arms. One by one, they take one in their hands, and let it float into the white spinning hole. The shapes float upstream against the lattices. The three teens float immovable against the lattices that still come out. These heavy shapes may pass through them. They may bounce off of their bodies, but they cannot push them from suspension. These upstream shapes transform as it gets closer to the opening. The lattices unfold into a grid; still glowing white and gold. And the grid breaks apart into strings, into threads.

The threads fall slowly into the iris. It floats in slow motion like dust kicked up from the floor. There might be a better word for it, the threads were *settling* into the iris. It's stitching together. The threads are weaving together. Underneath, over, back over, underneath. Between two sides. Closing two sides.

The light is faded. The spinning disc looked like a light caustic swirled in a whirlpool: shimmering, and sparkling. It's dim now, and soon, it will cease to rotate and emit shapes. The Field is quiet again. It's still.

Soon, the iris will have its light extinguished. Clearly, foreseeing, the future is tracking towards one single point. The branches fall off inside the Map like they are rotted. Along the one path in the future, they see the dark. There is a time line safe from these primal shapes and their random nature.

Sara says, "The light is fading."

Sam felt it too, "You two feel it, don't you?"

Their hearts pound. This situation was theirs to solve. As far as they can see, they must rectify the situation. And they couldn't have it both ways. If they exit the Field, they burst the seams of the curtain. And they end up where they were before.

Lindsey: "If we go back, then everything gets undone..."

Sara: "But we'll be with everyone."

Sam: "But they can't be safe."

But they also know if they close the two sides, the wishes will be lost forever.

The world rebuilds somehow. They'll untangle the mess. Years. The world will forget. Creation will follow destruction. Highways will be rebuilt. Money will be paid out by insurance after prolonged court battles. A decade. People will wonder if strange things ever happened.

People will look up at night and in a fugue, wonder where it all began. And who can say? And what could convince them that this new beginning happened at the turn of the century?

So seasons pass without their children. Old conversations in the night that discuss fate and free will recall their importance. The two families grow closer in the years following. To grieve alone, to live through those years alone, to separate entirely was never considered. They continue to search for their children until old age, until their bodies fail them, until the end of their lives.

* * *

Through the time line, it cycles back to the end of their summer. There has to be more than one direction. By their will, they'll find more than one way. To create new directions, they'll need their imagination. They'll turn the machine of the Field against itself. They'll stabilize all the things they've changed.

Lindsey: "There is something different here."

Sam: "I know what you mean. I know exactly what you mean."

Lindsey: "But..but what is it?"

Sara holds out the Map in her palm. It's illuminating. They share a thought. It is incredibly concrete, and synchronized to the very word; to the very cadence:

"Time and change."

They take these shapes and let go of them. Much like how the curtain was formed, the shapes dissolve into threads. They seem like laser lights but bent and amorphous. Like there was some kind of invisible haze in the Field, the threads shone brighter when they undulate through it. These illuminated threads stretch and stretch. They float—rather aggressively—out. They move to the farthest reaches in this Field, far to places where gray tones change to vibrant color. And then the shapes begin to finalize the structure that was intuited by those three.

The curtain has not sealed completely. It does not need to. A sliver of light shines into the Field.

This machine would be the largest structure in the universe if it was in their reality. It is a monumental machine. It's not a machine that does work, but a machine that works against work. In their conception: it is a tremendous lock. Long lines of light draw between shapes. Each shape lights up in the Field as threads latch on, and the threads pull taut. One by one, line by line, every shape joins into the chain. Every one of them becomes locked in place. They are frozen and suspended. The shapes are locked in space and in time.

The lock shimmers like a spider web caught in the morning sun. The lock has an unending depth to it. In the same way that the multiplying reflections of the Bubble created darkness, the visual overlap of lines makes the Field look no different from blue satin. But satin with its weave loose, and the black of the Field as its background.

These threads, together, look tessellated and networked, but it is all one chain. All of the shapes are frozen in space and in time. And they must realize that they must not make a wish so that this tenuous balance won't be disturbed. The lock becomes a monument to their summer, held in illuminated sapphire.

Sam: "Sara, it looks like the map we made with the lines."

Sara: "A little bit."

Lindsey stares into the iris; the last ray of light in the Field. Mixed inside there were the last vestiges of his star. He turns to look at Sam and Sara. Behind them was the lock. His star was out there too, in a different form. He wonders if the Bubble's map would look like the lock's chain structure.

They take a last look at the Field: a trillion trillion lights strung together and suspended in space. Then they return to a world without wishes.

* * *

The Dusk family takes their place in a long line to check in. They didn't have anything for bag check except their water bottles, kindly gifted by the Lovitt-Chen family. At the desk, they begin their process.

Bradley: "We were thinking about going to a national park for summer vacation, not flying back home. There goes the vacation fund."

He takes out his emergency credit card. He thinks aloud, "Well, it'll only be half of the credit limit."

Bradley: "Well, here."

Sara grabs her dad's wrist. "I just remembered that Sam and I have to go to Florida."

Bradley shakes his head incredulously, "What?"

Sam: "Oh that's right. Today's the day. Dad, we have to go to Florida."

Camille: "We don't have the money for that. And why do you have to go to Florida?"

Sam: "We met some strangers in Peru and they invited us to a party by the beach."

Bradley: "Excuse me? Come again?"

Mom: "What? What? What?" Each what was more worried and elongated than the last. The handling agent stands by watching the commotion unfold.

Sara: "Look. Don't worry about the money."

Sara turns to the handling agent, "How much for four seats to Florida?"

"Uh," the handling agent says. She prepares her hands over the keyboard, "Which airport?"

Sara: "Um, what's closest to Daytona Beach?"

Agent: "Daytona Beach."

Sam: "Check the price for us?"

She looks at the parents, and slowly types in to her terminal.

Bradley as Dad: "When did you go to Peru?"

Sam: "Uh ...when we were grounded."

Camille morphing into Mom: "And, pray tell, Sara Dusk, how will you pay for these tickets to Florida."

Dad: "Grounded means grounded. Tell your kids we can't afford to go. We have to go home."

Mom: "*My kids?*"

The handling agent tells them the price.

Sara, to Sam: "Hey, you have my card right?"

Sam: "Yeah."

Sam pulls out the ATM card. It looks different. Instead of a bank insignia on it, the ATM card has the logo of a major credit card company on it. He hands the credit card to the agent. "Just run it through," he tells the agent, "please."

"Hold on," their dad takes the card, and turns it over. It's real. "Florida. It's nice, isn't it?" he asks the agent.

The agent shrugs.

Mom: "I need a vacation."

Sara: "Florida's nice."

Sam whispers to the agent, "Swipe it."

The handling agent looks at the parents for approval. They nod for her to run the card.

* * *

Outside of Lindsey's house, the road and the houses returned to normal. Inside, they still have a hole in the roof. Seems like everything that was affected by the Field returned to normal except...except whatever actions they took to keep the world from becoming chaos...seemed to have consequences. Lindsey muttered to himself out loud; recounting disasters (that they caused) on his fingers, "...the roof, broken shipping containers, trees in the forest...oh crap, all the cars on the highway..."

Peter: "Hey, buddy, are you okay?"

Lindsey reaches back to what he learned on the singular time line, "Yeah, insurance will take care of it. They'll take care of everything."

Kacey: "What? Dad's asking if you're okay."

Lindsey fills a kettle with water. He asks his parents, "You two want coffee?" They nod no. Their son is a strange one. He rinses a mug. He takes the coffee can and scoops some instant coffee into the mug. And just a light dash of sugar, since he prefers the bitterness now.

Lindsey tells them, "But yeah, I think I'm okay. I mean as okay as I can be right?"

He paces around waiting for the water to heat up, but not too hot that it boils. Lindsey just wants the coffee as soon as possible.

They could do the only thing that anyone could do at this time: to just clean up the mess in their house. Peter takes plastic bags from a cabinet and passes them to Kacey. While the parents pick up the big pieces of wreckage, Lindsey sweeps up the dust and the smaller debris. He drinks his coffee before tackling the dust on the kitchen island. The refrigerator, the dishes previously left out to dry are wiped. They'll be cleaned again before eating.

For five hours, they turn the house upside down to clean it up. Bags of garbage pile up outside. California weather is agreeable when you have a hole in your roof.

Peter: "Our TV is still fine."

Lindsey: "Put on a movie then."

Kacey: "I could go for a movie."

Lindsey asks if they want coffee. Compared to his kitchen in the Bubble, the layout at his home wasn't his preferred layout. He sighs and slaps his head. He mutters to himself, "I could have tried skateboard flips into the foam pit. Dammit."

Kacey: "What was that?"

Lindsey turns to watch a shot of an ocean on the screen. A startling remainder comes into his head.

Lindsey: "Oh crap. I just realized I have to go to Florida. Mom, where's the sunscreen?"

"Are you going to be back?" Kacey asks.

"I'll be home in like five hours," Lindsey says.

"Sunscreen is in the top left cabinet," she responds.

He goes out the front door, slathering sunscreen on his arms and face. The blue sky is so different from the Field's lock. Trees rustle. Wind cross his arms. By intuition, he feels for the wind currents that lead him to Florida. But still, he feels the ground through his sneakers, and gravity never felt stronger. Staring at the blue sky, he wonders if the lock grounded him from flying.

Peter walks out the front door with popcorn still in hand, "What are you waiting for? We'll see you in a bit." Kacey comes up to Peter's side, and throws a couple of popcorn into her mouth.

She tells Lindsey, "Just come home in one piece."

Lindsey looks up at the blue sky. In a breeze, he is over Florida's skies looking for the signal smoke of the bonfire.

* * *

In a rental car, paid with Sara's card, the Dusk family takes a short drive into Daytona beach. Bradley drives the car, telling Sam and Sara how he used to have a motorcycle once.

"Their mom begins speaking to them, Sara...Sam..." She taps her fingers on the passenger side door trying to find the right words to say. But she'll just say it.

"You can say it, Cammy," Bradley says.

She says, "I think you two got the wishes from me."

"Where did it come from?" Sara asks.

"I don't know," their mom says.

A necklace with an ornate cube hangs off Sara's neck. The southern sun hangs low in the sky waiting for its retirement into night. Sara looks outside, yellow lights from high rise buildings stand out against the purple atmosphere.

Sara tells them, "I'm going to find out."

Dread and worry creeps into their parents *soul*. The worry buries itself in their very bodies and digs deeply. Bradley grips the steering while Camille beads sweat even when the air conditioning is on. The two of them cannot even imagine what their children could do given time. Regardless, Bradley tells Sara,

"Be careful."

The car pulls into the beach's parking lot. Bradley and Sara exit first. Sam looks at the crowds of people filing into the beach. The people look like ball bearings going into a funnel. The closest phenomenon he could compare it to was the shapes flowing and feeding into Lindsey's star. Sam turns to his mom and says, "I just need to protect them."

They hear the ocean roar—now that they're on the ground. But it is the bonfire that is the draw and the attraction. The wood is stacked at least as high as the two teens. The fire spins and at its apex, spirals back into the air. Deep in between the logs, the space glows white.

Sam notices how hot the fire is, even from afar.

"That's radiation," his dad says. "It's like how the sun or a radiator works. The heat affects you from far away."

Their mom says to them, "You two can go there. We're going to stay back." Mom takes off her shoes and digs her toes into the cooling sand. Dad collapses backwards and prepares himself for a short nap, "What a day."

Four silhouettes are outlined by orange firelight. They're all about the same height. One of them seems familiar, but he couldn't be that tall, could he? He turns to look at them. Lindsey is that tall. Sara looks at Sam, too. Sam's grown also.

Lindsey waves them over. It's Eric, Fiona, and Isla. Without the dirt of adventure on them, they're like ordinary people. Seeing them in bright tank tops and shorts instead of dirt-covered beige is a bit disorientating.

Eric: "I'm glad both of you came."

Fiona: "Did you two um...fly in like Lindsey?"

Sam: "Uh, flew in by plane..."

Sara: "Then our parents drove us here."

Eric: "Oh. Okay. Not what I was expecting but alright. We got burgers on the grill and some soda by the bucket. It's not much after what happened, but it's something."

Lindsey: "I could go for a burger."

Isla: "What happened today...that was you three, right?"

Sam: "Some of it."

Fiona: "A lot of the strange stuff just went away, but there's still some damage around."

Sara hesitates, but then says it anyway: "Yeah, the damage is our fault."

Eric: "Can you undo it?"

Sam shakes his head, "Not right now. We can't undo the damage without making things worse."

Fiona: "But you were able to fill up the hole in Peru."

Eric: "What changed?"

Sara takes the Map and tucks it into her shirt, out of view. Lindsey glances over at Sara, and then returns to the conversation.

Lindsey tells them, "We made a decision that we can't go back on. We won't be able to fix the damage."

Isla: "But everything is okay?"

Sara: "Yeah."

Isla: "Just be careful."

Eric: "Come on, let's get some food in you all. We can talk about other stuff. We need to celebrate the end of summer!"

Isla: "You're right. I do tend to mull on things."

Later in the night, Sara talks to Isla about what an anthropologist does. Sam is going to ask Fiona and Eric about the sciences. But before they do...

Sam: "Can you give us a second?"

The older trio nods, and walks away.

Sara: "Hey, Lindsey."

Lindsey: "What's up?"

Sara: "So before we got here, what were you talking to them about?"

Lindsey's tone changes to solemn. "Well," he bows his head down, and lightly puts his fist on his chin (it's a valiant attempt at Rodin's Thinking Man), "I told Isla how we...you..."

Sam: "What did you tell her?"

Lindsey: "I told her about how...how you fell off my skateboard. Jeez." He bursts out laughing. "It was so bad. No, no, no. I was talking to them about why would you build a bonfire in the middle of summer. It's hot, and they're just making it hotter."

While Lindsey was blabbering, Sam was processing a thought in his mind. *Lindsey's still able to fly. So whatever wishes we've made before are still in effect. Whatever we've locked in the Field didn't carry over to what's already happened. I think we've also made some wishes that haven't been granted. Huh. I don't think granted is even the right word.*

"I think. Hmm. Sam made a wish in the Field so that all these things happening could stop. But it didn't go through," Sara tells Lindsey. Lindsey looks at Sam, who's nodding along. Lindsey might not be the most emotionally intelligent person, but Sara was telling him something special. So he listens.

She continues, "Then he gave the wish to me. Which I guess is kind of poetic since I started this whole mess."

Lindsey holds back a quip that she did start the whole mess.

Sara takes a breath, "We knew when we created the lock that we can't make wishes anymore. We know that whatever is in the Field are also the same things causing wishes to come to life. But we had to stop the Field from changing anymore so that we can keep our home safe. But I think we need the wishes here. We need the wishes for people. What I'm really trying to say is that...hmm...um...every lock has a key. When the time comes, there's only one person we trust to use the key."

She puts her hand on Lindsey's shoulder. He'll later recall that was the heaviest weight he's ever had to bear. They've made him into both Excalibur and King Arthur simultaneously. In another way, he's the weapon and the detonation device. But a tool is only a weapon in the hand that wields it.

He takes the time to remember this moment. He closes his eyes. He holds the crackling fire inside of him. He holds the roaring ocean. He holds through the dark of his eyelids: the Field, and the link of the wish that *binds* him to it. He holds Sam and Sara close; for they were his brother and sister. And light is the burden that is shared between family.

By the bonfire, they all felt that this summer wasn't a loss of innocence; the summer was something more. Mistakes made were lessons to be learned. There is a realization that arrogance was hope—that each obstacle encountered and pain felt was fuel for a future.

"Thank you. I don't know what to say."

Sam tells him, "It's yours. You don't have to say anything."

"Honestly, I'm out of ideas of things to wish for," Lindsey says to them. The bonfire's ash gets swept into the wind. They look at all the people on the beach in all directions. Sara's Map is going to grow in an unfathomable rate, creating an infinite perimeter in a finite space—with what Lindsey is going to say next:

"Maybe we should find a candidate."

"Not a bad idea," Sam says.

They mingle into the crowd.